Best Short Stories 1995

Best Short Stories 1995

EDITED BY GILES GORDON AND DAVID HUGHES

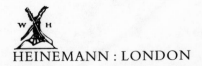

HEINEMANN : LONDON

First published in Great Britain 1995
by William Heinemann Ltd
an imprint of Reed Consumer Books Ltd
Michelin House, 81 Fulham Road, London SW3 6RB
and Auckland, Melbourne, Singapore and Toronto

A CIP catalogue record for this title
is available from the British Library

ISBN 0 434 00088 4

Typeset by Deltatype Limited, Ellesmere Port, Cheshire

Printed and bound by Clays Ltd, St Ives plc

Contents

Introduction

As usual we have chosen from a year's output of stories in English from Great Britain and the Commonwealth twenty-five worlds that all differ. Some are evoked and realised by the best writers in the language. By any standard Barnes, Boyd, O'Brien, Munro, Spark and Trevor make up quite a sextet; and there are, in our view, plenty more stories by other authors at least as stimulating.

This annual offering of *Best Short Stories*, now in its tenth year, comes up with novelties as well as favourites. The form is in good health. It gives satisfactory challenges to writers, not to mention readers. There is little new to say about the state of the art of the short story, beyond mentioning its vigour. Short fiction is appearing in an ever-widening variety of publications from *Granta* to *The Big Issue* and finding more of a slot on Radios 3 and 4. More newspapers are printing short stories than for many years. Last year and this the *Daily Telegraph* gave over a page a week to new fiction. The quarterly *Raconteur* is packed with talented narrative and offers cash prizes to its storytellers. An annual volume from the BBC lends further respectability to the craft. And so on.

The stories we assemble here from sources as varied as *Ambit*, *The New Yorker*, *Stand* and the *Spectator* are to our mind the best of the year's bunch, to be read, thought over, lived, enjoyed and remembered.

Giles Gordon and David Hughes

Interference

JULIAN BARNES

HE LONGED FOR death, and he longed for his gramophone records to arrive. The rest of life's business was complete. His work was done; in years to come it would be either forgotten or praised, depending upon whether mankind became more, or less, stupid. His business with Adeline was done, too: most of what she offered him now was foolishness and sentimentality. Women, he had concluded, were at base conventional: even the free-spirited were eventually brought down. Hence that repellent scene the other week. As if one could want to be manacled at this stage, when all that was left was a final, lonely soaring.

He looked around his room. The gramophone stood in the corner, a monstrous varnished lily. The wireless had been placed on the washstand, from which the jug and bowl had been removed: he no longer rose to rinse his wasted body. A low basketwork chair, in which Adeline would sit for far too long, imagining that if she enthused enough about the pettinesses of life he might discover a belated appetite for them. A wicker table, on which sat his spectacles, his medicines, Nietzsche, and the latest Edgar Wallace. A writer with the profligacy of some minor Italian composer. 'The lunch-time Wallace has arrived,' Adeline would announce, tirelessly repeating the joke he had told her in the first place. The Customs House at Calais appeared to have no difficulty allowing the lunch-time Wallace through. But not his 'Four English Seasons'. They wanted proof that the records were not being imported for commercial purposes. Absurd! He would have sent Adeline to Calais had she not been needed here.

His window opened to the north. He thought of the village nowadays solely in terms of nuisance. The butcher lady with her motor. The farms that pumped their feed every hour of the day. The baker with *his* motor. The American house with its infernal new bathroom. He briefly thought his way beyond the village, across the Marne, up to Compiègne, Amiens, Calais, London. He had not returned for three decades – perhaps it was almost four – and his bones would not do so on his behalf. He had given instructions. Adeline would obey.

He wondered what Boult was like. 'Your young champion,' as Adeline always characterised him. Forgetting the intentional irony when he had first bestowed this sobriquet on the conductor. You must expect nothing from those who denigrate you, and less from those who support you. This had always been his motto. He had sent Boult his instructions, too. Whether the fellow would understand the first principles of Kinetic Impressionism remained to be seen. Those damn gentlemen of the Customs House were perhaps listening to the results even now. He had written to Calais explaining the situation. He had telegraphed the recording company asking if a new set could not be dispatched contraband. He had telegraphed Boult, asking him to use his influence so that he might hear his suite before he died. Adeline had not liked his wording of that message; but then Adeline did not like much nowadays.

She had become a vexing woman. When they had first been companions, in Berlin, then in Montparnasse, she had believed in his work, and believed in his principles of life. Later she had become possessive, jealous, critical. As if the abandoning of her own career had made her more expert in his. She had developed a little repertoire of nods and pouts which countermanded her actual words. When he had described the plan and purpose of the 'Four English Seasons' to her, she had responded, as she all too regularly did, 'I am sure, Leonard, it will be very fine,' but her neck was tight as she said it, and she peered at her darning with unnecessary force. Why not say what you think, woman? She was becoming secretive and devious. For instance, he pretty much suspected that she had taken to her knees these last years. *Punaise de sacristie*, he had challenged. She hadn't liked that. She had liked it less when he had guessed another of her little games. 'I will see no priest,' he had told her. 'Or, rather, if I so much as smell one I shall attack him with the fire tongs.' She hadn't liked that, oh no. 'We are both old people now, Leonard,' she had mumbled.

'Agreed. And if I fail to attack him with the fire tongs, consider me senile.'

He banged on the boards and the maid, whatever was her name, came up at a trot. '*Numéro six*,' he said. She knew not to reply, but nodded, wound the EMG, put on the first movement of the Viola Sonata, and watched the needle's stationary progress until it was time, with swift and practised wrists, to flip the record over. She was good, this one: just a brief halt at a level crossing, then the music resumed. He was pleased. Tertis knew his business. Yes, he thought, as she lifted the needle, they cannot gainsay that. '*Merci*,' he murmured, dismissing the girl.

When Adeline returned, she looked questioningly at Marie-Thérèse, as she always did.

'*Numéro six*,' replied the maid.

The first movement of the Viola Sonata. He must have been angry; either that or suddenly fearful over his reputation. She had come to understand the shorthand of his requests, to read his mood from the music he asked to hear. Three months ago he had heard his last Grieg, two months ago his last Chopin. Since then, not even his friends Busoni and Sibelius; just the music of Leonard Verity. The Second Piano Quartet, the Berlin Suite, the Oboe Fantasy (with the revered Goossens), the Pagan Symphony, the Nine French Songs, the Viola Sonata . . . She knew the articulations of his work as once she had known the articulations of his body. And she admitted that in general he recognised what was finest in his output.

But not the 'Four English Seasons'. She had thought, from the moment he had first talked about it, then blocked it out with his thinned fingers on the piano, that the scheme was misconceived.

When he told her it was in four movements, one for each season, beginning with spring and ending with winter, she judged it banal. When he explained that it was not, of course, a mere programmatic representation of the seasons but a kinetic evocation of the memory of those seasons filtered through the known reality of other, non-English seasons, she judged it theoretical. When he chuckled at the notion that each movement would fit perfectly on the two sides of a gramophone record, she judged it calculating. Suspicious of the early sketches, she had liked the work no more in published form; she doubted that hearing it would convert her.

They had always agreed, from the beginning, to value truth above mere social form. But when truths collide, and one of them is dismissed as the squalid personal opinion of an ignorant, foolish Frenchwoman, then perhaps there was something to be said for social form. Heaven knew, she had always admired his music. She had given up her career, her life, for him; but instead of weighing with him this now seemed to count against her. The truth was, she thought – and this was *her* truth – that some composers had a fine late flowering and others did not. Perhaps the elegy for solo cello would be remembered, though Leonard grew suspicious nowadays at her too frequent praise of it; but not the 'Four English Seasons'. Leave such things to Elgar, she had said. What she had meant was: you seem to me to be courting the country you deliberately left, indulging a nostalgia of the kind you have always despised; worse, you seem to be inventing a nostalgia you do not truly feel in order to indulge it. Having scorned reputation, you now appear to be seeking it. If only you had said to me, triumphantly, that your work would not fit on to gramophone records.

There were other truths, or squalid personal opinions, that she could not transmit to him. That she herself was not well, and the doctor had talked of surgery. She had replied that she would wait until the current crisis was over. By which she meant, until Leonard is dead, when it will not matter to me whether I submit to a surgical intervention or not. His death had priority over hers. She did not resent this.

She did, however, resent being called a *punaise de sacristie*. She had not been going to Mass, and the idea of confession, after all

4

these decades, struck her as grotesque. But everyone must approach eternity in their own way, and when she sat alone in an empty church she was contemplating extinction, not its palliation by ritual. Leonard would pretend not to see the difference. 'Thin end of the wedge,' he would say – had said. For her, it was simply that they adopted different stances before the inevitable. Of course he did not like or understand this. He was growing more tyrannical as he reached the end. The weaker his strength, the more he asserted it.

The fire tongs sounded the opening of Beethoven's Fifth on the ceiling above. He must have heard, or guessed, her return. She ran heavily upstairs, banging an elbow on the turn of the banister. He sat in bed with the tongs aloft. 'Brought that priest of yours?' he enquired. But for once he was smiling. She fussed with his blankets and he pretended to object; but as she bent beside him, he laid his hand on her nape, just below her coiled and greying bun, and called her *ma Berlinoise*.

She had not anticipated, when they moved to Saint-Maure-de-Vercelles, that they would live quite so separately from the village. Pedantically, he had explained once more. He was an artist, did she not see? He was not an exile, since that implied a country to which he could, or would, return. Nor was he an immigrant, since that implied a desire to be accepted, to submit yourself to the land of adoption. But you did not leave one country, with its social forms and rules and pettinesses, in order to burden yourself with the parallel forms and rules and pettinesses of another country. No, he was an artist. He therefore lived alone with his art, in silence and in freedom. He had not left England, thank you very much, in order to attend a *vin d'honneur* at the *mairie*, or to tap his thigh at the local *kermesse* and offer a cretinous grin of approval to a squawking bugler.

Adeline learned that she must deal with the village in a swift and necessary fashion. She also found a way to translate Leonard's *profession de foi* into less rebarbative terms. M'sieur was a famous artist, a composer whose work had been played from Helsinki to Barcelona; his concentration must not be disturbed, lest the wonderful melodies forming within him be interrupted and lost for ever. M'sieur is like that, his head is in the clouds, it is just that he does not see you, otherwise, of course, he would tip his hat, why, sometimes he does not even notice me when I am standing in front of his face . . .

After they had been living in Saint-Maure for ten or so years, the baker, who played third cornet in the band of the *sapeurs pompiers*, shyly asked her if M'sieur would as a special honour write a dance, preferably a polka, for their twenty-fifth anniversary. Adeline pronounced it unlikely, but agreed to put the request to Leonard. She chose a time when he was not working on a composition, and seemed to be of sunny temperament. Later, she regretted that she had not chosen a moment of foul temper. For, yes, he said, with a curious smile, he would be delighted to write a polka for the band; he, whose work was performed from Helsinki to Barcelona, was not so proud that he would not do such a thing. Two days later, he gave her a sealed manila envelope. The baker was delighted and asked her to convey his particular thanks and respects to M'sieur. A week later, when she entered the *boulangerie*, he would not look at her or speak to her. Finally, he asked why M'sieur had chosen to laugh in their faces. He had scored the piece for three hundred players when they had only twelve. He had called it a polka but it did not have the rhythm of a polka; rather, that of a funeral march. Nor could Pierre-Marc or Jean-Simon, both of whom had made some musical studies, discern the slightest melody in the piece. The baker was regretful, yet also angry and humiliated. Perhaps, Adeline suggested, she had taken the wrong composition by mistake. She was handed the manila envelope and asked what the English word 'poxy' meant. She said she was not sure. She pulled out the score. It was headed 'Poxy Polka for Poxy Pompiers'. She said she thought the word meant 'bright', 'vivid', 'shining like the brass on your uniforms'. Well then, Madame, it was a pity that the piece did not appear bright and vivid enough to those who would not now play it.

More years passed, the baker handed over to his son, and it was the turn of the English artist, the irregular M'sieur who did not even tip his hat to the *curé* when he met him, to ask a favour. Saint-

Maure-de-Vercelles was just within range of the British Broadcasting Corporation. The English artist had a high-powered wireless that enabled him to pick up music from London. Reception, alas, was of greatly varying quality. Sometimes the atmosphere caused problems, there were storms and bad weather, against which nothing could be done. The hills beyond the Marne were not of great assistance, either. However, M'sieur had discovered, by deduction, one day when every single house in the village had fallen silent for a wedding, that there were also local forms of disturbance, from electric motors of all kinds. The butcher had such a machine, two of the farmers pumped their feed by this method, and of course the baker with his bread . . . Could they be prevailed upon, just for an afternoon, as an experiment, of course . . . Whereupon the English artist heard the opening bars of Sibelius's Fourth Symphony, that grave grumble from the lower strings and bassoons, which was normally below the threshold of audibility, with a sudden and refreshed clarity. And so the experiment was to be repeated from time to time, by permission. Adeline was the go-between on such occasions, a little apologetic, but also playing on the snobbery of the notion that Saint-Maure-de-Vercelles had living in its midst a great artist, one whose greatness embellished the village, and whose glory would shine the brighter if only the farmers would pump their feed by hand, the *boulanger* would confect his bread without electricity, and the butcher lady would turn off her motor as well. One afternoon Leonard discovered a new source of disturbance, which took powers of detection to locate and then delicacy of negotiation to disarm. The American ladies who were fair-weather occupants of that converted mill house beyond the *lavoir* had naturally installed all manner of appliances, which in Leonard's view were quite superfluous to life. One of these in particular affected the reception on M'sieur's high-powered wireless. The English artist did not even have a telephone; but the two American ladies had had the decadence, and the impertinence, to install a water closet operated by electricity! It took a certain tact, a quality Adeline had developed increasingly over the years, to persuade them, on certain occasions, to delay their flushing.

It was difficult to explain to Leonard that he could not require the village to fold its shutters every time he wanted to listen to a concert. Besides, there were occasions when the American ladies simply forgot, or appeared to forget, the Englishman's demand; while if Adeline entered the *boulangerie* and found that the baker's old father, still third cornettist for the *sapeurs pompiers*, was in charge, she knew there was little point in even asking. Leonard tended to become irate when she failed, and his normal pallor was blasted with puce. It would have been easier had he felt able to offer a word of direct thanks himself, perhaps even a small present; but no, he acted as if countrywide silence was his prerogative. When he first became seriously ill, and the wireless was transported to his bedroom, he wished to hear more and more concerts, which strained the sympathy of the village. Happily, over the last few months he had wanted nothing but his own music. Adeline might still be dispatched to obtain a vow of muteness from the village, but she would only pretend to go, confident that by the time the concert was due to begin Leonard would have decided not to bother with the wireless that evening. Instead, he would prefer her to wind up the EMG, shuffle the horn, and play him the Oboe Fantasy, the French Songs, or the slow movement of the Pagan Symphony.

Those had been brave days, in Berlin, Leipzig, Helsinki, Paris. England was death to the true artist. To be a success there you had to be a second Mendelssohn: that was what they were waiting for, like a second Messiah. In England they had fog between the ears. They imagined themselves talking about art but they were only talking about taste. They had no concept of freedom, of the artist's needs. It was all Jesus and marriage in London Town. Sir Edward Elgar, knight, Order of Merit, Master of the King's Musick, baronet, husband. 'Falstaff' was a worthy piece, there was fine stuff in the 'Introduction and Allegro', but he had wasted his time with Jesus, with those infernal oratorios. Parry! Had he lived long enough, he would have set to music the entire Bible.

It was not permitted to be an artist in England. You might be a painter, or a composer, or a scribbler of some kind, but those foggy brains did not understand the essential precondition behind all these subsequent professions: that of *being an artist*. In Continental

Europe they did not laugh at such an idea. He had had fine times, brave days. With Busoni, with Sibelius. His walking tour in the Tyrol, when he had read his beloved Nietzsche in the German. Christianity preaches death. Sin is the invention of the Jews. Chastity produces as much foulness of soul as lust. Man is the cruellest animal. To pity is to be weak.

In England, the soul lived on its knees, shuffling towards the non-existent God like some butcher boy. Religion had poisoned art. 'Gerontius' was nauseating. Palestrina was mathematics. Plainsong was ditchwater. You had to leave England to find the upper slopes, to let the soul soar. That comfortable island dragged you down into softness and pettiness, into Jesus and marriage. Music is an emanation, an exaltation of the spirit, and how can music flow when the spirit is pegged and tethered? He had explained all this to Adeline when first he had met her. She had understood. Had she been an Englishwoman, she would have expected him to play the organ on Sunday and help her bottle jam. But Adeline had been an artist herself at the time. The voice had been coarse but still expressive. And she had seen that if he was to pursue his destiny, her art would have to be subordinate to his. You could not soar if manacled. She had understood that, too, at the time.

It was insistently important to him that she admire the 'Four English Seasons'. She was becoming ever more conventional and foggy between the ears: such was the penalty of age. She had at last spotted before her the great immensity of the void and did not know how to respond. He knew. Either you lashed yourself to the mast or you were carried away. He therefore kept ever more sternly and deliberately to the rigorous principles of life and art which he had spent so long enunciating. If you weakened, you were lost, and the house would soon enough contain the priest, the telephone, and the collected works of Palestrina.

When the telegram from Boult arrived, he ordered Marie-Thérèse not to mention the fact to Madame, on pain of dismissal. Then he placed an additional pencil cross against Tuesday's concert in *Radio Times*. 'We shall listen to this,' he informed Adeline. 'Alert the village.' As she looked over his fingers at the paper, he could sense her puzzlement. A Glinka overture, followed by Schumann and Tchaikovsky: hardly the preferred listening of Leonard Verity. Not even Grieg, still less Busoni or Sibelius. 'We shall discover what my young champion does with this old stuff,' he said by way of explanation. 'Alert the village, do you see?' 'Yes, Leonard,' she replied.

He knew it was one of his masterpieces; he knew that were she to hear it truly, she would recognise this. But it must come upon her suddenly. That opening enchantment of the remembered bucolic, with a pianissimo *cor anglais* wrapped in the quietest rustle of muted violas. He imagined the soft transformation of her face, her eyes turning towards him as they had done in Berlin and Montparnasse . . . He loved her enough to see it as his task to rescue her from her own later self. But there must be truth between them, too.

As she straightened his blanket he therefore said, abruptly, 'This business won't be cured by *le coup du chapeau*, you know.'

She scurried from the room in tears. He could not judge whether they were caused by his acknowledgment of death or by his reference to their first few weeks together. Perhaps both. In Berlin, where they had met, he had failed to arrive for their second rendezvous, but instead of taking offence, as other women might have done, Adeline had come to his room and found him prostrate with an influenza cold. He remembered her straw hat, worn despite the lateness of the season, her full, clear eyes, the cool chord of her fingers, and the curve of her hip as she turned away.

'We shall cure you with *le coup du chapeau*,' she had announced. It was apparently some medical practice or, more likely, superstition among the peasants of her region. She declined to elucidate, but went away and returned with a wrapped bottle. She told him to make himself comfortable and to put his feet together. When they formed a soft *puy* in the bed, she found his hat and placed it over his feet. Then she poured him a large tumblerful of cognac and told him to drink. At the time, he had preferred beer to strong liquor, but he did as he was told, marvelling at how improbable such a scene would be in England.

After two deep glasses, she asked if he could still see his hat. He replied that of course he could. 'Keep watching it,' she had said, and poured him a third glass. He was forbidden to speak, and had no memory now of what she had chattered on about. He merely drank and watched his hat. Finally, midway through his fifth glass, he had started to giggle and announced, 'I can see two hats.'

'Good,' she said with sudden briskness. 'Then the cure is working.' She had played the same spread chord on his forehead and left, taking the bottle with her. He fell into a coma and awoke twenty hours later, feeling much better. Not the least reason for this was that when he opened his eyes and looked down towards his feet there was no hat to be seen but only the profile of his already beloved Adeline, sitting in a low chair reading a book. It was then that he told her he was going to become a great composer. Opus 1, scored for string quartet, flute, mezzo-soprano, and sousaphone, would be called 'Le Coup du Chapeau'. Using his newly discovered method of Kinetic Impressionism, it would depict the travails of a suffering artist cured of influenza and lovesickness by a beautiful helpmeet and a bottle of cognac. Would she accept the dedication, he had asked. Only if she admired the piece, she had replied with a flirtatious tilt of her face.

'If I write it, you will admire it.' The statement was not vain or authoritarian but, rather, the reverse. Our destinies, he meant, are now joined, and I shall consider worthless any composition of mine that fails to please you. This is what his words intended, and she had understood.

Now, downstairs in the kitchen, stripping the fat from some beef bones to make Leonard's bouillon, she remembered those first few months in Berlin. How jolly he had been, with his cane, his sly wink, and his repertoire of music-hall songs; how not at all the stiff Englishman of racial stereotype. And what a different patient he had made in those days when she had given him *le coup du chapeau*. That had been the start of their love; now she was tending him once more, at the end of it. In Berlin, when he was recovered, he had promised that she would be a great singer and he would be a great composer; he would write his music for her voice and together they would conquer Europe.

It had not happened. She had doubted her own talent more than she doubted his. They made instead an artists' pact. They bound themselves together, twin spirits in life and in music, though never in marriage. They would fly free of the constraints that governed most people's existences, preferring the higher constraints of art. They would rest lightly on the ground so that they might soar the higher. They would not entangle themselves in the pettinesses of life. There would be no children.

And so they had lived: in Berlin, Leipzig, Helsinki, Paris, and now in a softly scooped valley north of Coulommiers. They had rested lightly on the ground here for over two decades. Leonard's fame had grown, and with it his reclusiveness. There was no telephone in the house; newspapers were forbidden; the high-powered wireless was used only for listening to concerts. Journalists and acolytes were denied entry; most letters went unanswered. Once a year, until Leonard became ill, they would travel south, to Menton, Antibes, Toulon, incongruous locations where Leonard would fret for his damp valley and the lonely rigour of his normal life. On these journeys Adeline would sometimes fall prey to a sharper lamentation, for the family she had quarrelled with all those years ago. In a café her glance might stop on the face of some lyrical young man, and she would briefly consider him an unknown nephew. Leonard dismissed these speculations as sentimental.

For Adeline the artistic life had begun in gregariousness and warmth; now it was ending in solitude and austerity. When she had nervously suggested to Leonard that they might secretly be married she had implied two things only. First, that she would be better able to protect his music and watch over his copyrights; and, second, selfishly, that she would be able to live on in the house they had shared for so long.

She explained to Leonard the inflexibility of the French law in respect of concubinage, but he did not want to hear. He had become irate, banging the fire tongs on the boards, so that Marie-Thérèse came running. How could she think of betraying the very principles of their life together? His music belonged to nobody and to the whole planet. Either it would be played after his death or it would not, depending on the intelligence or stupidity of the world; that was all there was to be said. As for herself, he had not realised when they had made their pact that she had sought pecuniary advantage, and if that was what exercised her, she should take what money she could find in the house when he lay on his deathbed. She might as well return to her family and pamper those imaginary nephews she was always bleating about. Here, take the Gauguin off the wall and sell it now if that is your concern. But do stop your wailing.

'It is time,' Leonard Verity said.

'Yes.'

'We shall see what my "young champion" is made of.'

'Oh, Leonard, let us have the Oboe Fantasy again.'

'Just turn it on, woman. We are nearly at the hour.'

As the wireless slowly warmed and hummed, and the rain played a soft pizzicato on the window, she told herself it did not matter that she had failed to alert the village. She doubted he would persist beyond the overture to 'Ruslan and Ludmilla', which in any case had sufficient stridency to pierce most atmospheric disturbance.

'Queen's Hall . . . Invitation Concert . . . Musical Director of the British Broadcasting Corporation . . .' They listened to the normal litany from their normal positions: he aloft in the bed, she in the low basketwork chair, close to the EMG in case the tuning needed adjustment. 'Change to the programme which has been previously announced . . . Glinka . . . new work by the English composer Leonard Verity . . . honour of his seventieth birthday later this year . . . "Four English . . ." '

She howled. He had never heard such a sound emerge from her before. She fought her heavy way downstairs, ignored Marie-Thérèse, and ran out into a wet dark afternoon. Below her, the village jangled with light and flashed with noise: gigantic motors turned and thrummed. A *kermesse* had started in her head with traction engines and flood-lamps, the comic frippery of the roundabout organ, the tinny clatter of the shooting range, the careless blast of cornet and bugle, laughter, fake fear, flashing bulbs, and stupid songs. She ran down the track to the first of these orgiastic sites. The old *boulanger* turned inquisitively as the wild, wet, under-dressed woman erupted into his son's shop, gave him a mad stare, howled, and ran out again. She, who for years had been so practical, so swift and necessary with the village, now could not even make herself understood. She wanted to strike the whole countryside into silence with fire from the gods. She ran into the butcher's, where Madame was driving her mighty turbine: a throbbing belt, a tormenting scream, blood everywhere. She ran to the nearest farm and saw feed for a hundred thousand cattle being churned and sluiced by a hundred electric pumps. She ran to the American house, but her knocking could not be heard above the antic flushing of a dozen electric water closets. The village was conspiring, just as the world always conspired against the artist, waiting until he was weakest and then seeking to destroy him. The world did it carelessly, without knowing why, without seeing why, just thumbing a switch with a casual clack. And the world didn't even notice, didn't listen, just as now they seemed not to hear the words in her mouth, these faces gathered round, staring at her. He was right, of course he was right, he had always been right. And she had betrayed him in the end, he was right about that, too.

In the kitchen Marie-Thérèse was standing in awkward conspiracy with the *curé*. Adeline went upstairs to the bedroom and shut the door. He was dead, of course, she knew that. His eyes were closed, either by nature or by human interference. His hair looked as if it had just been combed, and his mouth was turned down in a final sulk. She eased the fire tongs from his hand, touched his forehead in a spread chord, then lay down on the bed beside him. His body yielded no more in death than it had in life. At last, she fell quiet, and as her senses returned she became loosely aware of Schumann's piano concerto stumbling through the static.

She sent to Paris for a *mouleur*, who took a cast of the composer's face, and one of his right hand. The British Broadcasting Corporation announced the death of Leonard Verity, but since they had so recently given the first performance of his final work, further musical tribute was judged inessential.

Three weeks after the funeral, a square parcel marked 'Fragile' arrived at the house. Adeline was alone. She chipped the sealing wax from the two fat knots, unfolded layers of corrugated cardboard, and found an obsequious letter from the recording manager. She took each of the 'Four English Seasons' from its stiff manila envelope and sat them on her knee. Idly, methodically, as Leonard would have approved, she ordered them. Spring, summer, autumn, winter. She stared at the edge of the kitchen table, hearing other melodies.

They broke like biscuit. Her thumb bled.

The Destiny of Nathalie X

WILLIAM BOYD

THE SCREEN IS BLACK

MAN'S VOICE (OVER): I once heard a theory about this town, this place where we work and wrangle, where we swindle and swive. It was told to me by this writer I knew. He said: 'It's only a dance, but then again, it's the only dance.' I'm not sure he's right, but, anyway, he's dead now . . .

FADE UP

Once upon a time – actually, not so very long ago at all, come to think of it – in east central West Africa, on one enervating May morning Aurélien No sat on the stoop of his father's house staring aimlessly at the road that led to Murkina Leto, state capital of the People's Republic of Kiq. The sun's force seemed to press upon the brown, dusty landscape with redundant intensity, Aurélien thought idly, there was surely no moisture left out there to evaporate and it seemed . . . He searched for a word for a second or two: it seemed 'stupid' that all that calorific energy should go to waste.

He called for his little brother Marius to fetch him another beer, but no reply came from inside the house. He scratched his cheek;

he thought he could taste metal in his mouth – that new filling. He shifted his weight on his cane chair and wondered vaguely why cane made that curious squeaking sound. Then his eye was caught by the sight of a small, blue van that was making its way up the middle of the road with what seemed like undue celerity, tooting its horn at the occasional roadside pedestrian and browsing cow not so much to scare them out of the way as to announce the importance of this errand it was on.

To Aurélien's mild astonishment the blue van turned abruptly into his father's driveway and stopped equally abruptly before the front door. As the laterite dust thrown up by the tyres slowly dispersed, the postman emerged from the auburn cloud like a messenger from the gods carrying before him a stiff envelope blazoned with an important-looking crest.

MARIUS NO: For sure, I remember that day when he won the prize. Personally, I was glad of the distraction. He had been emmerding me all morning. 'Get this', 'Get that', 'Fetch me a beer'. I just knew it had gone quiet for ten minutes. When I came out on to the stoop, he was sitting there, looking even more vacant than normal, just staring at this paper in his hands. 'Hey, Coco,' I said to him. 'Military service, mm? Poor *salaud*. Wait till those bastard sergeants give you one up the *cul*.' He said nothing, so I took the paper from his hands and read it. It was the 100,000 francs that had shocked him, struck him dumb.

When *Le Destin de Nathalie X* (*metteur en scène* Aurélien No) won the Prix d'Or at the *concours général* in Paris of L'Ecole Supérieur des Etudes Cinématographiques (ESEC), the Kiq Minister of Culture (Aurélien's brother-in-law) laid on a reception for 200 guests at the ministry. After a long speech the minister called Aurélien on to the podium to shake him publicly by the hand. Aurélien had gathered his small tight dreadlocks into a loose sheaf on the top of his head, and the photographs of that special evening show him startled and blinking in the silvery wash of the flash bulbs, some natural flinch causing the fronds of his dreadlock sheaf to toss simultaneously in one direction as if blown by a stiff breeze.

The minister asked him what he planned to do with the prize money.

'Good question,' Aurélien said and thought for ten seconds or so before replying. 'It's a condition of the prize that I put the money towards another film.'

'Here in Kiq?' the minister said, smiling knowingly.

'Of course.'

DELPHINE DRELLE: 'It's impossible,' I said when he called me. 'Completely out of the question. Are you mad? What kind of film could you make in Kiq?' He came to my apartment in Paris, he said he wanted me to be in his new film. I say I don't want to be an actress. Well, as soon as I started explaining, Aurélien saw I was making sense. That's what I like about Aurélien, by the way: he is responsive to the powers of reason. Absolutely not, I said to Aurélien, never in my life. He said he had an idea, but only I could do it. I said, look what happened the last time, do you think I'm crazy? I've only been out of the clinic one month. He just smiled at me. He said, what do you think if we go to Hollywood?'

Aurélien No turned out of the rental park at LAX and wondered which direction to take. Delphine Drelle sat beside him studying her face intently in the mirror of her compact and moaning about the dehydrating effect of international air travel. In the back seat of the car sat Bertrand Holbish, a photographer and ex-boyfriend of Delphine, squashed in the cramped space left by the two large scratched and dented aluminium boxes that held the camera and the sound equipment.

Aurélien turned left, drove 400 metres and turned left again. He saw a sign directing him to the freeway and followed it until he reached a hotel. Dollarwize Inn, he saw it was called as he pulled carefully into the forecourt. The hotel was a six-storey rectangle. The orange plastic cladding on the balconies had been bleached salmon pink by the sun.

'Here we are,' Aurélien said. 'This is perfect.'

'Where's Hollywood?' Bertrand Holbish asked.

'Can't be far away,' Aurélien said.

BERTRAND HOLBISH: Immediately, when he asked me, I said to Aurélien that I didn't know much about sound. He said you switch it on, you point the volume. No, you check the volume and you point the, ah, what's the word? . . . What? Ah, yes, 'boom'; I said: you pay my ticket? You buy me drugs? He said of course, only don't touch Delphine [laughs, coughs]. That's Aurélien for you, one crazy guy.

DELPHINE DRELLE: Did I tell you that he is a very attractive man, Aurélien? Yes? He's a real African, you know, strong face, strong African face . . . and his lips, they're like they're carved. He's tall, slim. He has this hair, it's like that tennis player, Noah, like little braids hanging down over his forehead. Sometimes he puts beads on the end of them. I don't like it so much. I want him to shave his head. Completely. He speaks real good English, Aurélien. I never knew this about him. I asked him once how he pronounced his name, and he said something like 'Ngoh'. He says it is a common name in Kiq. But everybody pronounces it differently. He doesn't mind.

When Aurélien went out the next day to scout for locations he discovered that the area they were staying in was called Westchester. He drove through the featureless streets – unusually wide, he thought, for such an inactive neighbourhood – the air charged and thunderous with landing jetliners, until he found a small cluster of shops beneath a revolving sign declaiming BROGAN'S MINI-MALL. There was a deli, a drugstore, a novelty store, a Korean grocery and a pizzeria-cum-coffee shop that had most of the features he was looking for: half a dozen tables on the sidewalk, a predominantly male staff, a licence to sell alcoholic beverages. He went inside, ordered a cappuccino and asked how long they stayed open in the evenings. Late, came the answer. For the first time since he had suggested coming to Los Angeles, Aurélien sensed a small tremor of excitement. Perhaps it would be possible after all. He looked at the expressionless tawny faces of the men behind the counter and the cheerful youths serving food and drink. He felt sure these gentlemen would allow him to film in their establishment – for a modest fee, of course.

MICHAEL SCOTT GEHN: Have you ever seen *Le Destin de Nathali X*? Extraordinary film, extraordinary. No, I tell you, I'd put it right up there with *Un Chien Andalou*, Todd's *Last Walk*, *Chelsea Girls*, Downey's *Chafed Elbows*. That category of film. Surreal, bizarre . . . Let's not beat about the bush, sometimes downright incomprehensible, but it gets to you. Somehow, subcutaneously. You know, I spend more time thinking about certain scenes in *Nathalie X* than I do about Warner's annual slate. And it's my business, what more can I say? Do you smoke? Do you have any non-violent objections if I do? Thank you, you're very gracious. I'm not kidding, you can't be too careful here. *Nathalie X* . . . OK. It's very simple and outstandingly clever. A girl wakes up in her bed in her room . . .

Aurélien looked at his map. Delphine and Bertrand stood at his shoulder, sun-glassed, fractious.

'We have to go from here . . . to here.'

'Aurélien, when are we going to film?'

'Tomorrow. Maybe. First we walk it through.'

Delphine let her shoulders slump. 'But we have the stock. Why don't we start?'

'I don't know. I need an idea. Let's walk it through.'

He took Bertrand's elbow and guided him across the road to the other side. He made half a square with his thumbs and his forefingers and framed Delphine in it as she lounged against the exit sign of the Dollarwize Inn.

'Turn right,' Aurélien shouted across the road. 'I'll tell you which way to go.'

MICHAEL SCOTT GEHN: . . . a girl wakes up in her own bed in her own room, somewhere in Paris. She gets out of bed and puts on her make-up, very slowly, very deliberately. No score, just the noises she makes as she goes about her business. You know, paints her nails, mascara on eyelashes. She hums a bit, she starts to sing a song to herself, snatches of a song in English. Beatles song, from the *White Album*, what's it called? Oh yeah: 'Rocky Racoon'. This girl's French, right, and she's singing in English with a French accent, just quietly to herself. The song sounds totally different. Totally. Extraordinary effect. Bodywide goose-bumps. This takes about twenty, thirty minutes. You are completely, but *completely*, held. You do not notice the time passing. That something so totally – let's not beat about the bush – banal, can hold you that way. Extraordinary. We're talking mundanity, here, absolute diurnal minutiae. I see, what, 250 movies a year in my business, not counting TV. I am replete with film. Sated. But I am held. No, mesmerised would be fair. [Pause.] Did I tell you the girl was naked?

'Turn left,' Aurélien called.

Delphine obliged and walked past the mirror-glass facade of an office building.

'Stop.'

Aurélien made a note on the map and turned to Bertrand.

'What could she do here, Bertrand? She needs to do some-thing.'

'I don't know. How should I know?'

'Something makes her stop.'

'She could step in some dog shit.'

Aurélien reflected for a while. He looked around him: at the cracked, parched concrete of the street, the dusty burnish on the few parked cars. There was a bleached, fumy quality to the light that day, a softened glare that hurt the eyes. The air reverberated as another jumbo hauled itself out of LAX.

'Not a bad idea,' he said. 'Thanks, Bertrand.' He called to Delphine. 'OK, go up to the end of the road and turn left.'

MICHAEL SCOTT GEHN: I've written a lot about this movie, analysed the hell out of it, the way it's shot, the way it manipulates mood, but it only struck me the other day how it works. Essentially, basically. It's all in the title, you see. '*Le Destin*'. The Destiny of Nathalie X. Destiny. What does destiny have in store for this girl, I should say, this astoundingly attractive girl? She gets up, she puts on her make-up, she sings a song, she gets dressed. She leaves her apartment building and walks through the streets of Paris to a café. It's night-time. She sits in this café and orders a beer. We're watching her, we're waiting. She drinks more beers, she seems to be getting drunk. People come and go. We wait. We wonder: What is the destiny of Nathalie X? (It's pronounced 'eeks' in French. Not 'ecks', 'eeks'.) And then? But I don't want to spoil the movie for you.

They started filming on their sixth day in Los Angeles. It was late afternoon – almost magic hour – and the orange sun basted the city in a warm, viscous light. Aurélien shot the sequence of the walk in front of the mirror-glass building. The moving cloudscape and the mirror-glass curtain wall was disturbingly beautiful. Aurélien had a moment's regret that he was filming in black and white.

Delphine wore a short, black skirt and a loose, V-neck, taupe cashmere sweater (no bra). On her feet she wore skin-coloured kid loafers, so fine you could roll them into a ball. She had a fringed suede bag over her shoulder. Her long hair was dyed a light sandy blonde and – after much debate – was down.

Aurélien set up the camera across the road for the first take. Bertrand stood beside him and pointed his microphone in the general direction of Delphine.

Aurélien switched on the camera, chalked SCENE ONE on the clapperboard, walked into frame, clicked it and said '*Vas y, Delphine.*'

Nathalie X walked along the sidewalk. When she reached the middle of the mirror-glass wall she stopped. She took off one of her shoes and peeled a coin of chewing-gum from its sole. She stuck the gum to the glass wall, refitted her shoe and walked on.

MICHAEL SCOTT GEHN: I have to say as a gesture of contempt for Western materialism, the capitalist macrostructure that we function in, that takes some beating. And it's not in the French version. Aurélien No has been six days in Los Angeles and he comes up with something as succinct, as moodily epiphanic as that. That's what I call talent. Not raw talent, talent of the highest sophistication.

BERTRAND HOLBISH: The way Delphine cut her hair, you know, is the clue, I think. It's blonde, right? Long, and she has a fringe, OK? But not like anybody else's fringe. It's just too long. It hangs to her lower eyelash. To here [gestures], to the middle of her nose. So she shakes her head all the time to clear her vision a little. She pulls it aside – like this – with one finger when she wants to see something a little better . . . You know, many, many people look at Delphine and find this very exciting, sexually, I mean. She's a pretty girl, for sure, nice body, nice face. But I see these girls everywhere. Especially in Los Angeles. It's something about this fringe business that makes her different. People look at her all the time. When we were waiting for Aurélien we – Delphine and me – used to play backgammon. For hours. The fringe, hanging there, over her eyes. It drove me fucking crazy. I offered her 500 dollars to cut it one centimetre, just one centimetre. She refused. She knew, Delphine, she knew.

Aurélien filmed the walk to the café first. It took four days, starting late afternoon, always approaching the café at dusk. He filmed Nathalie's *levée* in one sustained twelve-hour burst. Delphine woke, made up, sang and dressed eight times that day in a series of long takes, cuts only coming when the film ran out. The song changed: Delphine sang Bob Dylan's 'She belongs to me' with the pronoun changed to 'he'. This was Delphine's idea, and a good one, Aurélien thought. The only problem was she kept forgetting. 'He's an artist, she don't look back,' Delphine sang in her flat, breathy voice as she combed her hair. 'He never stumbles, she's got no place to fall.'

Every evening they would go to the pizzeria and eat. Aurélien insisted that Delphine get drunk, not knee-walking drunk, but as far as woozy inebriation. Of course the waiters came to know them, and conversation ensued. 'What you guys doin' here anyway? Making a movie? Great. Another beer for the lady? No problemo.'

After a week's regular visiting Aurélien asked the owner, a small nervy man called George Malinverno, if they could film at the pizzeria, outside on the 'terrace', for one night only. They agreed on a remuneration of 200 dollars.

MICHAEL SCOTT GEHN: Have your ever heard of the Topeka Film Festival? That's Topeka, Kansas? No? Neither have

I. So you can understand that I was kind of pissed when my editor assigned me to cover it. It ran a week, the theme was 'Kansas in the Western 1970–1980'. It's not my subject, my last book was on Murnau, for Christ's sake, but let's not get embroiled in office politics. The point is I'm on my way to the airport and I realise I've left my razor and shaving-foam behind. I pull into this mini-mall where there's a drugstore. I'm coming out of the shop and I see there's a film crew setting up a shot at the pizzeria. Normally I see a film crew and chronic catatonia sets in. But there's something about this one: the guy holding the boom mike looks like he's stoned – even I can see that it keeps dropping into shot. So I wander over. The camera is set up behind these plants, kind of poking through a gap, like it's hidden or something. And there's this black guy behind the camera with this great hair with beads on it. I see he's DP and clapperboy and director. He calls out into the darkness and this sensational-looking girl walks into the pizzeria terrace thing. She sits down and orders a beer, and they just keep filming. After about two minutes, the sound man drops the boom, and they have to start over. I hear them talking – French. I couldn't believe it. I had this guy figured for some wannabe homeboy director out of South Central LA. But they're talking French to each other. When was the last time a French crew shot a movie in this town? I introduced myself, and that's when he told me about *Nathalie X* and the Prix d'Or. I bought them all some drinks, and he told me his story and gave me a video cassette of the movie. Fuck Topeca, I thought, I knew this was too good to miss. French underground movies shooting next door to LAX. Are you kidding me? They were all staying in some fleabag motel under the flightpath, for God's sake. I called my editor and threatened to take the feature to *American Film*. He reassigned me.

The night's shooting at the pizzeria did not go well. Bertrand proved incapable of holding the boom aloft for more than two minutes, and this was one sequence where Aurélien knew he needed sound. He spent half an hour taping a mike under Delphine's table and snaking the wires round behind the potted plants. Then this man who said he was a film critic turned up and offered to buy them a drink. While Aurélien was talking to him,

Delphine drank three Margaritas and a Negroni. When they tried to restart, her reflexes had slowed to such an extent that when she remembered she had to throw the glass of beer, the waiter had turned away, and she missed completely. Aurélien wrapped it up for the night. Holbish wandered off, and Aurélien drove Delphine back to the hotel. She was sick in the parking-lot and started to cry, and that's when Aurélien thought about the gun.

KAISER PREVOST: I rarely read *film/e*. It's way too pretentious. Ditto that creep Michael Scott Gehn. Any guy with three names and I get irrationally angry. What's wrong with plain old Michael Gehn? Are there so many Michael Gehns out there that he has to distinguish himself? 'Oh, you mean Michael *Scott* Gehn, I got you now.' I'd like a Teacher's, straight up, with three ice-cubes. Three. Thank you. Anyway for some reason I bought it that week – it was the issue with that great shot of Jessica, no, Lanier on the cover – and I read the piece about this French director Aurélien No and this remake *Seeing Through Nathalie* he was shooting in town. Gehn – sorry Michael Scott Gehn – is going on like this guy is sitting there holding God's hand, and I read about the Prix d'Or and this *Nathalie X* film and I think, hmmm, has Aurélien got representation? This is Haig. This is not Teacher's.

MICHAEL SCOTT GEHN: I knew, I just knew when this young guy Kaiser Prevost calls me up, things would change. 'Hi, Michael,' he says, 'Kaiser Prevost here.' I don't know jack shit about any Kaiser Prevost but I do know I hate it when someone uses my Christian name from the get-go – what's wrong with Mister Gehn? Also his tone just assumes, just oozes the assumption that I'm going to know who he is. I mean, I am a film critic of some reputation, if I may be immodest for a moment, and these young guys in the agencies . . . There's a problem of perspectives, that's what it comes down to, that's what bedevils us. I have a theory about this town: there is no overview, nobody steps back, no one stands on the mountain looking down on the valley. Imagine an army composed entirely of officers. Let me put it another way: imagine an army where everyone *thinks* they're an officer. That's Hollywood, that's the film business. No one wants to accept the hierarchy, no one will admit they are a foot soldier. And I'm sorry, a young agent in a boutique agency is just a GI Joe to me. Still, he was a persuasive fellow and he had some astute and flattering things to say about the article. I told him where Aurélien was staying.

Aurélien No met Kaiser Prevost for breakfast in the coffee shop of the Dollarwize. Prevost looked around him as if he had just emerged from some prolonged comatose sleep.

'You know, I've lived in this town for all my life and I don't think I've ever even driven through here. And as for shooting a movie . . . It's a first.'

'Well, it was right for me.'

'Oh no. I appreciate that. I think it's fresh, original. Gehn certainly thinks a lot of you.'

'Who?'

Prevost showed him the article in *film/e*. Aurélien flicked through it. 'He has written a lot.'

'Have you got a rough assembly of the new movie? Anything I could see?'

'No.'

'Any dailies? Maybe you call them rushes.'

'There are no dailies on this film. None of us see anything until it is finished.'

'The ultimate *auteur*, huh? That is impressive. More than that, it's cool.'

Aurélien chuckled. 'No, it's a question of – what do you say? – *faute de mieux*.'

'I couldn't have put it better myself. Look, Aurélien, I'd like you to meet somebody, a friend of mine at a studio. Can I fix that up? I think it would be mutually beneficial.'

'Sure. If you like.'

KAISER PREVOST: I have a theory about this town, this place, about the way it works: it operates best when people go beyond the bounds of acceptable behaviour. You reach a position, a course of action suggests itself, and you say, 'This makes me morally uncomfortable', or 'This will constitute a betrayal of friendship'. In any other walk of life you withdraw, you rethink. But my theory goes like this: make it your working maxim. *When you find yourself in a position of normative doubt then that is the sign to commit.* My variation on this theory is that the really successful people go one step further. They find themselves in this moral grey area, they move right on into the black. Look at Vincent Bandine.

I knew I was doing the right thing with Aurélien No because I had determined not to tell my boss. Sheldon started ArtFocus after ten years at ICM. It was going well but it's clear that the foundations are giving. Two months ago we lost Larry Swiftsure. Last Saturday I get a call from Sheldon: Donata Vail has walked to CAA. His own Donata. He was weeping and was looking for consolation, which I hope I provided. Under these circumstances it seemed to me at best morally dubious that I should go behind his back and try and set up a deal for Aurélien at Alcazar. I was confident it was the only route to take.

The gun idea persisted, it nagged at Aurélien. He talked about it with Bertrand, who thought it was an amusing notion.

'A gun, why not? Pam-pam-pam-pam.'

'Could you get me one? A handgun?' Aurélien asked. 'Maybe one of those guys you know . . .'

'A prop gun? Or a real one?'

'Oh, I think it should be real. Don't tell Delphine, though.'

The next day Bertrand showed Aurélien a small, scarred automatic. It cost 500 dollars. Aurélien did not question him about its provenance.

He reshot the end of Nathalie's *levée*. Nathalie, dressed, is about to leave her room, her hand is on the doorknob. She pauses, turns and goes to a dresser, from the top drawer of which she removes the gun. She checks the clip and places it in her fringed suede shoulder bag. She leaves.

He and Delphine had a prolonged debate about whether they should reshoot the entire walk to the restaurant. Delphine thought it was pointless. How, she argued, would the audience know if the gun were in her shoulder bag or not? But *you* would know,

Aurélien countered, and everything might change. Delphine maintained that she would walk the same way whether she had a gun in her bag or not; also they had been in Los Angeles for three weeks and she was growing bored; *Le Destin* had been filmed in five days. A compromise was agreed: they would reshoot only the pizzeria sequence. Aurélien went off to negotiate another night's filming.

BOB BERGER: I hate to admit it but I was grateful to Kaiser Prevost when he brought the *Nathalie X* project to me. As I told him, I had admired Aurélien No's work for some years and was excited and honoured at the possibility of setting up his first English-language film. More to the point, the last two films I exec-ed at Alcazar had done me no favours: *Disintegrator* had only grossed thirteen before they stopped tracking, and *Sophomore Nite II* had gone straight to video. I liked the idea of doing something with more art quality and with a European kind of angle. I asked Kaiser to get a script to me soonest and I raised the project at our Monday morning staff meeting. I said I thought it would be a perfect vehicle for Lanier Cross. Boy, did that make Vincent sit up. Dirty old toad (he's my uncle).

KAISER PREVOST: I'll tell you one fact about Vincent Bandine. He has the cleanest teeth and the healthiest gums in Hollywood. Every morning a dental nurse comes to his house and flosses and cleans his teeth for him. Every morning, 365 days a year. That's what I call class. Have you any idea how much that must cost?

Kaiser Prevost thought he detected an unsettled quality about Aurélien as he drove him to the meeting at Alcazar. Aurélien was frowning as he looked about him. The day was perfect, the air clear, the colours ideally bright; more than that he was going to a deal meeting at a major minor studio, or minor major depending on whom you were talking to. Usually in these cases the anticipation in the car would be heady, palpable. Aurélien just made clicking noises in his mouth and fiddled with the beads on the end of his dreadlocks. Prevost told him about Alcazar Films, its money base, its ten-picture slate, its deals or potential deals with Goldie, Franklin Dean, Joel, Demi, Carlo Sancarlo and ItalFilm. The names seemed to make no impact.

As they turned up Coldwater to go over into the valley, Prevost finally had to ask if everything was all right.

'There's a slight problem,' Aurélien admitted. 'Delphine has left.'

'That's too bad,' Prevost said, trying to keep the excitement out of his voice. 'Gone back to France?'

'I don't know. She's left with Bertrand.'

'Bitch, man.'

'We still have the whole last scene to reshoot.'

'Listen, Aurélien, relax. One thing you learn about working in this town. Everything can be fixed. Everything.'

'How can I finish without Delphine?'

'Have you ever heard of Lanier Cross?'

VINCENT BANDINE: My nephew has two sterling qualities: he's dumb and he's eager to please. He's a good-looking kid too, and that helps, no doubt about it. Sometimes, sometimes, he gets it right. Sometimes he has a sense for the popular mood. When he started talking about this *Destiny of Nathalie* film I thought he was way out of his depth until he mentioned the fact that Lanier Cross would be buck naked for the first thirty minutes. I said get the French guy in, tie him up, get him together with Lanier. She'll go for the French part. If the No fellow won't play, get the Englishman in, what's his name, Tim Pascal, he'll do it. He'll do anything I tell him.

I have a theory about this town: there's too much respect for art. That's where we make all our mistakes, all of them. But if that's a given, then I'm prepared to work with it once in a while. Especially if it'll get me Lanier Cross nekkid.

MICHAEL SCOTT GEHN: When I heard that Aurélien No was doing a deal with Vincent Bandine at Alcazar I was both suicidal and oddly proud. If you'd asked me where was the worst home possible for a remake of *Nathalie X* I'd have said Alcazar straight off. But that's what heartens me about this burg, this place we fret and fight in. I have a theory about this town: they all talk about the 'business', the 'industry', how hard-nosed and bottom-line obsessed they are, but it's not true. Or rather not the whole truth. Films of worth are made, and I respect the place for it. God, I even respected Vincent Bandine for it and I never thought those words would ever issue from my mouth. We shouldn't say: look at all the crap that gets churned out; instead we should be amazed at the good films that do emerge from time to time. There is a heart here and it's still beating, even though the pulse is kind of thready.

Aurélien was impressed with the brutal economy of Bob Berger's office. A black ebony desk sat in the middle of a charcoal grey carpet. Two large, black leather sofas were separated by a thick sheet of glass resting on three sharp cones. On one wall were two black-and-white photographs of lily trumpets, and on another was an African mask. There was no evidence of work or the tools of work apart from the long flattened telephone on his desk. Berger himself was wearing brushed banana linen, he was in his mid-twenties, tall and deeply tanned.

Berger shook Aurélien's hand warmly, his left hand gripping Aurélien's forearm firmly as if Aurélien were a drowning man about to be hauled from a watery grave. He drew Aurélien to one of the leather sofas and sat him upon it. Prevost slid down beside him. A great variety of drinks were offered, though Aurélien's choice of beer caused some consternation. Berger's assistant was dispatched in search of some. Prevost and Berger's decaff espressos arrived promptly.

Prevost gestured at the mask. 'Home sweet home, eh, Aurélien?'

'Excuse me?'

'I love African art,' Berger said. 'What part of Africa are you from?'

'Kiq.'

'Right,' Berger said.

There was a short silence.

'Oh. Congratulations,' Berger said.

'Excuse me?'

'On the prize. Prix d'Or. Well deserved. Kaiser, have we got a print of *Nathalie X*?'

'We're shipping it over from Paris. It'll be here tomorrow.'

'It will?' Aurélien said, a little bemused.

'Everything can be fixed, Aurélien.'

'I want Lanier to see it. And Vincent.'

'Bob, I don't know if it's really Vincent's scene.'

'He has to see it. OK, after we sign Lanier.'

'I think that would be wise, Bob.'

'I want to see it again, I must say. Extraordinary piece.'

'You've seen it?' Aurélien said.

'Yeah. At Cannes, I think. Or possibly Berlin. Have we got a script yet, Kaiser?'

'There is no script. Extant.'

'We've got to get a synopsis. A treatment at least. Mike'll want to see something on paper. He'll never let Lanier go otherwise.'

'Shit. We need a goddamn writer, then,' Prevost said.

'Davide?' Berger said into the speaker phone. 'We need a writer. Get Matt Friedrich.' He turned to Aurélien. 'You'll like him. One of the old school. What?' He listened to the phone again and sighed. 'Aurélien, we're having some trouble tracking down your beer. What do you say to a Dr Pepper?'

BOB BERGER: I have a theory about this town, this place. You have people in powerful executive positions who are, to put it kindly, very ordinary-looking types. I'm not talking about intellect, I'm talking about looks. The problem is these ordinary-looking people control the lives of individuals with sensational genetic advantages. That's an unbelievably volatile mix, I can tell you. And it cuts both ways; it can be very uncomfortable. It's fine for me, I'm a handsome guy, I'm in good shape. But for most of my colleagues . . . It's the source of many of our problems. That's why I took up golf.

LANIER CROSS: Tolstoy said: 'Life is a *tartine de merde* that we are obliged to consume daily.'

'This is for me?' Aurélien said, looking at the house, its landscaped, multi-levelled sprawl, the wide maw of its vast garage.

'You can't stay down by the airport,' Prevost said. 'Not any more. You can shoot in Westchester but you can't live there.'

A young woman emerged from the front door. She had short chestnut hair, a wide white smile and was wearing a Spandex leotard and heavy climbing boots.

'This is Nancy, your assistant.'

'Hi. Good to meet you, Aurélien. Did I say that right?'

'Aurélien.'

'Aurélien?'

'It's not important.'

'The office is in back of the tennis court. It's in good shape.'

'Look, I got to fly, Aurélien. You're meeting Lanier Cross seven thirty a.m. at the Hamburger Haven on the Shore. Nancy'll fix everything up.'

To his surprise Kaiser Prevost then embraced him. When they broke apart Aurélien thought he saw tears in his eyes.

'We'll fucking show them, man, we'll fucking show them. Onward and upward, way to fucking go.'

'Any news of Delphine?'

'Who? No. Nothing yet. Any problems, call me, Aurélien. Twenty-four hours a day.'

MATT FRIEDRICH: *Le Destin de Nathalie X* was not as boring as I had expected but then I was expecting terminal boredom. I was bored, sure, but it was nice to see Paris again. That's the great thing they've got going for them, French films, they carry this wonderful cargo of nostalgic francophilia for all non-French audiences. Pretty girl too, easy on the eye. I never thought I could happily watch a girl drink herself drunk on beer in a French café but I did. It was not a wasted hour and a half.

It sure freaked out Prevost and Berger, though. 'Extraordinary,' Prevost said, clearly moved, 'extraordinary piece.' Berger mused awhile before announcing, 'That girl is a fox.' 'Michael Scott Gehn thinks it's a masterpiece,' I said. They agreed, vehemently. It's one of my tricks: when you don't know what to say, when you hated it or you're really stuck and anything qualified won't pass muster, use someone else's praise. Make it up if you have to. It's infallible, I promise.

I asked them how long they wanted the synopsis to be: sentence length or half a page. Berger said it had to be over forty pages, closely spaced, so people would be reluctant to read it. 'We already have coverage,' he said, 'but we need a document.' 'Make it as surreal and weird as you like,' Prevost said, handing me the video cassette, 'that's the whole point.'

We walked out into the Alcazar lot and went in search of our automobiles. 'When's he meeting Lanier?' Berger said. 'Tomorrow morning. She'll love him, Bob,' Prevost said. 'It's a done deal.' Berger gestured at the heavens. 'Bountiful Jehovah,' he said, 'get me Lanier.'

I looked at these two guys, young enough to be my sons, as they crouched into their sleek, haunchy cars under a tallow moon, fantasising loudly, belligerently, about this notional film, the deals, the stars, and I felt enormous pity for them. I have a theory about this town: our trouble is we are at once the most confident and the most insecure people in the world. We seem bulging with self-assurance, full of loud-voiced swagger, but in reality we're terrified, or we hate ourselves, or we're all taking happy pills of some order or another, or seeing shrinks, or getting counselled by fakirs and shamans, or fleeced by a whole gallimaufry of frauds and mountebanks. This is the Faustian pact – or should I say this is the Faust deal – you have to make in order to live and work here: you get it all, sure, but you get royally fucked up in the process. That's the price you pay. It's in the contract.

Aurélien No was directed to Lanier Cross's table in the dark rear angles of the Hamburger Haven. Another man and a woman were sitting with her. Aurélien shook her thin hand. She was beautiful, he saw, but so small, a child-woman, the musculature of a twelve-year-old with the sexual features of an adult. He found it hard not to stare at her breasts.

She introduced the others, an amiable, grinning, broad-shouldered youngster and a lean, crop-haired woman in her forties with a fierce, strong face.

'This is my husband,' she said. 'Kit Vermeer. And this is Naomi Tashourian. She's a writer we work with.'

'We love your work,' Kit said.

'Beautiful film,' echoed Lanier.

'You've seen it?' Aurélien said.

'We saw it two hours ago,' Lanier said.

Aurélien looked at his watch: Nancy had made sure he was punctual – 7.30 a.m.

'I called Berger, said I had to see it before we met.'

'We tend to sleep in the day,' Kit said. 'Like bats.'

'Like lemurs,' Lanier said. 'I don't like bats.'

' – like lemurs.'

'It's a beautiful film,' Lanier said. 'That's why we wanted to meet with you.' She reached up and unfastened a large plastic bulldog clip on the top of her head and uncoiled a great dark glossy hank of hair a yard long. She pulled and tightened it, screwing it up, winding it around her right hand, piling it back on the top of her head before she refastened it in position with the clip. Everyone remained silent during this operation.

'That's why we wanted you to meet Naomi.'

'This is a remake, right?' Naomi said.

'Yes. I think so.'

'Excellent,' Lanier said. 'I know Kit wants to put something to you. Kit?'

Kit leaned across the table. 'I want to play the waiter,' he said.

Aurélien thought before answering. 'The waiter is only in the film for about two minutes, right at the end.'

'Which is why we thought you should meet Naomi.'

'The way I see it,' Naomi said, 'is that Nathalie has been in a relationship with the waiter. That's why she goes to the restaurant. And we could see, in flashback, you know, their relationship.'

'I think it could be extraordinary, Aurélien,' Lanier said.

'And I know that because of our situation, I and Lanier, our marital situation,' Kit added, 'we could bring something extraordinary to that relationship. And beautiful.'

Lanier and Kit kissed each other, briefly but with some passion, before resuming the argument in favour of the flashback. Aurélien ordered a beer and some steak and french fries as they fleshed out the relationship between Nathalie X and her waiter-lover.

'And Naomi would write this?' Aurélien asked.

'Yes,' Lanier said. 'I'm not ready to work with another writer just yet.'

'I think Bob Berger has another writer – Matt Friedrich.'

'What's he done?' Kit said.

'We have to let Matt go, Aurélien,' Lanier said. 'You shouldn't drink beer this early in the morning.'

'Why not?'

'I'm an alcoholic,' Kit said. 'It's the thin end of the wedge, believe me.'

'Could you guys leave me alone with Aurélien?' Lanier said.

They left.

LANIER CROSS: I have a theory about this town: the money doesn't matter. THE MONEY DOESN'T MATTER. Everybody thinks it's about the money but they're wrong. They think it's only because of the money that people put up with the godawful shit that's dumped on them. That there can be only one possible reason why people are prepared to be so desperately unhappy. Money. Not so. Consider this: everybody who matters in this town has more than enough money. They don't need any more money. And I'm not talking about the studio heads, the top directors, the big stars, the people with obscene amounts. There are thousands of people in this town, possible tens of thousands, who are involved in movies who have more money than is reasonably acceptable. So it's not about money, it can't be, it's about something else. It's about being at the centre of the world.

'She loved you,' Kaiser Prevost said. 'She's all over you like a rash.'

'Any news of Delphine?'

'Who? Ah, no. What did you say to her, to Lanier? Bob called, she'll do it for nothing. Well, half her normal fee. Sensational idea about Kit Vermeer. Excellent. Why didn't I think of that? Maybe that's what swung it.'

'No, it was her idea. How are we going to finish the film without Delphine?'

'Aurélien. Please. Forget Delphine Drelle. We have Lanier Cross. We fired Friedrich, we got Tashourian writing the flashback. We're in business, my son, in business.'

NAOMI TASHOURIAN: I have a theory about this town, this place. Don't be a woman.

Aurélien sat in the cutting-room with Barker Lear, an editor, as they ran what existed of *Seeing Through Nathalie* on the Moviola.

Barker, a hefty man with a grizzled ginger goatee, watched Delphine sit down at the pizzeria and order a beer. She drank it down and ordered another, then the sound boom which had been bobbing erratically in and out of frame for the past few minutes fell fully into view and the screen went black.

Barker turned and looked at Aurélien who was frowning and tapping his teeth with the end of a pencil.

'That's some film,' Barker said. 'Who's the girl? She's extraordinary.'

'Delphine Drelle.'

'She a big star in France?'

'No.'

'Sorta hypnotic effect, she has . . .' He shrugged. 'Shame about the boom.'

'Oh, I don't worry about that sort of thing,' Aurélien said. 'It adds to the verisimilitude.'

'I don't follow.'

'You're meant to know it's a film. That's why the end works so well.'

'So what happens in the end? You've still got to shoot it, right?'

'Yes. I don't know what happens. Neither does Delphine.'

'You don't say?'

'She gets drunk you see. We watch her getting drunk. We don't cut away. We don't know what she might do. That's what makes it so exciting – that's the "Destiny of Nathalie X".'

'I see . . . So, ah, what happened at the end of the first film?'

'She goes to the café, she drinks six or seven beers very quickly and I can see she's quite drunk. She orders another drink, and when the waiter brings it, she throws it in his face.'

'You don't say? Then what?'

'They have a fight. Delphine and the waiter. They really hit each other. It's fantastic. Delphine, she's had this training, self-defence. She knees this guy in the *couilles*. Boff!'

'Fascinating.'

'He falls over. She collapses, crying, she turns to me, swears at me. Runs off into the night. The end. It's amazing.'

Barker rubbed his beard, thinking. He glanced at Aurélien covertly.

'Going to do the same thing here?'

'No, no. It's got to be different for the USA, for Hollywood. That's why I gave her the gun.'

'Is it a real gun?'

'Oh yes. Otherwise what would be the point?'

BARKER LEAR: I definitely had him for a wacko at first, but after I spent an afternoon with him, talking to him, it seemed to me he really knew what he was doing. He was a real calm guy, Aurélien. He had his own vision, didn't worry about other people, what other people might think about him. And it was the easiest editing job I ever did. Long, long takes. Lot of hand-held stuff. The walk had a few reverses, few mid-shots, dolly shots. And the film was kind of exciting, I have to admit, and I was really quite disappointed that he still hadn't shot the end. This girl Delphine, with this crazy blonde fringe over her eyes, there was definitely something wild about her. I mean, who knows, once she got loaded, what she might have done. Maybe Aurélien wasn't a wacko, but she definitely was.

You know, I have a theory about this town, this place. I've been working here for twenty-five years and I've seen them all. In this town you have very, very clever people and very, very wacko people, and the problem is – and that's what makes this place different – the very clever people *have* to work with the very wacko people. They have to, they can't help it, it's the nature of the job. That doesn't happen other places for one simple reason – clever and wacko don't mix.

Aurélien stood by the pool with Nancy, enjoying the subdued

play of morning light on the water. Today Nancy's hair was white blonde, and she wore a tutu over her leotard, and cowboy boots with spurs. She handed him a pair of car keys and an envelope with 1,000 dollars in it.

'That's the new rental car. Celica OK? And there's your per diem. And you've got dinner at Lanier Cross's at six thirty.'

'Six thirty p.m.?'

'Ah, yeah . . . She can make it six if you prefer. She asked me to tell you it will be vegetarian.'

'What are all those men doing? Is it some kind of military exercise?'

'Those are the gardeners. Shall I make them go away?'

'No, it's fine.'

'And Tim Pascal called.'

'Who's he?'

'He's an English film director. He has several projects in development at Alcazar. He wanted to know if you wanted to lunch or drink or whatever.'

The doorbell rang. Aurélien strode across the several levels of his cool, white living room to answer it; as he did so, the bell rang twice again. It was Delphine.

KAISER PREVOST: I have a theory about this town: it doesn't represent the fulfilment of the American dream, it represents the fulfilment of an American reality. It rewards relentless persistence, massive stamina, ruthlessness and the ability to live with grotesque failure. Look at me: I am a smallish guy, a hundred and thirty-eight pounds, with pretty severe myopia, and near average academic qualifications. But I have a personable manner and an excellent memory and a good head of hair. I will work hard and I will take hard decisions and I have developed the thickest of thick skins. With these attributes in this town nothing can stop me. Or those like me. We are legion. We know what they call us but we don't care. We don't need contacts, we don't need influence, we don't need talent, we don't need cosmetic surgery. That's why I love this place. It allows us to thrive. That's why when I heard Aurélien had never showed for dinner with Lanier Cross I didn't panic. People like me take that kind of awful crisis in their stride.

Aurélien turned over and gently kissed Delphine's right breast. She stubbed out her cigarette and hunched into him.

'This house is incredible, Aurélien. I like it here.'

'Where's Holbish?'

'You promised you wouldn't mention him again. I'm sorry Aurélien, I don't know what made me do it.'

'No, I'm just curious.'

'He's gone to Seattle.'

'Well, we can manage without him. Are you ready?'

'Of course, it's the least I can do. What about the pizzeria?'

'I was given 1,000 dollars cash today. I knew it would come in useful.'

MATT FRIEDRICH: I have to admit I was hoping for the *Seeing Through Nathalie* rewrite. When Bob Berger fired me and said that Naomi Tashourian was the new writer, it hurt for a while. It always does no matter how successful you are. But in my case I was due a break and I thought *Nathalie* was it. I've missed out on my last three Guild arbitrations, and a Lanier Cross film would have helped, however half-baked, however art-house. Berger said they would honour the fee for the synopsis I did (obfuscation takes on new meaning), but I guess the cheque is still in the post. But, I do not repine, as a great English novelist once said, I just get on with the job.

I have a theory about this town, this *Spielraum* where we dream and dawdle: one of our problems – perhaps it's *the* problem – is that here ego always outstrips ability. Always. That applies to everyone: writers, directors, actors, heads of production, d-boys and unit runners. It's our disease, our mark of Cain. When you have success here you think you can do anything and that's the great error. The success diet is too rich for our digestive systems: it poisons us, addles the brain. It makes us blind. We lose our self-knowledge. My advice to all those who make it is this: *take the job you would have done if the film had been a flop.* Don't go for the big one, don't let those horizons recede. Do the commercial, the TV pilot, the documentary, the three-week rewrite, the character role or whatever it was you had lined up first. Do that job and then maybe you can reach for the forbidden fruit, but at least you'll have your feet on the ground.

'Kaiser?'
  'Bob?'
  'He's not in the house, Kaiser.'
  'Shit.'
  'He's got to phone her. He's got to apologise.'
  'No. He's got to lie.'
  'She called Vincent.'
  'Fuck. The bitch.'
  'That's how bad she wants to do it. I think it's a good sign.'
  'Where is that African bastard? I'll kill him.'
  'Nancy says the French babe showed.'
  'Oh, no. No fuckin' no!'
  'It gets worse, Kaiser. Vincent told me to call Tim Pascal.'
  'Who the fuck's he?'
  'Some English director. Lanier wants to meet with him.'
  'Who's his agent?'
  'Sheldon . . . Hello? Kaiser?'

GEORGE MALINVERNO: I got a theory about this town, this place: everybody likes pizza. Even the French. We got to know them real well, I guess. They came back every night, the French. The tall black guy, the ratty one, the blonde girl. Real pretty girl. Every night they come. Every night they eat pizza. Every night she ties one on. Everybody likes pizza [bitter laugh]. Everybody. Too bad I didn't think of it first, huh?

They film, one night. And the girl, she's steaming. Then, I don't know, something goes wrong and we don't see them for a while. Then he comes back. Just the black guy, Aurélien, and the girl. He says can they film, one night, 1,000 bucks. I say for sure. So he sets up the sound and he sets up the camera behind the bushes. You know it's not a disturbance, exactly. I never see anybody make a film like this before. A thousand bucks, it's very generous. So the girl she walks up, she takes a seat, she orders beer and keeps on drinking. Soon she's pretty stewed. Aurélien sits behind the bushes, just keeps filming. Some guy tries to pick her up, puts his hand on the table, like, leans over, she takes a book of matches, like that one, and does something to the back of his hand with the corner. I couldn't see what she did, but the guy gasps with pain, shudders like this, just backs off.

Then we get a big party in, birthday party, they'd already booked, fourteen people. She sits there drinking and smoking, Aurélien's filming. Then we bring the cake out of the kitchen, candles all lit. Whenever there's a birthday we get Chico to sing. Chico, the little waiter, tubby guy, wanted to be an opera singer. Got a fine, strong voice. He's singing 'Happy Birthday to You' – he's got a kind of drawn-out, elaborate way of singing it. Top of his voice, *molto vibrato*, you know. Next thing I know, the girl's on her feet with a fuckin' gun in her hand, screaming in French. Nobody can hear because Chico's singing his balls off. I tear out from behind the bar, but I'm too late. POW. First shot blows the cake away. BAM. Second one gets Chico in the thigh. Flesh wound, thank God. I charge her to the ground, Roberto jumps on top. We wrestle the gun away. She put up quite a fight for a little thing. Did something to my shoulder too, she twisted it in some way, never been the same since. Aurélien got the whole thing on film. I hear it looks great.

Aurélien sat outside the Alcazar screening-room with Kaiser Prevost and Bob Berger. Berger combed and recombed his hair, he kept smelling his comb, smelling his fingertips. He asked Prevost to smell his hair. Prevost said it smelt of shampoo. Prevost went to the lavatory for the fourth time.

'Relax,' Aurélien said to them both. 'I'm really pleased with the film. I couldn't be more pleased.'

Berger groaned. 'Don't say that, don't say that.'

'If he likes it,' Kaiser said, 'we're in business. Lanier will like it, for sure, and Aurélien will apologise. Won't you Aurélien? Of course you will. No problem. Lanier loved him. Lanier loved you, didn't she, Aurélien?'

'Why are we worried about Lanier?' Aurélien said. 'Delphine came back. We finished the film.'

'Jesus Christ,' said Bob Berger.

'Don't worry, Bob,' Kaiser said. 'Everything can be fixed.'

Vincent Bandine emerged from the screening-room.
Aurélien stood up. 'What do you think?'

VINCENT BANDINE: I believe in candour. I have a theory about this town, this place: we don't put enough stock in candour. I am into candour in a big way. So I take Aurélien aside, gently, and I say, 'Aurélien, or whatever your name is, I think your film is goatshit. I think it's a disgusting boring piece of grade-A manure. I wouldn't give the sweat off my balls for your goatshit film.' That's what I said, verbatim. And I have to give it to the kid, he just stood there and looked at me, sort of slight smile on his face. Usually when I'm this candid they're in deep shock or weeping or vomiting by now. And he looks at me and says, 'I can't blame you for thinking like this. You're not a man of culture, so I can't blame you for thinking like this.' And he walks. He walks out jauntily. I should have had his fucking legs broken. I've got the biggest collection of Vuillard paintings on the west coast of America. I should have had his fucking legs broken. We had to pay the waiter fifty grand not to press charges, keep the Alcazar name out of things. The girl went to a clinic for three weeks to dry out . . . Aurélien No. Not a man of culture, eh?

KIT VERMEER: Ah, Lanier took it badly. Do you mind? Thank you. Bats and lemurs, man, wow, they didn't get a look in. Bats and lemurs. Story of my life. *Weltanschauung*, that's what I'm up for. No, *Weltschmerz*. That's my bag. Bats and lemurs. Why not owls and armadillos? No, I'm not looking at you, sir, or talking to you. Forsooth. Fuckin' nerd. Wank in a bath, that's what an English friend of mine calls them. What a wank in a bath. Owls and armadillos.

MATT FRIEDRICH: Aurélien came to see me before he left, which was gracious of him, I thought, especially for a film director, and he told me what had happened. I commiserated and told him other sorry stories about this town, this place. But he needed no consoling. 'I enjoyed my visit,' he said. 'No, I did. And I made the film. It was a curious but interesting experience.'

'It's just a dance,' I think I remember saying to him. 'It's just a dance we have to do.'

He laughed. He found that funny.

END ROLLER

BOB BERGER

is working from home where he is writing several screenplays

DELPHINE DRELLE

plays the character Suzi de la Tour in NBC's *Till Darkness Falls*

KAISER PREVOST

works for the investment bank Harbinger Cohen in New York City

BERTRAND HOLBISH

manages the Seattle band Morbid Anatomy

MARIUS NO

is in his first year at L'Ecole Supérieur des Etudes Cinématographiques

NAOMI TASHOURIAN

has written her first novel *Credits Not Contractual*

MICHAEL SCOTT GEHN

is chief executive critic and on the editorial board of *film/e*

KIT VERMEER

is a practising Sikh and wishes to be known as Khalsa Hari Atmar

LANIER CROSS

is scheduled to star in Lucy Wang's film *Charles Baudelaire's Les Fleurs du Mal*

VINCENT BANDINE

has announced Alcazar Film's eighteen-picture slate for the coming year

GEORGE MALINVERNO

has opened a third pizzeria in Pacific Palisades

BARKER LEAR

lives in San Luis Obispo

MATT FRIEDRICH

has taken his own life

'NATHALIE X AUX ETATS UNIS'

has been nominated for an Academy Award in the Best Foreign Film category

AURÉLIEN NO

is not returning your calls

Sure to Rise

FIONA FARRELL

WHEN HER MOTHER died Elizabeth drove south thinking about roly poly. The floury smoothness of it after it had been rolled beneath a milk bottle to a near-rectangle on the bench. When Jono was a baby his bottom reminded her of roly poly too, that firm cool curve under her hand. You shaped the dough roughly, then spread it with raspberry jam. Then you peeled back the long edge and rolled, pleating the ends to keep the jam inside. Then you furled the thick hank into the baking dish, the Pyrex one with the chipped handle, stained from all the preceding roly polys and crumbles and fruit sponges. And you poured over hot water, butter and sugar which transformed in the oven to a sticky syrup. And you ate it in slices with the top-of-the-milk.

She drove south thinking about roly poly.

She thought too about stew, with carrots and onions and mashed potatoes, and corned beef, pink and sweaty in mustard sauce, and pineapple-upside-down-pudding, and soup, the mutton knuckle boiled to bare bone among swollen barley beads. She thought of chicken broth with rice to sweat out a fever. And baking. All that baking: afghans crumbling at a single bite to brown flakes, cinnamon oysters, shortbread and peanut brownies which her mother made whenever she or her brother or sister had exams because peanuts were brain food, like fish and sweetbreads.

45

Even when they had left home, they studied with a tin of peanut biscuits from home beside them on the bed in flat or hostel, so that Jen's anatomy text book and Chris's car manuals and Elizabeth's Pitman's course were for ever after gritty with cake crumb.

Peanut biscuits. Ginger crunch. Albert squares. And birthdays were Cheerios popping from torn skins and butterfly cakes with red jelly eyes and marble cake miraculously technicolour. And Christmas was a roast chicken with new peas and new potatoes, taken in triumph from the garden because it was always a bit of a race against the weather and the Boltons' spaniel who was forever breaking through the fence and wrecking the place.

And after their father had died, exploding in a final fatal rage at Patch's excavations amongst the spring onions, scarlet and twisting, arm in mid-air with a handy piece of four-by-two, there were the gifts of food Mort Watson took to bringing round and leaving on the porch: three muddy brown trout, a whole salmon, its flesh lolly pink. A swan which he plucked in their wash house where its black head flopped like a snake from the copper. Wild pork, smelling of pea. And once, just once, a pukeko he'd shot because they were a bloody nuisance tearing the stacks to pieces.

Oh what a shame, said Mum, fingering the shimmering indigo feathers. Oh what a shame. She'd always liked them and there weren't nearly as many of them around as there had been when she was a girl and she made him promise not to do it again. 'But,' she said, a bird in the hand, 'it's no use letting good food go to waste.' She casseroled it slowly the way she cooked rabbits and they ate it with cabbage and mashed turnips from Mort's bottom paddock and it was nice, though you had to pick carefully through the intricate tracery of tiny bones.

As she accelerated on to the straight near Ashburton, Elizabeth tried to remember what they had had to follow the pukeko. Chocolate self-saucing pudding? (Mort had a soft spot for chocolate.) Apple pie? She thought perhaps they had eaten the pukeko on a Sunday, and if it was a Sunday, it would have been a sponge, since they always had sponge on Sunday. Their mother popped one in the minute they got in from church and it cooled on the window sill while they ate their meat and veges and then they had it for dessert, cut in thick wedges and spurting cream, its surface lacy with icing sugar dusted through a paper doily. A slice of lacy sponge and a cup of tea. Mort would wipe icing sugar from his top lip and say their mother's one-egg-sponge knocked all the others he'd ever tasted into a cocked hat.

Their aunty Vi had married an electrician in Gore and her speciality was Spanish Cream but Mum's was the one-egg-sponge. That's what people asked her to bring to spring afternoons or socials. One of your sponges, they said. One of Vera's sponges. Mum said there was nothing to it: the egg at room temperature, always beat by hand and always in the same direction to keep the air in. Elizabeth had tried often to follow the instructions but it never seemed to work. Her sponges had never been as high or as light. Her mother had the knack.

Elizabeth crossed the Rangitata and thought about sponges and her mother lying on the kitchen floor in the unit in Bevis Street. That was where the community worker found her: by the stove. She had been making a cup of tea and that's how the neighbours had guessed something was wrong. The kettle had whistled and whistled as it boiled dry and they had broken a window and found her. She had died with a teaspoon in her hand.

And Elizabeth wanted to think about that and why she hadn't been down to visit for months but it had seemed such an effort in the middle of renegotiating the marriage contract, as David put it, and finding out after a month's debate that one of the clauses was Rosalyn, software specialist and recent appointee to the staff at DigiTech. And crying and slamming and six weeks of Marriage Guidance with Stanley who advised them to express their needs clearly using 'I' statements, and more slamming because David said, 'What I want is to sleep with Rosalyn.'

And moving out of the villa on Bish Street which she had found on their first day back in New Zealand after two years of confinement in a tiny flat in Camden Town, and which she had loved on sight for its roses and mulberry tree and space for Jono and which she had refused, resolutely, to leave, though David had said, 'Move In and Move On, that's the way up in real estate.' ('It's a home,' she said. 'Not a property.')

And ringing Jono, grown lanky now and shaven-headed, who

47

said whatever she and Dad decided was fine with him no worries, and hey, he had a contract to paint a bistro in Parnell: Flash Tucker. He thought a kind of rural-punk look, very Kiwi in-joke, see you Mum, take care. And finding the other place, the rented town house in Porscholt Place, a cul-de-sac only ten minutes' walk from her desk in the pleasantly impersonal chrome-trimmed buzz of reception at Haye Eaton, Complete Accounting and Management Service. Ample Client Parking.

In the cul-de-sac, back against Hislop Park, she had not bothered to unpack. Here, her books, plates and blankets stayed stored in boxes in the bedroom. Here, she lay on a bare carpet looking out through a fog of white sheers to winter playing fields and a single conifer, firmly corsetted to form a perfect little sphere and nothing, absolutely nothing, laid claim to her attention.

She did not want to pay attention. She did not want enquiry or curiosity or commiseration.

Her mother rang. 'What went wrong?' she said. Puzzled. Probing. She had liked David. Everyone liked David. 'I don't mean to pry. But he seemed such a nice man. You seemed so well-suited. He didn't hit you, did he?' 'No,' said Elizabeth. 'Because I was reading about that just the other day when I was getting my blood pressure done at the doctor's,' said her mother. 'In a magazine. It said that children who have seen violence in the home expect it in their own marriages. That's what they call the Abuse Cycle.'

'David didn't hit me,' said Elizabeth. David wouldn't hit. David was nice. David was civilised. 'I mean,' said her mother, 'I've sometimes wondered if I should have left Trevor when you were little, but I thought if you had made vows you should stick to them. People did, in those days.'

'Look,' said Elizabeth, 'stop feeling guilty. You did your best. You might have made a mistake to begin with but when Dad died you chose better, with Mort. And Chris and Jen and I are just fine.' 'But none of you are married,' said her mother. 'None of you.' 'Well, I lasted twenty-two years,' said Elizabeth. 'So you can hardly say I didn't give it a good try. And Jen has had a couple of failures but she's more or less living with Ron now and Chris just likes being single in Sydney. And whatever we are anyway, it's not your fault.' 'But what went wrong?' said her mother. 'With you and David?' A pause. 'He met someone,' said Elizabeth. 'Oh,' said her mother.

A pause. A thrush lands on the conifer. Thinks better of it. Flies away.

'And you're looking after yourself?' said her mother. 'You're getting enough sleep? You're eating properly?' 'Yes,' said Elizabeth. (Stop fussing. I'm not dead. Just abandoned. Alone. But I like being alone. It's simple. She stretches on beige Axminster.) Her mother was speaking. It was, she was saying, only too easy to stop taking care of yourself when you were on your own. After Trevor's death, difficult and all as he had been, she lost all interest in food and really if it hadn't been for them, the children, she wouldn't have bothered at all: just lived on tea and biscuits. She would have got quite run down. 'I'm fine,' said Elizabeth. 'Truly. I'm sleeping well. I'm eating heaps.' 'What did you have for tea?' said her mother. 'A samosa,' said Elizabeth. (She honestly couldn't remember. There was a plate beside her on the floor with some kind of smear on it. A samosa probably. Or an avocado. Or bean salad, perhaps. Something quick, snatched up from the deli at Big Fresh on her way home.) 'What's a samosa?' said her mother. 'A sort of pastry,' said Elizabeth. 'With curry in the middle.' 'You used to hate curry,' said her mother. 'I made it once when Mort shot a goat. You made such a fuss about the smell. I cooked you all macaroni cheese and you ate it in the garden. You said the smell made you feel sick.' 'Well, it doesn't make me sick now,' said Elizabeth. 'I suppose you got a taste for that sort of thing when you were overseas,' said her mother.

Overseas. Elizabeth remembers her mother sitting at the corner table at the Americana when she came to visit, the winter Elizabeth had moved to Dunedin and her first job. She had prodded doubtfully at her Maryland Chicken. 'They've put fruit on it,' she said. 'Whatever next?'

They didn't eat out, her and Mort. If they went for a drive she would pack a thermos and some sandwiches. That way you ran no risk of dirty hands in unknown kitchens. You knew what you were eating. And Mort couldn't stand paying fancy prices for fancy muck and some pansy dancing round taking orders while he looked down his nose. Not for them the corner table and the long deliberation over the menu in its black plastic jacket. Give them the car and a cup of tea and a view, even if the view was drizzling or blowing. On holiday, they had the van. A 1972 Volkswagen AutoHome with swivel cab seating, stainless steel two-burner grill/cooker, sink, fridge/freezer, chemical toilet and convertible double bed. Mort stencilled its name on the rear: Morvera.

In Morvera they were free. They could pull over and brew up wherever they wanted. They could cook a whole dinner. Morvera was a boon. Uneasy in the Americana, Vera scraped the pineapple from her chicken. 'And will you look at that?' she said. 'Fancy beetroot. That must be how they do it Overseas.' 'Just eat it,' said Elizabeth. (The Americana had been her idea. She wanted to bring her mother here, take her out for dinner, on the proceeds of her first pay packet.) 'It's crinkle-cut. But it tastes just the same as the flat kind.'

When she came home at Christmas her mother cooked a roast chicken. 'And look,' she said, as she handed Elizabeth her plate. In a nest of shredded lettuce drenched in Highlander Milk mayonnaise lay three slices of crinkle-cut beetroot. 'I bought a tin at the dairy. You can't say we don't keep up with the times down here!'

Crinkle-cut beetroot. Elizabeth thought about crinkle-cut beetroot as she drove along the coast at Katiki eating peppermints, the sea rolling on her left in slanting summer evening light, the hills stretching back on her right to the Horse Range. Crinkle-cut beetroot. And sweetcorn. And persimmmons. All the food she had tried, at intervals, to share with her mother. The coq au vin for example. With plain boiled potatoes, green beans and a simple salad. Apple pastis to follow. The first meal she had cooked for her mother and Mort in the new house, the old villa on Bish Street which they'd bought for a song ('Worst house in the best street,' said David. 'That's the strategy.') Her mother had said they'd be coming through Christchurch on Saturday on their way north. They'd call in.

Elizabeth planned the meal so carefully. For a week she sat up in bed reading recipes at night before sleep. It must be something nice: not too complicated or rich (Mort had an ulcer), but stylish, sophisticated. Coq au vin, she decided. They'd had coq au vin in Angers the summer they'd spent jolting around France in a rusty Deux Chevaux, from cathedral to city square to vineyard, nibbling and sipping away the weeks before David began work with DigiTech.

They had had coq au vin looking over a languorous blue plain and afterwards, in a hotel room where the pipes hummed to themselves all night, she had conceived Jono.

On Saturday morning she selected exactly twenty tiny onions from the bin at Prasads'. She had the bacon cut in cubes from the bone at the butchers. She bought three kinds of lettuce for the salad: endive, red and buttercrunch. David opened a Stony Bay claret which had had good reviews and Jono picked flowers for the table: all the heads off all the tulips, but she floated them in a clear glass bowl and they looked beautiful, stems or no, on the wooden table she had found splattered with paint in a junk shop in Amberley and stripped painstakingly back to gleaming kauri.

Then Vera rang about five from a garage near Tinwald. They were running a bit behind schedule and Mort was keen to get as far up the road as possible so they wouldn't be rushing for the ferry the next day. They'd drop in for a few minutes, just to say hello. 'But I've cooked a special dinner,' said Elizabeth. 'Oh,' said her mother. 'You shouldn't have bothered.' 'But I have,' said Elizabeth. 'I thought you were going to stay the night. Jono thinks you're going to spend the night.' Her trump card. Vera wavered, said, well, in that case . . .

Morvera lumbered into the drive at six. Mort liked his dinner no later than 6.30. Because of the ulcer. But Elizabeth was ready. The coq au vin bubbled, the potatoes and beans waited in their pots, the table was laid. Vera looked at the tulip heads, the place mats Jono had crayoned for them, the fire in the grate for it was early spring and chilly, still, in the evenings. 'Oh, you've gone to so much trouble,' she said. 'I said you shouldn't bother.' It's not a bother, said Elizabeth, and would they like to take a look round before dinner? Jono wanted to show them his room, and there were all the renovations: the deck by the back door, the french doors which let so much more light into the living room, the cunning little mini-cellar where David could store his collection of New Zealand wines.

'Can I help you?' said Vera. 'Oh no,' said Elizabeth. Everything was under control. All she had to do was make a dressing for the salad. 'Oh,' said Vera. 'Let me do that. I'll make a dressing while you attend to the meat.' No, said Elizabeth. It wouldn't take a second and the kitchen was much too small as it was at present for two to work in comfortably. And she shut the door to reach down the plates from the corner cupboard. Through the wall she could hear Jono. 'Here, granna, here. This is mine room, this one with the train.' She added one dozen button mushrooms to the casserole. And she tossed the salad. A light vinaigrette. She removed her apron. Dinner was ready.

Mort said no thanks to the wine. Made him blow up like a balloon. Vera said just a little chicken thanks, and a small potato, and was that garlic in the salad? Because garlic didn't agree with her. The pastis was more successful. Mort had two helpings, said you couldn't beat apple betty and that Elizabeth took after her mum and no mistake. She was a dab hand at the cooking. Vera said, my, it was rich wasn't it?

They went to bed early in Morvera. They would have to make a smartish start, before breakfast, if they were going to make it to the ferry without a lot of fuss and bother. Before they said goodnight Mort popped out for the couple of ducks he'd been keeping for them in the van freezer. And Vera brought in a tin of ginger crunch.

Elizabeth looked out at the van parked on the drive as she was getting ready for bed. The cab light was on. 'They're still up,' she said. Her hair was tangled. She brushed at it furiously. 'I bet they're out there eating cheese on toast. I bet she had another dinner ready all the time.' 'Don't be daft,' said David. 'You always take things too seriously.'

But it was serious. It mattered.

They never visited overnight again. Just passed through. Dropped in. An hour here on their way to the Coast, an afternoon coming back from a van rally in Hanmer.

And then Mort died one Easter landing a twelve-pound brown in the Clinton.

Elizabeth went down for the funeral. Vera flung open the freezer lid. 'Look,' she said. 'Who's going to help me get through all this?' The cabinet was crammed with bird carcasses, fish in frozen slabs, chunks of meat and dozens of dinners, pre-cooked, labelled and ready for Morvera. 'You'll have to take some,' she said. 'There's no point,' said Elizabeth. 'We're vegetarian.' 'Since when?' said Vera poking a forequarter labelled Goat, August '83. 'Since Jono did a project on hamburgers,' said Elizabeth. 'He simply refused to touch meat and kept telling us about the rain forest being destroyed to make way for beef production and then he moved on to hens in battery cages and little calves being kept in the dark so the flesh would stay white and all the rest of it and in the end if seemed simpler just to stick to lentils.' 'Oh,' said Vera. 'Remember when Chris decided he was a dog and would only eat from a bowl? And Jen refusing to touch anything with raisins because they looked like eyes?' 'It's not a phase,' said Elizabeth. 'It's real. It's important. The planet's being destroyed by meat consumption. I'll send you one of Jono's books. I'll send you the project.' Vera knocked ice from a tray of chops. 'What about some lamb?' she said. 'What about a nice pork roast? You can't say no to a nice pork roast. Everybody likes a nice pork roast.'

Pork roast. With apple sauce. And crackling dribbling fat down your chin. And Brussels sprouts. And baked potatoes.

Vera stayed on in the house eating her way steadily through the freezer. 'In a way,' she said, 'it's just as well it's there because I've gone off shopping. I used to like it, collecting all the coupons for specials then driving into town on a Saturday to the Freshamart. It was quite an outing. But it's not the same on your own. Nothing's the same on your own. Shopping. Cooking. Eating.' She turned on the telly at midday and ate one of the Morvera dinners. Mince and peas. Mutton stew. Steak and kidney.

She perked up eventually. She sold Morvera. (Driving wasn't the same on your own.) But she took up bridge and went to bowls and she moved into the unit on Bevis Street. And Elizabeth lived on in Christchurch where Jono went to school and she went to her desk at Haye Eaton and David edged his way along the corridors of DigiTech (NZ) from software specialist to project manager to programme manager to South Island manager and an office on the sunny corner overlooking the river. On and on until the night of the pre-Christmas drinks. They always did pre-Christmas drinks for the staff.

Elizabeth was standing by the table making sushi. She had spread white rice in a rectangle on the nori and the little bamboo mat and she was cutting pickle into neat strips. David was trying to decide between the Rothesay and the 1988 Te Mata Chardonnay. He uncorked a bottle. There was something he wanted to talk about, he said.

'What?' said Elizabeth, the knife slicing steadily through pink radish flesh. 'Us,' said David. He thought it was time, now that Jono had left and they were both well-established in their careers to perhaps, ummm . . . (he sipped) . . . renegotiate the terms of their contract. 'You mean us?' said Elizabeth. 'You mean you and me?' Well, yes, said David. He did mean that. He wanted more space. Not, he assured her, because there was someone else. But it was quite common, he believed, in mid-life, once the children had left, for people to reassess their priorities, determine their objectives in life.

Elizabeth placed a sliver of pickle on the rice and turned to the cucumber. 'Do they?' she said. Oh yes, said David. (He thought the Rothesay after all. It was a fine year. He should have bought a few more bottles while he had the chance.) The knife slipped from watery flesh and gouged a tiny hole in the kauri table. But it didn't matter. It was only the kitchen table now, cut and scraped after years of use and marked with Jono's scribblings. They'd stopped using it for best long ago.

These things could be done in a civilised fashion, David was saying. There was no need for dramatics. They were both adults after all. He had arranged a flat in Merivale. He thought perhaps she should look for something similar. They'd put the villa on the market. It had been a good buy, now that the area had become popular. It would fetch a good price.

Elizabeth laid cucumber alongside the pickle and began to roll, but she must have pressed too hard because when she peeled back the mat the shiny seaweed tube had burst and sticky rice clung to the bamboo webbing. 'Oh, God,' she said. 'What a mess. Look what a mess I've made.'

And it was a mess and not civilised at all. There were arguments, dramatics, tears, bewilderment and a kind of furious renegotiation which ended in retreat to the cul de sac and the empty carpet while David moved within the month to Rosalyn's. Rosalyn was cool and fair and when she had asked them to dinner soon after she joined DigiTech she had produced seemingly without effort, crayfish à l'amoricaine and a kirsch soufflé while discussing the merits of fixed price projects versus time-and-materials. Light and beautiful, elegant and easy.

The day before she left Bish Street, Elizabeth opened every single one of David's bottles. She lit a candle at the kauri table, spread pâté from the deli on crackers, and drank. A gulp from each bottle.

And now her mother has died. And Elizabeth hasn't cried. She has driven all the way to Invercargill from Christchurch without stopping, eating peppermints the whole way. The funeral has all been planned. Her mother has told her exactly how it is to be conducted. No fuss, she said, on the phone back when her blood pressure first started to waver. No fuss, remember? Cremation and the lawn cemetery, and afterwards, tea at The Oaks on Dee Street. The woman who ran The Oaks played bridge with her and she brought along nice sandwiches and cakes which could have passed for home-made. Rima would do a good job of the afternoon tea.

'You'll do it properly?' she said. And Elizabeth said yes, she'd do it properly.

She drives south thinking about roly poly. And when she gets to Bevis Street the door opens on a quiet room, still furnished but already a little cold. She switches on the radio and looks in the fridge. There's butter, and a bottle of milk and in the cupboard she finds flour and jam. Blackberry, but it will do. The baking bowl is under the bench. She measures it all out: a cup, a teaspoon, a quarter of a pint. She rubs, but not too heavily or the dough will be tough. She rolls and spreads and furls and then she bakes the pudding in the little bench-top stove.

And when it's done, she sits at the table and eats.

And, at last, she can begin to take her mother seriously.
And, at last, she can cry.

Light

JANE GARDAM

IN THE FURTHEST Himalayas there was a child born with a single eye. You might think that this would have been to its advantage, for a single eye is frequently considered a sign of the greatest holiness. But this was the rumoured kingdom of Imlac and its religion was not altogether orthodox. It was a country even further and higher than Ladak, across wastes of unmarked snows, up a precipice with a float of clouds half-way up it and at the top of a vast tableland, scarcely peopled, scarcely visited, because of the avalanches sent by its gods, in particular the Snow Leopard.

The Snow Leopard was said to send the avalanches to kill interference from the outside world, from politics, accepted religions, medicine and foreign artistic endeavour (they were a conceited people) and, some said, as punishment for their sins.

But the holy idea of the single eye shining from the forehead had filtered into Imlac in a related interpretation and what made the plight of the baby, a little girl called Keril (which means shadow), hazardous and unfortunate was that her mother had promised her to the priests to be their goddess.

In the region of Imlac, as in Nepal today, a little girl, the most beautiful that can be found, was taken at two years old into a closed monastery and worshipped there as a goddess until she was about thirteen, or until the day of her first menstruation. When this occurred she was sent home. Women came to undo the tight bun of her hair and led her back to her family again, a family completely strange to her. She came back illiterate. For ten years she had been taught nothing except how to sit utterly still as, hour by hour, day by day, year by year, the monks filed past her bowing and chanting and worshipping. At other times honoured suppliants from the world outside approached and reverently spread at her feet presents that the monks then removed.

In Imlac there were secret initiation ceremonies for these little girls as there are today in Katmandu, and it is said that potions given to encourage the goddess's docility were powerful and carefully guarded. Certainly, when she was taken through the city on her throne, hung between poles and carried by a full football team of chanting, ruby-red, orange-helmeted monks, she stared blankly ahead as if there were other and sad scenes before her kohl-encircled eyes. A third great eye painted on the forehead glared out black, vermilion and gold beneath her jewelled triple crown. Bumping about unsmiling above the heads of the crowd, the child looked like a small bronze statue, quite unable to recognise her mother and family who would be somewhere there watching, filled with pride but often weeping.

In Imlac it was beginning to be harder to acquire one of these goddesses – as it is in Katmandu today. Mothers were refusing and the priests were troubled. The given reason for refusal was always unworthiness for such an honour, but the real reason was that when the goddess was returned home she was a useless zombie, unable to clean a floor, make a cheese, bake a loaf and accustomed to continuous admiration.

And marriage was uncertain. Cobwebs of magic still hung about these girls. They were said to have secret knowledge and husbands tended to die mysteriously in the first matrimonial year (which is still said to be true in Nepal) and snakes were said to issue from the girls' vaginas during intercourse. The mother of Keril had for some years been living in the remotest part of the kingdom to try to escape the notice of the monks, for twice now she had had the misfortune to produce daughters of exceptional beauty, twice the monks had sent for them and twice she had refused. These daughters had died.

She lived a hard life now out in the furthest and coldest part of the region where it was said there was only one day a year of summer, eight months of weather so hard that no other tribe could endure them and four months when the cold drove even this community underground to live in deep chambers cut into the rock, clamped down under great iron lids. The one day of summer, however, was of delirious beauty.

It was out of exhaustion that the woman promised the monks her next daughter and they told her it would be her passport to heaven. There, they said, she would find summer every day in the territory of the Snow Leopard whose realm is of no known world.

So the baby was conceived as she knew it would be. There is little help for it in an underground village with nothing else to do for four long months and everyone in a heap and who knows who it is who fumbles for you in the dark. The mother prayed constantly that the child would be a boy, that if it were a girl it might be ugly and that the Snow Leopard would bless her whatever happened.

The first two requests were not granted. The child was female and very beautiful. It took time to determine that her blindness constituted the answer to the third request, the blessing.

For blind she seemed. The eyes were obviously there, but closed. The long, tilted, lashless Himalayan eyelids were so delicately drawn that they looked as if they might be prised apart by the gentle stroking of a finger-tip. But no. This was illusion. The lines were unbreakable, the pale and luminous skin integral to cheek and brow, the gentle mounds of the hidden eyeballs as smooth and seamless and sealed as well-poached eggs.

It was several days before the mother found the third and operative eye that lived down in the baby's throat, an eye that the child must presumably close whilst feeding, an eye that flashed at the mother one morning as she looked down at the sweetly sleeping bundle strapped warmly to her breast as they stood on the windy plateau. The eye flashed as the cold sun shone on to the triangular mouth which was opening in a yawn. The mother died quite soon afterwards, not necessarily altogether from shock, for she was already worn out, but the revelation was certainly not conducive to survival.

The grandmother took the child then, and when the emissary of the monastery appeared two days later to take the baby, she gave no hint about the hidden eye. She had kept it secret from everyone. And yet a whiff of something unsavoury had somehow reached the city, something sinister about the new goddess on the plateau who seemed always to be asleep.

When the emissary looked down at the child's sealed eyes, he took his leave at once without her, not even pausing to make the ritual tests of purity, the cleansing of the orifices: the flour for the ears, the lamp for the eyes, the incense for the nose, the herbal ointments for the sexual organs and, most importantly, the washing of the mouth with rice. He swirled off and fled, the eyeless morsel lying golden and almost divinely fair on the smelly black goat-skins near the mouth of the river dwelling.

The baby, of course, knew nothing of her beginnings. She never knew that she had been carried in the funeral procession of her mother, or that it had been then suggested that it would be better for a blind girl to be put out beside her to die on the mountain and picked clean by the birds. As she grew older she did not greatly miss her two eyes for (sworn to secrecy by her grandmother) she held her mouth open whenever she felt like it, sometimes in wonder, sometimes out of curiosity, sometimes for convenience when she was sewing or for safety when she was on the icy slopes. All this seemed quite normal, if very slightly retarded.

And can you believe in such a society nobody knew about the eye in the throat except the grandmother? Well, it is true. Keril was a silent child and the grandmother was not a gregarious woman and kept her apart. She was slightly feared, too, the old creature, humped-down, hook-beaked, dressed always in rusty black and brown instead of the brilliant costume of the land. She was given to talking and muttering to herself sitting out on the hillside, the only one who did not seem to long for the one summer's day. In all possible weathers she would sit gazing down for hours at the two great converging rivers that could be seen, sometimes even heard, thundering between drifts in the clouds. Even Keril, who showed little emotion about anything, was afraid of her grandmother.

She grew up, then, almost as remote from her tribe as if she had been the little goddess. She was different. For a start she was clean. Her nose did not run with thick, green mucus that left a pale track down a filthy cheek and was never wiped away. Nor did she wheeze and cough and die before she was ten, as one in six of the other children did. Her voice was soft and she moved quietly about on pretty feet. She wound up her hair with delicacy as she grew up and arranged it high in her fan-shaped head-dress of gold coins that were to be her dowry, in an almost royal way. She sang to herself, as she sat with the goats beside her grandmother, in a voice that made the hardest men fall silent. She seemed quite untroubled by her hidden abnormality. Watching her gaze open-mouthed at the sky above, down at the great valley or up and away above her home to the tablelands towards Tibet where the yetis live, they said, 'It's as if she sees.'

'It's as if she sees,' they said uneasily to the grandmother.

'She is praying to the Snow Leopard,' said she.

As a baby Keril had never cried, at least not visibly, and as a girl she grew to be brave and self-sufficient. Nobody ever saw down her throat. She ate with small bites, never had tonsillitis, was fortunate enough in having no toothache, and if she had a little bit of goat's sinew stuck between her teeth, she flew at once, and only, to her grandmother. She made sure never to laugh loudly, sing in company or let her jaw drop in surprise. After babyhood she never again yawned without politely covering her mouth and she sat away from the village, listening to the wind and the rivers, opening her mouth only to the turning eagles above her, allowing herself to laugh and gape only at the yetis when they came blundering up close. Yetis often slink about these far villages and are given pet names. They have to be shooed away from eating the sunflowers that sprout into glory on the one summer's day.

Keril's danger began with puberty and the following months of darkness in the underground tomb. By long tradition boys and girls were separated down there at night until it was thought that the girls were old enough for marriage or child-bearing. Keril, at fourteen, was still too young and had managed to keep a private space for herself between the sour-smelling, skin-hung wall and the bony back of her grandmother. But in the soft light of the butter-lamps and the heat and reek of the place, particularly the butter with which everyone was daubed like oven-ready chickens (Keril never larded herself like the rest, yet she never felt cold and her skin remained soft and the colour of ripe corn), there were men to whom this beautiful girl was becoming an obsession. They showed it by shouting at her, flinging hard work at her, pressing her hands down on hot pots, saying she did not earn her keep and made an excuse of her blindness. She brought them bad luck, they said. Why had they kept her? Why did they keep her? In the night she would awaken to furious quarrels between them and her grandmother who kept them off with threats of demons and the wrath of the Snow Leopard.

There was a village boy who could have any girl he wanted. There always is. He was eighteen years old with beautiful, narrow, black eyes and he was fascinated by Keril's blindness because he felt that even sitting in her darkness she could see him; that she knew him. He was angry because she hid from him more than from the others. And he was angry because he knew that she wanted him.

When the open weather came he watched her on the plateau. When the glorious summer day drew near and it was the annual festival of the goddess down the mountain, he asked the grandmother's permission to take the girl with him.

And when this was refused he took some coins and goatskins, dressed himself in the wonderful clothes of his region, the diamond-patterned woollen stockings, the midnight-blue wool shirt, the tunic of scarlet and purple with the white wool skirt beneath, the white cuffs turned back like Oliver Cromwell (but buttoned with knobs of jade), and made off alone. After three days he returned with a necklace for Keril made of sky-blue turquoises and the village girls hated her because she could not even see it. She sat there fingering it, holding it high, open-mouthed, until the grandmother came and took it away.

And then the summer's day arrived. The underground chambers were cleared and the goats led out from them, and the butter-lamps and the dung and the skin and the gallons of pale, weak whisky re-stored above ground, and all the stew and darkness of winter blew away. Flowers, like miracles, appeared in the melting snow.

The boy looked endlessly at Keril as she sat, still mittened and booted and shawled but lifting her face to the sun and smiling. While the grandmother was rearranging their quarters for the period above the ground, the boy came and took Keril by the wrist, away behind the rocks, pulled her down and kissed her. She did not struggle even when his mouth took the light away from her and his tongue came into her mouth urging and probing about like a live animal. And it came upon the eye.

She had of course closed the eye, but he felt it. He rolled off her, took her face between his two dark, goat-boy's hands and pressed until her mouth was forced open. He hauled her small head towards him and shook it, and down in the throat the eye opened, liquid and gleaming.

He screamed. He screamed and fled, leaving her lying. Much later the grandmother came with water and alcohol and made her drink it.

The grandmother knew that the eye within was weeping, for the girl choked and gulped and clung to her. The grandmother knew too that Keril would have to die. Nothing so terrible, secret and watchful as Keril's eye had ever been known.

So the next day, with the village all standing close together, far away and silent, and the boy nowhere to be seen, the grandmother and Keril set off upwards into the highest places where it is always winter and there is no life that can survive except for the few animals who live a paralysed existence as sustenance for the Snow Leopard. If, of course, the Snow Leopard exists, for few claimed to have seen him.

The two women, one black and bent, one upright and slender as a summer fern, set off up the mountain plateau and over the table-top snows. They passed a couple of yetis on the way who ambled up on their great feet, but Keril did not notice them and the grandmother eased them away with the palm of her hand as if they were nuzzling cattle. On the two women went until the going became too hard for the old woman and they stopped and looked back. A whirling, untimely snow seemed to be gathering below. 'Go back now,' said the girl. 'I shall go on until there is somewhere to rest. Then I shall cover my face and go into the dark.'

So the old woman went hobbling down the mountain and night fell. The girl sat in the cleft of the rocks in her ceremonial clothes but without the blue necklace. Her hair was coiled round the fan of her head-dress which did not now jingle and jump with the gold-coin dowry left her by her mother. This too had been taken from her. For hundreds of miles about her the mountains turned violet and orange-red, lemon and sickening green as the night fell, and she wrapped herself in her woollen shawl and waited to die.

But as the dawn came she was still not dead. All night she had sat, tranced as a child goddess in the thin, almost non-existent air. In the cold that should have burned her body into the rock, she had sat neatly, quite warm, breathing easily, and as the sun rose she dropped the shawl from her face and turned her eyelessness up to it. She heard a soft sound near her and the Snow Leopard on his silken feet approached and brushed her shoulder and snuffed her cheek. Then he licked the sealed eyelids and her eyes flew open to the sun. At the fullness of light she screamed, and as she screamed the third eye shot out of her mouth and lay in the snow, a wet, black beetle. It rolled away from her and gathered snow and within a moment it had gathered enough to be the size of a man's head, and then a yeti's head and then the dome of a huge round Dzong. And then it was the size of a rotunda temple on the plain, and then it was the size of the great monastery of the city.

Then the snow of the whole mountainside seemed to be sucked towards it and, high as a range of hills, it rolled over the precipice gathering snows a mile wide and hundreds of metres deep, and down it dropped surging like oceans to engulf the village.

Then it roared on to engulf the realm below, the city itself, the temples, the markets, the streets of noble, painted houses. Then it took mile upon mile of little farms, with their gardens of herbs and roofs shiny with capsicums like splashes of blood. It rolled even further down the valleys of serpentine rice terraces, to where the dark-green corn grew among apple trees that blossomed and fruited twice a year among the meadow flowers. And it covered them too.

Only the rivers it could not subdue, and so it merged with them and soon the great valley kingdom was water, green, icy water, deep as the sea.

The girl Keril survives, however. Occasionally an intrepid and partly-snow-blinded explorer gets a sight of her riding the sky on the Snow Leopard's back, her eyes as clear and beautiful as the stars.

The Take-Over

MICHAEL HAMBURGER

IN MY MOTH-PROOFED old uniform, the insignia of an outmoded war, I make my way across the square to discover what's in store for me under the new régime. The odd militia men in front of public buildings stare at me with variable mixtures of wonder, amusement and contempt, but neither shoot nor pounce. I ask one of them to direct me to the appropriate office. He tells me that all offices are closed for the emergency and advises me to stay at home. 'They'll come for you when they want you.' I dare not ask him who, or for what. We haven't been told what faction brought off the coup. Rumour favours the National Revolutionaries, a group never represented in parliament but said to have been widely supported in the armed forces, the police, and what remained of big business after the recession. The King, it seems, has not been deposed. Just before our receivers faded out and the newspapers ceased to appear he was shown on the Palace balcony between unknown men in civilian clothes, but did not speak, merely waving to what must have been a television camera in the otherwise empty forecourt. All the ministers in the former government, and who knows how many senior civil servants, are said to have been arrested and taken away for reconditioning. It was a bloodless coup.

I could have saved myself the uniform and the walk. When I get

back to my flat the door is open. The place has been ransacked by
secret police officers, who are busy packing my papers and books.
Their spokesman tells me to take off the uniform and put on a
garment that looks like a straitjacket. It turns out to be reversible,
depriving the wearer of the use of either his right arm or his left.
They have already noted that I am right-handed. They call it a
reconditioning suit. They're polite enough, even good-hum-
oured. While I'm changing the spokesman pinches my cheek,
saying that I've been chosen for a special privilege, a special
freedom. 'The Director has always wanted to revive the ancient
institution of the court fool. You have been earmarked for the job.
The reconditioning suit, in your case, is a mere formality,
indispensable for one known to have written books. Once
installed, you will have the use of your old clothes – or of any other
clothes you may choose to wear. Any except the relic, that is,' he
adds with a titter, stuffing the uniform, campaign ribbons, badges
and all, into my Ideal boiler – itself a relic – then throwing in my
gold fountain pen, awarded to me some twenty-five years ago for
my 'services to literature'. 'The last of its kind,' I can't help
muttering wistfully, more to myself than in protest, and meaning
fountain pens in general rather than that particular one, the
uniform or the boiler. At that moment, as though coming out of
anaesthesia, I remember my wife and son, away in the country.
Before I can open my mouth to ask what's to become of them, the
fellow says: 'Court fools don't need pens – nor families. Your wife
and son will be taken care of. It will be best for you to put them out
of your thoughts for the time being. Presence of mind is one of the
requirements of your employment.'

They take me to a suite in the Palace. To my astonishment
they've brought my record-player and what looks like my
complete record collection. 'The Director wants you to be
comfortable and relaxed. Music, his advisers tell him, is intrinsi-
cally unpolitical, even though it can be combined with words,
dangerously so, or, in its purely instrumental form, adapted for
corporatively therapeutical uses, as a stimulant or sedative, as the
occasion demands. The austerity of your taste and that intrinsic
autonomy allow us to give you the freedom of music. The
Director believes that this freedom may help you to break the

forbidden habit of literary composition – an altogether pernicious pursuit, as he has decreed. Words will be published only in their proper place – the State-controlled media. You alone will have the right, and the duty, to indulge in verbal spontaneity – for the Director's exclusive benefit. No, you will find no reading matter here, any more than writing materials.' The spokesman reacts with lightning speed to my apprehensive inspection of the place. True enough. Not even a desk or table. Only a radio and a television set. But armchairs, exquisite carpets and tapestries, a couch and a cocktail cabinet, a silver cigar box engraved with the royal arms. 'That telephone, by the way, is not for external or outgoing calls. It will convey instructions to you and summon you to the presence. Let me unfasten the suit. You will find your clothes in the bedroom.'

Left alone there, for a moment I catch myself identifying the 'presence' with the King's, as though the man hadn't made the position clear enough. In spite of what he said about clothes I hesitate before choosing an old sweater and corduroys. Anyway, it seems unlikely that my services will be called upon today. The problem is how to pass the time. Much as I like music, I'm in no mood to listen to it now – and here. I don't drink when I'm alone and have never cared for cigars. Fortunately they emptied my uniform pockets before burning it and didn't confiscate the cigarettes. But one packet won't last me very long. The windows don't help. They overlook a courtyard, three walls with shuttered windows. Not a tree, not a bird – let alone those famous flower gardens, avenues, fountains and ponds. Will they keep me cooped up here? An outdoor man, despite my sedentary profession, happiest in the open country? And expect me to be equal to my function, whatever a court fool's function may be in this day and age? The telephone rings. A male voice tells me: 'The grounds are at your disposal now; and will be, whenever you are not on duty. A closed-circuit receiver will be issued to you in due course, so that you can be recalled when you are needed.'

Days pass without employment, without mail, without communication of any kind. A meal buzzer activates a dumb waiter. Cigarettes appear with the food, though I haven't asked for them. The rooms are cleaned, laundry is collected and returned, while

I'm out in the grounds. Phrases form in my head as I walk, but I resist the temptation to scratch them on to bark or soil. For hours I stand by the fish-ponds, envying the contentment of carp, orfe, rudd, tench in their element. Mated or single in this summer season they bask or shoot or leap as though made for this one patch of water, totally contained by it, totally fulfilled; unaware that they've been placed in it quite arbitrarily, as a momentary distraction from a boredom beyond their comprehension. Such is their freedom, and such is mine between the palace suite and the grounds, where I never meet so much as a gardener, though they are immaculately maintained. Not a sound reaches them from over the walls. No traffic, no human voice, no heels on pavements. Even rail and air services must have been suspended. Yet something, a great deal, must be going on somewhere. All behind closed doors? And not here, when this must be the centre of power in the new order, more than in the old?

At last I see a figure at the other end of a long avenue. A mistake, surely, after so many solitary walks. Should I turn back? I am sure that I should, but curiosity and days of tedium make me walk on. If only it isn't the Director! Whoever he turns out to be, I haven't the slightest wish to confront him before I must. But after some thirty paces I recognise the figure. It's the King! He too stopped for a moment, then walked on. Without thinking I bow to him. He looks me over, then says: 'Who the devil are you? Never seen you before. They tell me I'm not to speak to anyone. And what the hell did you bow to me for? To make fun of me? I suppose you're one of his people. Well, say something, man.' I'm sure that we're under surveillance, or that this encounter is due to some technical error that could cost me my constitutionals. So I whisper to him: 'Let's go into the maze, sir. I'm not one of his men. I'm here under duress – the court fool, they call me. It might be unwise for us to be seen talking.' We make for the maze, keeping clipped hedges between us and the Palace. 'Court fool, did you say? Never heard of such a thing. Never had one at my court – though there was never any lack of fools. And what did you do before you came here?' I introduce myself, telling him that I'd been a writer, and explaining how I come to be here. 'Suppose I ought to have heard of you. Never had much time for reading. Interesting, though. Because, in a way, we're in the same boat. He's keeping me on, too – for "consultation", he says. Damnable insolence. To make a fool of me, he means. To inflate his monstrous arrogance with the knowledge that I'm at his beck and call whenever he feels like questioning me about the old times. Won't let me go into decent exile, as hundreds have done before me. Worms everything out of me. Endless gossip and tittle-tattle about what statesman said what, when, who went to bed with whom. Consultation my foot. Cheap entertainment. Yes, now I get it: I'm his court fool! But in that case you're redundant, as those politician fellows used to put it.' I reflect on that. 'Well, sir, I think my function may turn out to be a rather different one – as a former writer, you understand. Like many people he may think that writers have the gift of the gab – when in fact they're the ones who find it hardest to express themselves because words matter to them more than to other people. I think he may be in for a surprise.' 'Sincerely hope so. Pleasure to meet you, anyway. See you again, I hope.' He does, much sooner than either of us expect. Although we part in opposite directions, we keep running into each other in the maze. When I bow to him again, he returns the bow – with a hint of a smile, I think. After that I merely wave. It takes me the best part of an hour to get out. And I don't know whether the King has got out before me or is still wandering about in the maze.

One morning, after breakfast, the telephone voice tells me that I'm to be taken to the Director. I have time to change, but refrain from putting on a suit. To appear casual is the least I can do. The Director, too, is casual, or appears so; rises not from a seat at a desk – I forget that writing has been abolished – but from an easy chair; shakes my hand, offers me another chair, but paces the room as he talks. I seem to recognise him without being able to put a name to the face. Then the circumstances come back to me: a successful arms dealer, rarely mentioned in public, but briefly interviewed once for a documentary programme, and eloquent enough about his activities to have left an impression. The name is still a blur – no more than two vowel sounds, making a spondee. The twinkling eyes, less fanatical than those of other 'leaders', ought to reassure me. They don't. Intelligence, in a man with his ambitions, is more formidable than fanaticism. 'So here we are', he says unnecessarily. 'I'm sorry that I couldn't see you sooner. Perhaps I'd better begin by removing any possible misunderstanding. The words "court fool", I'm told, were used to prepare you for your employment. You'd better ignore the title – a mere *faute de mieux*, I assure you. No, your function is unprecedented and unique. It is to replace the written word, and all those liberal, humane and individualistic "values" once associated with it. As you know, I have had no choice but to ban it – and them – from the public sphere; but I am determined not to make the same mistakes as my historical predecessors. Which of them could afford the luxury of an opposition? You are to be my opposition – at complete liberty to say whatever is on your mind. And there's no need for you to clown, to be funny, when you're not in the mood. Amusement of so high an order is in the eye of the beholder, as it were. Your business is only to be truthful, by your lights. You can be Polonius rather than Feste, sententious rather than witty. Nothing is banned in our sessions, not even religion, though that, too, has had to be publicly proscribed, beyond those externals of observance which have been almost correctly described as the "opium of the people". "Bromide of the people" would be more accurate, since it doesn't hallucinate. Your special knowledge of literature is another qualification. You shall be my mobile museum, the live depository of dead cultures.' Silence. A long silence. He looks me in the eyes. 'Call me Jack, by the way. There is to be no formality between us.' That's the last straw. I am to be denied the distance of subordination, of deference. At last I blurt out: 'You're making a great mistake – Jack. You've got the wrong man. I've absolutely forgotten everything I ever read – except the things I learned by heart at school, Latin tags, some lines of verse, a date or two. And I'm completely tongue-tied in company, always have been. Couldn't bear to read out my stuff – let alone extemporise anything. If I was ever witty on paper, that was because the theme generated wit. And goodness knows where the themes come from. They were simply there, inside me. Not imposed on me from the outside like the spontaneity you demand. Get rid of me now, or you'll regret it.' He laughed. 'Excellent, excellent. An excellent start. You've only to keep that up, and I shall be

constantly entertained. Tongue-tied indeed! Forgotten everything! Just wait till you see what real illiteracy, real amnesia are
like. We're experts in the art of inducing them.' 'Bless you, Jack,' I
answer, inadvertently falling into my new role. 'All the kids will
love you for that. You're the answer to every hippie's and pop
fan's prayer.' He doesn't laugh at that. I can feel that I'm dismissed
– for the day.

The routine takes over. Day after day I walk in the grounds never
to meet the King again. Most days a dumb official escorts me to the
'presence'. I've taken to solitary drinking, but the whisky could be
lemonade for all the effect it has on me. The more the Director
tells me about his reconditioning programme, his agents in foreign
countries busy creating power vacuums everywhere, his tighten-
ing stranglehold on the world commodity market, the re-employ-
ment, one by one, of the few people I used to respect, the less
capable I become of serious comment. Tom-foolery is my only
refuge. There were times when I responded to his boasting with
harangues, protests, appeals. I recall those outbursts with shame.
They served only to titillate his frivolity, which is limitless
compared to mine, because his manipulations and machinations
become other people's realities. 'I alone have succeeded in
abolishing the past,' he brags. 'I shall leave no future that isn't a
continuation of my presence; no going back, and no starting from
scratch.' I salute him: 'Yes, indeed, your Nothingness, sir. Like the
founder of the Millennial Reich that lasted a dozen years. He also
tried to re-create the world in his image, which was nothingness,
so as to usurp God's attributes, and nature's; until the people for
whom he had "sacrificed" himself proved unworthy of him,
because they couldn't see how endless subtraction could amount
to anything but zero . . .' I goose-step round the room, then
collapse on the floor. He chuckles. 'Kid stuff, as well you know.
More vulgarly monumental than Bismarck's Reich, and full of
built-in atavisms. Killing off its own population, instead of putting
it to good use. There hasn't been a single execution under my rule,
not even of a so-called criminal. And I shall achieve my objective
without a single military action.' I lower my head and charge. He
tries to step aside, but has to use his hands to break the impact. It's

my turn to laugh. 'Jack, Jack, the joker in the pack. Never dirties his hands, but mustn't turn his back.' He rings the bell. For the guards? No, for my dumb escort.

One thing he hasn't abolished, yet, is the seasons. The fish grow torpid, then active again. Frogs appear from nowhere to couple and croak in the ponds. I catch a pair of them and release them during the session. His squeamishness is genuine. He jumps out of his chair and almost screams for the guards, who remove the harmless creatures. I know so much about him now, even about the personal life that consists in having none – no friends, no wife, no mistress – that he will have to get rid of me soon. My boredom will precipitate the thing, just as my boredom has made me break the supreme interdict. I've written all this in my suite, with coffee, wine or jam, on to old shirts. It's a slow business, but just what I need to keep me sane. The shirts can be wrapped around my chest and chucked over one of the high garden walls. I don't care what becomes of them, or of me. The act of writing is enough, now that he has made it the ultimate act of defiance. If I had the slightest hope of being able to write anything more after this it would be not about him or against him – that is dependence – but what I should be writing if he didn't exist. Listening to music proved too passive an occupation: I didn't want to be enthralled or edified. Nor have I ever switched on the radio or television. I know from the cook's mouth what pap is ladled out to the public. My 'privilege' is to be the only one to whom he needn't bother to lie – a stand-in for the conscience he lacks. As such I prepare for my last walk in the palace gardens; and for the final session.

Preposterous to the end, I have to write my account of it before the event so that I can add this scrawl to the bundle. I have laid out my one passably good suit, a dark one. This occasion, after all, is a solemn one, although yesterday the Director consummated my indifference by informing me that my wife and son are 'well and happy' – 'your wife in a rather senior administrative capacity, your son as a trainee in the secret service, with excellent prospects, I'm told.' Even before that last confidence – probably intended to allay 'counter-productive' anxiety, and as likely to be true as all the other case histories he has chosen to tell me – my apathy was penetrable only by dream fragments of my former life, landscapes with figures that were they, and others. Now they, too, are part of a past he has abolished – for the time being, at any rate.

He receives me as genially as ever, after a slightly quizzical look at the suit. 'Dressed to go out,' he said, savouring another little advantage over me. 'How observant of you,' I answer. 'How perspicacious. I am, Jack, I am. The fact is I'm here to give notice of precisely that. Too late, I think, for you to make the necessary arrangements for my replacement. Too late, that is, for you to institute a training scheme for the function I cannot and will not perform. I warned you at the start. We verbalisers need a special kind of freedom that's beyond your power to bestow. It is not a luxury but prerequisite of our work. Nor can it be a prerogative separable from the condition of those who are denied it. They may not want this freedom, nor exercise it when they have it. They may even dislike it, or fear it – as you do. But its availability to them is our first and last need. The spontaneity we used to voice was only our own if, potentially, it was anyone's. Where that spark has been put out we have nothing to say.' Silence. A long silence. He paces the room, then tries again: 'A fine piece of rhetoric. I see now why it wouldn't have done to deliver it in your usual outfit. But I don't see what you hope to achieve by it.' I'm ready for that: 'Yes, you do. My release, that's what I shall achieve by it. And you can't withhold it. Your only choice is between one way or another of granting it.' He is still playing for time, reluctant to call the guards. 'It may also interest you to know that I've been writing again,' I add, to give him the push he needs, 'and that I intend to write more.' He glares at me. 'Liar,' he shouts. 'Trying to trick me, after all I've done for you.' I pull a table napkin out of my pocket. On it, in letters of oxtail soup, under the royal crest, I have printed one word:

FOOLPROOF

I wave it at him. He runs to the bell.

The Sarum Twins

CHRISTINE HAUCH

It was a year so topsy-turvy, so scarifying in its shocks and cruelties as to make the toe-nails crack. Spring came in February. It tempted the bluebells up through the earth before they were ready and fretted the pregnant ewes under their too-hot coats. On Lady Day it lifted my mother's skirts to the lecherous intentions of a passing mercenary on his way home from who knows what butchery. There will always be wars enough to go round for men who hanker to fight in them.

The day after my conception.

(Our conception, surely, the case for 'my' in the phrase 'my mother's skirts' being arguable.)

The day after our conception, however, the promise of summer was abruptly withdrawn. Chilblains sprouted on knee-backs and knuckles, icicles tapered from the well-head. Our grandparents watched our mother vomiting and bewailed the loss of her purity and the waste of the food she had eaten.

When warmth finally returned in the middle of June it was too late to restore a balance to the seasons. Trees that had uncurled their fingers early in March found them frost-bitten in April. Seven weeks of dusty heat dried the stream-beds and scored a tracery of cracks across the fields; then followed another seven of ceaseless rain. The people of our village muttered about devils and spirits, but despite their prayers and ritual sacrifices what crops had survived rotted on the stems.

All this she and I were told much later.

Floating heads down alongside each other, I and my sister, who is also I *(yes, I am who am she, but so far and no further)*, we sucked our thumbs through drought and downpour. For as long as we were fed by the cord of life, we could give our mouths to comfort all day long.

(This entire account of the time before our birth is, I should add, a matter on my sister's part less of poetic licence than of gratifying the imagination. However, the writing of this story is her decision and I may interject but not prevent it. That much we have agreed. For the present.)

After such an ominous gestation our birth was as normal as such things can be. The midwife would have drowned us like kittens, but our mother heard our mewing through her pain and clung to us. She never spoke about our early childhood. I can only suppose that we ate and defecated, grew hair and teeth, as infants do. We crawled not at all, and walking came late. It must have seemed that we were to be denied that erectness which sets humankind apart from the beasts of field and forest. We have had to find our own way to acquire humanity.

I and my sister, who are one person, were kept well hidden from neighbours and gossip. As far as our mother was able, she made us invisible. My grandparents were convinced we were the work of the evil one and a curse on the family. I would never blame them for that. She who is I and I who am she have between us two heads, four arms, four legs, four breasts, two hearts, two livers, two wombs, one vagina, one anus, and no buttocks. Tied back to back by a malign creator, we are trapped together for life and death *(and in the Life Everlasting, though she refuses to believe in its existence, despite my prayers)*. We are the Sarum twins. You may have read about us in the literature. We have been examined by men of science and expatiated upon in monographs. Before Phineas Taylor Barnum thought to add spice to his greatest show on earth by exhibiting Eng who is also Chang, the Chinese brothers born in Bangkok, thereby making all conjoined siblings Siamese no matter where they had been born, there was a short time when Wiltshire might have claimed the honour of providing the label. To commemorate the diocese of our birth, there were British doctors ready to describe our condition as Sarum syndrome. But our fame, such as it is, cannot compete with the spangles and flourish of Mr Barnum's set pieces.

We are not unique, or so we have been told, but we are unquestionably rare. We are also unlike almost all women of our time and station in one other important respect: we have received an education. However I may weep for my outward shape, I shall never cease to be glad that my mind has been trained.

(With that, at least, I can wholeheartedly concur.)

At first, we found it disturbing to be treated as specimens for examination, even if interest on the part of others has seldom given way to unkindness. But children can become inured to much. Indeed, as we acquired the ability to read and write, we began to make our own notes on those who came to view us. It has been a simple exercise to develop a secret coded written language, a Sarumish. Although he knows that we can read, the bishop still believes that our writing is gibberish.

(I regret that we continue to deceive him on this point. However, there is no denying that were I to tell him the truth he could not be trusted to keep it to himself. And, while there are times when my sense of spiritual proximity to the bishop, or George, as he has asked me to call him, outweighs my loyalty to her, the fact remains that I am bound to her by the most extreme form of consanguinity. Moreover, she has left me in no doubt that disclosure of our cipher to George, or to anybody, would result in a physical response by her of such frenzy that I should have to fear for the life of my child.)

Besides, no fools we, since our mother has relinquished her claims to us, it has become clear that our very survival depends on the fact that we are known to people of reputation who will feed and clothe us, even if we are to remain in captivity. Given who we are, we do not harbour many illusions about the freedom available to us. A cage in the circus is probably the best we could look forward to. Our only hope of anonymity would be to return to the house of our grandparents; but there is no guarantee for our safety in such a step. Were there to be another summer like the one before our birth, the villagers might come looking for a sacrificial victim, or two, to placate the wrath of nature. *(We have quarrelled so fiercely over this point that I shall not unduly delay her narrative by iterating here all my arguments on the subject. I shall say merely that her love of fanciful hyperbole must by now be apparent to all.)*

We cannot remember when we first became aware of our otherness. I would say that the initial experience of such things has little meaning in any case, that their effect is cumulative. She would try to recapture the original sensation. That is how we are, general and particular. I the broad sweep of things, she the finicky. *(I the fineness, she the unruly.)* I the wayward child, she the prim and priggish miss. *(She the mischief-maker, I the prudent keeper of the peace.)*

We agree, at least, that it is the bishop who has done most to bring home to us our plural singularity.

It never worried my mother that we were not baptised. She had not been able to disguise the signs of our impending arrival; and, since scandal flies round village kitchens fast as dragonflies, she would have expected the news to reach the old rector. At the due time he would be sure to come in search of new lambs for the flock. When he ignored our arrival she assumed that our unusual nature had been made known to him and that he, too, had dismissed us as the spawn of Lucifer.

'I'd not let him near my children, in any case,' she'd have said. 'The last time I prayed to his god was when I found I was expecting them. He did nothing for me then, he'd do no more now.'

(The attribution of such ungodliness to my mother is not to be borne. And I give warning that I shall find some means to put an end to this account unless these provocations cease. She may threaten damage to the unborn, but she knows that I am not without an arsenal of my own. There are many ways in which I could make her life much less comfortable without myself incurring undue suffering.)

In fact, there were no such excommunicatory motives behind the rector's neglect of us. He was a squeamish thing, who had taken to the study of toadstools as soon as his wife started coughing, and was out in the woods with his specimen basket when the consumption finally claimed her. The village midwife, while she had little enough respect for him, knew that, as long as he rather than another continued to dispense morality in the parish, it would be easier to help her patients out of difficulties, and no questions asked. So she had no wish to see him go, and fearing the sight of us would tip him into the grave, she told him we had been a phantom pregnancy. If he never scented the least whiff of gossip about us after that it was probably because the midwife had suggested to her customers that it would be better so.

When I-she were beginning to master the awkwardness of walking at around the age of seven or eight, a new god-man came to the parish. *(The meaning is clear, I suppose, though I could wish for a more respectful title. I hope also that it will be clear to any reader that her portrait of the old rector is simply more of her tarradiddle. Since my censure usually leads to her committing yet further outrages, I am endeavouring to control my natural revulsion at her flagrant falsehoods.)*

The old rector had died, and not from eating a misidentified fungus, but from the same blight that had shrivelled his wife. For the first time in forty years a different voice was promising eternal salvation from the pulpit, and with startling vigour. Desperate for new souls, he was. Somebody told him about us, although little enough, and he came to offer us an afterlife. I laugh about it now. The years of contact with educated minds have given me a more refined sense of humour. Imagine the knotty problems we must have posed for him. How many souls do we have? What is St Peter to do with us at the pearly gates? One entry ticket to paradise, or two? For paradise must be our destination if there is any justice.

To give the young rector his due, he never treated us as if we were a deformity, more perhaps an aberration, a cause for wonder at the diversity of his god's creation. After his first tactful visit, eyes carefully trained at a point between our two heads, he bade us goodbye at the cottage door and we did not see him again for several months. We were not to know that we had become a topic of conversation at the episcopal dinner-table. Our spiritual shepherd had attended the university with the bishop's son and was a frequent guest at the larger houses in the cathedral close. The bishop himself had his curiosity whetted and offered, as a favour to his son's friend, to grace our parish with his presence in order to take the next confirmation service.

After admitting a small group of girls into full membership of the Anglican communion, the bishop postponed his return home for long enough to make a short tour of the neighbourhood. He admired the view from the top of Gibbet Hill and waved a ringed hand at a scattering of stone-picking children who scarcely looked up as he passed. The arrival of his carriage at the end of our lane brought us out of the house to see what had happened. The only time any vehicle stopped there was when they brought my grandfather home drunk from the ale-house, but that was Saturday-night business, and this was Sunday afternoon.

(It is difficult for me to say exactly how, difficult to select the precise word or phrase that offends, but there is something sardonic here. The facts are probably more or less accurate, but the manner of their telling sneers.)

The bishop beckoned us towards him, and as we began our scuttling crab-like progress along the track he took out a pair of wire-framed spectacles and looped the ends round his ears. A trick of the light made the discs of glass look opaque and my sister, who is not always me, took fright. She tried to turn back while I would have carried on. Equally determined, we both tugged the other in the direction we wanted to go. The bishop found us a startling sight. He ran towards us, then changed his mind and stood, panting from his burst of exercise, at a distance of about thirty feet.

He held out a gingerly hand in front of him, as town people do when they are suddenly confronted by cattle and need to make a gesture of propitiation and good will. She, glimpsing the movement, took it for a threat and made an extra effort to run away. We fell over.

I was very angry and caught her a satisfying slap across the fleshiest part of her right leg. She tried to hit me back, and we were soon too absorbed in our awkward attempts to hurt ourself to notice that the bishop had come closer, close enough indeed to bend over and try to stop us.

His intervention united us in a common hostility towards this stranger who had effectively laid us low by his approach. But small children, even in pairs, have few tools of aggression to deploy against fully grown men. She-I scrambled to our feet and fled homewards, yelling and screaming for the largest weapon in our armoury, our mother.

An angry woman, our mother, with cause enough to be so, goodness knows, she never let her indignation run amok, but marshalled all the forces of it to deliver perhaps a single sentence of such concentrated and unanswerable scorn that the recipient would retire defeated after the first salvo. Mother saw the bishop off. She wasted little time on the young rector, too, when he came a week later to offer her money to allow us to be taken away by important people who might, as he put it, be able to do something for us.

'And what sort of a something would that be?' she asked. 'A rosy future, is it? Fame and fortune? Or a satin-lined box for my daughters to live in while the public pay to gawp at them?'

My grandfather could see no harm in the suggestion. The sum of money mentioned by the rector represented a good few months of drunken Saturday nights. He and mother argued about it for several days, and for the first time I heard ourself alluded to as a sport of nature, an entry in the human family album of curiosities, albeit not in those terms. However, as I said, that's my recollection. I don't speak for her, my sister, though there are plenty have thought I do. (*Only, I might add, because she opens her mouth at times when I find it more prudent to keep mine closed. She accuses me of playing the hypocrite, of allowing her to voice my less agreeable thoughts while myself maintaining through silence the appearance of untainted virtue. I have not consciously sought to make her my scapegoat, but honesty compels me to admit that her outspokenness has spared me the necessity to expose my own occasional dissentience to general view. She has a choice. Since she has decided to play the dog, why should I bark?*)

Two years passed before we were taken. There had been a grudging agreement that my mother should stay under her parents' roof – which was not theirs at all but belonged to Farmer Sedgely – so that she could care for us; but as soon as we were old enough to be left at home occupied in some useful task, she was forced out to work on the land.

As we sat on the doorstep in the April sunshine picking out the best of last year's peas to be sowed, the bishop's carriage again drew up at the end of the lane. This time it was our grandfather who descended from it and beckoned. As a special treat for being good girls we were to be given a ride. And good girls that we were, we climbed in without a fuss and waved grandpa goodbye. On our jolting journey through the countryside we were allowed to survey the scenery, but once the outskirts of the city were reached the bishop moved us to the floor, where our only view was of his booted calves.

Wrapped in a rug, to avoid frightening the servants, we were carried through a side door in the bishop's palace, past the portraits of his predecessors lining the stair-well, and up to the loft. There two dormer windows, with a low colonnade edging the parapet beyond them, admitted light and the astonishing sight of the cathedral, a stone leviathan basking in a sea of grass. We had never imagined there could be anything so immense and assumed that our privileged view of this wonder was part of our reward for goodness. For some time we stood at the window, in silence. She and I only talk to each other when we disagree, and not always then. It is a waste of breath to speak out loud to her alone when all I am doing is echoing her thoughts.

Shortly afterwards the bishop himself brought us white bread and butter, two glasses of milk and two small sweet cakes covered in a chocolate coating that looked like eggshell but melted on our fingers. Even she began to doubt that anything we had done could merit prizes on this scale. And my-her suspicions were justified. It was not for what we had done, but for what we were that a double bed had been set up there under the roof and a lock put on the door, to which only the bishop had a key.

He was not an unfeeling gaoler, however. He did his best to reassure us that our sleeping in the bed was part of some prearranged plan of which our mother had approved. It seemed plausible. We had grown accustomed to spending nights without her. Farmer Sedgely had recruited her labours in his kitchen the previous Christmas, when a large house-party and an epidemic among his household staff had necessitated drafting in extra workers. His appreciation of her beauty had led to further occasional invitations, both to scour the pots for a penny, and to perform additional services for the promise of his protection. If Mrs Sedgely knew, she turned a blind eye, grateful no doubt that the risks attendant upon a further confinement were to be foisted on to some other victim.

(Lest there should be any who could imagine this idle and calumnious speculation to be proven truth, I have no choice now but to interrupt. Our grandfather's drinking habits are unfortunately too much a matter of

general knowledge to deny, which is why I made no comment earlier, although it is not necessary to draw attention to them. But her transcription of rude gossip concerning mother and Farmer Sedgely is the last straw. My dear sister, in her no doubt admirable efforts to paint the lives of hard-working country people in their real colours, has a tendency to dwell upon squalor. I shall impute no evil motives to her. But the blamelessness of the end does not always exonerate the means. Whatever her intentions, her wilful disregard for the basic tenets of good behaviour and for the sensibilities of those to whom she owes respect and love is no longer endurable.)

Mrs Sedgely always treated our mother well.

A down quilt is a considerable improvement on a blanket of uncertain origin and several layers of sacking. Under the elegant episcopal roof we slept the sleep of fear-free innocence until the bishop woke us with breakfast, warm water to wash in, and clean clothes. He withdrew, saying that he would come back when the cathedral bells started ringing for matins. The clean clothes were finer than anything worn in our family, but did not fit. And yet the problem was not so much that they had been made for two separate people. We could have contrived some semblance of decency had they not been much too small.

I have no doubt that the bishop had done his best to prepare the two men with whom he returned for the sight of us, but there are phenomena for which words are inadequate. The way in which we are joined has necessarily entailed our appearing to lean away from each other since we first learned to sit or stand. But the bodices with which we had now been provided were so small that we were only able to fasten them by rounding our shoulders still further, as though each were shrinking in horror from the other. Even the bishop, who must by then have grown accustomed to our general outline, was taken aback.

'Gentlemen,' he said, endeavouring to regain his composure by an observance of the conventions. 'May I present to you the Misses Dibden, Mary-Anne and Mary-Jane.'

The taller of the two visitors introduced himself as Dr Stillwater, physician and surgeon. He expressed himself delighted to make our acquaintance and went immediately to the window to admire the view, as he said. The other man was more voluble.

'I am Charles Wicks,' he said, and stared at us, unabashed. 'I have heard so much about you. As a man of science I have always taken a particular interest in the variety of the human condition. You will perhaps be generous enough to afford me the opportunity to further my investigations into the daughters of Eve.'

(She cannot possibly recall so precisely what he said.)

He baffled us. Indeed, most of the people who came to see us during the first months of our life here spoke to us in language which might as well have been Polish or Pushtu for all the sense we could make of it. But, as I have said, the bishop has been no Barnum. Although he brought his friends and, later, a wider circle of spectators to visit the living whims of Dame Nature in his vivarium under the eaves, he also supplied us with schooling and books and eventually gave us access to his library. That he should have conducted such experiments on our cognitive faculties is not perhaps so surprising. Whatever his other failings, his curiosity may be accounted a moral strength and his kindness a blessing. Even under the present circumstances, when most people would not have condemned him if he had let us loose to fend for ourselves, he has cared for her, if less for me, with as much solicitude as a doting grandfather.

(I feel a weakness in her, at last. And how just it is that it should be a recognition of George's goodness that is undermining her misanthropy. With the help of his Blessed Redeemer, God made Man, I shall persevere in my efforts to feel compassion for her who rails so against her fate. It is she who has brought me to my present condition, whether I would or no. But now that I have been granted this chance to fulfil my purpose as a woman I owe her some gratitude.)

With the freedom to choose our own reading matter, admittedly from within the limits of the bishop's collect, I found intellectual independence from her.

(And I, thanks be to God, from her.)

Travelling with Aeneas and Gulliver, with Falstaff and Candide, I was able for the first time to leave her behind.

(She drifts. And as her firmness of purpose wanes, so mine waxes. I will no longer confine myself to comment. I shall emerge from my parenthetical existence. This story shall be mine.)

Yet, how should I best tell it? If I return to our birth, amending her account in the interests of veracity, it will seem small-minded. She has brought us to the bishop's palace, and it is here that our true lives began. For we have been given the best possible gift, one not to be measured against riches, noble birth or beauty: the knowledge of the Love of God. In His Wisdom He has created us. Every vessel, however misshapen, may receive His Body and Blood.

The strict chronology of events is unnecessary. In due season we reached womanhood. Precisely when matters little. Since there is no record of our birth in the parish register nobody can be sure of our exact age. Although we were not forewarned of the ways in which our maturity would become visible (being almost entirely divorced from the company of our own sex from the day we were abducted to the time of our first bleeding) *my faith in the benevolence of Providence was by then sufficient to allay her fears* (and the bishop, noticing certain undeniable symptoms, arranged that we should have an older female servant to attend us).

Despite George's assurances of my innocence, I cannot help reproaching myself that I did not do more to quell the spirit of perversity in her or to discover the paths along which it was taking her. The books she read did not interest me. Her silences and fits of abstraction I took to be similar in nature to my own: a time given to the proper contemplation of higher things. Since there is no deviousness in my own nature I sought no other motives in her behaviour than would have influenced my conduct.

(Ha!)

Although we have never been out in the world, I have had no cause to resent our enclosed existence. The dangerous notions she plays with, equality, self-determination, liberation, are will-o'-the-wispish. Seduced by their false allure, she has threatened to sink us both. But an all-merciful Father has seen fit to allow that some good may come of her errors.

(Overt persecution would be preferable to this regretfulness for my misdemeanours. Her condescension saps my resistance.)

It is natural enough for a woman to seek the joys of motherhood. I had simply assumed that we had been chosen for a different life and had put all such ideas from me. But not she. For how long she had entertained her vile schemes I shall never know since she has solemnly sworn the most impious oaths never to speak of them. It may be that motherhood was not her aim at all, but that she was seeking to arouse in a man, any man, that emotion which leads rightfully to wedlock.

(I have been foolish, I admit it, but not so naïve as to believe in the possibility of a sensual attraction towards me. Of course I wanted to bear a child, a creature in my image who could yet be free of her.)

During the weeks between a late Easter and Ascension Day George was called away to attend his dying father. He had never left us for more than a week since bringing us to the close. But Eliza, our servant, had always proved equal to the task of caring for us during these short absences, and he had no reason to doubt but that she would do so on this sad occasion also. As the days lengthened, the afternoons we spent reading in the library stretched further into the evening. Eliza came later and later to fetch us – we never went up or down the stairs without an escort for fear we might fall; and one evening, it being too dark to read, we waited for her by the open window, leaning side by side on the sill to relish the scents of the garden.

A young man appeared from near the stables which stand at the end of the east wall. She waved to him. Perhaps she smiled. Since I must stand with my back to her I cannot know. He walked towards us, hesitantly as it appeared.

(And no wonder. What monster must have he been led to expect?)

He came close enough to see our faces clearly, said his 'good evening' and walked back to the stables. I dismissed the episode from my mind. But the next afternoon she, under pretext of difficulty with small print, insisted that we sit right by the window so that she could watch for him. He did not come. She fretted. I asked what was disturbing her. She said it was the heat.

For three days we sat by the window that she might benefit from the light, the breeze, the delightful perfume of the wisteria, and at last her patience was rewarded. The young man returned. This time he walked straight up to us. She asked his name. He muttered a reply.

(Hugh. His name is Hugh.)

When Eliza came for us he was still standing there. She told him to be off to where he belonged, but she smiled at him, indulgently. 'The coachman's nephew, young charmer he is. You'll need to watch yourselves with that one, my Marys.' And she laughed.

(It was a laugh directed at us, or so I felt it to be.)

Once more he came to see her, earlier than before, so that there was less chance of his being found with us. He moved round us until he was facing her. I could scarcely make out his continued presence without turning my neck until it hurt. They talked together so quietly that I could not hear their words, mouthing like fish over their love-play.

(Jealous, ah yes. How she betrays herself. Does she imagine I was after billing and cooing? All I ever wanted was my child.)

He did not return. She no longer asked to sit near the window. She complained of headaches and asked me to read to her. She tired of my voice and suggested that we conduct an experiment. She had been reading, she said, of the work of a Mesmerist newly established in London. According to his theories, it was possible for one person to relieve pain in another through animal magnetism. We were both to be blindfolded that we might concentrate on transmitting the necessary influences between us, and then I was to wish her headache away.

Against my better judgment, I agreed that she should tie her sash around my head. I thought only to humour her in her migraine. She knotted it so tightly that I cried out, but before I could protest further I found myself tipped forward. I shall not describe in any detail the horrors of what followed. When she allowed me to breathe again and released the blindfold we were alone in the room with our ruptured maidenhead.

(And now my child moves inside us, but it dances to the rhythm of her heartbeat. Too impetuous, too desperate fully to consider the consquences of what I longed to do, I had made no allowances for the blind thrust of male seed. Spurning my welcoming womb, it entered hers who would have rejected it. And now in the weeks of waiting my barren emptiness continues to weep the red tears of its loss month by month as though nothing had happened, while she grows fat and contented around my future. How should I not 'rail against fate', as she puts it, when I have sacrificed so much in order to achieve so little.)

Because her monthly bleeding continued, it was not immediately apparent that I was to have a child. When my body swelled and Dr Stillwater was summoned to examine me, there was talk of a dropsy, or worse. It was not until I finally determined to break my vow of secrecy and disclose the nightmare that had befallen me in the library that the true nature of my condition was diagnosed. My shame upon learning of it is hardly to be imagined. And yet, with George's help, decency will triumph. Although I was unable to name the father of my child, not having seen him, my suspicions as to his identity were confirmed by her eventual confession.

(A confession extracted from me under the severest moral torture. I was given a choice: to see all the menservants in the bishop's household brought before the law accused of attacking us, and thus under threat of hanging or transportation, or to name the one man who might then be coerced into marrying her and so give the child a name.)

I am to be wed next month. Tomorrow the banns will be read for the first time. It is understood that this marriage is being solemnised for the sole purpose of providing my child with a legitimate birth. My husband will continue to groom the horses. She and I will continue to live under George's protection. Our apartments will be extended to include a nursery.

(You may think me powerless now, but while there is breath in our body I can curse your stony-hearted piety. For the moment you have appropriated our story, but the ending is still to be written. And who can say how matters will turn out? The child kicks impatiently. Will it wait until you have exchanged your unmeaning vows with Hugh? Were I to implore your god for anything, it would be for the patience to bide my time.)

She is silent. Once I might have tried to penetrate her thoughts, but they no longer interest me. I have my own concerns. I pray God that He will see me safely delivered in the hour of my greatest need, and that I may be given the strength to raise my child as a true Christian. Soon George will sit beside me, and together we shall recite the words of the Magnificat. 'My soul doth magnify the Lord and my spirit doth rejoice in God my saviour . . . he hath shewd strength with his arm: he hath scattered the proud in the imagination of their hearts . . .'

Feel our child, sister. Even you cannot ignore it. It will be born.

Books and Records

NICK HORNBY

'Already two lovers and she wished she could cancel the first and, if she and Hank broke up, there would be a third and she would be going the way of her sisters who had recovered, she thought, too many times from too many lovers; were growing, she thought, cynical; and when they visited home, they talked about love but never permanent love any more . . .'

Andre Dubus, *Finding a Girl in America*

THERE WERE TWO deep alcoves on either side of the fire place, with two strong shelves in each. They put the amp and the record and cassette decks on the bottom shelf on the right, nearest the window, and the speakers on the two top shelves. Phil pats the nearest box.

'Shall we start putting them up, then?' He's talking about the records. He's got seven or eight hundred albums and maybe fifty 12-inch singles. Juliet has less than quarter that number.

Juliet shrugs. 'Sure.'

'How do you want them filed?'

'Well, alphabetical, I suppose.'

Phil rolls his eyes. 'Yeah, I'd worked that bit out. Which kind?'

'The A–Z kind?'

'Yeah, but . . .' He lassoes the sharp edge of his voice and hauls it back. 'First name or surname?'

'Surname?'

'OK, so where would you put Danny Wilson?'

'I'll say "W". Then you can tell me why I'm wrong.'

'Because . . . because Danny Wilson is the name of the group. There isn't anyone called Danny Wilson in it.' It's the first time all day that he's been really animated. 'See, if you put Danny Wilson under "W", you might as well put . . . I dunno . . . the Velvet Underground under "U". And what about Teena Marie? Two first names, see?'

'OK. Use first names, then.'

'You sure?'

'Yeah. Christ, Phil.'

'And are we going to have a separate classical section?'

'You haven't got any classical.'

'Yeah, I know, but we're putting the two lots together, aren't we? Yours and mine?'

Juliet starts to pick holes in the plastic sheeting covering the sofa. 'Ju?'

For some reason she feels she ought to care about this, but she's tired and she just wants to get the boxes off the floor.

'You do what you want, love.'

'OK. Well, I'll put the two together and we won't have a separate classical section.'

'Fine.'

'But . . . hold on. Problem.' He makes the noise of a police siren, 'Da da, da da.' Juliet smiles, not because of the noise, which he always makes whenever there's any kind of tiny crisis ('Last tea bag. Da da, da da.'), but because of his absorption in what he's doing.

'What?' She didn't mean to make that big a hole. Phil said to leave the plastic on until all the painting is done. She shifts position slightly to cover it.

'Where are we going to put Bach? Under "B" or "J"?'

'What do you want to put him under "J" for?'

'Johannes. See, otherwise you'll have David Bowie under "D" and Bach under "B". Oh no! Aaaargh!' He clutches the top of his head.

Juliet gives a little laugh and feels her impatience draining away.

'So put the classical somewhere else, then.'

'Right.' Phil nods decisively. 'One more thing. Philip Glass. Classical or pop? Discuss.'

'Classical.'

'Fine.'

He tears the sticky tape off the first box.

An hour later he calls her in.

'There you are. Look pretty good, don't they?'

The records nearly fill the alcoves. Juliet likes the sheer bulk of them, but she wishes she had listened to the niggly little voice she'd heard earlier on, when Phil asked her about putting the two lots together. She'd imagined that adding her records to his would be like adding milk to coffee, that the two lots would come togther to make something of a slightly different complexion. This, she now realises, was a fanciful notion. Girly, Phil would call it. Actually, adding records to records was more like adding water to water. Or anything to anything. In fact, adding records to records is such a mundane thing to do that it's silly even thinking of a simile for it.

By the time they come to argue about the books, Juliet has more energy. Phil wants a straight A–Z in three different categories: fiction, non-fiction and drama. But Juliet points out that only a couple of the shelves are big enough for hardbacks, which means that a straight A–Z is impossible. In any case, she says, she'd like to keep all the same size books together, maybe even the same colour paperbacks.

'What, like all the Penguin Modern Classics?' He has a sneer on his face.

'Why not? It looks nicer.'

'I used to do that when I was seventeen.'

'So did I. I ate when I was seventeen too. Doesn't mean it's an adolescent activity though, does it?'

'So you want all the Viragos together? And all the Pelicans?'

'Yeah.'

'Just so they'll look better?'

'Yeah.'

'Only you'd think of that.'

'I'd like to claim the idea as my own, Philip, but I think someone else might have had it first.'

'Girls, I expect.'

Juliet sighs. 'Just what would you find so difficult about my idea?'

'Because . . . because . . . I wouldn't be able to find anything. It'd be like Foyles in here.'

Juliet gets her way in the end.

When they have finished putting up all the books and all the records, Phil feels kind of cheated. He thought they were going to have more fun doing it. After all, aren't all these hardbacks and paperbacks and albums some of the reasons they have decided to live together? And on top of that, he's maybe a bit disappointed in Juliet, because he thinks he has discovered that Juliet cares more about what things look like than what they are. And guilty, too, about how easily his records have swallowed up hers, because he remembers that the same thing has happened before.

Juliet guesses this, and she feels a bit resentful. And she's disappointed in Phil. She's not going to find the book system difficult because she can remember the size and colour of every book she's ever owned. So she thinks she has discovered that Phil is more interested in buying books than reading them.

One more thing. When everything is in its correct place somewhere on a shelf, they discover (Phil counts them) that they have 117 duplicates. And not just two copies of *The Catcher in the Rye* and *Born to Run*, either. There are two copies of *The Sportswriter* (both hardback), two copies of all the Rickie Lee Jones albums (including the *Girl At Her Volcano* ten-inch), and three copies of *The Stories of Raymond Carver*. (Phil always keeps a spare to give to people.) They have nineteen Elvis Costello albums and twenty-six Graham Greene novels, all Penguins.

Of course, as many couples know, this is in no way coincidental. For one thing, there is their shared passion for the Picador. And for another, they spent the first few months buying each other their own particular favourites as if neither would be satisfied until they had made their new lover into an exact replica of themselves.

'It looks daft,' says Phil.

Juliet looks at the two copies of *Money* with their tacky silver and black spines.

'Yeah, but what can we do about it?'

'We could always flog them. We'd get sixty or seventy quid if we took them to Record and Tape or somewhere. And we could do with the cash. It'd pay for the blind.'

Working out whose they are going to sell is a bit tricky. They decide to keep anything of sentimental value – twice Phil grabs books out of Juliet's hands before she has a chance to open the title page – and the copies in the best condition. The only other problem is with some of the classics, which have margin notes written with a youthful enthusiasm and earnestness that both of them lost around the time their lives became more serious. Juliet's copy of *Jude the Obscure* has TRAGIC! in faded red ink alongside the scene where Jude and Sue find their children hanging from the coat hooks. Phil's *A Passage to India* has 'She was asking for it!' in pencil as an explanation for what happened in the Marabar Caves. For various reasons they decide to keep these.

Juliet has the next day off. She goes back to sleep after Phil has gone to work, and wakes up again around nine. She makes a cup of tea, and then starts to put all the spare books and records in carrier bags. She told Phil last night she'd take them down to Notting Hill this morning.

But as she's sliding her copy of *Marvin Gaye's Greatest Hits* into a bag (hers is more scratched than Phil's) she has a strange thought. She has no idea where it came from and its arrival is as sudden and violent as that of someone crashing through the sitting room window and on to the carpet. Her thought is this: how do I know that the next one has got this record?

She holds this idea up to the light, looks at the seams, tries it on. It's a sad thought, sure, but the simplicity and truth of it almost make her giggle. Because there will be a next one, she's sure of that. One day, Phil's little siren noise is going to sound like a real siren going off right in her ear, and then she will have to take all these books and records and put them somewhere else. Maybe at Sarah's, if she's got a spare room at the right time. And she'll live there for a little while and have fun and feel wistful, and people will look after her and phone her a lot and make sure she's always got something to do at weekends. And then she'll meet someone called Tim or Paul or Martin or Nick, maybe at work, maybe at, oh, Robert and Fran's little girl Becky's third birthday party (maybe even her second – she's one next week), a boozy do where the adults stay on late and flirt. And after a few cautious months she'll borrow Dad's Volvo Estate and all the cardboard boxes will be on the floor again.

And how does she know Tim has got *Marvin Gaye's Greatest Hits*? How does she know he likes Marvin Gaye, or has even heard of him? He might be bookish and isolated, or a classical musician, or her older man. Or he might never have got round to buying it. (Perhaps he sold his because Annaliese had one.)

If she knew his name or his phone number, she could phone him up and ask him, but she hasn't so she can't. She unpacks all the carrier bags and starts sorting out a new system instead.

Unperformed Experiments Have No Results

JANETTE TURNER HOSPITAL

YOU COULD SAY it began with the man in the canoe rather than with the dream, though I can no longer be certain of the sequence of events. It is possible, after all, that the letter arrived before either the dream or that frail and curious vessel, though I do not think so. I used to be without doubts on this matter. Chronology used not to be even a question. But since the disappearances, trying to catch hold of any kind of certainty has been like catching hold of water.

Sometimes, when a tradesman or a parcel delivery man comes to the door, I have to restrain myself, by a fierce act of the will, from grabbing him by the lapels or by the denim coverall straps and demanding: 'What do accidents mean, do you think? Do you have an opinion? Are you a gambling man? Have you ever been spooked by coincidence?' The truth is, I have become obsessed with the patterns of chance – the neatness of them, the provocation such neatness gives – but chance is a subject that very much resists scrutiny, and the more I ponder random conjunctions of events, the more intensely I try to focus my memory, the hazier things become. You cannot, as the physicists keep telling us, engage in the act of close observation without changing the thing observed. Of course I resort to such analogies because it is Brian who is dying.

Nevertheless, though it may or may not be the first cause, I will start with that afternoon on my dock and with the man in the canoe. It was a late summer afternoon and very humid, and the forecast – for thunderstorms – was sufficient to keep most boats in marinas. There were whitecaps on the lake and the river. When I looked east, I could see the pines on the tip of Howe Island bending like crippled old men in the wind. Westward, past the Spectacles, past Milton Island, I thought I could just see one of the ferries, veiled in great fans of spray, crossing the neck of the lake. Wolfe Island, directly opposite, was invisible, or almost so, behind a billowing indigo cloud that threw the whole head of the river into twilight, although it was only about four o'clock in the afternoon.

I was right at the end of my dock, and I had a book propped on my knees, but the wind kept buffeting my light aluminium deck-chair to such an extent that I began to wonder if it was aerodynamically possible to be lifted up on a gust and dumped into the water. I kept looking up over the page, partly to assess my chances of staying dry, but mostly to enjoy the extravagant theatre of wind and water. And then, startled, I thought I saw a canoe emerging from the bateau channel between Howe Island and the shore.

I'm imagining things, I decided, rubbing my eyes. Who would be so foolhardy on such a day? Or so strong, for that matter. Here, the currents are swift and ruthless. Every summer, bits and pieces of our ageing dock disappear, and end up, no doubt, somewhere around Montreal; every winter the pack-ice brings us splintered paddles and fragments of boats bearing registration marks from Toronto, Niagara, and even, once, from Thunder Bay. I shaded my eyes and squinted. Nothing there.

Wait . . . Yes, there it was again, a canoe, definitely, with a solitary paddler, heading upriver against all this mad seaward-running energy.

It is by no means impossible to paddle upriver – I have done it myself – but even without a headwind it is very hard work and is rarely tried solo. Astonished, I kept my eyes on the paddler. He must have muscles like steel ropes, I thought. His chances of capsizing seemed extraordinarily high. Clearly, he was someone who liked danger, someone who was excited by risk, perhaps even someone who got a certain kick out of pain, or at any rate, out of enduring it. But for how long, I wondered, could his arms take such punishment?

> *Do not undertake anything unless you desire to continue it; for example, do not begin to paddle unless you are inclined to continue paddling. Take from the start the place in the canoe that you wish to keep.*

Old advice, three centuries old, but still as sound as when Jean de Brébeuf sent his letter home to Paris full of tips 'for the Fathers of our society who shall be sent to the Hurons'. I always think of them, those French Jesuits, *voyageurs*, when I see a canoe pitching itself against the current. I think of them often, as a matter of fact, since I moved out here on to the river. I keep their *Relations* on my bedside table, I frequently browse through those lively, detailed, sometimes despairing reports to their superiors. Paris, Rome: it must have seemed as uncertain as prayer, dispatching words by ship.

> *The Relation for 1649 to the General of the Society of Jesus at Rome: I have received, very Reverend Paternity, your letter dated January 20, 1647. If you wrote to us last year, 1648, we have not yet received that letter . . .*

With canoes, they had more reliable, more intimate relations.

> *The Relation for 1637: You must be prompt in embarking and disembarking; and tuck up your gowns so that they will not get wet, and so that you will not carry either water or sand into the canoe. To be properly dressed, you must have your feet and legs bare; while crossing the rapids, you can wear your shoes, and, in the long portages, even your leggings.*

I imagine them with their blistered European hands and their cassocks hoisted up around their thighs, paddling full pelt up their *Great River St Lawrence* (they wrote of it with such affectionate possessiveness, with such respect for its stern powers), dipping their paddles towards their deaths, skimming past these very rocks that buttress (and will eventually smash) my dock, heading west

97

with their mad cargo of idealism, dedication, and wrong-headed-ness.

> *You must try and eat at daybreak unless you can take your meal with you in the canoe; for the day is very long, if you have to pass it without eating. The Barbarians eat only at Sunrise and Sunset, when they are on their journeys.*

I could see the flash of the paddle now, knifing into the water, keeping to the right side, pulling closer to shore. His arms are giving out, I thought. He is going to try to beach on this stretch. Now that the canoe was close enough, I could see that it was neither fibre-glass nor aluminum, but birchbark. It wasn't until the next day that I was struck by the oddness of this, and by the fact that I had never seen a bark canoe before, except in photographs and museums. At the time it seemed quite unsurprising, or at least, not significant. I merely noted it, wondering exactly where the canoeist would reach shore, and if he would manage this before capsizing.

And then, gradually, it became clear to me that the paddler had no intention of trying to land. He's crazy, I thought. Shoulders hunched forward, head slightly down, eyes on the prow of his craft, he was bent on defying the current and continuing upriver, parallel to shore and now only about thirty feet out. It seemed incredible. He was all manic energy and obstinacy, and I fancied I could hear the pure high humming note of his will above the general bluster of the wind. His strength, which seemed superna-tural, was oddly infectious. It was as though infusions of energy were pumping themselves into my body, as though the paddler's adrenalin was an atmosphere that I inhaled. I couldn't take my eyes off him. *Go, go, go,* I urged, weirdly excited.

It is odd how certain body shapes, certain ways of moving the body, are retained like templates on the memory. So we recognise a voice, a face – we take this as unremarkable – but so also a gesture or a way of walking can be recalled. I could still see only the outline of the figure (though I'd assumed from the start the paddler was male), and he was wearing a hooded windbreaker so that he (or even she) could have been anyone. And yet, watching the way the shoulders lunged forward, the way the arms dug into the water, the sharp thought came to me: *This reminds me of someone. Who is it? Who? Who?*

It was maddening. It was like meeting someone at a party and *knowing* you have met that person before somewhere, but being unable to summon up a name or a context. This sort of incomplete recollection can drive you crazy. The canoe was drawing level with my dock now, and I wished I'd brought my binoculars down. The plunge and lift and dip of the shoulder blades, oh, it was at the tip of my mind, who did that movement remind me of? Now the canoe was level with the end of my dock, but the hooded head kept its eyes resolutely on the prow and the water, the paddle flashed.

Oh please look up, I willed.

And he did.

'Good God!' I cried out, thunderstruck. '*Brian*!'

Brian – no, of course not Brian, I was aware almost instantaneously that it couldn't possibly be Brian, who was either in Australia or Japan – not Brian, then, but the man in the canoe simply sat there, resting his paddle and staring at me, startled, which naturally meant that he scudded back downstream very swiftly. He dug the paddle furiously into the water, dip, dip, dip, until he drew level again, closer this time. He rested his paddle and stared. I felt, as the current again bucked him backwards, that I had to do something potent and instant to stop time unwinding itself, but I could neither speak nor move, the resemblance to Brian was so eerie. I was experiencing something like vertigo, and a pain like angina in my chest.

I was dimly aware that my book had fallen into the water and that I was on my hands and knees on the dock. I watched the canoe draw level a third time, and the paddler and I stared at each other (he was very pale, and there seemed, now, to be no expression at all on his face), and then he, Brian, I mean the man in the birchbark canoe, turned away and lowered his head, and resumed paddling more fiercely than ever.

I watched until he disappeared from sight, which seemed to take hours. I have no idea how long I stayed on my hands and knees. I know that when I tried to climb the steep steps up our cliff, my legs felt like jelly and kept shaking so badly I had to stop and rest several times.

People climbing mountains and cliffs hyper-ventilate, this is common knowledge. They see things. Visitations alight on them.

Between the fiftieth step and the fifty-first, the past distends itself like a balloon, and I climb into it. I can feel its soft sealed walls. *Trapped*, I think. And simultaneously, pleasurably: *home*. I can smell the rainforest, smell Queensland, feel the moist air of the rich sub-tropics again.

Brian is a few feet ahead of me, both of us drenched, both feeling for handholds and footholds, both of us (I realise it now) equally scared, but too proud to admit it.

(This would have been our last year in high school, and this was something we did every year, spend a day in our own bit of rainforest – we thought of it that way – on the outskirts of Brisbane, climbing the waterfall. But our last year in high school was the year of the floods. I think we both gulped a little when we saw the falls, but neither would ever have been the first to back out. We were both given to constant high anxiety, and both temperamentally incapable of backing away from our fears.)

So. Every handhold slips, every foothold is algae-slick. My fingers keep giving way. My heart thumps – thud, thud, thud – against its cage. Delirium, the salt flavour of panic: I can taste them. Just inches above my eyes, I see the tendon in Brian's ankle. If I were to touch it, it would snap. I tilt my head back and see his shoulder blades, corded tight, lift like wings, pause, settle, lift again. He reaches and pulls, reaches and pulls, he is a machine of bodily will. The energy field of his determination – pulses of it, like a kind of white light, bouncing off him – brush against me, charging the air. This keeps me going.

At the top of the falls, we collapse. We lie on the flat wet rocks. We do not speak. Our clothes give off curls of steam that drift up into the canopy, and creepers trail down to meet them. We float into sleep, or perhaps it is merely a long sensuous silence that is sweeter than sleep. I dream of flying. I have languid wings. I can feel updrafts of warm air, like pillows, against my breast feathers.

'Mmm,' I murmur drowsily at last, 'I love this heat. I could lie here for ever. How come the water's so cold, when it's so hot here on the rocks?'

'I'm not even going to answer that, Philippa,' Brian says lazily. 'It's such a dumb question.'

'Piss off,' I say. I inch forward on my stomach and peer over the lip of the falls. I can't believe we have climbed them. I watch the solid column of water smash itself on the rocks below. I feel queasy. I can see four years of high school shredding themselves, all the particles parting, nothing ever the same again. 'Where do you reckon we'll be five years from now?' I ask him. I have to shout. My voice falls down into the rift and loses itself in spray.

Brian crawls across and joins me. Side by side, we stare down ravines and years, high school, adolescence, childhood, we've climbed out of them all. There is just university ahead, and then the unmapped future.

'Where will we end up, d'you reckon?'

'Not here,' Brian shouts. 'We won't be in Brisbane.'

'Bet we will. And even if we aren't, we'll come back. Let's do this every year for the rest of our lives.'

'Not me,' Brian says. 'After uni, I'm never coming back.'

The shouting takes too much energy, and we crawl back to the relative hush of the flat rocks ringed with ferns.

'So where will you be?'

'I don't know. Cambridge. Japan, maybe. There's some interesting stuff coming out of Tokyo. Wherever's best for the kind of physics I'm interested in.'

'What if you don't get into Cambridge?' I ask, although I know it's another dumb question. It's like asking: what if you don't get to the top of the falls?

Brian doesn't bother to answer.

'I'll probably still be here,' I say.

'No you won't.'

'You're such a bloody know-it-all, Brian.'

'I know you and me.'

'You think you do.'

'Philippa,' he says irritably, with finality. 'I know us well enough to know we won't stay in Brisbane. You'll end up somewhere extreme, Africa, Canada, somewhere crazy.'

'You're nuts,' I say. 'Anyway, wise guy, wherever I am, you can bet I'm going to stay close to water.'

'Yes,' he says. 'You win that one. We'll both be near water.'

In the dream, I am at the end of my dock, reading, when I notice the most curious light over Wolfe Island. The whole island seems burnished with gold leaf, and there is an extraordinary clarity to things, to individual trees, for instance, as though each detail has been outlined with a fine-tipped black brush. I can see vines, orchids, staghorn ferns against the tree-trunks. I can see that Wolfe Island has gone tropical, that it is thick with rainforest, that lorikeets and kingfishers are flashing their colours on the St Lawrence banks.

Then I note that there is a suspension bridge, the catwalk kind, with wooden planks and rope sides, the kind sometimes strung a hundred and fifty feet up in the rainforest canopy to allow tourists to see the aerial garden running riot up there. This bridge starts at the end of my dock and crosses the river to Wolfe Island, but it is submerged.

What catches my eye first are the ropes tied to the end of my dock, just below water level. I lie flat on my stomach and peer down. I can see the arc of the bridge, little seaweed gardens swaying on its planks, curving down and away from me.

There is someone lying on his back on the bridge, or rather floating with it, just above the planks, just below the rope siderails. It is Brian. His eyes are open but unseeing, his skin has the pallor of a drowned man, algae spreads up from his ankles, tiny shell colonies are crusting themselves at all his joints. Seaweed ferns move with him and around him. He looks like Ophelia. *There with fantastic garlands did she come . . .*

'Alas, then,' I say to him, 'are you drowned?'

'Drowned, drowned,' he says.

No one would be too surprised by the fact of my dream. First I see a man in a canoe who reminds me of someone I know, and that very night I dream of Brian. A canoeist in a storm is at risk; I dream of death. There is a simple logic to this sequence of events; anyone would subscribe to it.

Nevertheless, I woke in a state of panic. I woke with the certainty that something was wrong. I hadn't seen Brian for, I had to count back . . . well over a year, it must have been. It was always hit or miss with Brian. Luckily, childhood friends had a slightly better chance of making contact with him than ex-lovers or his ex-wife, but no one alive could compete with the sharp scent of a new hypothesis. I used to picture him literally *living* in his research lab, Melbourne or Tokyo, either city it was the same. I used to imagine a rollaway bed tucked under the computer desk. The last time we met for dinner in Melbourne he said, sometime after midnight:

'My God, the time! I've got to get back to the lab.'

'You sleep there?' I asked sardonically.

'Quite often,' he said.

On principle, Brian never answered his phone. He kept it unplugged (both in his lab, and at the home address he rarely used) except for when he was calling out. I knew this. Nevertheless I called, Melbourne and Tokyo, both, and of course got no answer.

I sent faxes and got no response.

I called the secretary at his research institute in Melbourne. 'Professor Leckie is in Tokyo,' she said, 'but no one has seen him for weeks. We still get his e-mail though, so he's all right.'

E-mail! I never remembered to check mine, I used it so rarely. I plugged in the modem on my computer, keyed in my password, got into the system, and opened my 'mailbox' on screen.

There was only one message, undated.

Philippa: I'm going away and wanted to say goodbye. Remember the falls? Those were the good old days, weren't they, when nothing could stop us? I often think of you. Of us back then. Pity we can't go backwards. Take care. Brian.

I sent a message back instantly.

Brian, I typed on to my screen. *Had a disturbing dream about you last night. Are you okay? I miss you. Take care. Philippa.*

Back then, on the day of the message on the screen, the order was still beyond question for me. First the man in the canoe, then the dream, then the message. I began to be less confident of this sequence after the letter from my mother in Brisbane. Not immediately, of course. But a few weeks after the letter, I had to make a point of reminding myself that the terrible thunderstorm weather had begun in late August, that my mother's letter was postmarked September, and that I could not anchor (by any external proof) either my dream or my e-mail to a date.

I bumped into Brian's mother in the city last week, my mother wrote. *She says something's the matter with Brian, some nervous system disorder, I think she said, something quite dreadful, there was a Latin-sounding word but I can't remember. She said she flew down to visit him in the Royal Melbourne, and he looked like a skeleton, he'd lost so much weight. He's not taking it well, she said. He's never been able to tolerate any kind of interference with his work, not even his marriage, as you know. She's terribly worried. He refused treatment and checked himself out and flew to Tokyo, can you believe that? You know he used to phone her once a week from wherever he was? Well, he's stopped doing it. She's quite depressed and quite frightened. I thought maybe you could get him to phone her, poor dear. Or maybe you'd like to write to her yourself? She must be awfully lonely since Mr Leckie died. We thought perhaps we should invite her for Christmas, but it's hard to tell whether she'd enjoy this or not. Maybe you should write to her, Philippa. You know her much better than we do.*

Every day I would begin a letter in my mind.

Dear Mrs Leckie: Remember when Brian and I used to go on rainforest treks and get home hours later than we planned? You used to worry yourself sick, and my parents too. But we always did show up, remember? Brian's just off on another trek, he's lost track of time, that's all . . .

No. Begin again.

Dear Mrs Leckie: Brian's gone on a journey, as we always knew he would, from which (both you and I have a hunch about this) he might not return. He carries everything he needs inside his head, and always has. In his own way, he misses us. I promise I'll visit when I'm in Brisbane next year. How is your frangipani tree? Remember when Brian and I . . . ?

I never sent these unwritten letters.

I began to ask myself whether I'd imagined the man in the canoe. Or whether I'd dreamed him. Or whether I'd dreamed the e-mail message which had vanished into electronic ether without a trace.

For my night-time reading, I followed records of lost trails. *The Relation of 1673*, for example, written by Father Claude Dablon:

He had long premeditated this undertaking, influenced by a most ardent desire to extend the kingdom of knowledge . . . he has the Courage to dread nothing where everything is to be Feared . . . and if, having passed through a thousand dangers, he had not unfortunately been wrecked in the very harbour, his Canoe having been upset below sault St Louys, near Montreal . . .

In Brisbane (two years ago? three?), on the verandah of the Regatta Hotel, a mere stone's throw from the university, a jug of beer between us, Brian said: 'D'you ever get panic attacks that you'll burn up all your energy before you get there?'

'Get where?' I asked.

'I shouldn't even answer that, Philippa. God, you can be annoying,' Brian said. 'Get to where you wanted to go.'

I couldn't concentrate. I stared across Coronation Drive at the Brisbane River. I could never quite believe that the present had inched forward from the past. 'Look at those barges,' I said. 'I bet they haven't replaced them since we were students. They're decrepit, it's a miracle they're still afloat. I could swear even the graffiti hasn't changed.'

'It hasn't,' Brian said. 'We come back younger because we're in orbit, that's all. Brisbane gets older, we get younger. A clock on a spaceship moves slower than clocks on earth, don't you know that, Philippa? If we went on a journey to Canopus, a few light-years out, a few back, we'd come back younger than our great-great-grandchildren. Got that? And we've moved light-years from Brisbane, haven't we? So it figures. The trouble with you arty types is you don't know your relativity ABCs.'

Dear Mrs Leckie, I could write. *Brian's in orbit. He's simply on a different timetrack, it's all relative. We could go backwards, and swing on your front gate again. We could unclimb the waterfall. We could go back through the looking-glass and watch the future before it came.*

I sent out daily e-mail messages to Brian's number. *Past calling the future*, I signalled. *Brisbane calling Far Traveller. Please send back bulletins. I miss you. P.*

I tried to goad him into verbal duelling: *Which clocktime are you travelling on? Please report light-year deviation from Greenwich Mean.*

Every day I checked my 'box'. There was nothing.

I called Brian's secretary in Melbourne again. 'When you said you were still getting his e-mail,' I asked, 'how often did you mean? And where is it coming from?'

'You never know where e-mail is coming from,' his secretary said. 'Actually, we haven't had any for several weeks, but that's not so unusual for him. Once he went silent for months. When he gets obsessed with a new theory . . .'

'How long has he been ill?' I ask.

'I didn't know he was ill,' she said. 'But it doesn't surprise me. We're always half expecting all our researchers to drop dead from heart attacks. They're all so driven.'

I think of the last time I saw him, in Melbourne. 'Why don't you slow down a bit?' I asked. 'How many more prizes do you have to win, for God's sake?'

'Prizes!' He was full of contempt. 'It's got nothing to do with prizes. Honestly, Philippa, you exasperate me sometimes.'

'What's it got to do with then?'

'It's got to do with getting where I want to go.' I could hear our beer glasses rattling a little on the table. I think it was his heartbeat bumping things. He couldn't keep still. His fingers drummed a tattoo, his feet tapped to a manic tune. 'I'm running out of time,' he said. I would have to describe the expression on his face at that moment as one of anguish.

'You frighten me sometimes, Brian. Sometimes, it's exhausting just being with you.'

Brian laughed. 'Look who's talking.'

'Compared to you, I'm a drifter. Wouldn't it be, you know, more *efficient*, if you just, even just a little, slowed down?'

'When I slow down,' he said, 'you'll know I'm dead.'

Between the soup and the main course of a dinner party, my mind elsewhere, I heard these words: *that birchbark canoe that washed up . . .* and *police inquiries . . .*

I had a peppermill in my hand at the time, and I ground it slowly over my salad. I took careful note of the sharp pleasing contrast made by cracked peppercorn against green leaf. I looked discreetly around the table. Who had spoken the words? *Had* they been spoken?

I could hear Brian say irritably: 'Honestly, Philippa, you never *verify* things. You live inside this vague world of your mind, you make things up, and then you believe they're real.'

'But so do you. You make up a theory, and then you set out to prove it's real.'

'*There's* the crucial difference,' he says. 'My hypotheses are verifiable, one way or the other. I chase details, I nail them down. I won't stop until my theory is either proved or *dis*proved. If I can't do either, I have to discard it.'

'Same with me,' I say. 'I put riddles on one side, and come back to them. I do realise the birchbark canoe could have been a figment of my mind and my bedtime reading. I'm checking around. What's the difference?'

'I'm not even going to answer that question,' Brian says.

'But don't you ever come back to your discards?'

'Of course I do. Some problem-sets have been passed on for generations. The trick is, you have to approach from a new angle every time. Half the battle is how you frame the question. Unperformed experiments have no results.'

'Exactly,' I say.

And over the candles on the dinner table at the other end of the world, I hazarded cautiously, flippantly: 'Did someone just say something about a birchbark canoe, or did I imagine it?'

Seven pairs of eyes stared at me.

'Sometimes, Philippa,' my husband joked, 'I swear you put one part of your mind on automatic pilot, and the other part is God knows where.'

'It's true,' I said disarmingly. 'So did I hear something about a birchbark canoe, or didn't I?'

'The one washed up on the ferry dock,' one of the guests said. She waved a ringed hand and smiled, courteously tolerant. ('Bit of a flake, isn't she?' I could imagine her saying to someone later. 'Where *does* she get to, between the crackers and the cheese?') 'The one the police are making enquiries about. I was just telling everyone that I'd had to go down to the station and make a statement. And John did too, didn't you, John? Didn't you see him? Yes, I thought so, I was talking to Milly on the phone. So that makes two of us. I mean, who saw the canoe when there was someone in it. Paddling.'

'I saw him several times, as a matter of fact,' John said. 'Came within ten feet of my boat once, when I was fishing. I waved – well, it's customary – but he didn't wave back. Funny, I only ever saw him paddling upriver. Beautiful canoe.'

'The Burketts,' someone else said, 'the ones who live on Howe Island, you know? – they said there was a hunter camped there most of July and August. No one knew where he was from, and no one was very happy about it, but that's who it must have been. I mean, they said he had a birchbark canoe and it's not as though you see them every day. And then he just up and disappeared. The Burketts gave the police a full description and they're putting out a trace, you know, for next of kin.'

'I expect they'll find the body eventually,' John said. 'I wouldn't mind buying the canoe, she was a real beauty. I suppose she'll go up on police auction sooner or later.'

'Won't they have to hang on to it as evidence until the body is found?' someone asked.

'I expect so,' John said. 'Yes, I expect so. Still, sooner or later. The police boats are out dragging every day.'

'I hope they don't find him,' I said.

Everyone looked at me.

Sooner or later, I think, evidence of one kind or another will cast itself up: a dream, a letter, an item in the newspaper. Every day, I read the 'Police and Fire Watch' column in the local paper. Every day, I am relieved that no body has been found. Of course this is ridiculous, and I know it. There's a name for it: *sympathetic magic*.

And there's that other matter too, for which Brian had a word: *synchronicities*.

What do they mean? I ask myself. What do they *mean*?

In the evenings, I read of doomed voyages.

The Relation of Christophe Regnaut concerning the martyrdom and blessed death of Father de Brébeuf . . . captured on the 16th day of March, in the morning, with Father Lalemant, in the year 1649. Father de Brébeuf died the same day as his capture, about 4 o'clock in the afternoon . . . I saw and touched the top of his scalped head. . . .

The Relation of 1702: Father Bineteau died there from exhaustion; but if he had had a few drops of Spanish wine, for which he asked us during his last illness . . . or had we been able to procure some Fresh food for him, he would perhaps be still alive. Father Pinet and Father Marest are wearing out their strength; and they are two saints, who take pleasure in being deprived of everything . . . For my part I am in good health, but I have no cassock . . . I am in a sorry plight, and the others are hardly less so . . .

I read also of survival against all odds.

The Relation of the First Voyage made by Father Marquette toward New Mexico in 1673: . . . his Canoe having been upset below the sault, where he lost both his men and his papers, and whence he escaped only by a sort of Miracle . . .

I check my e-mail every day, I send out messages, I wait. I spin theories and discard them. I shuffle sequences as I might shuffle a pack of cards.

The joker comes up every time. Any riddles for recycling? he grins. Any letters for uncertain destinations? Any unperformed experiments to go?

I'm not even going to answer, I say.

The Lobster Season

BARRY HUNTER

GEOFFREY NDOLA WOKE up smiling, a full bladder adding potency to his erection. With the UDP taking sixteen of the twenty-nine parliamentary seats in Monday's general election, he was in opposition again. To his left, a wooden bowl containing three limes and a tube of Johnson & Johnson lubricating jelly held his attention briefly before his dark eyes settled on a naïve seascape with twig figures, an unframed canvas by local artist and marijuana evangelist Walter Tsambas, perched experimentally on the skirting-board beside the air conditioner. On his right, her buttocks connecting coolly with his own like washed fruits in a plastic bag, Samantha J. Hopper was dreaming of her father's death for the umpteenth time since he passed away on the jetty at Caye Caulker, chewed to the bone on his right side by a hammerhead he had encouraged out on the reef in the days before the marine reserve at Hol Chan began charging three dollars a head. (In Sammy J's dream, Samuel Hopper II is never killed by a fish. Instead, he dies over and over again in his suite at the Hotel Palenque, close to the Mayan ruins, when a ceiling fan drops out of the sky like a monstrous insect, hovering now and then on its slow-motion descent towards a torso protected only by a Conrad reader in paperback.)

'Way to go, Sammy J,' whispered Geoffrey Ndola. 'Of course, we live as we dream – alone.'

He swung his legs off the hammock, stepped into his pants, and pulled on his PUP vest. It was going to be a fine day for sure. The United Democratic Party may have won the election, but the returned opposition member for Belize Coastal South had a majority of 305 votes to celebrate. Geoffrey Ndola was a constituency man. While the People's United Party campaigned for tougher restrictions on American investment along the barrier reef coast, the Honourable Member kissed his Louisiana exile under the stars on the roof of the Sundowner Hotel where she worked and lived. Geoffrey Ndola believed in mutual understanding. He liked to wait and see. One day, he and Sammy J would sling the hammock of their dreams between the coconut palms at St George's Creek, where the fish snap at dragonflies and rare birds call out in the night. Until then, what was the harm in a few shell-pink condos on the Ambergris coast?

Geoffrey Ndola eased the noose of his PUP tie over his head and tightened it, relieving himself quietly into the sink. He picked up his briefcase and shoes and slipped out to the verandah overlooking the hotel beach. Above him, the Island Airways 'Early Bird' service to the municipal airport and Goldson International cleared the Sundowner's corrugated roof with a roar and banked immediately towards the mainland. Geoffrey Ndola watched it climb above the sun. From below, the drone of the engine was gradually replaced by the scratching in the sand of Charlie's seaweed rake as the hotel handyman cleared up after the squall. Two glass-bottomed boats in the shallows beside the Amigos del Mar sports jetty creaked at their moorings and beyond, near the Texaco pump and the watertaxi rank, a pelican broke the surface at the edge of Geoffrey Ndola's vision and reclaimed the air with a cry. The Honourable Member paused in the sand at the bottom of the wooden stairs to slip on his shoes, then stepped into the sunlight on Front Street. He walked unshaven down a dirt road towards the radio bunker with the stray dogs of San Pedro.

'What's new, Miller?' asked Geoffrey Ndola as he sat down in the studio and picked up the guest headphones.

'Gonna find out right now, councillor,' said the Cuban DJ with exaggerated sing-song lilt. He pressed home the news jingle cassette and handed his visitor a sheaf of faxed pages. 'Coming up in a few moments, the Honourable Geoffrey Ndola MP will be telling us how it feels to be re-elected to represent this wonderful constituency of ours. But first, at just before six thirty on Wednesday fifteenth July, the news headlines . . .'

Miller wiped his mouth with the back of his hand and read from the faxed bulletin. 'With the start of the lobster season still two days away, police in Belize City have made a number of arrests in connection with illegal lobster harvesting along the coast. During a series of dawn raids in the city yesterday, three separate stockpiles of frozen lobster tails with a combined street value of four thousand dollars were seized and later sold at market, the proceeds destined for various charities in Belize City.

'Security is to be reviewed for the second time this year at the city's notorious Queen Street Prison following last night's break-out in which sixteen inmates escaped. New Interior Minister Remijio Montalzo has promised an independent enquiry into the incident and urged those still at large to give themselves up immediately. Six prisoners who absconded were recaptured within half an hour when they were discovered drinking beer at a popular cabaret venue just two blocks from the prison.

'At the Americas Trade Association summit in Guadalajara, final agreement on US import quotas is expected later today after a stormy two-day debate during which the Honduran delegation twice walked out in protest at proposed banana restrictions.'

It was enough to be going on with. Cuban Miller spiked the final item about the Governor General inaugurating a new incinerator for the pathology department at Belmopan's central hospital. He nodded his satisfaction, hit the jungle tape again, and cued Geoffrey Ndola.

She shivered in the draught of the oscillating fan and pressed her hands together between her thighs. She stretched in the shuttered half-light and switched on the radio behind her head. Sammy J lifted the sheet from the tiles below. She pulled it across her body and up around her throat where a gold chain tightened momentarily and then relaxed against her skin. Is there a time between sleeping and waking when the earth stops turning and the night sky merges with land and lake, all stars denied? She walks arm in arm with her father towards a temple pyramid, a structure dim, crepuscular, not yet revealed but defined by scaffolding and hedged with flame of the forest trees. Around his neck hang a loaded Leica and two light meters, and in her hand a Polaroid print draws its moist shellac across the view: this ruined wedding cake of a building and, behind it, the blood blister of the sun.

'Jesus,' she said softly, turning up the volume and extending the telescopic aerial to maximum. Sammy J splashed her face with tepid water and wiped her armpits with a discarded Nike singlet. As she dressed in mannish checked shirt and loose-fitting cotton dungarees, Geoffrey Ndola was speaking slowly and clearly into the microphone on the boom arm beside him.

'In conclusion, ladies and gentlemen, let us recall that when Jesus chose Peter to be the head of the church, the first Pope, he said: Thou art Peter and upon this rock I will build my church. So Saint Peter is the rock and an appropriate name for our beloved township.'

He paused and swallowed. Beside him, the lean Cuban broke off from ringing diagonal letter groupings in a dog-eared puzzle book and passed his visitor three ready-made reefers. 'In a world where the dollar is god and nothing seems permanent,' continued Geoffrey Ndola, 'it is more important than ever that we hold before us an example of constancy, of stability and of integrity – our patron saint, San Pedro.'

Sammy J switched off the radio and returned to the basin in order to vomit. She was fifty-two days pregnant. As she wiped her mouth she remembered tonight was Chicken Drop night at the Sundowner Hotel. Every Wednesday, beers half price.

She pocketed her key and took the lift to the ground-floor lobby where Charlie was being sworn in as temporary daytime receptionist by a fat manager in his underpants. The Sundowner had two shift managers (one fat, both patronising) and a melancholic receptionist in exile whose wife disappeared around dawn in a camouflaged truck between Guatemala City and the shores of Lake Atitlán in '88. Now he too was prone to early disappearances, arriving calmly at his post beside the pigeon holes in the middle of the morning with five dollars for Charlie and an excuse for the manager. One day he resuscitated a hypoglycaemic Arab in an overflowing upstairs bathtub after tell-tale droplets fell on his forehead from the polystyrene ceiling tiles of the reception area. In our earthly lives, he told Sammy J privately, we must learn to recognise the signs from above.

She said good morning, picked up the courtesy kart keys and headed out to Front Street. Charlie knew she was bound for the airport to meet the first flight from the mainland, and to collect two valises from Walter Tsambas's place on the lagoon side of the caye. By the time she returned with two prospective guests, the handyman was ready for her. He had cleared a space behind the ketchup jars at the back of the walk-in refrigerator and left a clean sheet as arranged. While Charlie checked in the mother-and-son combination from London, Sammy J tucked a cool white sheet round two identical red suitcases and returned to the reception desk. For the English new arrivals, she stowed twenty-five rolls of unexposed Kodachrome 64 in the lobby bar cooler, next to a pineapple and something soft wrapped in foil, then poured two Diet Cokes. She noticed that the long-haired English boy in jogging pants and trainers wore two gold hoops at his right ear and a leaping fish on his bicep. She already knew he was blind.

'I'll have a *piña colada* and the young man will have what I'm having,' she announced with whisky voice to the barman-cum-waiter at the Blue Parrot.

Geoffrey Ndola looked up from his *huevos rancheros* to watch her park her bottom on the stool, swing her legs into position and rest her feet on the crossbar. Her legs were long. She wore blue deck shoes and ivory slacks with foot straps like ski-pants and a turquoise long-sleeved blouse which buttoned high at the throat like a Chinese jacket. Around her neck, her sunglasses swung on a cherry red lanyard.

'Too late for breakfast, too early for lunch,' she added with a thin smile in Geoffrey Ndola's direction, shrugging her shoulders and then gripping the young man's elbow as he slipped in beside her. Her face was tanned and freckled and as lined as any old Africa hand's. She wore neither make-up nor jewellery. With her grey hair swept back tightly and drawn into a bun at the nape of her neck, she could have been Eva Peron on safari. It was impossible to say how old she was.

She took off her sunglasses and placed them on the bar deliberately. Releasing the young man's arm, she fished a portrait lens from a leather duffel bag which was strapped like a quiver across his back, then brought out a battered Nikon with motordrive attached. She clicked the lens into position and fired off twenty frames at the relaxed member of parliament before introducing herself. 'My name is Elizabeth Barrett and this is my son, Matthew.'

Geoffrey Ndola rose from his chair and took her hand. 'Mrs Barrett, Matthew . . . welcome to our island. I trust your stay will be a pleasant one.' He sought out the young man's hand and shook it robustly, then returned to his table and gathered up his papers. 'I'm afraid you must excuse me, though,' he added. 'I have my surgery in half an hour.'

Geoffrey Ndola slipped a ten dollar bill under his coffee saucer, snapped his briefcase shut and approached the Englishwoman with his PUP card proffered. 'At your service,' he said with ironic gravity, then ambled through the door beside the jukebox.

Elizabeth Barrett drained most of her drink in one draught and stirred the remainder with a straw. She glanced at the TV screen (Bill Clinton, the weather) which looked over the place like an umpire from its wooden gantry. She took in the garish papier mâché birds hanging on gilt perches from the palm fronds above, counting parrots, toucans, cockatoos, macaws.

'Charming man, wouldn't you say?'

Matthew sipped. He pulled a wad of banknotes from his shorts and fanned them out on the bar like playing cards for the man to select. When they finished their drinks they walked hand in hand across the sand to Ma Baker's watersports shop which had its own private jetty. The thatched hut was homely and decorated with sponges and cuttlefish bones, plus the jaws of some small sharks fished from deeper waters beyond the reef. Elizabeth Barrett recognised Charlie from the hotel as he hosed down a stack of wet suits, fins, face masks and snorkels. Without his baseball cap, he was quite bald.

Of course, Ma Baker had reservations about the crazy Englishwoman with the cameras and her blind son who wanted to go snorkeling at Hol Chan. Nevertheless, she stored their things and talked to Charlie and then waved all three of them off in a large speed boat fitted with a sun shade and stocked with water. Soon it would be the hottest part of the day.

When they arrived at the reef, Charlie paid the entry fee to a boatman at the edge of the marine reserve and nosed forward, looking for a good spot to drop anchor. In the water, all three stood on the tips of their fins while Charlie explained that the idea was to avoid damaging the corals by touching them or snapping their brittle stems. The sun flashed on their face masks. Elizabeth Barrett looked down. She saw the seabed stretching ahead and behind and to the side like a fabulous desert strewn with conch shells and fan corals and great boulders of brain coral studded with brilliant fish. Matthew spat into his snorkel and held Charlie's hand as they swam through the shallows close to the wrecked lighter. When his guide broke away to harry a crayfish, the blind boy floated at the surface of the ocean with fathoms below him and fathoms above. He felt the sun on his back and the salt on his skin. Honour the lord, and the lord will honour you. That was what he told himself.

By the time Sammy J lay down for her siesta, the sting was already going out of the day. Through the open shutters of her room she watched the sea turn silver as the sun began to dip and dazzle and dance in spots across her retina. She has been here before: this sacred valley in unknown Mexico which can be accessed only on foot. The year is 1892. Leaving his mule at the entrance to the valley, her father follows his Indian guides into the holy precinct. Some of the men are in a considerable state of excitement, having fallen under the influence of their magic plant. They are anxious to meet with the gods as soon as possible. After an hour's march along the side of the valley they descend for a thousand feet to a small clearing just above the river where the God of Fire, following extensive travel, has taken up residence in the temple devoted to him. In the realm of the Huichol, this location is the most sacred. Rendered crudely in volcanic ash, an idol stands in front of the doorway at a height of some eighteen inches. The statue is dirty and caked with dried blood, except for a hole on the right side where the raw material shows through cleanly. (It seems that when healing shamans visit the temple they scrape off a portion of the god's body with their fingernails in the belief that to eat it is to acquire a knowledge of mysterious things.) By the time he has made three exposures, the white man's guides rejoin him after swimming in the river. And he, tired by the exertions of the day, insists on resting here for the night. But they will hear none of it. They volunteer to bring him water and fresh hikuli to boost his strength, and he consents to their medicine, hoping the plant will help him recover. He swallows the bitter sap without difficulty. It slakes his thirst and allays his hunger. His fatigue is removed and he feels stimulated, as if he has taken some strong liquor. The effects, moreover, are immediate. He ascends the hill quite easily, pausing only to adjust the photographic apparatus on his back and to draw a full breath of air. At night he lies with an Indian youth on a carpet of oleander leaves and it seems the boy's tongue is a lizard's.

The sky was bruised black and blue when Walter Tsambas arrived at the Sundowner Hotel for the last time. He was in high spirits.

He chained his bicycle to a lime tree on the edge of Front Street and walked round the side of the building to the crowded verandah bar on the sea front where Sammy J was selling numbered tickets for the Chicken Drop. She was standing barefoot behind a trestle table in a simple cotton dress, a strap hanging off her shoulder and an unlit cigarette in her mouth. Walter Tsambas watched her explain the rules of the game to a man in long shorts who lit her cigarette and selected his tickets from the bucket on the table. As Sammy J noted names and numbers, a fluorescent light above her head flickered off and on briefly before snuffing out the night.

Walter Tsambas paid for a bottle of beer. He held the liquid in his mouth while he pictured himself at the embassy in London, surrounded by luxurious paintings, mingling with critics and second-world diplomats on the opening night of a successful exhibition for promising artists of the Caribbean. He had addresses in Croydon and Ladbroke Grove at which to stay. What he required was spending money.

He started towards the patio. He watched Geoffrey Ndola exchange words with Sammy J, then embrace her, then turn to confront a group of well-wishers who shook his hand and patted him on the back. As he passed the smiling politician, Walter Tsambas squeezed his elbow and congratulated him too. He waited beside Sammy J until she took a pair of keys on a string from around her neck and handed them to him. Close up, he could smell her perfume.

'They're in my room upstairs.' She spoke rapidly in his ear. 'Room twenty-four, on the second floor. Two red suitcases with sixty tails in each as agreed. The kart's on Front Street. Keep the keys till you get back with the money. You should go now. You'll miss your flight.'

People wanted tickets. She turned from Walter Tsambas and smiled at the tall Englishwoman and her son.

'You're just in time here tonight. How many numbers will you guys have?'

'Just the two, thank you,' said Elizabeth Barrett. She took her son's hand and guided it towards the plastic bucket. There were about a dozen tickets left. Matthew picked out numbers seventy-eight and four. He could smell the patchouli which lingered on Sammy J's skin.

'So how does it work?' he asked her.

'You'll see,' she said without thinking. 'Actually, it's very simple. If the chicken shits on your number, you get the jackpot. That'll be two dollars, please. The only thing is, if you win you have to clean up the chicken shit before you get your money.'

The patio filled up around the numbered board. As Sammy J sold the remaining tickets to a tourist from Des Moines, she was joined by Geoffrey Ndola. He bowed slightly across the trestle table.

'Mrs Barrett, a very good evening to you,' he said. 'No camera to record our cultural showpiece tonight?' He put one arm round Sammy J's waist and signalled with the other to Charlie at the back of the patio. 'May I present my fiancée, Samantha Hopper?'

Then Charlie arrived at the crowded table with a large wicker basket and it was time to play the game. As Sammy J made her way with Geoffrey Ndola and Charlie towards the numbered board, she felt a hand seize her wrist and then release it. It was the Englishwoman's. She pressed a small monochrome photograph into Sammy J's palm and mouthed: 'I knew your father as a Yucatan man.' That was all she said.

Sammy J reached the space at the centre of the small crowd. In front of her was a painted grid of squares numbered one to one hundred at random. When Charlie took the lid off the basket, she reached in with both arms, dropping the photograph as she picked up the bird. Many of those assembled began to cluck and flap their wings but she neither saw nor heard them. She placed the chicken in the blind boy's hands and gently extended his arms over the grid. The bird dropped to the ground, slipped and regained its footing. For a full minute it crouched immobile in the middle of the board, deaf to all entreaty, as the flashguns popped. Then, setting off in the direction of the beach, it released a sudden stream of excrement which all but obscured the painted number beneath.

Sammy J picked up the chicken and put it back in the wicker basket. She walked through the bar to the reception desk and collected a house key to her room. Alone on the second-floor verandah, she stared at the darkness beyond the jetty lamps and saw the spume of the reef phosphoresce in the moonlight. Pretty soon she heard the roar of the last flight to the mainland as the aircraft cleared the hotel roof and headed out to sea. She listened as the noise of the engine came and went and watched the plane turn back towards the coast. As it lost height suddenly, she had a vision of Walter Tsambas smiling serenely at the twinkling lights of San Pedro and waving at her through the window. Then the aircraft hit the water in the shallows beyond Ma Baker's jetty and buried its nose in the sand. Sammy J thought about her friend and the lobsters in his luggage. She imagined startled fish dashing from the crash scene in silent shoals. A hundred yards from the shore, the tail of the plane rose out of the darkness like the handle of a shocking sword. It was the most amazing thing she had ever seen.

Three Miles to One Inch

ELIZABETH JOLLEY

THE AUNT WANTED to get out by herself. The aunt said she wanted quiet and fresh air. She said she would walk alone, the nephews must walk with their grandmother. 'This once,' the aunt said, 'your grandmother would like a walk. Go with your grandmother.' The aunt said the nephews could not go with her unless they walked first with the grandmother. The nephews could come with her later – she did not want the grandmother to explore with them along the cliff. The cliff path, the secret path on the rocky cliff, the aunt said, was uneven. The grandmother would not manage the path, she said – all those rocks.

The grandmother thought about the aunt's wanting to walk alone. She thought it might be because the aunt wanted to meet someone, but if the aunt wanted to meet someone all by herself, the grandmother did not know who it could be. She hoped that no harm would come to the aunt. She was afraid that the aunt might be hurt in some way.

The grandsons told the grandmother that they did not want to walk. They did not want to walk anywhere. Because of this, the walk, as it turned out, was something of an ordeal for the grandmother. The grandsons started straightaway to race ahead, disappearing in the gardens all along the road. They disappeared for such a long time that the grandmother thought they must be lost, or that they might have turned back and gone home.

The grandsons, reappearing as if from nowhere, climbed like monkeys into the street trees, and, with strange inhuman noises, burrowed into the woody hibiscus and oleander bushes. The grandmother feared hidden broken glass and thought of their bare, fragile feet.

The grandmother called the grandsons to come out from the bushes. The grandsons, obeying, walked immediately behind the grandmother, almost treading on her heels. She turned, smiling, and told the grandsons to look yonder, at the lemon tree there in the deep green of someone's back garden. She admired, for them, white roses and a variety of hibiscus, apricot-coloured, the flowers, she said, as big as dinner plates. 'Look you,' she said to the grandsons, 'at that pretty house and the pretty fence.' A white fence, she told them, is nice with geraniums climbing over the pickets.

Crappy house. That's a crappy house, the grandsons told each other, and a crappy fence, they said. Crappy crap. Another crappy house; the grandsons counted the crappy houses, one after the other. Crap, one grandson said. Crap, the other replied. It was all crap, they agreed. Yeah. The grandsons disappeared once more.

In the corner shop, the grandmother said that the grandsons could choose a chocolate bar each. The grandmother told the grandsons that the coin-operated game would not work without money. She told them to leave the knobs and handles alone. As the grandsons unwrapped their chocolate, she noticed suddenly how small their hands were, still. She hoped, as they all three walked slowly home, that the aunt would not wait and wait on the cliff path for someone who, having promised to come there, would not come.

When it was time to do the shopping at the supermarket, neither of the grandsons wanted to go with the grandmother. First one, then the other, said they would wait at home for the aunt. They would be perfectly all right by themselves, they said.

During a previous visit the grandsons had made a dash for the shopping trolleys, one each, which they took, with their own engine noises and remarkably realistic squealing brakes, down the first aisle and round the corner and back up the next aisle and down the third while the grandmother was still studying her shopping list. She had told the first grandson, as he rushed by, soap powder. She'd moved quickly out of his way as he put himself in reverse. She told the second grandson detergent and floor polish, but he was already too far away, in bread, cakes, biscuits, rolls, and muffins. The supermarket had resounded with their engines as they changed from first gear to second and up to third somewhere inside their thin, narrow chests.

It could be, the grandmother thought, as she prowled in the strangely quiet supermarket, that she might go, on one of these days stretching out into evenings when the aunt went out alone, to the path along the river. It was possible that she might see someone, and, from a little distance, of course, sum him or her up at once.

'It's vascular,' the doctor said when the grandmother tried to explain that the noise in her head was like a pump going. He went on to say that he'd had head noises himself for years. 'Bells,' he said, 'and not bicycle or church.' Everyone had noises in their head, himself included. Not like mine, the grandmother told him. Sometimes, she said, she was embarrassed that people might be listening to her head and what was going on in there.

While the doctor wrote a prescription for her, the grandmother thought about the long grass in her orchard and the way in which this dry, bleached grass pursued her, as if on fire, whenever she made her way up the slope. She thought of the plums – the satsuma, the golden drop, and the blue prune plums. They would be ready for picking. The Australian prune plums in particular never failed to surprise her; they were like something in a fairy-tale illustration, an intense blue, hanging secretly in the deep green of the leaves. The bloom on these small, vividly coloured fruits gave an impression of a delicate mist hovering about the trees. She often picked some plums early and put them along the kitchen windowsill to ripen. Forgetting about them, she was agreeably surprised to see them whenever she went into the kitchen.

Some mornings, like this morning, early, the grandmother would study an old road atlas, three miles to one inch – just certain pages, of course. Her family had moved to Australia when she was young, and so she was familiar with only two or three small areas in Great Britain. She put on her reading glasses and held the magnifying glass over the maps.

This morning, she could not seem to find Sparkbrook. She had the Stratford Road, all right, out of Birmingham. Farm Road (there was no farm) went off Stratford Road. Sparkbrook was marked, she was sure, but perhaps where one map joined another. She knew the Stratford Road through Henley-in-Arden to Stratford. Once, she had ridden a bicycle all the way to the edge of the Cotswolds, where her boarding school was. The way went through Henley-in-Arden, through Stratford-upon-Avon – there it all was, clearly on the map – through Shipston-on-Stour, on to Upper Brailes and Lower Brailes, and on to the three villages of Sibford Ferris, Sibford Gower, and Burdrop. The names and the recollections were a kind of poem. At the end of that term, her last, she rode all the way back on the bicycle, the sixty-seven miles to Solihull, the place her own grandmother moved to when she left Sparkbrook.

The grandmother, waking too early before it was light and before the birds, was overwhelmed with dismal thoughts. There was the family visit and the shoutings of the grandsons' father the day before, and an unexpected reproach and criticism of herself during an early birthday telephone call for the aunt from the middle daughter, living on the other side of the world. (The aunt had refused to come to the telephone.) But worse was the anxious expression in the gentle eyes of the elder grandson and the indecision shown by her youngest daughter, the grandsons' mother, faced with the father's loud, angry voice. And then there was her own stupid and unforgivable forgetfulness about small but important items – the wholemeal bread, for one thing. *That bread.* The aunt said, What does *bread* matter for heaven's sake? And she added that the grandmother should *not* have answered the phone at lunchtime when the whole family was milling around in the kitchen. The aunt went out for the rest of the day by herself.

The nephews piled all the nicest things they could find in the house in the doorway of the aunt's room.

As the light crept up the sky outside her window, the grandmother heard the first soft chirpings of the birds. Tentative bird voices, scarcely a song, little bird whisperings, as one, then another made the first bird sounds. It was like hearing the grandchildren waking up and beginning to talk to each other in the room across the passage, the way her own children, the three sisters, had, years ago, played small, quiet games together at daybreak.

The grandmother has never forgotten the way in which the aunt, waiting her turn, took and held first one new-born nephew and then the second nephew when he was newly born. It seemed to the grandmother that the aunt held each new baby somehow in the palms of her large hands. It was as if the lineaments of both children's distinctive and separate features were carved, in advance, for their expected coming into these capable and empty hands. It was as if the stick-like little thighs and arms fattened and dimpled visibly in the caress of the aunt's hands, cupped to receive first one and then the other. The aunt's love for her nephews lit up her plain face and softened, with a previously hidden tenderness, her angular body. Whenever the nephews came to visit, the aunt made them hers, in her looking at them, in her sitting and walking with them, in their going to bed, and in their getting up. Her voice, which was deep, became deeper and softer when she spoke or read to them. The nephews, right from the beginning, every time they visited, came into the aunt's world. The grandmother knew it was because of the aunt that they were still willing, now that they were no longer tiny children, to come. She did not mind at all, and took pleasure in their visits and the wrecking of the ordinary childless tidiness of her home. It was decided that the grandsons should stay (they called it 'sleeping over') because of its being the aunt's birthday the next day, even though the aunt declared she had no birthdays now.

The journey to school on the three-miles-to-one-inch map held many pleasures. For one thing, the grandmother liked her school uniform very much. She liked it so much that she never liked to dress up in her red jumper and skirt on changing days (Wednesday and Saturday afternoons, after games). The school uniform was a green tunic with a square neck. It was loose, with three box pleats, front and back, and gathered at the waist by a woven belt called a 'girdle' also green. The tunic was worn over a cream-coloured blouse, with a school tie, or, in winter, over a dark-green jumper with the school colours of brown and gold showing at the neck and wrists. Later, she became very fond of her nurse's uniform.

Sometimes she wondered why she preferred uniforms. Perhaps, she thought now, it simplified life, giving the wearer a plain but recognised status – if that was what was needed. It also meant that a person did not stand out to be criticised or laughed at because of an odd choice in clothes. The uniform, she knew now, made for the safe and the ordinary. A long time ago, the grandmother recalls, someone's mother passed on a navy-blue tunic that was too big for her. Long before she was old enough for school, she dressed up in it, bunching it up in front with the girdle, and, going in to where her father sat at his desk, she told him that if anyone came calling for her he was to tell them she had left and gone away to school.

When the very young mother of the new grandson, the firstborn, cried because breast-feeding presented a problem, the grandmother sat on the side of the young mother's bed and, with authority, pressed the grandson's head and his anger towards the engorged breast. The grandmother felt competent in her clean cotton frock, especially as the grandson's regular swallowing was at once the only sound in the room. The young mother forgot her tears and laughed, saying that, because of the crisp blue stuff of the grandmother's sleeves, it was like having a real nurse at home looking after her.

Perhaps, the grandmother thought, as she put away the three-miles-to-one-inch maps, she should consider these days now, these times, these early mornings, as being the happiest in her life, since there was no way of knowing what lay ahead. She tried then to remember where she had left her gardening gloves. She would make a point of pulling up weeds for ten minutes every day. She had, she knew, great strength and determination in her fingers. With this last thought, she remembered once more the power of the pretend uniform and the quiet, relaxed but subdued laughter both she and her youngest daughter allowed themselves in the presence of the hungry baby. Pushing the remnants of discord and unhappiness from her mind, she looked forward to the afternoon, when she would drag the tenacious grass out from the lavender, and possibly sweep up a wine box full of fallen leaves and tip them on the rose bed with the hope of enriching the worn-out earth.

Sometimes, during the afternoons, there was something about the changing light as the sun moved over the trees which made the grandmother forget how many years had gone by. She would find herself expecting her own three daughters to come home from their schools and immediately begin trying on each other's clothes, or borrowing from each other pens and books and earrings and hats, calling out, all the time, teasing remarks and items of schoolgirl gossip.

Sometimes, just after putting away the precious inches of the road atlas, the grandmother dropped things: a knife clattered in the metal sink, or a bowl chipped and cracked on the tap. The quickness of thought, she told herself then, is too quick for the body. It was surprising that she should remember so much when she was very forgetful. She wondered why this was.

It was the Stratford Road, out from Birmingham to Spark-brook, that brought the grandmother's own grandfather's voice – the sound of his voice and his head coming, grizzled, round the door of the room where she and her sister sat. They sat playing together on the carpet, in front of the fire, with the Christmas dolls and all the little piles of folded dolls' clothes. Did they know, their grandfather asked, how many little girls like themselves were either kidnapped or run over and killed on the Stratford Road, just down there where Farm Road went off Stratford Road, just a little way down from where they, their grandfather and grandmother lived?

A kidnapping, her grandfather said then, was as bad as a road accident, because children belonged to their parents and grand-parents right from before they were born. And they were cherished. Did they, the two of them, there on that carpet, understand just how much they were cherished? Cherished, he said, and brought up with nothing spared, and then, in a flash, taken away suddenly. Kidnap and sudden death in an accident were, he said, as if the earth itself had cracked open, revealing a black, bottomless cave into which the child just disappeared for ever, leaving broken hearts to make do and mend the best way they could. Broken hearts, broken like this, he said, never do mend, not properly. Kidnap and road accidents were not the only way children disappeared, he said, not at all the only way they disappeared.

The grandmother, in her own reading later, much later, fitted fairy story and legend and real life together. It seemed to her that legends were attempts to explain happenings that were too painful and hard for human endurance. She wanted to explain something of this to the grandsons. One day, on a rug on the lawn, the grandmother read aloud to the grandsons. She held them each by an ankle, one hand to one ankle on each grandson. She sat with the book in her lap. She was, she told them, going to read them the story of Proserpina and the pomegranate seeds and how the little girl Proserpina, disobeying her mother, disappeared one bright, sunny day while playing on the seashore. The story, the grandmother explained, described the way in which Proserpina's mother, Ceres, was heartbroken. She searched all over the world, asking everyone she met had they seen her little girl, her most precious possession. The grandmother explained that Proserpina was also known as Persephone, and that her mother then was called Demeter. It was important, she said, to be correct with the names. Ceres or Demeter, she said, was the goddess of the corn, of the harvest. The grandmother told the grandsons to listen to the part of the story which described how Ceres, during her search, stops at a castle to look after a baby prince who was unable to thrive. She read to the grandsons:

> Ceres sat before the hearth with the child in her lap, and the firelight making her shadow dance upon the ceiling overhead. She undressed the little prince, and bathed him all over with some fragrant liquid out of a vase.

The grandmother paused to explain that the baby laughed and clapped his little hands and then:

> Ceres suddenly laid him, all naked as he was, in the hollow among the red-hot embers. Then she raked the ashes over him and turned quietly away.

When the prince's mother saw this, the grandmother said, she was very upset and grabbed her baby out of the hot coals. Ceres was scornful and asked the mother if she imagined that children could become immortal if they were not tempered in the greatest heat of the fire.

It was during this part of the story that the grandsons simply slipped from the grandmother's grasp and disappeared with a slight rustling of dry leaves into the surrounding bushes.

Alone on the grey rug, in the deeply shaded garden, the grandmother began to understand that it was not until she was a grandmother herself that she, because of her own love for her grandsons, realised how much she, as a small child, had been loved. And the pity was that it was too late now to acknowledge this to anyone. It was no longer possible to offer, unsolicited, a kiss, a caress, or a tender phrase backwards, as it were, over the shoulder. Recalling momentarily the pain of the telephone reprimand – well deserved, she was sure, and only one of many – the grandmother came to a very real truth, which was that the great love that holds the mother to the child does not necessarily travel in the other direction, from the child to the mother. She understood also that she would not be the only person in the world to have discovered this. She had at times during her life found herself offering thanks even to the cross old man, her own grandfather, in small, silent words, scarcely moving her lips, but still with fervour, as if saying a prayer.

Ancient legends, she said to herself on the rug, come from real and unbearable grief. She thought she would write to the grandsons and equip them with this truth. She would include the inescapable suffering of bereavement, of rejection, of jealousy, and of remorse. The grandsons, she was sure, would read in time the great writings which included all these. In the meantime, they would have her letters. Children, even when they would not listen, would, out of curiosity, gobble up written words. Children were naturally curious.

The grandmother, reassured by the noise, the steady beating as of a piston and a cylinder, in her head, folded up the rug and went indoors. Sometimes it was as if a valve, or something like that, were permanently open, stuck, so that there was, in her head, a steady pouring as of an ancient pump, well into its stride – the water flowing without effort. She did not mind this, either. It was, in a way, reassuring that there was something sustained and continuing. Mostly she had other things to think about: the aunt, for example. The grandmother's eldest daughter was a teacher. She was tall, too tall – tall enough to have wept, at one time, about being too tall. She walked with long steps, like a man – mannish, the grandmother thought, but kindly, remembering the boyish little girl. The aunt was the manager; she had all the keys in a bunch of her own. The grandmother never minded. There had never been any thought or possibility of a marriage. In the world inhabited by the aunt, either the men were married or they preferred the company and the affection of other men, or, covertly, both. There were also those men who chose women on whose reputation, social standing, and income they could depend. They, these men, described themselves as being in special occupations, as consultants in management, in real estate, in fashion, and in food. They were agents selling other people's products on secret commission. They wrote up wine and restaurants and the elegant homes of the affluent in lyrical but repetitive language. Sham, but, believing in themselves, what else could they do? The grandmother thought about the thick hedges of coarse, bleached hair and the slack lips. She had noticed the quick, sidelong glances of deception in the presence of wives innocent of certain business dealings. She understood that there was place enough for all this, and perhaps more besides. The important thing, she thought, was recognition and acceptance that they were not for the aunt.

Even when the youngest daughter was writing out her wedding invitations, the aunt (who was not an aunt then) wept silently, admitting in her desperation that, as the eldest, she should have been the first to be married. Even as she was saying this, she said she knew the idea was an ancient one from fairy tales and romantic novels, and she laughed while she was crying. Whenever the grandmother thought about this, it was not hard for her to remember the tears trembling along the aunt's eyelashes.

The grandmother thought of the aunt wanting, as she had said, to walk alone. Hours had passed, and she had not come back. The grandmother imagined the aunt sitting high up where the riverbank was a cliff. She would be sitting there watching the changing colour of the water as the day moved slowly through the afternoon towards the evening. The river there was wide. From one hour to the next there could be, on its surface, an ice-blue calm changing to a greenish blue and, a little later, to a sea-green metallic sheet, and then, almost at once, the water would be as if whipped up into waves with frothy white crests, an animation threatening a storm. Later still, the waves would settle once more, this time into slate-purple peacefulness, matching the evening sky at sunset.

This river had been ever a reminder to the grandmother and the aunt that they and the two younger sisters had travelled. This place, with all the differences – and the river was one of these – had become their home. The three-miles-to-one-inch was an atlas of roads in that other place, the major roads in red and the minor in blue. The forests, the hills, the mountains, the cities, the towns, and even the smallest villages – everything connected by roads could be found. And the English rivers – the Cam, the Thames, the Wey, and the Severn – these in particular, from the grandmother's experience and memory, were little by comparison, making this river look, in places, like a wide blue lake. Sometimes, even from the clean sand of this river, it was possible to catch a moment of the special fragrance of those other rivers, a reminder of the brown water between narrow grass-covered banks often mud-trodden by cows being herded for milking, and overhung with willow trees, their thin branches and leaves trailing over and in the water.

The grandmother knew that the grandsons came to visit because of the aunt. She understood, too, that it was a possibility that the aunt, by walking alone, by insisting on taking a walk alone on that high-up place (and she really did walk alone, for who was there of any worth to match her?), was giving the nephews to the grandmother for the whole afternoon.

The grandmother understood, too, without being told, that the aunt would not, if she was seeing someone, bring him or her home, in case it never came to anything. The aunt was shy. She was shy and gentle; both qualities demanded privacy.

The grandmother told the grandsons that it was high time the aunt came home. She told them that they would go together to look for her. They would stalk the aunt if stalking became necessary. They must follow her tracks and catch her. They, the grandsons, must show her, the grandmother, the secret paths along the river. She would, she said, manage the rocks. For hadn't she herself taken the aunt for walks there long ago? It was important, she told the grandsons, that they find the aunt. They must hurry, she told them as they set off at dusk. The grandmother hoped that the river paths, unlike the roads and houses in the suburb and the trolleys in the supermarket, were not crap. She hoped that the aunt's game and the secret paths, the rocks and the rock pools along the river beaches, would remain uncrapped for as long as possible.

Little lights were beginning to appear along the far bank as the grandmother and the grandsons followed a single pathway, about the width of a man's boot. It reminded the grandmother of the path made by a small flock of geese as they followed the gander. Five geese to a gander − a hand of geese, the grandmother remembered − walking one behind the other through the grass. The path was the width of the aunt's shoe, one foot being placed, in the manner of geese, directly in front of the other as she walked. Small half-moons of trodden grass on either side suggested the thin, nimble feet of the grandsons running and leaping, repeatedly following and leading the aunt.

A flock of black cockatoos, showing white flashes in their wings, flew screaming, breasting the purple-brown river. The black cloud of marauding birds seemed suddenly to dip down into the water, then, rising with fresh screams, the birds turned and flew in the other direction.

The sweet yet sharp fragrance of the warm evening reminded the grandmother of her own small orchard and the pleasure of walking there on summer nights. The air rose cool and damp from the river, picking up the scent of the dry grass and the dry leaves and the few late flowers remaining after the hot summer. Because water is the last thing to get dark, the river was too pale and made a poor background for the path the fast-rising moon tried to provide. The grandsons, running like little dogs to and fro and in circles, made one of their disappearances, sliding with hardly any sound down an old watercourse. The grandmother, remembering, thought of their torn and sand-stained clothes. In the following silence, she heard the river water whispering along the foot of the small cliff, and from the surrounding grass there was a thin, persistent, motonous music from the grasshoppers and other insects. The grandmother told herself that she should have taken this walk long before now. She should have, on one of the afternoons stretching into the evenings, walked out to where the aunt would be, and there she, the grandmother, might have seen someone and known, in one glimpse, whether he or she was worthy or unworthy of the aunt.

Once, long ago, when playing on the grass-covered pit mounds of her childhood, the grandmother had come near to a sinister and forbidden place, an old pit shaft fenced with single wires attached to rotted and leaning posts. The coarse tufted grass grew up to and over the edges of the shaft so that it was not possible to guess the true edges. It was not possible, either, to know how deep the shaft was, and it was a surprise to discover the horror that it was not deep at all but filled in almost to the top and furnished with all the ugliness of displaced human existence. An old sofa lay there on its side, the flock and springs bursting, as if through infected wounds in the discoloured cloth, as if someone, hiding, were living there and would return at nightfall to this remnant of an ordinary household, hideous in the desolate place.

The grandmother, catching sight briefly of the grandsons ahead of her in the fast-falling dusk, called out to them to keep away from fenced-off hollows along the river, places where sand and rocks had been quarried and where water collected out of sight, and you could never know (her voice cracked as she called to them), you could never know how deep that water might be; and you could never know what or who might be lurking in the castor-oil bushes, thriving as they do in deserted places, like stinging nettles, encroaching, in the wake of human habitation and human use of the land. They were approaching just such a place, and the grandmother, recalling that there had been a derelict house there at one time, felt suddenly afraid. The grandsons had disappeared as if gone for ever. It was almost too dark to make out the path. The rocks were troublesome underfoot, and her voice had lost all power. Her skirts caught in the woody stems of ancient bushes; eucalyptus, redcurrant, and rosemary, she thought, as she stumbled down into the damp and overgrown hollow. Fearful of hidden, jagged corrugated iron, coils of old wire, old timber with rusty nails protruding, she thought suddenly of snakes. All at once she was seized on both sides, her clothes clutched by thin fingers, and the clutching was accompanied by the familiar small rustlings that seemed, from the start, to be characteristic of any movements made by the grandsons. They, one on each side of the grandmother, seemed to be hauling her upward as stones and loose gravel gave way beneath her feet. The grandmother, even as she was dragged upward, wondered at the strength of the grandsons, knowing, as she did, how slender and vulnerable their little, boyish bodies were beneath her apparently merciless scrubbings when she bathed them – like little frogs, she thought, then, as they slid from her soaped cloth and disappeared under the warm water.

Just as quickly as they appeared, the grandsons disappeared once more into a deep, dry ditch, another watercourse left from last winter's rain. She heard them ahead, their catcalls rising and falling, echoing and fading.

The moonlight was romantic and pretty now, a real path shining across the river. It was then that the grandmother saw the aunt sitting, a little way ahead on a tilted flat rock on the edge of a part of the cliff that was higher than the rest. It was a lookout point; the grandmother thought she remembered it. Behind the aunt, and leaning over her, was a figure indistinguishable in the gathered darkness. The grandmother, pausing for breath, wondered who could stand so still leaning over the aunt, who did not turn her gaze from the river to speak to him. The air was fresh with the ever-rising mist, and the grandmother could make out the grandsons as they scrambled up on the rock. The tall, dark man continued to lean. He seemed not to notice the nephews as they made themselves comfortable, one on each side of the aunt. The grandmother supposed that the aunt would be wearing her usual heavy lisle stockings and her sensible shoes. The grandmother wondered for a moment, as she approached slowly, if the leaning figure, the man, the stranger, perhaps not a stranger to the aunt, had noticed the aunt's clothes and, if he had noticed, whether he minded them.

The grandmother often, with admiration and pleasure, saw young, bare legs on bicycles as their owners, apparently without much effort, travelled along the quiet roads from one suburb to the next. She regretted not having noticed her own youthfulness before it passed with such remarkable speed into old age. This was a repeated thought, and it was possible that the aunt, walking in seamed stockings and an unfashionable skirt, would notice these young people and have similar feelings of regret over the passing of her own youth. The grandmother consoled herself with the thought that the aunt, once in the classroom with her students, would forget what was, after all, only a fleeting moment of regret. The grandmother did not need to remind herself that such considerations were unprofitable. Even so, there was the recollection, which rose unbidden, of the time when she opened the bathroom door into the fragrant steam just as her eldest daughter (not yet the aunt) was standing up in the bath and reaching for her towel. There she was, suddenly grown up, tall, long-limbed, graceful, and rounded, her skin glowing pink with the hot bath and her own youth. The grandmother had closed the door at once, not saying anything then or later about the beauty of her daughter's body, perhaps because at the time it seemed untouched, untroubled and innocent. Whenever the grandmother recalled this moment, she understood that she herself had never been rosy pink at the edge of innocence and smooth youthfulness. She had never once considered how she might have looked as a young woman, either dressed or naked.

The grandmother, treading carefully, advanced slowly along the last remaining path. The man, the stranger, did not alter his position. He leaned as if in supplication towards the aunt. The grandmother felt relieved that there seemed to be no threat in the way in which he stood. She paused once more for comfortable breath and wondered who would be a suppliant to the aunt, and could she be refusing to acknowledge his presence until it suited her to do otherwise. Perhaps this was the undiagnosed fault in the aunt's nature. Perhaps she, as mother, should have seen this earlier and corrected the daughter.

The grandmother recalled the one time the aunt agreed to go on a holiday, a special tour in Europe. The aunt, despising tourists, agreed with reluctance to join a guided tour with an experienced mountaineer; the grandmother could remember some of the place-names: Appenzell and Grindelwald and Zermatt in the Swiss Alps. The aunt had returned, apparently unchanged by the experience, and silent. The grandmother wondered now, when it was much too late to have such thoughts, whether the aunt's uncompromising attitude, which she could see plainly ahead of her, was the reason that the aunt had had nothing to say about either the famous mountaineer or the other travellers when she returned from the holiday. The grandmother pressed on towards the little group ahead.

The previous year, the nephews had eaten the aunt's birthday chocolates. To be more accurate, they had each picked out the ones they liked, leaving a ravaged box of chocolate papers, nuts, and hard centres. This year, the aunt not wanting her birthday even mentioned, let alone celebrated, there were no chocolates. Of course, the grandmother remembered it was the aunt's birthday, and clearly she was waiting out the day there along the riverbank. There were people who did things like that. They endured. They endured something alone and in silence till it passed.

The grandmother came close to where the aunt and the nephews sat beneath the black shape, which still did not move but continued to lean over them. The grandmother, with an extra strength, marched straight up to confront the stranger. It occurred to her that she might be taking a stupid risk. This unknown man might easily have, as people did nowadays, a knife. The knife might be at the aunt's back and that might be why she did not turn round to him. The man might mistakenly be thinking that she had money on her. He could have *her* money, the grandmother told herself; she never went anywhere without her purse. He could have her purse and her pension cheque, he could have her library-book tickets. It would be safer to offer all she had. There was no need for him to strangle her and snatch her purse. She would hold it out to him and tell him he could have it and be off. She would tell him in plain words.

Then the grandmother saw and remembered, just in time, a big old pear tree at the back of the rock. It was nothing more than a leaning stump now, but substantial, for all that the branches had, at different times, been lost to firewood thieves. She did not speak to the stump. She pushed her purse back deep into her pocket and sat down on the edge of the rock to rest and to gaze, as the others were doing, across to the moonlight which trembled now on the calm and dark water. The crushed grass all round the rock gave off a sweetness that comes from hay during the night. There in the peacefulness, in that steady and pleasant orchestration of small night sounds, undisturbed by intruders of the gentle sort, the grandmother came to the conclusion that this riverbank had no place and no scale in the road atlas. But, taking the scale given there, this walk, this little journey, even with all its immensity, was in fact, if you put it into scale, just a little short of an inch.

The Web

FRANCIS KING

THE PORTLY, BEDRAGGLED black mongrel, rheumy eyes half-closed, was standing in such a way, her legs with their prominent dewclaws widely splayed for balance, that Liz's first attempt to squeeze past her was a failure. When she attempted the other side, she was barred by the bitch's harness, gripped in the hand of a young man in a dingy cloth cap and dark glasses, who, oblivious of her, was carrying on a conversation with the old woman slumped beside him. 'Oh, she's choosy,' he was saying. 'Amazingly choosy. You wouldn't believe. More like a cat than a dog.' His voice, with its flattened vowels, had a whiny twang to it.

'Excuse me!' Liz said. The young man went on talking. '*Excuse me*! I can't get past.'

'It's no use trying this way, love. Her lead's this side. In my hand.'

'Well, I can't get past on the other side either. I've got to get round her somehow. I can't spend this whole journey standing here by the driver. Can I? And what about other people trying to get on?' Her voice was sharp. 'Please move her!'

The man put out a hand and gave a tug at the harness. Then he transferred the hand to the dog's rump and swivelled her towards him.

Liz edged past, the straps of two bulging shopping bags biting into her palms.

'What a way to speak to a blind person!' the old woman next to the man said in a loud, indignant voice. Clearly she intended Liz to hear.

'Oh, don't let it bother you, love. Happens all the time. One gets used to it.'

Liz wanted to turn and protest: 'He's not blind. I've seen him in the Library. Without that dog. In the Reference Room.' But she decided not to do so. She sat down, placing the bags on the seat beside her. She gazed out of the window.

As, minutes later, the bus lurched round the corner from Church Street into Kensington High Street, the man staggered to his feet. He was wearing a grubby anorak with yellow fluorescent bands sewn to it and unpolished brogues worn down at the heels. 'Come on, old girl!' he said to the dog, which, having long since lain down, now stirred from sleep, grunted and eventually tottered to her feet. 'It was nice talking to you,' he told the elderly woman.

'Take care,' she said, and then: 'Bye!' As, followed by the dog, the man slowly edged himself off the bus, she then remarked to no one in particular: 'Poor chap!'

Liz watched him through the window. He and the dog were both peering around them. Then the dog went over to a lamp-post and squatted beside it. Urine gushed out of her, flooding over the pavement and splashing into the gutter, where it steamed in the winter air. The man smiled to himself, raising a hand to adjust first the dingy cap and then the dark glasses. A moment later, he looked over at the bus, stuck at the traffic-lights. His gaze locked with Liz's.

She would show him what she thought of him. She put out a tongue.

The man threw back his head and laughed. He had large, white teeth and his neck was thick and strong.

Then, as the bus jerked forward, he raised two insulting fingers.

A few days later, Liz saw the man again. He was huddled in a doorway of a block of flats in Kensington High Street, the dingy cap pulled down low over his forehead and the collar of his soiled, tattered tweed overcoat turned up, his chin sunk into it, so that it was impossible to see more of his face than the eyes, now without the dark glasses, and the nose. His greasy, dishevelled hair cascaded to his shoulders. The dog, who now seemed even more portly than on the previous occasion, was asleep beside him, oblivious of the people hurrying past, often so close that a misjudged step might easily have struck her. The man's hands, clasped around his knees, were grey and waxen with dirt. The laces of one of the brogues were untied and the other brogue had a crack across the instep. Beside him, propped against a chipped enamel mug, was a piece of cardboard, on which he had written in large, straggling letters: STARVING. PLEASE HELP.

The middle-aged woman ahead of Liz put down her Marks & Spencer shopping-bag, balancing it between her sturdy legs, and fumbled in her purse. She then dropped a fifty pence piece into the enamel mug. She put out a hand and patted the dog's head. The dog made no response. 'Isn't she sweet?' she said. 'It *is* a she, isn't it?'

The man nodded. 'She'll be glad of something to eat. And so will I,' he added.

The woman picked up her bag and hurried on. Shoulders thrown back, her pace was now much brisker. Her negligible act of charity had clearly exhilarated her.

Liz approached. She stopped and stared down at the man. He stared up at her. Then she said: 'If you're really starving, why don't you eat your dog?'

'Cunt!'

As she walked away, she could hear his derisive laughter.

Having finished her shopping, Liz went into British Home Stores for something to eat before returning home. She picked up a wedge of quiche, some salad and a cup of coffee, and found a table in a corner to herself. She folded her *Guardian* at the crossword and, between mouthfuls, studied it.

Suddenly she was aware that the man was standing over her, one hand gripping a tray while the other rested on the back of the chair opposite to her. She scowled up at him.

'May I?'

'Certainly not!'

But he merely set down the tray, pulled out the chair and edged himself on to it.

'I said No!'

'But you didn't mean it.'

'I most certainly did. There are plenty of empty tables.'

'What's wrong with a little company?'

'I certainly don't want your company.'

'What a lucky coincidence I found you here! I'd have thought you'd be eating at somewhere much more posh.'

He picked up his knife and fork from the tray. His hands no longer had that waxen, grey look. They were scrupulously clean. The dingy cap and the soiled, tattered overcoat had been abandoned. He was now wearing grey flannel trousers, a white open-necked shirt, and a sports jacket made of a loosely woven dark-green tweed.

'Where's your dog?'

'In the van. Which is on a double yellow line. I just hope it doesn't attract the attention of a warden.' This certainly was not the accent, its vowels whiningly flattened, with which he had spoken to the old woman on the bus. He might have been one of Liz's male cousins – except that, with his dark eyes under thick eyebrows which almost met each other, his aquiline nose and his strong, dimpled chin, he was more handsome than any of them.

'You have a van?' She was incredulous.

He nodded. 'That's where I change. Out of all that filthy gear. Into these.' He indicated the clean clothes with a downward sweep of both hands.

She stared at him with a mixture of amazement and indignation.

'You're shocked.'

'Yes, of course I'm shocked.'

'It's just another way of ripping people off. Why not? All business is a process, in one way or another, of ripping others off. Isn't it?' He pointed at the Harrods shopping bag on the chair between them. 'If that name wasn't on that bag, you wouldn't have paid as much money as you have for the things in it. Would you? Just as, if I didn't look as filthy as possible or as helpless as possible, no one would bother to give me any money. It's all a question of appearances.'

'You deceive people – pretending to be destitute, pretending to be blind. But what of the people who are really destitute, really blind?'

'You mean I'm in unfair competition with them?' His fork raised to his mouth and head tilted on one side, he gazed at her quizzically. He chewed on the piece of chicken. Then he laughed. 'Oh, don't be such a prig!'

Later she had difficulty in believing in the reality of what had happened after they had left the store. Had she suddenly lost her mind? Or had he, in the course of their increasingly friendly conversation, exerted some kind of hypnotic power over her? Or had it all been an extraordinary dream? She had had lovers certainly, she had even had an occasional one-night stand. But in retrospect the casual promiscuity of her behaviour on this occasion frightened and shocked her. 'Let me give you a lift up to Notting Hill Gate,' he had offered, having already learned from her that it was there that she worked in a small firm of graphic artists; and when she had said No, thank you, she needed the walk, he had pushed that aside – 'Oh, come *on*!' Uttering no further refusal, all resistance mysteriously disintegrating, she had then followed him down one side-street and up another, with an extraordinary mingling of apprehension and excitement.

Suddenly he had turned to her. 'You know what I want, don't you?'

She shook her head. But weirdly, frighteningly she knew, oh yes, she knew already.

'As soon as I saw you on that bus – when I had to pretend I couldn't see you . . . I fell for you at once. You're a class act, you know. So cool, elegant, snooty. And very beautiful,' he added. He put an arm around her shoulder. 'You know what I want, don't you?' he repeated.

Yes, yes, I know! And I want it too! But she did not say that. She said nothing.

'Oh, shit!'

'A ticket?'

He jerked the piece of paper out from under the windscreen

wiper, crumpled it up, and chucked it into the gutter. He gave the loud, explosive laugh with which, in the days ahead, she was to become so familiar. 'With any luck that'll be the end of it. They can't chase up everyone. They haven't the staff.'

He had opened first one of the deeply scratched and dented doors of the van and then the other. There was a whimper like a startled, muffled cry. From the darkness within, as from some cave, two points of light gleamed. Then, muzzle lowered, the bitch crept forward.

'No! Go back, back! *Back*!'

The bitch retreated.

When, at a gesture from this stranger – was she crazy, utterly crazy? – Liz had clambered into that cave, she found it unpleasantly damp and hot and full of the smell, not only of the dog, but of what, strangely, appeared to be resin. Her companion clambered in after her and then jerked shut first one of the doors and then the other. A chink of light remained.

'Someone might come. Someone might see us.'

'So what? Anyway, it's highly unlikely.' He pushed away the dog with an exclamation of annoyance, as she began to sniff at his face. Then he put out both arms and heaved Liz towards him.

His name was Gavin. His father, who had been a captain in the Navy, was dead and his mother, remarried to an American much older than herself, was living in Florida. He had been educated at a minor public school and at Oxford, after which he had taken up a job with a merchant bank. Ten months before he had been made redundant.

On two more subsequent occasions they made love in the van. Then he persuaded her to travel out with him to his two-room flat in Bedford Park. Norman Shaw had been the architect of the house, he told her with pride. He also told her that none of the other occupants had any idea of how he now earned his living. 'Aren't you afraid that one day one of them might see you?' Liz asked. His reply was once more to give that loud, explosive laugh. 'Too bad if they do! I like to live dangerously. Anyway what could they do about it?'

Holding her in his arms on the narrow, low divan, with the bitch snoring beside them, he told her: 'The odd thing is that, when I'm out on the job, I really do seem to become that blind man, that derelict who's starving . . . Perhaps I'm really an actor *manqué*. I know all about that blind man. He was an orphan, brought up in a special school. His girlfriend jilted him and he can never settle to a proper job. That derelict is a schizophrenic who was released from a mental hospital now closed. Often he forgets to take his pills – or decides not to take them. Then he suffers horrendous – or, sometimes, wonderful – hallucinations. You see? I know everything about the two of them. That's why I can convince people. That's why they give me money.'

'How much money?'

'How much? Oh, on a good day – well – say, fifty, sixty pounds. But there are sometimes even better days than that . . . And, of course, worse ones. There are certain days – don't ask me why – when everyone is in a giving mood. And then there are other days when everyone is feeling as mean as hell. As soon as I settle at my pitch, I know just how it is to be. I suppose actors feel the same when they first walk on to a stage. Within seconds they know if the house will be a good one or a bad one.'

One day, as she sipped from a glass of wine in his tiny kitchen, Liz mused: 'I wonder if I could do it?'

'Do what?'

'What you do.'

'Why not?'

'Would I have the nerve?'

'Why not?'

The next Saturday afternoon she tried it, close by Earls Court Station. She had dishevelled her hair under a black crocheted beret and she had made her face, devoid of any make-up, look grubby and greasy. Her tights were laddered and there was a hole in the voluminous, dusty black skirt arranged about her. She earned in that one afternoon as much as he had ever earned in a whole day. 'A pity you didn't have a baby with you,' he commented. 'Then you would have made even more.'

Squatting on the pavement, from time to time extending a hand to some compassionate-looking passerby, she had felt humiliated. But she had also felt a dizzy exhilaration. Suppose someone she knew saw her there? She now understood what Gavin meant by the excitement of danger. This excitement on the pavement, with the traffic thundering past, was oddly similar to the excitement which she had experienced in the dark, malodorous cave at the back of the van.

Gavin had a number of what he called 'dodges'. Seated on a bench outside the Commonwealth Institute, Liz had watched him 'work' one of these.

He leaned on a stick with a rubber ferrule. He limped from time to time, grimacing with pain, along the pavement. His face – how did he achieve that? – looked grey and clammy.

He approached a distinguished-looking elderly man in wide-brimmed black hat and black coat with an astrakhan collar. The elderly man also carried a stick; but, slender with a silver knob, it was clearly decorative, not functional.

Liz knew what Gavin would be saying to him, since already he had told her. 'Excuse me, sir . . . I'm terribly sorry to trouble you, but I wonder if you could help me. I'm in something of a fix. I have an appointment at the Marsden Hospital for a scan and, because I've never been there before and because I'm not from London, I've rather lost my way. If I'm late, I'm afraid I may lose my appointment. If I didn't have this problem with my spine, it wouldn't be all that far for me to walk, I suppose, but as it is . . . I'll have to take a taxi, and the trouble is – well, what with the train fare from Birmingham and so on, I am, well, skint . . .'

The elderly man looked irritated. He sighed and pulled a face. But eventually, with extreme reluctance, he tugged his wallet out of the breast-pocket of his suit and removed a five pound note. 'I'm an old age pensioner,' he said in a peevish voice. 'I can no longer afford this kind of thing. But there you are!'

As Gavin limped past the bench, he gave Liz a wink. Then a moment later he was approaching a young girl strenuously pushing a pram towards the entrance to Holland Park. She listened to him, head tilted to one side and full, moist lips parted. Once or twice in the course of his narration, she said 'Sorry?', not understanding. She was foreign, probably an *au pair*.

Eventually she produced a pound. 'I have no more,' she said.

Gavin bowed and smiled. 'That's terrific! Bless you, my dear!'

It was Gavin who thought up the idea for Liz. He had been reading the biography of a famous novelist, Julia Granger, who had been the lover of an obscure poet, Gloria Destinne-Franks. Both women were now dead. He had reached out from the bed on which he and Liz were lying and had picked up the telephone book on the floor beside it. 'I wonder,' he said, impatiently flicking over the pages. 'I wonder if there's a Destinne-Franks . . . Yes!' He stabbed with a finger. 'It must be someone from the same family. No two families could share such a silly name. Living in Fulham. We're in luck.'

'What do you mean? I don't get it.'

Gavin explained.

The small, mean house was one of a row of small, mean houses. Gavin had parked the van in Lilley Road. He told Liz that he would wait there for her.

The gate hung askew on a rusty hinge and the small front garden contained a number of straggling hydrangea bushes, the few blooms of the previous year shrivelled and browned on them. Having failed to hear the bell ring, Liz raised the knocker, a rusty metal fish, and let it fall.

A tiny, elderly woman, with unnaturally red hair tumbling in curls around her triangular face and a smear of lipstick across a cheek, put her head round the door. 'Oh!' She sounded disappointed, as though she had been expecting someone else.

'You don't know me,' Liz said. 'Please forgive me. I'm a – a niece of Julia Granger, well, a sort of niece, really a cousin once removed.'

Liz had feared that the woman would not know whom she meant. But, pulling the door wide open, she cried out, her face irradiated with pleasure: 'A niece of Julia Granger! Oh, what a lovely surprise! Do come in. I thought it was my meals-on-wheels. One never knows when they'll come.'

'I don't want to waste your time,' Liz said, edging into a narrow, fusty hall, a cat-basket, a Siamese asleep in it, all but blocking any further progress. 'It's just that . . . I'm in a terrible fix.' Like Gavin when he became the blind man or the derelict, she now felt that she had really become the dead novelist's relation.

'Don't worry about Ming. Just step over him. That's right.'

The old woman preceded Liz down the hall to a tiny conservatory, choked with plants most of which seemed to be dead, at the far end of it. 'Do sit,' she said, carefully lowering herself into one of the two folding metal chairs placed at either end of a wooden table covered with packets of insecticide, bottles of fertiliser, secateurs, bast, string.

Liz sat down on the chair opposite the old woman's. She leaned forward. 'I feel terrible about bothering you – throwing myself on your mercy. But I'm in such a fix, I don't know what else to do.'

Twisting her hands in her lap, Liz told the story of how she had come to London from the Wirral to have an interview for a job as a window dresser at Dickens and Jones. After the interview she had gone into the café of the store for a cup of coffee and a Danish before catching her train back home, and it was then that the terrible thing had happened. Someone had taken her bag, containing everything she possessed. No, she had no idea who could have done it, no one had seen anything. Well, at that hour, just after one, that café was *packed*. The staff had been awfully kind about it all, they had told her not to worry about paying, and one of the girls – wasn't it sweet of her? – had even given her a pound. But the problem was that her return ticket to Liverpool had been in her bag. How on earth could she buy another one? Everything she possessed had been in that bag. 'I know no one in London, absolutely no one. But then I remembered that Aunt Julia – I always called her Aunt – had told me that this relative of her great, great friend lived somewhere in Fulham. And so I looked you up in the telephone book. You were my one hope. Thank goodness I found you in.'

The old woman had been clucking, now with sympathy and now with indignation, as Liz had gone through her story. Now she put out a claw and gripped the hand which Liz had rested on the table before her. 'Oh, you poor dear! So what can I do to help?'

'Well, if you . . . if you could possibly lend me the money for the ticket . . . Of course, as soon as I get home, my father will send you a cheque for it.'

It was all so easy – 'How gullible people are!' Gavin was to exclaim derisively when Liz rejoined him in the van. 'Fancy swallowing such a story!' The old woman fetched her bag from upstairs and began to empty it on to the table. 'I just hope that I have as much as you need. If not, we can go down to the cashpoint together.' She looked up and smiled. 'I think my bank balance will just about stand it. I got an unexpected little dividend the other day. I was lucky to get a hundred Powergen shares when they had that issue.' She began to count out first notes and then coins. 'I'm sorry it's all going to be in dribs and drabs.' Then she looked up again. 'I know that Gloria – my sister – would have wanted me to do everything possible to help a relative of Julia's.'

When Liz had eventually pocketed the notes and innumerable coins, she stood at the window of the conservatory, gazing out at the surprisingly large, dishevelled garden, while the old woman, tip of tongue caught between upper and lower lips, wrote out her name and address in large letters on a sheet of writing paper. An ancient hand-mower stood by a flower-bed, so rusty that Liz could not imagine that it had been used for years and years. She could read the name engraved on its cast iron: TURFMASTER. When Liz had been a child, the gardener, a wiry, gypsy-like little man, had cut the lawns with a Turfmaster, but one much bigger than this one.

'There!' the old woman said, handing Liz the address. 'But there's no hurry.'

'I'm so grateful to you. I really am. I don't know what I'd have done without you.'

The old woman offered Liz some tea. When that was refused, she asked if Liz would like to see some photographs of Julia Granger and Gloria Destinne-Franks. Liz shook her head. 'I'd love to see them. But I must catch a train back home as soon as possible. Otherwise my parents will be frantic.'

The old woman then kept Liz talking for minutes on end by the front-door – the locks and bolts on it had cost a fortune, she said, but these days, with so many burglaries taking place, one couldn't be too careful, could one? People had become so dishonest. It had not been like that when she was young. Then all the family could go out leaving the front-door unlocked and even the windows wide open.

Seated in the van beside Gavin, Liz was silent.

'What's up?' Gavin asked.

Liz shrugged. She thought of the old woman, head lowered, counting out those fifty, twenty, ten and five pee pieces on the table with fingers knobbly and twisted with arthritis. She thought of the shabby bag from which she had emptied them. She thought of those Powergen shares. Finally she thought of that Turfmaster rusting away in a corner of the garden, the grass high and silvery around it.

'What's up?' Gavin repeated.

'Nothing.'

But somehow something which had been so swiftly knitted had now, with no less devastating precipitancy, begun to unravel.

The Occupation; A Guide For Tourists

MIKE McCORMACK

MY JEEP WAS one of a dozen vehicles tailed back from the checkpoint. Up ahead the border security were swarming over the first trucks, searching under the bonnets and under seats. One of the guards had disappeared into the security hut with a handful of visas. An air of surly menace hung over the guards, as if they had been ordered to complete some despicably menial task by way of punishment. Everyone of them needed a shave and a new issue of fatigues. The thirty-year occupation showed in every filthy and frayed piece of webbing and in the corroded state of their ancient weaponry: and this was the occupying army.

Ours were the first vehicles to gain entry to the occupation in fifteen years. We were a detail of Amnesty observers coming to verify rumours of horrific and systematic human rights abuses. Somewhere to our rear a massive convoy of relief aid under UN guard was wending its way through the desert.

It was possible to believe that these soldiers were taking the recent UN resolution as something of a personal insult. Only such lofty approbrium could account for the sheer sense of affront excuded by the soldier who was making his way towards me. He was handing back the visas to the other travellers without a word. When he stood before me I saw that he had also handed out a second document. I read it through and quote it here in full. It was titled, 'The Occupation: A Guide For Tourists'. It went on:

1

While travelling in a foreign country you come upon a terrible scene. Atop a hill a young man is being put to death before a small crowd of onlookers. He has recently been nailed to a cross. Blood streams from his side and his body is faced into the full glare of the sun, he does not have long to live. Do you;

A Feel outrage and disgust and immediately cut the man down from the cross.

B Pass quickly without saying a word, you will not presume to meddle in the judicial procedures of your host country. Besides, the man was obviously a notorious criminal who got what was coming to him.

C Admire the skill with which the whole tableau has been staged and resolve to seek out the theatre company and make them a lavish contribution.

If your answer is A, proceed to 2A if B to 2B if C to 2C and so on.

2A You take the man to a small hospital on the outskirts of the city and sign him in at casualty as a relative. You undertake to pay the medical fees in foreign currency. You spend several days in the city while the man is in the intensive care unit.

2B You have put the incident quickly out of your mind and spend a few days touring the city and outlying countryside. You discover scenes of waste and devastation. The occupying armies have requisitioned crops and animals and the city is crawling with paupers. The thoroughfares of the commercial centre are a *chevaux de freize* of broken glass and strewn metal.

2C You trace the theatre company to an abandoned ware-house by the railway station. They are a small company specialising in a particularly vivid brutalism. Productions of *Hamlet* and *Oedipus Rex* have taken a devastating toll on the players. You make an offer of funding and it is accepted with gratitude. You are treated like a messiah.

3A After four days the young man regains consciousness. He is catered to by a retinue of a dozen men his own age. He is singularly lacking in gratitude when told of your intervention. He accuses you of having thwarted his destiny and of meddling in things of which you know nothing.

3B An explosion in the commercial area of the city results in many casualties. You sign up at a mobile blood transfusion unit and donate 500ml of blood. Pandemonium reigns in the streets and you volunteer to do relief work in one of the mobile field hospitals.

3C You learn that the company has a constant fear of infiltration by the authorities, it has been targeted as the source of resistance propaganda. Several productions in the past have been shut down by the security forces.

4A After ten days your relationship with the patient has not improved. He is uncommunicative and evasive. No one will reveal his identity and local police have no record of him having committed a crime.

4B You are contacted at the hotel by the transfusion unit who inform you that you have a developed case of HIV. You spend the rest of the day drinking heavily at the hotel bar. Outside there is a heavy military presence. Rumour has it that there are several more incendiary devices triggered to go off.

4C The company has planned a final production of an ancient morality play. It will have an overt polemical theme; it is hoped that it will incite the city to all-out and unified resistance against the invaders. At their request you take on a minor but significant role in the production.

5A Psychological tests show that the patient suffers from a complex of neuroses ranging from severe paranoia to extensive credulity in the occult and New Age religions, healing crystals and tarot cards. The psychologist remarks that his condition is not unusual, the circumstances of the occupation have given rise to several such cases. He will not venture a prognosis.

5B After four days wandering the city in a drunken stupor you sober up near a brothel. Your mind is now clear. You enter and promptly engage in several acts of anal intercourse with under-age boys. You then refuse to pay. There follows a tense scene when a search by bouncers reveal that you are carrying no currency whatsoever. You calmly await the arrival of the police.

5C Rehearsals are continuing smoothly and you are now enjoying your privileged status within the company. Furthermore you have discovered a talent for acting and your performance has drawn praise from the other actors.

6A The patient's attitude has changed to outright hostility. You narrowly escape serious injury when he attacks you with scissors in the recreation room of the hospital. You are rescued by four male nurses. The psychologist explains that you have now assumed demonic status in the patient's imagination. Not only are you responsible for a salvation he did not need but also for the political failure of his death. He suspects that you are a spy for the army.

6B You co-operate fully with your interrogators and admit to having no funds whatsoever. You astonish them further by confessing to six attempted murders via the sexual act. Your captors are in a quandary, they would like to prosecute but are unsure of the grounds on which to proceed. The emergency laws make no provisions for dealing with aliens. On a sheet of paper you outline the charges against yourself and draw up details of an emergency bill covering the crime of murder by sexually transmitted disease. You advise that the bill be made law as quickly as possible and waive the right to a preliminary hearing. You are scheduled to stand trial in three days.

6C You have now begun to covet the lead role in the play. The principal player is a buffoon whose every word and gesture grates on your soul. You resolve to turn him over the authorities. You begin to circulate information about him in various bars and cafeterias.

7A You now have misgivings about the wisdom of your intervention. It is revealed to you that the patient is one of the leaders of the resistance and that you have interfered with a mythopoeic event essential to the salvation of the city and its people. After much soul-searching you resolve to make amends.

7B Your trial begins in the ruins of a religious museum. The witnesses testify from the pulpit and the judge is seated behind the altar. The jury is made up of patients from a nearby infirmary. You conduct your own defence but limit your examination to apparently pointless questions on the history of the occupation. In your closing speech you plead guilty and urge that the maximum sentence be handed down. In his summative speech the judge congratulates you on the skill and clarity of your defence. He speaks at length on the ground-breaking nature of the trial and assures that your name will merit a chapter to itself in the judicial history of his country.

7C On his way home from rehearsals the principal actor is picked up by the security forces. After interrogations and beatings he signs a detailed confession, outlining various subversive activities and intentions. Morale in the company plummets when several more members are implicated. The company is now gutted of a large part of its artistic and administrative talent, its future is in real jeopardy. You move quickly to take charge of the production, promptly casting yourself in the principal role and allocating the lesser ones in such a way as to throw light on your performance. There is a feeling of renewed confidence.

8A You outline your plan to the patient and after consultation with his cadre it is decided that it will go ahead. You are issued with a new identity which places you immediately in the pantheon of resistance heroes, who have kept the flame of national salvation burning. Within days you are being greeted surreptitiously as the hidden king.

8B After only two hours' deliberation the jury file back into the pews and the foreman returns a guilty verdict. You congratulate yourself on having conducted a successful defence. The judge congratulates the jury on their verdict and then draws a black cowl over his head before delivering the sentence. You hear that your execution will be expedited immediately – there are no provisions for an appeal.

8C The day of the production is drawing close. Advertising has been distributed and a large crowd is anticipated. The dressmaker works long into the night preparing your costume, there are numerous alterations to be made before it will fit.

9A The patient briefs you on the details of your mission. You overcome crippling fears with the thought that a whole nation is depending on you. Besides, events have now taken on a momentum of their own. You are robed in a regal gown and a makeshift crown is placed on your head. You are paraded through the slums of the city to a summit on its outskirts, the site of your ascension. On your journey various thugs take the opportunity to indulge in indiscriminate violence. There are several scuffles. By the time you reach the summit you have sustained several injuries and your cloak has been ripped away.

9B You are led from the museum into the sunlight wearing a sign which details your crimes. You are taken through the streets where the crowds are gathering to view some sort of pageant. Upon reading your crimes they grow incensed and start to attack you. They seem to have a ready supply of whips and chains. By the time you reach the execution summit your body is running with blood.

9C The routes are lined with crowds and the production is going off without a hitch. You move serenely at the head of your supporting cast who have handed out whips and chains and stones. They now urge the onlookers to play the part of persecutors. They work your body in passing and by the time you reach the summit your body is a tracery of lacerations and you have begun to hallucinate. Your entire focus is on the lines of your parting speech.

10   Beneath the cross you are given a final moment with which to address the crowd. An expectant hush descends, you have their full attention. You begin haltingly, it is your first public address, but gradually you gain in confidence and your speech becomes a ringing affirmation of life, the sacredness of resistance and the necessity of justice. The murmur of assent grows until a wave of applause breaks over you; it is sustained while the soldiers take you bodily and hoist you on to the cross. As the nails are driven in you feel no pain, your ecstasy has lifted you beyond sensation. From your perch you can see out over the crowd down on to the ruins of the city. This is your kingdom and auditorium, your panopticon, and it remains fixed in your mind until consciousness, like the daylight, drains away to darkness.

The dirt road beyond the checkpoint curved past an isolated grove of cedars, wending its way to the top of a low summit. Half way up the slope a woman led a donkey, carrying a huge bundle of fardels. Beyond the hill the city cast up a grey pall of smoke, shrouding the top of the hill. Beneath the smoke vague shadows moved. I took my binoculars and gazed into the fugue: I saw that the joiners were already working on the crosses.

Creatures of the Earth

JOHN McGAHERN

IN WILD, WET January weather, two months after Mr Waldron's death, Mrs Waldron and her daughter, Eileen, closed their big house outside Castlebar and moved to their summer cottage on Achill.

The whole family – two other daughters, their husbands, two sons, their wives and three grandchildren – had gathered in the big house that Christmas. They would have preferred it to be kept open until at least the summer, but their mother was determined to move, even on her own. The Waldrons were an unusual family, all of them secure in good professions, and they had little interest in their inheritance other than for it to be settled according to their parents' wishes. Their chief inheritance, a good education, had already been given. Michael Flynn was to be kept on two days a week to look after the gardens and grounds, and Eileen, a solicitor, who worked in Castlebar, might sometimes use the house in bad weather or whenever there were late court sittings. With some reluctance it was agreed that the horses and the few cattle that had been their father's main diversion would be sold. In a year's time they could look at the situation again. With relief and some nervous laughter it was settled that nothing more had to be done or said. They could start opening the wines they would have with the Christmas dinner.

Eileen would have been as happy to stay as to move. There was a man her own age in Castlebar who interested her. It was she who had been the closest to her father. She did not like the idea at first of his horses being sold, but had to admit that keeping them made little sense. Secretly she was glad of the hour-long drive from Achill to Castlebar: it might help shake off the listlessness and sense of emptiness she had begun to feel once her initial anger at the death had passed. And she had come to that unnerving time when youth is rapidly disappearing into early middle age.

The wind rocked the heavy, white Mercedes as they crossed the Sound to the island the January Saturday they moved, the sea and sky rain-sodden and wild. They had taken very little with them from Castlebar. The only precious thing they took was an old, trusting black cat they were all very attached to. The black cat had four white paws and a white star on her forehead and was called Fats.

In the evenings the cat used to wait for the surgeon's car to come from the hospital. Often Mr Waldron carried her indoors on his shoulder, and when he went over the fields to look at the cattle or horses the cat went with him, racing ahead and crying to be lifted on to his shoulder whenever the grass was wet. All through his final illness the cat slept at the foot of his bed. Whenever Mrs Waldron attempted to remove her from the folded quilt, he woke instantly. 'No. Leave her be. *She* has not deserted us' – a humorous reference to the apparent avoidance of them early in the illness, especially by many of the people who had worked for years with him at the hospital. All through their long life together it had been agreed that it was vanity, a waste, to consider how they appeared in the eyes of others.

In merriment they had often recalled walking behind the professor of philosophy on a clear winter's morning when they were undergraduates on their way to the Saturday market and hearing him demand after each person passed, 'Did they *snub* us or did they *not* see us?' Over the years it had become one of the playful catch-phrases of the house: 'Did they not see us or did they *snub* us?'

At first Mrs Waldron did not believe that his colleagues were avoiding him, thought indeed it was all in his imagination: 'You'll be as paranoiac as old Professor Ryan soon if you're not careful.'

'I don't think so. In fact, I'm glad they're avoiding us. Most of the time I'm too tired to receive them if they did want to visit.'

Then, when it was clear he would not recover, she noticed the wives melt away to another part of the supermarket, the husbands disappear down side-streets in the middle of the town.

'We are no longer useful. It is as simple as that.'

'It can't be that simple.'

'Not complicated, then, either. They work with sick people but they are not ill. They are outside and above all that. They have to be. They loom like gods in the eyes of most of these poor creatures. Now that I am sick I simply am no longer part of the necessary lie that works. I have to be shut out. Gods can never appear ill or wounded.'

'*You* never behaved that way.'

'I like to think I was a little different, but maybe not all that different either. Anyhow . . .'

The day before he died, he woke briefly, recognised her and said, 'I think we were a good pair,' and almost at once the heavy, monotonous breathing resumed. They were the last words he spoke, and broke her heart, but they were a deep source of solace in the days ahead. She lifted the cat from the foot of the bed, burying her face in the fur, and left the darkened room to the nurse who came behind her and closed the door softly.

'What do you think of all this?' Mrs Waldon said as she stroked the cat stretched like a lion on the dashboard of the car. The black cat suddenly yawned, rose to her feet and looked gravely down on the surging water of the Sound.

The cottage was by a stream beyond the village, well below the road, which gave some protection against the storms. At high tide the ocean covered the rocks on the other side of the raised road. When the tide was out, there was a long, bright strand between two curving headlands. The cottage was whitewashed in the traditional way, with blue stone slate roof and a small porch in front. A garage had been added to the side that faced the stream, and a large living room and bathroom were hidden at the back.

Mrs Waldon loved the slow, crunching sound the car tyres made as they rolled down to the porch.

Each morning, before Eileen left for work in Castlebar, the two women rose and had breakfast together. 'I know there's no need for me to get up so early, but it helps give shape to the day.' After Eileen left, Mrs Waldron tidied the house, fed the cat in the shelter of the porch, watching her with an amusement that was pure affection as she performed her toilet, with ceremony and great gravity, in the black earth beneath the escallonias. Then Mrs Waldron read. Even during the busiest times of her young life in the town, if she had not managed to set at least an hour aside for reading she felt that the day had lacked concentration, had somehow been dissipated and lost.

Now her only interruptions were rare telephone calls – and when her reading brought her face to face with some affection or sharp memory. 'She had done more than she wanted to, less than she ought.' She found herself repeating the sentence long after she had closed the book, seeing elements of her own life and people she knew reflected in it, elements of that life seen and given a moral sweetness that was close to smiling.

'Smith told me he's given up reading!' her husband informed her boisterously one evening years ago after he came home from the hospital.

'What's so funny about that?'

'He told me it's too passive. He's going to concentrate on hill and mountain climbing!'

'Then he'll be happier climbing.'

'Oh, love, don't be so serious.' He tried to waltz her away from whatever she was preparing for dinner.

'Are you sure you've not been drinking?'

'Not a drop. But I intend to have a stiff drink before dinner. We have to examine Smith's momentous decision. Will you join me?'

Without reading, she would feel her whole life now to be spiritually idle. All through their marriage she and her husband had talked to one another about the good things that they'd happened upon, that lightened and deepened life, gave recognition and pleasure.

After a light lunch she rested and then set out on her walk. In all but the worst weather she walked, and never varied it unless the wind forced her in another direction, but these walks were never as enjoyable as the ones she and her husband took together in the last years when they were alone.

She went by the harbour. It was empty now of boats except for four old curraghs resting upside down on concrete blocks, roped down against the storms. There were a few wooden crayfish creels along the short pier wall and these were also weighted down, as was some torn and tangled netting. Passing the harbour she could choose between several sheep paths through the heather, but generally she went by the path closest to the ocean. The only person she met on her walks that February was a fat little old man in green oilskins with a pair of binoculars. Always he was in the same place, resting in the shelter of a big boulder and looking out to sea. Only after she'd passed him several times did he look at her and nod. Then, sometimes, she was the first to smile and nod. He seemed pleased, but still they did not speak. She thought he might be a relict, like herself, who had taken up bird-watching, or someone just fascinated by the power and beauty of the ocean, ever changing. What did *he* see there?

A school fife-and-drum band marching past the cottage to early Mass woke both mother and daughter to St Patrick's Day. The weather was warmer. People suddenly seemed to be in better spirits. Along all the cottages on the road to the harbour, people were digging their kitchen gardens, spreading manure and seaweed, shovelling the rich, black earth. Some waved to her with their spades or shovels as she passed.

'God bless the work.'

'And you, too, Missus, when you're at it.'

At the harbour they were scraping and tarring the boats. A man was lovingly measuring a square of calico over weakened timbers before covering it with a boiling mixture of tar and pitch from a tin jug. She loved the smell of the boiling tar in the sea air. There was a crazy doctor by the name of Doorley she remembered from her childhood who believed in the healing properties of tar, and each summer he tarred his ten children from head to toe. All of them were disturbed in later life. One became a beggar on the roads.

Two committed suicide. Though her father, who was also a medical doctor, and others complained about his behaviour, nobody was able or willing to bring it to a stop. Everybody was too afraid. Authority could not be questioned then, especially when vested in a priest or doctor. How rapidly all that had changed. Sometimes she could hardly believe it had all taken place in the brief space of a lifetime.

As soon as the weather turned, the man with binoculars discarded his green oilskins for a thick jersey of unwashed grey wool with a worn black suit and a cloth cap. One day she stopped to talk to him, and the stop became almost mandatory. He had worked all his life in England, near Didcot, on buildings and line maintenance. Tommy McHugh was his name. He had five children, all grown. When they were growing up he saw them at Christmas and a few weeks each summer. During the war he didn't see his family for four years. A child conceived during one visit was three years old when he next returned. Dog-tired after the boat and train journey, he woke in the morning to see a small boy standing at the foot of the bed, saying to all who'd listen, 'That's my Daddy!' His wife and he had never lived together until he returned for good. She thought it must have been hard for them to come together after such absences, but she noticed he never talked about his wife unless she reflected a part of his own life.

'Is it the colours you watch or the sea birds or just the ocean itself?'

'I'd not be stupid enough to be watching anything like that,' he replied slowly, a sly smile in his eyes. He looked at her with approval, as if she had laid a clever trap and he had danced clear. 'I'd have no taste for watching anything like that. I'd be watching those sheep over there.' He gestured towards the Head and handed her the binoculars. What were white specks beforehand grew into clear shapes.

'Sheep are very stupid animals,' he confided. 'Hardly a week goes by but one of them doesn't fall off.'

'What do you do then?'

'Sometimes you can get them back on their feet. More times they're finished.'

'Are you not too far off here?'

'You can see better from here than on the Head, and it's a cruel climb. The trouble is that it's a very tasty bit of land.'

From that day on he always handed her the binoculars to look at the sheep. Over and over he told her about his hard life in England, the monies he sent home out of every pay-packet, how difficult it was to pass the time after work, but fortunately there was everlasting overtime.

One day he had with him a beautiful black-and-white collie pup on a long line of binder twine, timid and anxious to please, its coat woolly still, and before long she found herself looking forward to seeing it each day. At first, the man was enamoured: he was going to train it into the best working dog on the island. But during the weeks that followed, as the pup grew into a young, eager dog, and the training proceeded, complaints replaced the early in-loveness and praise. Sometimes the collie was 'as stupid as the sheep' he rushed and scattered. She observed how self-absorbed the man was, how impatient. Increasingly, she disliked that the young dog was in his control. She found herself wondering what his wife was like and how had she coped with his return? Thinking of the man and his life, and the dog and sheep, without warning, a buried memory of her father scattered the day. It was summer. She was home from college. Her father was late returning from a round of sick calls. Lunch was already on the table, and she was standing with her mother in the open bay window, when her father's car came up the laurelled avenue and turned on the big square of gravel. Instead of coming straight into the house, he went around the car and took a whole side of lamb from the boot, placing a towel on his shoulder to carry it proudly in. The lamb was probably some payment in kind.

She saw no significance in the memory other than it had displaced this actual day of her life and the disturbance her observations of Tommy McHugh had caused. Her life with her father and mother had passed. Her life with her husband had now passed. Was her whole life, then, all nothing? Was it just what happened and the memory of those happenings, like the old classmate she had once chanced upon in the ship's restaurant during a Holyhead–Dublin crossing? The classmate had grown old, was only dimly recognisable, as she herself had grown old, having to be asked if, indeed, she was the girl at Earlsfort Terrace who played hockey and married one of the medical students. The memory of her father, though, had not grown old, had come to her out of all those dead years with more freshness and vividness than the actual sea thistle and heather between the rocks at her feet high above the pounding ocean. It could not all be nothing. 'A mind lively and at ease with itself is content to look at nothing,' she recalled a favourite passage from Jane Austen, 'and that nothing will always answer back'; and suddenly the recollection itself gave heart and belief to her walk. That was what always answered back, all that we had loved, all that we had cared for. Love is never tired or dispirited. Love is ever watchful and lively and at ease.

The black cat was waiting for her return to the cottage. She lifted her on to her shoulder and carried her into the house just as her husband used to do on his return from work. The cat, at least, seemed to have taken on a new lease of life since the move to Achill. She had started to hunt again and had brought mice and small birds, even a frog, into the bedroom through the partially open window as she had done in Castlebar when she was young. Other times she sat out on dry stones in the middle of the stream, gazing down studiously at the small trout streaking about or lying still in the pools. Mrs Waldron didn't like the offerings of the mice or small birds in the bedroom. She hadn't liked it in Castlebar, but her husband had said, 'What harm is it anyhow? It's her nature,' and as he had sanctioned it, she did not want to be the one to end it now. After meticulous crunching of small bones, she heard a vigorous licking, then loud purring as the cat curled into the eiderdown, declaring to all her own approval of the good, providing cat she knew herself to be.

In the evenings Mrs Waldron prepared dinner for herself and Eileen. Mostly they talked of Eileen's day, of practical things that concerned the house and gardens in Castlebar and of Michael Flynn. They never talked other than glancingly of the dead man, and when they did the conversation was quick to move.

Hotels and restaurants on the island began to reopen for Easter, and the Waldrons returned to Castlebar for two weeks of the holiday. Nearly all the family came back over Easter, but for no more than a day or two, and all of them arrived and left separately. After they left, Mrs Waldron was more eager than ever to get back to Achill. For the time being, Eileen still didn't mind the hour-long drive on and off the island. 'It fills a space where loss can't get in.'

The summer was unusual, dry and hot, with hardly any of the usual soft rain. The island became crowded. Motor bikes roared past. People carrying blaring transistors walked or cycled by the cottage. Wild music came through open windows of passing cars and into fields sloping down to the harbour where whole families were saving hay. There was much broken glass along the roads. Eileen had taken holidays and gone to France for two weeks. Then her sister and brother and their families came to the house in Castlebar, and there was much to-ing and fro-ing between the house and the island, so much so that Mrs Waldron was seldom alone. She was fond of all of them and glad to have them, but glad too to have two whole days to herself before Eileen came back.

The morning Eileen was due she felt too excited to concentrate on anything, and after feeding the black cat she cleaned the entire cottage. Then she went to buy some staples that were running low. Close to the shops she came on a van selling fresh fish and bought a sea trout for dinner. She thought it a lucky or happy omen for Eileen's return: though this place was surrounded by the ocean, it was difficult to obtain fresh fish. With all the preparations for the homecoming, she was later than usual setting out on her walk. Tommy McHugh kept her talking for a long time, and he was full of complaint about the young collie who cowered now more than ever when approached. This changed her mood so much that she took a different route back to the cottage to avoid them. There was a lack of feeling, of sensitivity, in the man that disturbed her, and she was beginning to regret ever having come to know him.

While Mrs Waldron was talking to Tommy McHugh, Murphy and Heslin came up the road to the cottage. They wore jeans and sneakers, and because of the heat they had taken off their shirts and knotted the sleeves around their throats so that the light cotton floated out behind them in the ocean breeze, leaving their torsos bare. Murphy carried a loud-playing transistor. Heslin had a large, canvas bag slung from his shoulder in which there was a pair of collapsible stools, swimming-trunks, three six-packs of lager and a deck of cards. They were both in their twenties, sold encyclopaedias for a living and had come to the island because they'd heard it attracted working-class girls from Scotland and Northern Ireland who were reputedly free with their favours. Heslin was the better-looking and more forceful of the two and was admired by Murphy. Three nights they had been on the island, and so far had had no luck with girls, even though they drank each night into the hopeful hours in several bars and discos. They never rose before midday.

The black cat was waiting between the gate and escallonias for Mrs Waldron, and when Murphy and Heslin paused she went towards them and rubbed her fur against the bars of the gate. As she had known nothing but kindness, she did not flee when Heslin stooped to lift her into the crook of his arm. She continued to purr as she was carried the first few yards from the house, but when she tried to get away he held her tight. Once she began to claw and cry he took her in his strong hands and thrust her into the canvas bag. The cat alternately tore and struggled, or cried plaintively, but every ploy she tried was ineffective.

They passed Gielty's Bar and the whitewashed cottage where Tommy McHugh lived with his wife beside another small stream at its entrance.

'You wouldn't be interested in a pint before heading for the bay?' Murphy suggested as they passed the bar.

'Not with the bloody cat.'

'What'll you do with it?'

'I'm not sure. We'll see.'

Cars passed them as they began to climb the Head. A gang of bikers roared past aggressively in red helmets and black leather, a blue insignia painted on the back of the jackets. Below them a solitary old woman was threading her way back through the sheep and rabbit paths. They kept their heads low as they climbed, but as soon as they reached the summit they could see the bright strand in the two arms of the bay, the high, dark cliffs rising on the far side. There were no boats on the ocean. They descended quickly, the cat crying and struggling in the bag. An ugly, flat-roofed concrete hut or storeroom stood on the road above the bay. The bikers had turned around, revving the engines before roaring back. There were a few cars parked in a lay-by past the concrete hut. A couple of families were picnicking on the roads between the cars and the strand. The sand was as white and unspoiled as it had looked from the summit and was completely empty. The tide was about to turn, and they walked far out to the water's edge, a white froth marking the tideline, a gentle, dirty backwash of water and sand curling back underneath the froth. A single man followed them out and searched along the froth until he found a green plastic oil can which marked a set line. He then began to lift the hooks, freshly baiting each one with sand eels taken from a red plastic bucket. His catch was small, three little plaice, a dogfish, the white head of a sea trout. Before removing the head and rebaiting the hook, he paused in obvious disappointment: by the size of the head the trout must have been two or three pounds, a prize catch but for the seals. Murphy and Heslin were afraid he'd be attracted by the cries from the canvas bag, but he didn't appear to notice. Throwing a metal weight on the end of the line far out into the tide when he finished, he disappeared up the strand with his bucket and the few fish he'd caught.

As he disappeared, Heslin handed the canvas bag to Murphy. He took a ball of fishing-line from his jeans, made a running noose on the end of it and cut off five or six feet with a penknife. Then he found a long, flat piece of rock and knotted the cut end of the line round its centre. Gingerly he inserted his arm into the bag Murphy still held. The cat cried, then went still, and he searched about until he could grip the fur on the back of the neck. Quickly he slipped the noose over her head before she could claw herself free. The cat shot away but was held by the line and rock. More strain and she would strangle herself. She tried to claw the noose free but it was too tight.

The two men fixed the collapsible stools on the ground, opened beer bottles, placed a towel between the stools, and Murphy cut the pack of cards and dealt two hands face down on the towel. Heslin turned the transistor high and drank the first of the bottles of beer. Behind them the black cat struggled against the incoming tide. An oldish, wiry man with a white terrier came on to the strand and seemed to notice the struggling cat. As he approached, Murphy and Heslin turned their stools to face him directly, lifted their beer bottles and put the transistor up to its full volume. The man paused and then, very reluctantly, turned away. A few times he looked back before leaving the beach. By then the black cat, through drowning or struggling or pure terror, floated about like any lifeless thing on the end of the line. The tide now washed around the stools, and the two moved further in as they continued playing cards and drinking. As they did so, they looked back for a long time at the incoming tide, but weren't able to pick out the cat being tossed about on any of the low waves.

Murphy and Heslin kept moving in, letting the tide take their empties. When the strand was half-filled, two curraghs were taken by a group of men from the concrete hut and carried upside down to the water. There were four men to each curragh. The men's heads and shoulders were covered by the black canvas so that the curragh looked like an enormous insect with eight legs advancing into the water. There they floated the boats and fixed the oars in their pins, and a white nylon net was passed between them before they rowed apart. After they'd stretched the net, a man in each boat waved what looked like a crudely made spear to a watcher on the high cliffs, who blew a shrill whistle by way of recognition. Heslin and Murphy stopped playing cards to watch.

The crude spears were made from the leaves of old car springs, sharpened to a blade and attached to the long poles. The men were fishing for basking sharks. The watcher, high on the cliff, was able to see the shadow on the bright sand as soon as the shark entered the bay, and through a series of whistles was able to tell the men in the boats where the shark was moving. Obeying the whistles, they rowed in a wide arc until they had encircled the shark with the pale net, and then they drew the net tight. They killed the shark with the homemade spears. What they had to be most careful of as they thrust the spear into the flesh was the shark's tail: a single flick would make matchwood of the boats. They could sit out there in the boats without anything happening for days on end, and then two or three sharks could come in during the course of a single evening.

Murphy and Heslin watched the boats for some time as they bobbed listlessly on the water, the men resting on their oars with occasional strokes to keep their position, but as nothing appeared to be happening they went back to playing cards. They kept moving in ahead of the tide, playing for small stakes, till they had the six-packs drunk. The tide was three-quarters full, but still the men rested on the oars in the boats out on the bay without anything happening. It was easier now to make out the watcher high on the cliff.

'I wonder what the fuck they're waiting about there in the boats for,' Murphy said.

'I don't know and I couldn't care less,' Heslin said fiercely as he slapped down a winning card.

The two men then decided to have a last game. Whoever lost would buy the drinks in Gielty's on the way back. Then they folded the stools and towel and put them into the canvas bag. Several cars passed them as they climbed the hill up to the main road. As there was an evening chill in the breeze, they put on and buttoned up their shirts. It was very dark in Gielty's after the sealight. They ordered pints of stout, and Heslin paid.

'Would you fancy a second?' Murphy offered as they rose to leave.

'No. We have the whole night to get through yet,' Heslin said. 'And if we hit fish we better be able to reel them in.'

They rose and left the bar and walked back down to the village. A white Mercedes stood in front of the cottage. Further up the small stream a boy was dabbling a worm in one of the larger pools.

'They must be rich,' Heslin said as they walked nonchalantly past the cottage.

'Wouldn't you just love to send them a video of what happened to the fukken cat?' Murphy replied.

Mrs Waldron missed the cat as soon as she came through the gate, so constant was her wait by the escallonias. She looked at the stone in the stream and saw the boy fishing, and then about the house, and thought no more about it. Perhaps she had caught a mouse or a bird and was sleeping somewhere. In the excitement of Eileen's return, the cat was forgotten. The presents she brought – a silk scarf, soft leather gloves and different kinds of mushrooms and herbs from a market in Rennes – had to be examined and admired. Readily, Eileen answered her mother's questions about the towns she'd stopped in, the hotels, the restaurants, the markets, the shops, châteaux, museums, cathedrals, but there was a slowness in the responses, as if something weighed on her mind. Seeing this, her mother concentrated on the preparations for dinner, content to wait. Over the sea trout, mushrooms and the bottle of dry white wine she'd brought back from Nantes, Eileen spoke about what had been on her mind since her return.

'I didn't like to tell you till I saw how it went . . . I was in France with someone I've been seeing for months.'

'I can hardly pretend to be surprised. Did it go well?'

'I think so. I'm afraid though that Father might not have approved of him.'

'What makes you say that?'

'He's not a professional man. In fact, he manages a supermarket. His name is John Quinn.'

'If he's decent and hard-working and kind, I don't think your father would have minded what he was. I hope you'll be happy.'

'Did anything happen to Fats while I was away?' Eileen asked suddenly, missing the cat for the first time and anxious to change the subject. 'It's not like her to miss fish of this quality.'

'She was here all morning, but I missed her when I got back. I am worried but I didn't want to bring it up. She always waited for me by the gate.'

'Why don't we look for her while there's still light?'

They searched the road on both sides of the cottage. The ocean pounded relentlessly on the strand.

'She might come yet through the window during the night.'

'That would be happiness.'

Two days later, Mrs Waldron said, 'Fats won't come back now. Something has happened to her.' The sense of loss was palpable. It was as if the dull ache of the surgeon's death had been sharpened to a blade. He was gone, and now the whole irrelevant playful heart of that time had gone too. They counted back the years that the cat had been part of their lives. She had been with them almost thirteen.

'I sensed it at the time and now I know it. Fats marked thirteen years of intense happiness . . . years of amazing luck . . . and they could not last. Yet we had all that . . . It's hard to imagine now. All that.'

Eileen returned to her work in Castlebar. Several times Mrs Waldron set out to walk, but each time found herself without heart to go further than the small harbour. She was ashamed of her own grief, the continual sense of absence instead of presence, glancing down at the stream and seeing only the bare stones by the pools.

Then one morning she woke up determined to walk the whole way out along the cliffs. The previous evening Eileen told her that she wanted to invite John Quinn to lunch the following Sunday. She looked forward with an excitement that was as much apprehension as curiosity, and knew that most of the weekend would go into planning the lunch.

She read all morning, made a light lunch and set out. 'A mind lively and at ease can look out on nothing, and that nothing will always answer back.' Was her mind at ease? Love was ever watchful. But was there a final going out of the light, a turning of the face to the earth? The light would belong to others then. They would watch. They would walk in the light.

She climbed away from the harbour, at once meeting the stiff breeze from the ocean, and was so intent on her path that before she noticed him she was beside Tommy McHugh. His face glowed with pleasure, and he came forward with an outstretched hand.

'You're welcome back. I was beginning to be afraid something had happened to you. There's not many of our kind left now.'

'My daughter came back from France. And we've had many visitors,' she said almost by way of apology.

'You're welcome back anyhow.'

'Where's Shep today?' she asked after a pause.

'It got so bad he'd do nothing I'd tell him. He was driving those sheep mad. So I took him . . . I took him and threw him – and threw him over the cliff, and I have peace ever since.'

She heard and didn't hear. She could see the petrified black-and-white shape blur in the air as it was flung out over the water. She had to get away quickly.

'Well. I'm glad to see you too,' she said as she started to move away.

There was something about the abruptness of her leaving, her distracted air, that displeased Tommy McHugh. He followed her disappearing figure for a long time, then said in the sing-song, confiding voice he had often used with the young collie when the two of them were sitting alone together above the ocean: 'I don't believe any of that stuff about the daughter coming from France, or the visitors. I wouldn't entertain it for even one holy, eternal minute. Let me tell you something for nothing, lad. Let me tell it to you for now and for ever and for world without end, Amen, deliver us, lad, that yon old bird is on her sweet effing way out,' he declared to the absent collie in a voice that sang out that they alone among all the creatures of the earth would never have to go that way.

A Nation Once Again

JIM McGOWAN

FOR THE LITTLE FELLOW democracy was a weapon wielded by his parents to deny him his human, civil and natural right to do what he wanted to do, when, where and how. He wasn't having any of this 'mocracy'. He was two-and-a-half years old. This was his house, his room, his bag of toys, and his Da.

So Paddy howled. He thumped his big brother, told him to get out, go in 'til the kitchen. His brother appealed. His Da canted his hands to the ceiling, shrugged one of his 'what-can-a-father-do' looks. The thumped one went.

Stephen the father, Paddy his son, got back to the royal business of building a city. They sat on the carpet. Trucks rolled, cranes dipped, bridges slotted into place.

'Gaffer,' Stephen was on his hunkers now, 'we need more cement.' He held out his watch, looked at the ceiling. 'Urgent. Got to get these roads finished before it gets dark.' He clapped his hands once. 'Here. Get on the blower.' He tossed Paddy the kitchen pastry-funnel.

The youngster looked intently at the funnel, then up at his father, and down. He gazed a long moment at the blue-and-yellow runners his mother had matched with yellow socks, blue jeans, blue jersey with red triangles and yellow stars.

He lifted his chin, his eyes severe.

'No,' he said. 'Me the gaffer. You go the blower.' He threw the funnel back across the Lego city and lined up two lorries beside the station platform.

'Now,' he said. 'Is ready. You call Jacko,' and he clapped his hands once.

Stephen held the funnel to his lips, drew a mighty breath till his cheeks pressed out.

'JACKO!' They looked into the ceiling sky, listened to the sound echo along Queen Street, down Royal Avenue, across the Lagan's Albert Bridge to Fortwilliam Road and Jacko's realm, far from matchbox ships and pepper tower blocks, far from the saucer of lake, where cornflake geese rested from their weary flight across the carpet sea from Newfoundland.

'Sshh.' Stephen placed a finger to his lips. The call was heard, Jacko heard the call, Jacko always heard the call, and through the skies of Belfast came the giant buckets of cement and Stephen's long arm arced them down, down, to tilt their load at last into Paddy's egg-cup train at Central Station. A nod from Stephen, Paddy clackety-clacked like the hammers, until the train gripped to a sucked halt at the little fellow's personal platform. Out waltzed giraffy longleg cranes; lorries filled, mixers tumbled, the dark was beaten. Paddy drummed his chest and looked in triumph at his Da.

'Ahah, begod, the Germans are only trottin' after you,' Stephen reached across and ruffled the small head. Standing, he put the funnel to his lips again. His eyes widened with the intake.

'Right-on Jacko. Jacko, send the bill.'

The door opened abruptly.

'In the name of God, Stephen, are you losing the bit you have left? Are you? The neighbours'll be in 'til take me away, assault and battery – Paddy, that's a lovely what it is, would you look at the pepper, me searching everywhere and what is this?'

Maura reached out to take the pastry-funnel. Stephen folded her in his arms, kissed her forehead.

'Do you know what, Maura, you're one beautiful, sensible woman.' He kissed her again.

She snatched the funnel and reminded him that Nigel and Geraldine would be arriving with her mother at seven, and would he ever tidy the place.

Stephen hunkered down again.

'Well, Paddy, master builder of the north, what do you think?'

'Is made. No dark.' His hands went over his head. Then he demolished the lot. The new Belfast was wrecked. Lake, towers, ships and bridge. One sweep of a small hand, everything went. This was his territory and he was king.

Stephen picked up the pieces.

Nigel Matthews was English, thirty-one, married to Maura's sister Geraldine. This was Nigel's fourth holiday in Belfast. Geraldine liked to make the trip home at least once in the year. She was pleased that this coming Christmas Maura, Stephen, the children and her mother would take the boat to Liverpool and be with herself and Nigel for the few days. Christmas was a great time, especially for the children.

The chat over dinner was school, football, music, and now, that state of politics in what Nigel described as 'this part of the united Kingdom'. Nigel had a great grá for Stephen, never failed to tease him on politics or religion, safe in the knowledge that Stephen wouldn't take offence.

'What's all the fuss about then, Stephen? Politicians dashing, London, here, here to Dublin; walking-in, walking-out?'

'They're talking, Nigel, wow, isn't that something, they're talking. See if they can sort out the mess you Brits created!'

'Oh aye, the impartial observer, Stephen, eh? Will you listen to him, Geraldine, blaming the British again and we going to feed him turkey and pudding. Well, sod that, after all we done for the Irish, putting manners on you.'

'That's the Irish for you, Nigel, bite the hand that feeds them.' Maura was full of sympathy.

'I heard the Paisley doctor on TV. He says the South won't talk?'

Stephen put the lid back on the jam, tapped it tight.

'Sir Ninian has the agenda signed and sealed. When they come to it the articles will be out there with all the rest for all to see and examine.'

Nigel looked around at the others.

'Ah, you know,' Maura said, 'the Irish Constitution, article two, it says, wait now, "the national territory consists of the whole island of Ireland, its islands and the territorial seas", that's it. Our Ian says the South are bullies.'

'Oh right, of course he would and so would I and wouldn't you now, Maura?'

Maura was suddenly serious.

'Did you ever,' she said, 'hear tell of the clash of the absolutes? The clash of the absolutes. That's what I think. That's where we are all the time – "we're right, you're wrong, you started it, no we didn't, you made your bed in '21 and if we did the gun was to our head," on and on and on, living the past, we'll have to move away from that.'

'You don't support the talking, Maura, then? All hogwash, is it?'

'Oh I do, I do. Oh God, I think it's wonderful, better talking than fighting. Oh yes, it's just I wish they'd get away from that, you know, "I'm absolutely right"; does it matter all that much, so long as we can be glad for each other, you know, nobody lording it over the other.'

'What about the nation once again, man, then?' Nigel glared at Stephen.

'Would you go 'way you, you bloody git of a Brit,' Stephen prodded a finger, his eyes bright. 'The Brits began it, getting in, the Brits can end it, getting out!'

Nigel stuck his fingers in his ears, wimpled his nose at his wife.

'Oh no, Geraldine. This is the hundred thousand welcomes? Over the sea we came, to be insulted? And didn't we only do our very best to educate these – these – people? Tell me, oh wise one, where did we poor British go wrong?'

'Easy! You planted a permanent majority here, gave it gerrymander roots, fed the world majority rule, sang the glory of democracy, hand-made in the British Empire. Pass us over the butter, will you, and hang your head in shame!'

'No butter 'til you learn to be civil. So, Stephen. Slogan on the wall solution then? Brits out, quick march, gone?'

'Ah no, wrong again there, Nigel. No. You go, yes, right? Go as a meddling mother, stay as a favourite aunt. Help us get on with a marriage in Ireland, that's my solution, speech over, that's the answer now, look at the time, it's all our fault, are we going to Mahaffy's or not? Come on, get a decent All-Ireland drink.'

The pub was fairly full when they nodded their way through to the lounge. Sean Maguire and the other musicians were there in their corner; not playing yet, enjoying a drink, giving the occasional run of the bow, the strum and pluck of strings.

Maura hoped her mother was all right at home with the five children. God knows, their own three were handful enough, but five! She hoped Geraldine and Nigel would enjoy the evening, especially Nigel. Poor Nigel, he was a dote. A totally English man, he loved his wife, his kids, his work and his home-place: he loved the Irish, a good pint, and an away-win for Liverpool – in that order, as he said himself. Oh yes, he had the tin whistle in his pocket, he assured her, and yes he would give it a go later when the throat was well wet and the fingers not shy.

Maura coaxed a move-up at a wall table, near enough to the music-makers.

Would this be Liverpool's year or was it going to be Leeds again? The two men argued the calibre of the Liverpool players, the women were into talk of school. A voice came over the loudspeaker. Phone call for Stephen MacMackin.

'Oh no.' Stephen put down his glass. 'It must be Terry Dugan. He can't get the bloody thing going, wait 'til you see, I bet you anything.'

'Get what going?'

'He took a loan of the video-machine – he has Americans over. Not big into technology.'

'Like some I know.' Geraldine smiled.

'I hope it's not my mother, anyhow, pleading with us to come home, please, please, rescue her from that lot.'

Stephen edged his way down to the far end of the bar where the public phone rested in the bubble booth. The receiver was off the cradle.

'Hello.'

'Christ, you took your time,' the voice was tense. 'OK. Be sure you get it right. Boyle's house. Lombard Street. 43. Front door. Bath, skylight. We reckon 9.50. Be in position 9.35, just in case. Remember, the zebra crossing at the lights. Wait. Wait 'til you hear the three crackers. Do it then. Our cars will rev up and go, as usual. Go out the back door. Walk the long-road back to Mahaffy's. Have you – '

Stephen felt a tap on his shoulder. He spun around and looked into the eyes of Finbar Hammond.

Finbar took the receiver.

'Hang on a sec,' he spoke calmly into the phone, then placed a hand over the mouthpiece. He held pen and paper in his hand.

'Stephen,' he said. 'You're in demand tonight.'

'Sorry, Finbar. I was called – '

'I heard. Try the lounge, the house-phone.'

'Right. Finbar, wait for me here, I won't be a minute, I, eh – ' Stephen went quickly to the lounge, lighting a cigarette as he went.

'There was a call for me?' The barman indicated the phone inside the counter.

'Hello.'

'Stephen, hello, how are you going, calamity struck, the Ireland video is in the slot, my American friends are here in their seats. I press the zapper, bingo – nothing but winter snow.'

'Course I have it plugged in, gimme a break, will you? Yeah, yeah, the TV too. The black lead? Oh yes. Into the video. And the TV. And the aerial, Jesus, yeah, that could be it, hang on. Who's a wally? There she goes, oh great, Stephen, you are one genius, America loves you, I love you – '

Stephen glanced toward the musicians' corner, saw Maura, Geraldine, Nigel, chatting away. He hurried back into the bar. Finbar Hammond wasn't there. He tried the men's room. Why hadn't he waited. The phone call was blatant. Christ, Finbar, of all people. He had taken his own road. In spite of all the argument. He was in it. Up to his neck. That smile. There was a terrible confidence in him, no fright in his eyes. Stephen stood at the bar counter, his fist tapping.

'No, nothing thanks,' he said to the barman. Finbar Hammond. Oh, good God.

Their friendship went back a long way. Rivals and friends. School, college, dances. Two men, one woman. Fiona, fiery, feminine, mad for dance, wild with words. She settled for Finbar. Two men, married now, three children apiece. Still neck-and-neck.

They were babies when it all blew up. Reared on Cow and Gate, the GAA, Civil Rights, Up Down, One Person One Vote. It was normal living now, the odd explosion, sad priests, and flagged coffins, women laughing in shops, lamp-posts, soldiers, children artistic, armoured cars.

Stephen opened the bar door, stepped into the street. Not a sign. What hurry was on him? He went back in, got a pint, sat down, lit a cigarette. What could he do? Could he do anything? After all their talk on the vomit of violence, the stink of killing, the dark madness of it all. He took a long gulp, looked at the people around him.

Self-defence was one thing, but not this. Even that night for Finbar, when he was fucked into the armoured car, him and the others, walking along minding their business, the rush of soldiers, carted off, RUC, the barracks. Even that, even what followed, the cell, questions, threats, blows, lies by police that colleagues had admitted guilt.

Stephen inhaled, blew smoke to the ceiling. Nothing could justify killing. To what purpose, for God's sake? The long hours he had spent with Finbar! And he had won the day, or so he thought. Now, by a throw of the dice, a quirk of fate, he had new knowledge. What was he called to do now, as friend?

He searched a way back through the lounge. The guy on the phone said 9.35. It was gone eight o'clock. Lombard Street was what – ten minutes if you put your mind to it? It needled him that Finbar hadn't waited. If the boot was on the other foot would he have waited? Yes. For Finbar Hammond he would have waited. They were important players in each other's lives. He would have waited.

Across the faces he saw Geraldine point to him, saw Maura turn, Nigel beckon. The musicians were into 'Antrim's Green and Mossy Glens'. At the table he put a hand on Maura's shoulder.

'Terry can't manage the video. It's only fifteen minutes, I think I better get over there. He has the Americans, they're off on tour tomorrow.'

'Has he no children?' Nigel laughed. 'The kids are the ones to deal with the new technology.'

'I'll go.' Stephen smiled to Maura and Geraldine.

'And you,' – to Nigel – 'don't you dare perform 'til I get back. Should make it before nine.'

He wasn't going to Terry Dugan's. He was going to 43 Lombard Street. Why not tell Maura? She would have barred his way, raised hell. Maura was a love-your-enemy woman. He smiled at the thought. 'You have to have enemies before you can love them,' he'd said to her one time but that only made her mad. This was not time for debate. He was his brother's keeper.

It was cooler now, hazy. He could smell the misted leaves of plane trees. There was no way out to the stars. He knew Lombard Street, knew the house. Was Sean Boyle in on it too, part of it? Or was he told to get out for a few hours or else?

He turned the corner at O'Neill's the newsagents, broke into a trot up Little Donegal Street. Still no sign. 'Be in position at 9.35.' Was it bombing, shooting, what? A radio contraption maybe? Long-distance mayhem? What was it like to cross the divide from light to dark?

The two women came to mind. Maura and Geraldine. Their spoken heroes: Bernadette Devlin, Martin Luther King. Their parents in the Northern Ireland Civil Rights Association. Peaceful protest. Internment, the Maze, hunger strikes. Peace women. Peace women! Peace women is right! At that film he went to with Maura and Geraldine, when a woman shot a rapist those two angelic women gave the gunwoman a standing ovation! Shift the emotions, women were no different. The trick was to put right on your side. Make yourself the good guy, you can blow anyone away. Unless, unless there was that inner energy, the greater force that stayed the hand.

His trot was a loping run now, along McCurtin Street, his thoughts on Paddy, two-and-a-half, on Lego roads, the good god Jacko who answered any call. He stopped at the corner of Lombard Street, got his breath back, had a good look up and down the street.

A street like any street, people strolling, a few shops still open, pubs busy as usual, in spite of recession, or maybe because of it. Up to the right, across the road, Boyle's house. Beyond Boyle's house the traffic lights. That would be it, the zebra crossing, my God, three crackers, cars revving. How do you turn all this into a glass of beer together, a touch of wishing well?

A hand fell of his shoulder.

'Stephen.' Finbar offered a cigarette.

They crossed the road, and walked slowly together without speaking. At number 43 Finbar turned to Stephen.

'Thanks.' He said it as 'goodbye', but when Stephen followed him into the lit hallway he made no protest. He looked fit, but then he always was, wasn't he, always moved like that, lightly, as if he might dance. He was excitingly calm.

Stephen struggled for sensible words. At the bottom of the stairs he managed a 'What's going on here, what is this, I mean, why, for God's sake?' His laugh was nervous.

Pausing on the stairs, Finbar half turned.

'Birthright? Heritage? Identity? Freedom? Today's bad words. Take your pick.' He stood on the landing, hands linked behind his neck, head moving in exercise. Stephen took out a hanky, put it back in his pocket.

'We were through all that. Talked it to death.'

Finbar opened the bathroom door, turned, stood close. 'So we have,' he said. 'We've been through a lot together, you and me. I haven't measured up, have I?'

Stephen avoided his eyes. When Finbar knelt beside the bath Stephen, his fists clenched, was astonished to hear himself say, 'I never thought I'd see the day. Fucking gangsterism, this is what you're into now? Hit-men, extortion, protection money, racketeers?'

Finbar undid the domehead screws on the bath panel. 'Or you could call it indirect taxation, or even Christmas Dues,' he said, lifting out the panel.

He stood, and rested a bundle of dark clothes on the bath.

'The dress suit,' he said, and pulled off pullover, shirt, trousers.

Stephen watched him dress, wanted to touch him, hold him even. Kneeling once more Finbar reached in, got to his feet, his hands intimate with a gun.

'Go, Stephen. When it happens they'll be all over the place. Any papist will do, even a good one.'

'What are you doing to yourself? Once you begin – '

'Wrong, Stephen. After the first it gets easy.'

Their eyes met.

Stephen flat-footed his way downstairs. At a break in the line of cars he crossed the street, stood with his back to Copeland's Emporium. He lit a cigarette. What time was it? Twenty to nine. A very different Finbar. He looked up at the roof of number 43, the chimney just visible in the black dark. He wanted to go back up there to Finbar Hammond.

Walking quickly down Lombard Street he turned into McCurtin Street. Three soldiers. An armoured car at the end of the short street. Shop windows, tailors' dummies, stock-still soldiers. In front, a soldier on one knee, then a soldier with back pressed to the bricks, the third looking to the armoured car. Still in their twenties, khaki, blackened faces, guns. Paid killers? Security forces? The clash of the absolutes. For a second as he passed eyes made contact.

Back in Mahaffy's Stephen gladly suffered Maura's reprimand and questions. He ordered a round of drinks. Nigel, on the stand with the bazooki-player, waved and shouted his 'thought you'd never come'.

Putting the whistle to his lips he sounded a few practice-notes and started into 'The Hare In The Heather'. On tables round about, fingers drummed, talk eased to gradual quiet. Nigel was going down a treat. So much so that he took his encore for granted and began to sing, his English accent resonant in the telling that 'He would once again wander with his Irish colleen, round the high rocky slopes of the cliffs of Doneen.'

Geraldine raised her glass and gave out one of her special whoops.

Stephen looked at his watch. It was gone half nine. He excused himself, headed for the toilet, went out, ran, ran, past the smell of plane trees, around the corner at O'Neill's, up little Donegal Street into McCurtin Street.

The armoured car. No sign of soldiers. In Lombard Street he saw them, frozen at Copeland's Grand Emporium.

He looked across at the black dark of number 43. He walked past two soldiers. On one knee he spoke urgent words to a man in his twenties on one knee, touched the soldier, flinched from the butt-swing of a gun, heard three shots sound, pain somewhere, cars, engines, screams, Paddy building Lego roads and Jacko swimming swimming into sweet sounds of Ireland Ireland its islands and its territorial seas.

A Silver Summer

SHENA MACKAY

IN THE SUMMER of 1962, a girl sits at the edge of the lunch-time pastoral in Lincoln's Inn Fields. Although she is alone among the flowers and the bees mumbling in old, sun-warmed stone, she is not a wallflower herself, merely waiting to be asked to join the dance. Meanwhile, she observes the quadrangle quadrilles, the furtive two-steps, a fandango of fantails in the blue air above the white discarded shirts and white legs in rolled-down stockings. Barristers stroll across the daisied grass, swinging the big blue bags that contain their official robes, and if any whiff of corruption escapes those tasselled drawstrings, Tessa, daydreaming in the scent of roses, cannot smell it and is reminded of shoebags on the pegs at the school she left three months ago, and thinks how far away it seems. Her glossy hair, cut in a fringe above green eyes, is iridescent like starlings' feathers in the sun. She has just made an appointment at Hebe's Hair Stylists, which will rather spoil it.

Her lunch-hour over, Tessa returns to Sheldon's Silver & Antiques in Chancery Lane. Mrs Sheldon has an art deco look, an aura of Chanel and Lalique and *poudre de riz* and Biarritz. She flies to the Riviera every January with her sister and has photographs of the two of them on the Promenade des Anglais at Nice, with a famous bandleader of the 1930s. Mrs Sheldon smokes Black Cat in an amber cigarette-holder, and her cough, like her rage, is formidable. Tessa worships her, and thinks she has a heart of gold. Well, silver-gilt perhaps. Pinchbeck, anyway. Tess is learning fast; she studies the little book of silver hallmarks on the train on her way home each evening. 'I've been rushed off my feet, Tessa!' Mrs Sheldon accuses. 'Get me a cup of tea, there's a good girl and then we'll need some boxes from over the road.'

The first order is fine, because Tessa likes going to the Italian cafe next door and saying, 'Tea for the lady, please,' as she'd been instructed, so that Alf will make it precisely to Mrs Sheldon's requirements. The cafe is always steamy, busy and noisy, with Ilda, Alf's sister, shouting, 'Chump chop and chips twice, right away!' to the cook.

The second command fills her with dread. Going across to Dodd & Dodsworth's, the legal stationers, to ask for spare boxes, is the only aspect of her job that she hates. 'The boy will take you down to the cellar for a look,' says courteous, obliging old Mr Dodsworth.

'For a feel, don't you mean?' mouths the Dodd & Dodsworth boy, through wet, slack lips, and then says loudly, 'Follow me, modom, *if* you please!' Paunchy at nineteen, in a shiny blue suit, with a complexion suggestive of solitary pleasures, the Dodd & Dodsworth boy leads the way. As soon as they are in the cellar, he switches off the light and pushes her against a stack of stationery. Today, Tessa escapes with a grazed lip and faint bruises on the arms that clutch a pair of cardboard boxes. 'Don't lounge there with your hands in your pockets, boy. Smarten yourself up,' Tessa hears old Mr Dodsworth say as he holds open the door for her.

'Yes, sir,' says the Dodd & Dodsworth boy. Mrs Sheldon is fuming, about to lose a sale.

Business is good. The tourists, Swedish and American, are buying, Nigerian law students in bright patterned cotton are buying gold, masons are buying seals and fobs and gold balls that open to reveal secret symbols for their watch-chains, nurses are buying filigree silver belt-buckles, judges are buying *Spy* cartoons to hang in their chambers. Mrs Sheldon's great-niece Natalie comes in to help sometimes, freeing Tessa to take and collect repairs from the bead-stringers in Hatton Garden, the engravers and silversmiths in Clerkenwell. She loves walking through

Leather Lane market, and climbing dark, splintery staircases in ancient buildings, trusted with precious things. And yet, sometimes in the hot, glittery streets and the gardens of Lincoln's Inn, she feels a little lonely.

A dealer, one of those mysterious men who pull diamonds and bits of jewellery in twists of tissue paper from hidden pockets, asks her for a date. He is at least forty, and Tessa is glad when Mrs Sheldon refuses on her behalf. A nice young barrister invites her to lunch, but she has to turn him down because he wears big black brogues. Mrs Sheldon is so pleased with Tessa's work that she gives her an old paste ring with a stone like a cabochon ruby. Tessa gives her mother a little gold brooch with MIZPAH on it. 'Wasn't there one that said "Daphne"?' her mother asks, but she wears the brooch every day, round the house. She tells Tessa not to worry, the right boy will come along some day.

It is a sultry afternoon, just before closing time, when a woman buys the Capo di Monte figures of the Four Seasons. Tessa is told to run across the road for a stout box. 'Please be quick, I'm in a hurry!' she pleads with the Dodd & Dodsworth boy, staying safely half-way down the cellar stairs.

'I'll bet you are!' He drags her off the step into the darkness as he flicks off the light, crushing her against him, pressing her closed fist on his swollen trousers, panting as they struggle, trying to get his hand up her skirt. 'Begging for it, aren't you? I've been watching you! I bet you've had it off with half the blokes down Leather Lane.' Tessa wrenches a hand free and hits him hard across the face. She gropes for the light switch and grabs a box. As she backs up the stairs, fearful of a hand shooting out to grasp an ankle, she sees, horrified, a pigeon's egg ruby of blood welling from the corner of his lip, where her ring had caught it.

'Shouldn't have done that,' he says.

A fat tongue flips the ruby into his mouth.

Cars brake and hoot as Tessa runs through the traffic and trips up the kerb.

'Hey, are you OK?' She sees a blur of olive skin, blond curls, blue denim, and feels a hand on her arm, helping her up.

'Yes, yes, I'm fine thanks.' She rushes inside. Her face is on fire, and her hands feel filthy and she swaddles the porcelain babies in newspaper and tissue and tucks them into a bed of wood-wool. Too humiliated to speak of the incident ever, to anybody, she plans desperate strategems for getting out of going to Dodd & Dodsworth's ever again, and scrubs her hands sore at the sink, dragging the cabochon ruby from her finger.

She is on her way to the tube, passing the Silver Vaults, when a boy falls into step beside her, making her jump. He pulls her back from the gutter on to the pavement. 'Is this your day for getting run over? I'm sorry – I didn't mean to startle you. I was hoping you'd come this way. Just tell me to get lost if I'm bothering you. I'm Tyler,' he adds, hopefully.

Tainted Tessa realises she is with the most beautiful boy she has ever seen. 'No, it's all right. I was just on my way home. I'm Tessa.'

'Well, Tessa, could I buy you a cup of coffee or something?' A shiny blue suit pushes past them, unnoticed.

'You're American, aren't you?' says Tessa as they walk on.

'From New York. On vacation. I'm just here in London for another few days before joining up with friends in Paris. Doesn't seem like such a hot idea now.'

'What doesn't?'

'Paris. Now that I've met you.' Tyler and Tessa are falling in love on High Holborn.

Tessa phones her mother to say she will be late. They walk, and talk, until they come upon a little restaurant called San Marino. Although it is still early, the waiter sets a candle in a Chianti bottle on their table and sings 'O Sole Mio' as he waltzes around with the cutlery, under the plastic vine leaves hung with coloured fairy lights. They can't get over how much they have in common – music, films, books – and the most amazing thing is, apart from the fact that they might never have met, that Tyler's mother used to sell jewellery in Bloomingdales. Later, they kiss on the Embankment under a green sky with faint hazy stars, while the tide tries to race away with the reflections of the shimmering glass globes that loop the river.

Alf is in a bad mood the next morning when Tessa goes in for Mrs Sheldon's tea and a cup for herself. 'That's the one for the *lady* . . .' he says, as if she didn't know by now. And Ilda is moaning about the veal or salami or something. 'Easy meat!' she mutters fiercely. Tessa's too excited to pay them much attention. Tyler is meeting her for lunch.

Mrs Sheldon is in a foul temper, too. Perhaps it's the weather; the sky is oppressive with heavy clouds like Old Sheffield plate with the copper wearing through. Business is slow. Mrs Sheldon abruptly tells Tessa to get on with cleaning some silver. She strides up and down the shop with a long ash on her cigarette. Silver shivers on the glass shelves at every sharp turn of her high heels, porcelain tinkles in fear. You could cut the air with the verdigrised knife Tessa is dunking in the malodorous Silver Dip. A fine powder drifts over her hair and dress, into her nose, as she brushes polish from grooves and interstices. By mid-morning her hands are grey. She sits like Cinderella, wondering what she has done wrong, while Mrs Sheldon serves the customers. At 12.45 p.m., she glances out of the window. Shock sucks the breath and colour from her as if with a straw, and blows it back again, flooding her face with icy red. Tyler is across the street talking to the Dodd & Dodsworth boy.

'Nn-oh!' Tessa screams, jumping up, upsetting the Silver Dip tangling with the long-coated schnorrer in the doorway, deaf to his curse. Tyler starts running. 'Tyler! Wait! Oh, please wait. Tyler!' She chases him to the tube, glimpsing his blond head, his long blue legs through gaps in the crowded pavement. She almost has him, and grasps air with her little grey hands. Then she knows she has lost him. Ilda's words 'Easy meat' slap her face like a raw, dirty slice of veal, with recognition of their meaning. The fat worm of lust and malice that lurks in those blue trousers has impelled the Dodd & Dodsworth boy to do his spiteful work up and down the Lane. She turns back towards the shop where everything is tarnished now. The loss of Tyler and the disgrace are too much to bear. She finds herself in Lincoln's Inn Fields, sobbing into the grass.

Eventually she sits up, wiping the falling tears with the backs of her hands, leaving great grey smears. 'I *will* find him again, whatever it takes. I'll go to Bloomingdales, to the Ivy League, whatever that is, they'll be able to help me.' Tessa walks back slowly, as the sky, like a battered old salver, starts oozing drops of

Silver Dip. People would say, 'There's no smoke without fire.' Throw a bit of mud, and some of it sticks, she knows. Well, sticks and stones might break her bones, but names would never hurt her! She is a drowned grey rat, but determined, by the time she reaches the shop, full of plans for making smoke without fire in a certain cellar, for which somebody else would be blamed, and for throwing mud and making it stick.

Bevis

DAVID MACKENZIE

'WILD ABOUT NOTHING' was written in large white letters in the middle of the six foot high brown brick wall at the base of which Bevis Marchment, seventy-six, set down his bucket of whitewash. The wall was a good thirty-five feet long and ran beside the dusty road up to the corner of the filling-station which was run by Bevis's grandson Jim. It was a wall that seemed to lack purpose. The filling-station was on the edge of town and was separated from the fields of the first big farm by an area of grass and heath locally known as The Walk. The wall in turn separated The Walk from the road but at the wall's end, the end farthest away from the filling-station, it just stopped. It didn't join up with a fence or a gate or anything; it just came to a halt as if the builder of it had said Well, that's far enough.

As he stood at this far end of the wall, the whitewash bucket at his feet, Bevis knew that he was about to embark on a significant act, something that would involve him in more than a small measure of commitment. He understood that with the first splash of white upon the wall he was committed all the way through to the last brush-stroke at the other end. But more than that, he knew he was fated to repeat the process at regular intervals because a white wall was too inviting, he was sure, too pristine a thing to stay unsullied for long. Soon, maybe even tomorrow (and he hadn't

189

even started the first painting of the wall yet) he would have to do it again and then again and again.

But this was understood. It was a problem but it was understood. 'Things have got to be clean,' Bevis said. 'There's no doubt about that. Things have got to be clean and smart and white, just like the Lord himself.'

He had thought of words too, words that he could write up when the whitewashing of the wall was complete. This would not be graffiti of course; this would be good news: 'Jesus Saves' perhaps or 'The Lord Jesus Christ is Risen'. But he had rejected this idea. He knew that some would take such slogans as a challenge. Graffiti would transform these messages into blasphemy and he did not want the Lord's name besmirched. Nor did he want to offer anyone an opportunity to sin any more than they had already. No, he was too old for that particular fight. At seventy-six all he could do was make the wall white and, with a little help from above, ensure that it stayed white for as long a time as possible.

Within forty minutes he was tired. The day was hot and, although there wasn't too much traffic, his brain was getting numbed by the sound of the cars slowing down to turn in at the filling-station or speeding up as they left. He had reached the middle of the wall anyway and 'Wild about' was duly erased; only 'Nothing' was left. He decided to take a break. He parked the bucket of whitewash and the brush in the shade of the wall and made his way slowly to the filling-station where his grandson Jim was sitting in the small cluttered office with his feet up on the desk.

Bevis's slight, stooped figure contrasted with the bulk of his grandson. Jim Lennard was a big man, six feet two and eighteen and a half stones. His extra-large denim shirt struggled to cope with his extensive beer belly and considerable strain was put on the forty-inch waistband of his jeans. Slowly, he moved his scuffed brown boots to the floor.

'Finished, Grandad?' he asked.

'Half,' Bevis replied. 'I've done half so there's half remains to be done.'

'I don't know why you're doing it. It seems like a waste of time to me.'

'I'll do it,' Bevis said. 'I'll do it and pray that the Lord gives me strength to complete it.'

Jim shook his head. From his office he could see through a Perspex screen into the tiny shop where he sold sweets and drinks and then out, through the front window, to the filling-station forecourt with its two pumps.

'White too,' he said. 'Why'd you choose white? It's an open invitation.'

'They used white.'

'So?'

'It covers the letters better. I don't want them to show through.'

'But they wouldn't,' Jim said. 'They wouldn't if you used a dark colour. They wouldn't if you used black, for instance.'

'Black?' Bevis looked surprised. 'Black?' he said again. The idea repelled him. 'No, not black,' he said. 'It's got to be white, clean and white like the Lord himself.'

A white Mercedes pulled in to the filling-station. Jim stood up. 'Well,' he said as he reached the office door, 'Jesus wasn't white anyway.' He stepped out into the forecourt and made his way across to the Mercedes.

Bevis entered the shop. He stuck coins into a drinks machine and got himself a plastic beaker of warm brown liquid. Between sips he continued the conversation quietly, with only himself as participant and audience. 'White,' he said. 'How could it be anything but white? What does he know about the true things of this life and how they are?' He shook his head. He looked down into the drink in his hand, drank some more and then dropped the plastic beaker into a lined litter bin. He stepped back into the office.

When Jim returned, Bevis said, 'What did you say?'

'What? What did I say about what?'

'About Jesus not being white. What kind of thing is that to say?'

'But he wasn't.'

'I'm talking about purity,' Bevis said. 'He was white, white and pure.'

'Pure I don't know but white he wasn't. I mean how he looked. He was a Jew, Grandad.'

'I know that.'

'Like Mr Cohen.'

'Like . . .'

Another car drew in to the forecourt, a grey Rover. Jim left his desk again. At the door he turned and said, 'Try worshipping Amos Cohen and see how it feels.' He laughed.

Bevis made his way slowly back to the wall. He despaired at hearing such blasphemy from his grandson's lips. Worshipping Amos Cohen, the very idea . . . For one awful moment he contemplated it. He stopped, still a few yards short of the whitewash bucket and he thought about it. He didn't like Amos Cohen. Amos Cohen was small and dark, almost swarthy. Bevis believed that he was darker, much darker than the average Jew, although he did not know many Jews. No, that wasn't true. He thought hard. No, he didn't, in fact, know any other Jews at all. Only Amos Cohen and his wife who wasn't Jewish. There, you see, Amos Cohen wasn't even a proper Jew anyway. Proper Jews only married other Jews. So, so . . . so that was taken care of.

It was nearly lunch-time when Bevis finished whitewashing the wall. He crossed to the other side of the road to get a better view of his handiwork and saw that 'Wild about Nothing' had gone, completely. It was impossible to detect where the words had been. He felt pleased. He allowed himself to smile.

When he reached the office, however, he remembered his earlier conversation with his grandson and his feeling of well-being was diminished. Jim was reading a newspaper and barely looked up when Bevis walked in.

'You've got no respect for me,' Bevis began.

'That's not true,' Jim said. 'That's not true at all. I've got a lot of respect for you but I haven't got much time for . . . for God and all that stuff, that's all.' He shook his newspaper to straighten it out and continued reading.

'It's all the same thing,' Bevis said.

'What do you mean?' Jim didn't look up from his paper.

'Me and what I believe. You can't separate us.'

'No? I think you can.'

'You can't,' Bevis said adamantly. 'You cannot.' After a few moments he said, 'I'll pray for you.'

'Fine,' Jim said.

The next day Bevis inspected the wall and found that no one had defaced it during the night. It was still as white as when he had made the last stroke of the brush the day before. Or not quite, in fact. He discovered that one small area of paint had been chipped off, a tiny area about an inch square. He decided that this was probably the result of a stone being flung against the wall, a stone thrown up by the wheels of a passing vehicle. The mark this made on the wall, the tiny patch of brown brick in the huge area of white was hardly significant; in fact, from the other side of the road it could not be detected at all. But Bevis painted it over anyway. Though the whole exercise took him over half an hour – the slow walk back to his house, the retrieval of the whitewash bucket and the selection of a small window brush – he did it and was pleased. He walked the length of the wall very slowly, looking over every inch of it, and he found three or four other chips or cracks or perhaps just areas that he had somehow missed. He painted them all.

But the following morning 'Wild about Nothing' was back in big black letters that stretched along most of the thirty-five feet of the wall's length. Bevis was saddened by the vandalism, saddened that someone, some young, lost person could be motivated towards such an act of desecration. But on the other hand he felt something that was close to being glad. Of course he was not glad, he was not happy, but there was undoubtedly a strange kind of satisfaction; it was clear to him now that he had been entrusted with a task, had been given a commission, he had been singled out for a small but important work. Standing on the grass verge on the opposite side of the road he bowed his head and prayed that he was equal to the task, prayed that he would triumph in his battle against evil.

Two hours later he was standing in the same spot examining his handiwork. It did not look good. He had covered the offending words with one coat of whitewash but he could still see them. They were faint, it was true, but they were there. He would have to wait for the whitewash to dry fully before applying another coat.

'Is it worth it?' his grandson asked when Bevis, tired and

dejected, sat down in the only other chair in the filling-station office.

'Yes,' Bevis said. 'It is.'

'Why?'

'Because I have a duty to do it.' The old man was breathing heavily and spoke slowly.

'That's no answer,' Jim said. 'Why have you got a duty to do it? I mean, what's the point?'

'Don't you want the place clean?' Bevis asked. 'Don't you want to stamp out this . . . this vandal behaviour?'

'Stamp it out? What do you mean stamp it out? You're actually encouraging it, don't you understand that? You've given them a white wall, a *white* wall. I told you already, you're just inviting them to do it. Can't you see that?'

Bevis, looking hurt but dignified, said, 'I don't expect you to understand.'

'No? Well, I'll tell you something I do understand. You're overdoing it, Grandad. You spent two or three hours on that wall the day before yesterday and you've spent, I don't know, another hour and a half today on it. You'll tire yourself out and do yourself an injury. And all for the sake of a sodding wall.'

'You'll not speak to me with such filthy language,' Bevis said.

'Oh God,' Jim said quietly.

'Nor take the name of the Lord in vain, either.'

Jim opened his mouth as if to speak but thought better of it. He shrugged. Then he said, 'I care about you, Grandad. It's bloody difficult at times but I do. I just don't want you to . . . hurt yourself, that's all.'

'Huh,' Bevis said, grumpily. He stood up. 'I'll be back this afternoon,' he added.

'Not to do any more painting, I hope,' Jim said.

'You can still see what they've written,' Bevis said. 'It needs another coat.'

'Oh, for crying out loud,' Jim said, allowing some of his frustration to show through. 'You'll be doing it for ever, don't you know that? If you must paint it, paint it black. At least then it'll be easier to cover it up if they carry on. Which they will,' he added.

Bevis stepped over to the door. 'No,' he said firmly. 'I know what I have to do. It's out of my hands, anyway. I'm going to paint it again and it will be white as before and if they write anything on it I will paint it again and again and again until they stop.'

'They won't stop,' Jim said.

'Oh, they will,' Bevis said. 'They will stop when they understand that they cannot prevail.'

'Right then,' Jim said. 'Better buy yourself a lot of whitewash.'

Bevis returned that afternoon and completed the second coat. He was still not fully satisfied with it but he decided it would have to do. At four thirty in the afternoon he got home and sat down in an armchair in the small living room of the house he had occupied alone since his wife had died fifteen years before. He was so tired that he fell asleep and did not wake up for three hours.

The next day 'Wild about Nothing' was back. He painted over it. The day after, it was there again. For a whole week Bevis set out each morning to erase the devil's work of the night before.

There were variations.

The colour changed from black to dark blue. This was a problem because, for some reason that Bevis could not understand, his white paint covered the dark blue less well than it had done the black. This did not seem right to him but there was little point in allowing it to upset him, he just had to carry on.

Then, on the eighth or ninth morning he found that 'Wild about Nothing' had been repeated seventeen times – he counted them – all over the wall in letters of various sizes. That day he did not complete his repainting until five o'clock and he was exhausted.

By this time Jim had given up trying to persuade Bevis to stop. He had decided to make things a little easier for him by picking up the white paint or whitewash from the nearest paint shop and storing it under his desk at the filling-station so that Bevis did not have to carry the heavy cans from his house.

'I don't know why I'm doing this,' Jim said on the tenth morning as he carried a tin of paint for Bevis from the filling-station to the end of the wall. 'I'm just helping you be more stubborn. I don't like it. I don't like it one bit,' he said as he put down the tin.

Bevis said only, 'Open it.'

Jim pulled a screwdriver from the back pocket of his jeans and began to prise off the lid of the tin. It was already warm and he was perspiring. Two drops of sweat from his forehead fell into the white paint when he managed to get the lid off.

'There,' he said. He looked back to the filling-station and saw a car, a dark red Vauxhall, drawing up beside one of the pumps. 'Damn it,' he said. 'You'll be the death of me yet.' He set off for the filling-station at a sort of heavy, slow, shambling run. Bevis pushed his new brush into the clean, flat circle of white paint with its two tiny drops of Jim's sweat sitting on the thick surface. He attacked the top of the 'W' of the first of the seventeen renderings of 'Wild about Nothing'.

At the beginning of the third week, Bevis decided to find out who his tormentors were.

He knew he would have to stay up all night, or at least a part of it, and this was a problem. However, he managed to complete the repainting of the wall in the morning and he slept for two hours in the late afternoon. From when he woke up until he left the house at ten thirty he thought hard about what he was going to do. He wanted to make it clear to these hooligans who were wild about nothing that he was determined to keep that wall clean. He could outlast them, old as he was, because he had right on his side. He wanted to show them the folly of their ways, to bring them to repentance. Somewhere inside him, though he was reluctant to admit it to himself, he felt he might even bring them to God.

But he had to admit that he was a little scared. As he passed the filling-station at twenty to eleven, he felt alone. He shivered in the unexpected cool of the evening. He reached the wall which still showed up clean and white in the light of the nearest streetlamp which was positioned at one end, the end nearest the filling-station. It was the last streetlamp in the town and beyond it, beyond the wall and the rough grass of The Walk, the light from it grew weaker and weaker and all that was left was the dark night and the distant twinkle of lights from a farmhouse window.

Bevis crossed to the other side of the road. He stood on the verge for a few moments and then stepped back to wait at the side of one of half a dozen beech trees that grew there. He began to feel more afraid than before and, every time a car passed, he flattened himself against the tree in order, he hoped, to make himself invisible. He was in this position, at about two in the morning, when a car slowed down and came to a halt opposite him, on the side of the road by the wall.

He recognised it as being an old, rather battered Volkswagen, but in the dim light from the streetlamp he could not make out its colour exactly; it might have been light blue or light green or even grey.

As Bevis peered round from behind the tree he could see six boys get out of the car. They were all whooping and shouting and making a great deal of noise which Bevis did not approve of. They were all wearing jeans or cut-aways and baggy sweatshirts. Two were wearing baseball caps with the peaks twisted round to the side. Those two were black; the other four boys were white.

The bonnet of the Volkswagen was raised and there was a scramble for the spray-cans of paint that lay inside the boot. Soon all six boys were at work. They were evenly spaced along the wall as if each had his own territory, his own six feet or so to cover with the legend 'Wild about Nothing' over and over again. They were counting, too, and Bevis, daring to look out at them from behind his beech tree, understood that some sort of competition was taking place – who could squeeze in most lines in his allotment of wall.

Within five minutes they were finished. Bevis could see that there was very little of the wall that was still white. Every inch seemed to have suffered the attack of the black or perhaps dark blue paint.

And when it was done, the boys piled into the Volkswagen and sped off, leaving the place suddenly very quiet again.

Bevis waited for some time before he stepped out from behind his tree. He found that he was shaking. He felt as though he had witnessed some strange ritual performed by another species of being altogether. It was difficult for him to believe that he shared with these boys a common humanity. A car sped by and he shrank back again. A little later, however, he managed to step off the verge and actually walk across to the other side of the road. He walked from one end of the wall to the other, in the direction of the filling-station, afraid all the time that the Volkswagen would return and hoping that, if that did happen, he would just appear to them to be an old man walking slowly home.

But no more cars passed and he was able to inspect the entire length of the wall and confirm to himself that it was more written on than ever before, that the amount of black writing seemed to outweigh the tiny areas of white. He was amazed that it had all been accomplished so quickly. He was overcome for a while by frustration, by an understanding of the futility of his own efforts, the huge amounts of raw time that he had spent in combating something so quickly and carelessly achieved. It was only half an hour later, when he was back home in his kitchen feeling the comfort of familiar objects around him, that he was able to contemplate again the work ahead of him, how huge that work was. It took a great effort of will to push back his feeling of despondency and convince himself that the next day, or rather later the same day, he would have to get up bright and early for he had a lot of work to do.

But, for the first time for many years, he overslept. He woke at 10 a.m. and lay for a full fifteen minutes before getting up. The tiredness that he felt seemed to have invaded his mind as well as his body.

The door-bell rang while he was still in his dressing gown. It was Jim.

'What are you doing here?' Bevis said, irritated to be found at nearly half past ten still in his pyjamas.

'I see,' Jim said. 'That's all the thanks I get for coming to see if you're OK.'

'Why wouldn't I be OK?'

'I haven't the faintest idea. It's just that you're usually up and about by this time.'

'I fancied a lie-in,' Bevis said.

'Glad to hear it. I wish you'd do it more often, take things a bit more leisurely.'

They went through to the kitchen and had tea.

'You're not at the station this morning?' Bevis asked.

'No, Alec's in. I start at twelve.'

'Nice for some,' Bevis said.

'Oh? I'm not allowed a morning off then, am I?'

Bevis grunted.

Later, when Bevis had dressed, they walked to the filling-station together. When they were half-way there, Jim said, 'Anyway, you don't have to paint the wall. It's been done.'

'You did it?' Bevis asked.

'Give you a break,' Jim said. 'It didn't take long, anyway.'

Bevis said nothing.

When they reached the filling-station Jim went in to take over from Alec. Bevis walked on to inspect the wall. Two minutes later he was back in the tiny office.

'You painted it black,' he said and he was not happy.

'It was easier,' Jim said.

'Easier isn't better,' Bevis said.

'No?' Jim picked up the newspaper that Alec had left behind and began looking through the sports pages. 'It'll last longer.'

'What do you mean by that?' Bevis asked.

'They're expecting white, aren't they? I mean tonight.' He looked up from his paper. 'If they come tonight they'll be expecting a white wall. So, unless they've got white paint with them they won't be able to do anything.'

Bevis was standing in the doorway. He was thinking hard and he said nothing for some time. Then he said, 'I don't like black.'

Jim folded his newspaper and put it down on the desk. 'It's done,' he said, 'and that's that.' He left the office to attend to a red Toyota van that had just pulled in to the station forecourt.

But Jim was right. The following day the wall was untouched, black and unmarked. Although he appreciated the day off from painting that this gave him, Bevis looked at the wall with distaste. For a few moments he even thought of repainting the whole thing white there and then, of restoring it to its pure stage. He even argued with himself that there would be an element of double bluff if he did so, that the vandals, now expecting a black wall, would be thwarted if he anticipated this move by painting it white. But he knew that he would only get away with it once. Soon they would arrive with spray-cans of different colours, ready for any move that he might make.

He was tired too. Physical tiredness he could deal with; it was just a matter of resting, restoring himself, getting on with the job. But what he felt more and more was spiritual tiredness. He found that he was struggling more and more to convince himself that he was doing the right thing. Was it really worth it, after all, to go through all this torment just to keep the wall white? Was it necessary? Did it achieve anything, either for God, for himself or for the six boys in the Volkswagen?

He thought hard about all this and was shocked to find himself so weak. He came to the conclusion that he was being tested and almost found wanting. It was a terrible realisation. He prayed long and hard for renewed energy, for the physical, mental and spiritual resolve, for the strength for the fight, for vigilance about his own failings. He prayed that he would be able to go on with this task that he had been given to do.

It became clear to him then that he would have to talk to the boys in the Volkswagen.

They didn't turn up till 3 am. By that time Bevis had been waiting for four hours. He had sat down at the base of the beech tree and had fallen asleep. When they woke him with their shouts and chatter he was stiff and cold and it took him a few moments to figure out exactly where he was and what he was supposed to be doing. He got to his feet slowly and leaned against the tree for support. Looking across he could see the boys already busy, spraying the wall. He thought, for a moment, about the different types of courage there were and how much more was being required from him because he had already witnessed the situation he was going to enter. He had seen these boys before and had shirked meeting them. Now he was back and he knew how hard it really was. But this time he had brought his Bible with him as a comfort, a talisman. Holding it tightly to his chest, he stepped out from the protection of the beech tree.

He was half-way across the road before he spoke.

'Why?' he began. 'Why are . . .'

But he couldn't finish because all six boys spun round in alarm. 'Jesus!' one of them shouted out. 'Who the fuck are you?'

Bevis found that he could not speak.

'Yeah, what do you want, old man?' another said.

'You some kind of pervert?'

'I . . .' Bevis began but he could go no further.

'You've got the coat for it,' someone said and they all laughed.

'Dirty brown mac.'

'Dirty old man.'

'Are your flies undone, eh?'

Bevis, involuntarily, looked down. This provoked hoots of laughter.

'I am the keeper of the wall,' Bevis found himself saying in a strong clear voice which surprised even himself.

This brought immediate silence.

'What?' one of them asked.

'A nutcase, pure and simple,' another said.

'I . . . I keep this wall,' Bevis said. 'I come in the name . . .'

'Wait a minute, wait a minute . . .' One of them began. He was tall, about sixteen years old and black. He was wearing a sweatshirt with 'Premium' written on the front.

'Hey, Premium, ask him if he's got holes in his pockets,' someone said.

'No, hold it, hold it,' Premium said. When there was silence he spoke to Bevis in a quieter voice. 'Are you the guy that paints this wall? I mean every day?'

'That's right,' Bevis said. 'That's what I do.'

'Every fuckin' day? No shit?'

'It's my work,' Bevis said.

'Why?'

Bevis became aware that they were gathering round him now and he began to feel afraid. They stood in their sweatshirts and baseball caps, spray-cans clutched in their hands, and formed a ragged semi-circle only a few feet away from him. They were relaxed and some of them were even smiling but he felt their menace.

'Because . . .' Bevis began, 'because I do the Lord's will. I do as he tells me to do . . .'

'He tell you to paint the wall, did he?' one of them asked. The others laughed.

'It's a matter of cleanliness,' Bevis went on. 'Purity, whiteness . . .'

'White?' Premium asked.

Bevis looked at him.

'White?' the boy repeated.

'As in purity,' Bevis said. 'White is the symbol of purity . . .'

'No shit.'

'White has always been . . .'

'What's that you got there?' Premium said, pointing to the Bible in Bevis's hand.

'The word of the Lord,' Bevis said.

'That so.'

'Yes.' Bevis no longer clutched the book to his chest. In the silence that followed he was able to relax a little. He held the book out before him, almost as if offering it to Premium.

'It's black,' the boy said.

'Colour itself . . .' Bevis responded, but he stopped. Then he said, 'Bibles have . . . have always been black. It's traditional.'

'Well, well.' Premium smiled. He turned and glanced at the two boys to his right. 'Tell you what, Grandad,' he said, looking at Bevis again. 'We'll just purify it.'

Before Bevis could speak the boy raised his spray-can and squirted a large white blotch onto the cover of the Bible. Some of Bevis's fingernails were also sprayed white.

Bevis fell back a couple of steps. He looked aghast at the violated cover of the Bible. Then he began to shout.

'Vandal!' he yelled. 'Blasphemer! You desecrator of the Lord's word! You . . . you!' As it seemed that no further words would come out he rushed forward, his arm raised as if he wanted to strike the boy with the book itself. Laughing, Premium caught Bevis's arms and held him without difficulty.

'Careful, old man,' he said. 'Don't bust a blood vessel or nothin' like that.'

Bevis sank to his knees. 'Violator,' he said, but more quietly now as his body slewed sideways and the boy let him down gently on to the grass. Bevis lay on his back, breathing heavily.

'Jesus,' one of the others said.

Bevis's mouth opened and closed like a fish gulping air on land. Then it closed and did not open again. His eyes closed too.

'Jesus H. Christ,' one of the boys said. 'The fucker's gone and died on us.'

But Bevis was not dead. He awoke in hospital. It was some time before he was able to put together again the events of that night. Jim helped him.

'But I just don't understand what you expected to achieve,' Jim said.

'I wanted to talk to them,' Bevis said. He was sitting up in his hospital bed, three pillows at his back.

'Talk to them?' Jim repeated.

'Reason with them,' Bevis said. 'Make them understand the error of their ways.'

Jim shook his head. He looked round the small ward that Bevis had been placed in. There were three other men in the ward, all of them of Bevis's age. One of them was asleep and snoring loudly.

'Who found me?' Bevis asked.

'Found you? What do you mean?'

'Who took me to hospital? Was it you?'

'Me? How could it have been me? I didn't know you were up at three in the morning preaching, did I?'

'I wasn't preaching,' Bevis said.

'Whatever. You should have more sense.'

'So who did it then?'

'They did.'

'Who do you mean?'

'Them, the boys at the wall, the lads with the spray-cans. Stuck you in their car and drove you straight here.'

Bevis could say nothing.

'Doctor said you were lucky to be alive. If they hadn't been so quick about it you'd be gone.'

It was three weeks before Bevis got out of hospital. He had to take things easy, go for short walks each day, get plenty of rest. On his third day back home, he walked slowly out to the filling-station.

Before going in to see Jim, he walked past the filling-station to inspect the wall. He approached it nervously, not knowing what to expect. Jim had said nothing of the condition of the wall and Bevis had not asked. Perhaps Jim had painted it again – perhaps even in white – and the boys in the Volkswagen had decided to leave it. Yes, that was probably it, Bevis decided. Jim had said nothing because it was going to be a pleasant surprise – a bright, new, white wall, completely free of slogans. Pure.

The wall was not there.

It had been knocked down and all the consequent rubble removed. All that remained was a thirty-five-foot length of broken brick which barely reached ankle height and, on the grass on either side, some traces of reddish-brown brick dust.

'I did it,' Jim said as Bevis entered the filling-station office. 'I did it and that's an end to it.'

'No,' Bevis said.

'Oh yes it is,' Jim said confidently. 'The wall did nothing anyway. It was a waste of time.'

'It was necessary,' Bevis said. 'It had a purpose.'

'Oh yes? And what was that?'

Bevis hesitated and then said, 'You wouldn't understand.'

'No? No, probably not.' Jim got to his feet. A pale blue Volkswagen had pulled in to the filling-station forecourt.

As Jim reached the office door Bevis said, 'I need bricks, cement. I'll get them.'

'You do that,' Jim said as he stepped out into the bright sunshine.

Hired Girl

ALICE MUNRO

MRS MONTJOY WAS showing me how to put the pots and pans away in her cupboard. I had put some of them in the wrong places.

'Just like our hired girls at home,' I said. 'The first few days, they were always putting things away where we couldn't find them. We called our maids hired girls, at home.'

'Did you?' said Mrs Montjoy. A moment of silence passed. 'And the colander on that hook there.'

Nothing about my life could interest or impress her.

Above all things, she said, she hated a higgledy-piggledy cupboard.

A couple of days before this, Mrs Montjoy had picked me up at the station in Pointe au Baril and brought me to the island. I had got the job through the woman in the Pointe au Baril store, an old friend of my mother's – they had once taught school together. Mrs Montjoy had asked this woman if she knew of a country girl who would take a summer job, and the woman had thought that I would be about the right age, and trained to do housework. Mrs Montjoy wore khaki shorts and a tucked-in shirt. Her short, sun-bleached hair was pushed behind her ears. She had leapt on board the boat like a boy, given a fierce tug to the outboard motor, and we were flung out on the choppy evening waters of Georgian Bay. For thirty or forty minutes we dodged among the rocky wooded islands, with their lone cottages, their boats bobbing beside the dock, and their pine trees jutting out at odd angles, just as they do in paintings.

I held on to the sides of the boat, and shivered in my flimsy new dress.

'Feeling sick?' said Mrs Montjoy, with the briefest possible smile – it was like a signal for a smile, when the occasion did not warrant the real thing. She had large, white teeth in a long face, and her commonest expression seemed to be one of impatience held decently in check. She probably knew that what I was feeling was fear, not sickness, and she threw out this question so that I – and she – need not be embarrassed. What she did not understand was that fear did not embarrass me.

Here was a difference, already, from the world that I was used to. In that world, fear was commonplace, at least for a female. You could be afraid of snakes, thunderstorms, deep water, heights, rats and the road through the swamp, and nobody thought any the worse of you. In Mrs Montjoy's world, however, fear was shameful, always something to be conquered.

The island that was our destination had a name – Nausicaä. It was written on a board at the end of the dock. This name seemed to me a good sign, and I said it aloud as I clambered out of the boat. I was anxious to appear appreciative and at ease.

'Oh, yes,' Mrs Montjoy said. 'That was its name when Daddy bought it. It's after some character in Shakespeare.'

I opened my mouth to say no, no, not Shakespeare, and to explain all about Nausicaä being the girl on the beach – the princess playing ball with her friends – whom Ulysses surprised when he awoke from his sleep. I was used to giving out information of this sort, without thinking about whether people wanted it. But some briskness in Mrs Montjoy's tone warned me off, this time. My superior knowledge gave me a familiar feeling, of satisfaction and misgiving.

The dress I was wearing was one I had made myself of pink-and-white striped cotton. The material had been cheap, because it was not really meant for a dress but for a blouse or a nightgown, and the style I had chosen – the full-skirted, tight-waisted style of those days, the early fifties – was a mistake. When I walked, the cloth bunched up between my legs, and I had to yank it free. Today was the first day the dress had been worn, and I still thought that the problem was temporary – with a firm enough yank the skirt could be made to hang properly. But I found when I took off my belt that the day's heat and my sweat on the train had created a worse problem. The belt was wide and elasticised, and it was of a burgundy colour, which had run. It had circled my waist with strawberry stains.

I made this discovery in the loft of the boathouse, where I was to sleep. I shared the loft with Mrs Montjoy's ten-year-old daughter, Mary Anne. Mary Anne was fair-haired and freckled, with a long face like her mother's. But she didn't have her mother's look of quick judgments waiting, marshalled right at the surface, ready to be tossed out at you. Her expression was benign and serious – she wore her heavy glasses even when she was sitting up in bed. It had taken two operations to get her eyes as straight as they were now. ('Daddy's eyes,' she called them.)

'That's too bad about your dress,' she said.

I said it was an old dress anyway. 'I didn't want to wear anything good on the train.'

All night long you could hear the water slapping against the boards of the boathouse. Morning came early here. A hundred miles north of home – could that make a difference? There was a window at each end of the loft. I got up and looked out.

Through one window the silky water, dark underneath but flashing back, from its surface, the light of the sky. The rocky shores of a little cove, the moored sailing-boats, the open channel beyond, the mound of another island, shores and channels beyond that. I thought that I would never, on my own, be able to find my way back to the mainland.

But maids don't have to find their way anywhere. They stay put, where the work is. It's the other people who come and go.

The other window looked out on a grey rock that was like a slanting wall, with shelves and crevices on it where little pine and cedar trees, and blueberry bushes, had got a foothold. Down at the base of the rock was a path – which I would take later on – through the woods, to Mrs Montjoy's house. Here everything was damp and almost in darkness still, though the sky was whitening at the top of the rock. The trees here were the strict and fragrant evergreens, with their heavy boughs that don't allow much growth underneath – no riot of saplings and brambles and grapevines such as you find in the hardword forest. Mostly damp ferns, blueberries. I had noticed this the day before, from the train, and it seemed to me that this was a more authentic forest than the bush lots we had at home – it had eliminated all the lavishness and confusion and seasonal change. And it went on more or less for ever.

This morning was the last time that I would feel the shock of this different place on my eyes and skin in this way. What happened after that? It wasn't a matter of things becoming familiar, or housewife's blinkers being put on my eyes – I was not that vigilant, or conscientious. It was just that a barrier went up. A transparent barrier. And perhaps 'barrier' is too strong a word – all I mean is that there was something like a heat shimmer in the air, not a warning so much as an indolent reminder. *Not for you.* As if it hardly needed to be said. *Not for you.* And of course I would not admit that such a reminder was there, I would never admit that I was in the least humbled or lonely, or even that I had really become a servant. But I started thinking differently, without admitting it to myself. I stopped thinking about leaving the path, going in among the trees, walking there by myself. I would have had to explain what I was doing, if anybody saw me, and the thought of that made the whole thing too much trouble.

Mary Anne liked to talk when we were lying in our cots at night. She told me that her favourite book was *Kon-Tiki* and that she didn't believe in God or in Heaven.

'My sister is dead,' she said. 'But I don't believe she is floating around in space in a white nightie. She's just dead, she is nothing.'

'My sister was pretty,' she said. 'Compared to me, anyway. Mother isn't pretty and Daddy is really ugly. Aunt Margaret used to be pretty, but she's fat now, and Nana used to be pretty, but she's old. My friend Helen is pretty but my friend Susan isn't. You are sort of pretty, but it isn't the same thing, because you're a maid. Does it hurt your feelings when I say that?'

I said no. 'I'm only a maid when I'm here.'

It wasn't that I was the only servant, even on this island. The other servants were Henry and Corrie, and they were not unhappy with their jobs – in fact, they were grateful. Henry and Corrie had come to Canada from Holland a few years before and had gone to work for Mr and Mrs Foley, who were Mrs Montjoy's parents. Mr and Mrs Foley spent the summers in a big white house with verandahs and awnings, on the highest point of the island. Henry cut the grass and looked after the tennis court and helped Mr Foley with the boats, the clearing of the paths, and repairs to the dock. Corrie did the housework and cooked the meals and looked after Mrs Foley. Mrs Foley spent every sunny morning sitting out on a deckchair on the grass, with her feet stretched out to get the sun and a little awning protecting her head. Corrie came and shifted her around as the sun moved, took her to the bathroom, and brought her cups of tea or glasses of iced coffee. (I often had to go up to the Foleys' house on some errand. I took things there, to put in the freezer, and I got things out. Home freezers were uncommon at that time.)

'You are not going to suck the ice cubes, are you?' I heard Corrie say to Mrs Foley one afternoon. She stood by and watched, and when Mrs Foley did begin to suck an ice cube, she said, 'Spit it out. Spit it right out in Corrie's hand. You didn't do what I say.'

'She could choke to death,' Corrie said to me later. 'But Mrs Montjoy, Mr Foley – they say, "Give her ice cubes like everybody else." So I watch her.'

I thought it might be interesting if Corrie talked about the war. But all she would say was that everybody had been very hungry and that they had made soup out of potato skins.

'No good,' she said. 'No good to talk about it.'

Corrie never just wiped the counters – she scoured them. Every move she made had the energy and concentration somebody would show when rowing a boat against the current, and every word she said was flung out as if against a high wind. When she wrung out the cleaning rag, she might have been wringing the neck of a chicken.

She and Henry were saving their money to go into business. They meant to start a nursing home. 'Lots of them like her,' said Corrie, throwing her head back to indicate Mrs Foley on the lawn.

'Soon more and more, because of the doctors; they are not dying soon. Who will be taking care?'

One day, Mrs Foley called out to me as I crossed the lawn. 'Now, where are you going to in this hot sun? You sit down by me and have a little rest.'

Her white hair was tucked up under a floppy straw hat, and when she leaned forward the sun came through the holes in the straw, sprinkling her face with pimples of light. Pink and pale-brown spots covered her face, anyway. Her eyes, too, were a pale – an almost extinct – brown, and red around the rims. Her shape was curious – a narrow, flat chest and swollen stomach, under layers of loose, pale clothing. The legs she stuck out into the sun where shiny and discoloured and faintly cracked, like old plates.

'I didn't put my stockings on,' she said. 'I'm afraid I'm having rather a lazy day today. But aren't you the remarkable girl, coming all that way by yourself? Did you get Henry to help you carry the groceries up from the dock?'

Mrs Montjoy waved to us. She was on her way to the tennis court, behind the Foleys' house. Every morning she gave Mary Anne a tennis lesson, and at lunch they discussed what Mary Anne was doing wrong.

'That's a woman who comes to play tennis,' Mrs Foley said. 'She comes every day, so I suppose it's all right. She must be a very dedicated tennis player.'

Mrs Montjoy said to me later, 'Did Mrs Foley ask you to come over and sit on the grass?'

I said yes. 'She thought I was somebody who brought the groceries.'

'Oh, yes. That was during the war – a girl used to come in a boat. There hasn't been any grocery delivery in years. Mrs Foley gets her wires crossed occasionally.'

'She said you were a woman who came to play tennis.'

'Did she really?' Mrs Montjoy said.

The work that I had to do here was nothing new for me. Like most country girls of my age, I could bake and iron, and clean an oven. This was the reason, in fact, that Mrs Montjoy had sought out a country girl. In some ways the work was not as hard as it was at home. Nobody tracked barnyard mud into the kitchen, and there were no heavy men's work clothes to wrestle through the wringer and hang on the line. But there was the business of putting every pot and spoon back in its special place and cleaning the burners of the stove after every use, so that it looked as if nothing had ever been cooked there, and polishing the glass door leading to the deck so that the glass disappeared and people were in danger of smashing their faces against it.

The Montjoys' house was modern, built of golden-brown wood, with a flat roof, a deck extending over the edge of the water, and a great many windows, which Mrs Montjoy would have liked to see as clean as the glass doors.

'But I have to be realistic,' she said. 'I know if you did that you'd be doing nothing else.' She was not by any means a slave driver. Her tone with me was firm and slightly irritable, but that was the way it was with almost everybody. She was always on the lookout for incompetence, which she detested. 'Sloppy' was a favourite word of condemnation. Others were 'wishy-washy' and 'unnecessary.' A great many things that people said or did or felt were unnecessary, and some of these unnecessary things were wishy-washy. Other people might have used the word 'arty', or 'intellectual', or 'permissive'. Mrs Montjoy swept all that away. Wishy-washy.

I ate my meals alone, at a table in the kitchen. Mrs Montjoy and Mary Anne ate their lunch on the deck. I took their salad and sandwiches and drinks out to them, on a tray, and then I did not have to wait on them any more. I read as I ate. I found a stack of old magazines – Life and Look and Time and Collier's – at the back of the broom closet. I could tell that Mrs Montjoy did not quite like the idea of my sitting reading these magazines as I ate my lunch. Was it because it was bad manners to read as you ate, or because I hadn't asked permission? More likely she saw my interest in such things as a subtle kind of impudence. Unnecessary.

All she said was 'Those old magazines must be dreadfully dusty.'

I said that I always wiped them off.

Sometimes a woman friend came over from one of the other islands, to play tennis and have lunch. I heard Mrs Montjoy saying

'. . . have to keep your girls happy, or they'll be off to the hotel, off to the port. They can get jobs so easily, these days.'

The other woman said, 'That's so true.'

'So you make allowances,' Mrs Montjoy said. 'You do the best you can.'

It took me a little while to understand that they were talking about me, that 'girls' meant girls like me. I wondered, then, how was I being kept happy? By being allowed to read those magazines, by being taken along on the occasional alarming boat ride, when Mrs Montjoy went to get our supplies? By being allowed to wear shorts and a blouse or even a halter instead of a dark-blue uniform with white collar and cuffs such as Corrie wore?

And what hotel was this? What port?

'What are you best at?' Mary Anne said. 'What sports?'

'Well – volleyball,' I said. We all had to play that, at school.

'Oh, I don't mean team sports,' Mary Anne said. 'I mean, what are you best at? Such as tennis? Or swimming or riding or what? My really best thing is riding, because that doesn't depend so much on your eyesight. Aunt Margaret's best used to be tennis and so was Nana's, and Grandad's was always sailing, and Daddy's is golf and Uncle Stewart's is sailing and golf, and Mother's is golf and swimming and sailing and tennis and everything, but maybe tennis a little bit the best of all. If my sister Jane hadn't died I'm not sure what hers would have been, but I think swimming, because she could already swim and she was only three.'

I had never been on a tennis court. The idea of getting up on a horse or going out in a sailboat terrified me. I could barely swim. Golf was something that silly-looking men did in cartoons. The adults I knew sat down and rested whenever they were not working. That was not often.

'Everybody I know works too hard to do any of those things,' I said. 'We don't have a tennis court in our town. We don't have a golf course, either.' (Actually, we had once had both, but there had been no money to keep them up in the thirties, and they had not been restored since.) 'Nobody I know owns a sailboat.'

I did not mention the hockey rink or the baseball park.

'Really?' said Mary Anne thoughtfully. 'What do they do, then?'

'They work,' I said. 'And they never have any money. All of their lives.'

I told her that most people never saw a flush toilet unless it was in a public building and that old people stayed in bed all winter (these were people too old to work) in order to keep warm. Children walked barefoot until the frost came, in order to save shoe leather, and died of stomach aches and fevers, because there was no money for a doctor. I said that sometimes people had eaten boiled grass for supper.

Not one of these statements – not even the one about boiled grass – was completely a lie. The one about flush toilets came closest to the truth, but it applied to country people – not townpeople – ten or twelve years earlier. But as I talked to Mary Anne, all the isolated incidents and bizarre circumstances I had heard about spread out in my mind, so that I almost believed that I myself had walked with bare, blue feet on frosty roads – I, who had been given cod-liver oil and inoculations and bundled up for school within an inch of my life, and had gone to bed hungry only because of a refusal to eat beef sausages or junket or bread pudding or liver. And this false impression I was giving seemed quite justifiable because of the real gulf that was there, that could never be made clear. What a difference there was, for instance, between the Montjoys' kitchen and the kitchen at home – but you couldn't explain the difference just by mentioning the worn-out linoleum of one and the perfectly shining surfaces of the other, or the fact that in one of them water was pumped into the sink from a cistern and in the other it came out of a tap. The fact was that one kitchen followed with absolute correctness an idea of what everybody's kitchen ought to be, and the other grew and changed, with improvisations and use, and belonged entirely to one family, to the years and decades of the family's life. And when I thought of that kitchen, with its blackened shelves behind the stove, the historical confusion deep in its cupboards, the smell of the barn clothes hung by the door, it seemed that I had to protect it from contempt – that I had to protect a whole precious and intimate though often unpleasant way of life from contempt, which I supposed to be nourished in the icy hearts of people like the Montjoys.

So I spun out the details of hardship and made no mention of the hired girls I had talked about to Mrs Montjoy. I eliminated soft, drowsy Olive, whom I would have liked to please, but couldn't because she lived in a fog of hymns and prophecies and curious prohibitions, also Annie, who marked the cups with lipstick and did her hair up in pin curls at night and kept a list of the boys she went out with, putting strange marks after their names – + + + ⋆ O – and Mavis, who hung the clothes on the line in an eccentric way, by one corner or leg or sleeve. Hired girls had become a thing of the past, anyway, when I got old enough to manage part of the housework. And now my sister was old enough.

'That isn't fair,' said Mary Anne. 'That's awful.' But then she added, 'Why don't they go and catch some fish?'

'They haven't got any fishing rods.'

'Couldn't they make some?'

'People who don't even need the fish have come and caught them all, anyway. For fun.'

I thought that would keep her quiet, but she could not stop mulling over the problem. 'Couldn't they go to the Salvation Army?'

'They're too proud,' I said.

'Well, I feel sorry for them,' Mary Anne said. 'I feel sorry for them, but I think that's really stupid. What about the children? They ought to think about their children. Are the children too proud, too?'

'Everybody's proud,' I said.

When Mr Montjoy came to the island on the weekends, there was always a great deal of noise and activity. Some of that was because there were visitors, who came by boat to swim or have drinks and watch sailing races. But a lot of it was generated by Mr Montjoy himself. He had a loud, blustery voice and a clumsy body. Every weekend he turned red from the sun, and during every week the burned skin peeled away, leaving him splotchy and pink and muddy with freckles, ready to be burned again. When he took off his glasses you could see that one eye was quick and squinty and the other boldly blue but stupid-looking and moving jerkily, as if it had been caught in a trap.

His blustering was often about things that he had misplaced, or dropped, or bumped into. 'Where the hell is the – ?' he would say, or, 'You didn't happen to see the – ?' so it seemed that he had also misplaced, or failed to grasp in the first place, even the name of the thing he was looking for. To console himself he might grab up a handful of peanuts or pretzels – whatever was nearby – and eat them as if not noticing what he was doing. You felt that he might look at the empty bowl, the minute he had finished eating, and say, 'Where the hell are the – ?'

One morning I heard him say, 'Now where the hell is my – ?' when he was crashing around out on the deck.

'Your book?' said Mrs Montjoy. She was out there having her morning coffee.

'I thought I had it out here,' Mr Montjoy said. 'I was reading it.'

'That Book-of-the-Month-Club book?' she said. 'I think you left it in the living room.'

She was right. I was vacuuming the living-room floor, and I had found a book pushed partway under the sofa. Its title was *Seven Gothic Tales*. That made me want to see what it was about, so I opened it, and even as I listened to this conversation on the deck I was reading, holding the book open in one hand and guiding the vacuum cleaner with the other: ' "Nay, I speak from my heart," said Mira. "I have been trying for a long time to understand God. Now I have made friends with him. To love him truly you must love change, and you must love a joke, these being the true inclinations of his own heart . . ." '

'There it is,' said Mr Montjoy. 'Good girl, you found my book. Now I remember. I was reading it on the sofa last night.'

'I just picked it up,' I said. 'It was on the floor.'

He must have seen that I was reading it. 'It's a queer kind of book,' he said. 'But sometimes you want to read a book that isn't like all the others.'

'I couldn't make head or tail of it,' said Mrs Montjoy, coming in with the coffee tray. 'We'll have to get out of the way here – Elsa has to get on with the vacuuming.'

Mr Montjoy went back to the city that evening. The next day I looked everywhere. I looked under the chairs and behind the curtains, in case he might have left the book behind. but I could not find it.

'I always thought it would be nice to live up here all the year round, the way you people do,' said Mrs Foley. She must have been thinking again that I was the local girl who used to bring the groceries. Some days she said, 'Now I know who you are. You're the new girl helping the Dutch woman in the kitchen, but I just can't recall your name,' and other days she let me walk by without giving any greeting or showing the least sign of interest.

'We used to come up in the winter,' she said. 'Sometimes the bay was frozen over and there would be a road across the ice. We used to go snowshoeing. Now can you tell me, why does nobody go snowshoeing anymore?'

She didn't wait for me to answer. She leaned towards me. 'Can you tell me where Jane is?' she said with embarrassment, speaking almost in a whisper.

I said that I didn't know. She reached out a hand, perhaps to touch my face, and I drew back, so that the hand grazed my chest instead. It was a hot day, and I was wearing a halter. I felt her touch on my bare skin just where my breasts divided. Her hand was light and dry as a wood shaving.

'I'm sure it's all right,' she said.

After that I didn't want to sit down beside her or speak to her again.

On a Saturday afternoon towards the end of August, the Montjoys gave a cocktail party. The party was given in honour of the friends they had staying with them that weekend – Mr and Mrs Hammond.

People arrived in motorboats and sailing boats. Some of them went swimming, then sat around on the rocks in their bathing suits or lay on the dock in the sun. Others came up to the house immediately and started drinking and talking in the living room or out on the deck. Some children had come with their parents, and some by themselves, in their own boats. These were not children of Mary Anne's age – Mary Anne had been taken to stay with her friend Susan, on another island – but of mine. Girls and boys fifteen or sixteen years old. They spent most of the afternoon in the water, diving and shouting and having races to the raft.

Mrs Montjoy and I had been busy since early morning, making all the different things to eat, which we now arranged on platters and offered to these people. This was fiddly and exasperating work – stuffing various mixtures into mushroom caps, sticking one tiny slice of something on top of a tiny slice of something on top of a precise fragment of toast or bread. All the shapes had to be perfect and of exactly the same size – perfect rounds, perfect squares, perfect triangles, perfect diamonds. Mrs Hammond came into the kitchen several times and admired what we were doing.

'How gorgeous everything looks,' she said. 'You notice I'm not even offering to help. It would just be a joke, I'm hopeless.'

I liked the way she said that. I admired her husky voice, its weary, humorous tone. *I'm hopeless.* I wished I were her, in a sleek, black bathing suit with a tan like dark toast, shoulder-length dark hair, and an exotic orchid lipstick, constantly reapplied. She did not look happy, but her air of complaint and sullenness seemed glamorous to me, her hints of cloudy drama enviable. She and her husband were an altogether different kind of rich people from Mr and Mrs Montjoy. They were more like the people I had already met in magazine stories and in books like *The Hucksters* – people who drank a lot, had love affairs, went to psychiatrists. Her name was Carol and her husband's name was Ivan. I already thought of them by their first names – something I had never been tempted to do with the Montjoys.

Mrs Montjoy had asked me to put on a dress, so I wore the pink-and-white stripped cotton, with the smudged material around its waist tucked under the elasticised belt. Nearly everybody else was in shorts or even in bathing suits. I passed among them, offering food. I was not sure how to do this. Sometimes people were talking or laughing so busily that they didn't notice me. I had to say, 'Excuse me – would you like one of these?' in a very determined voice, to get their attention. Then they looked startled and amused. 'Why, thank you,' they said as if my interruption were a further joke.

'Enough passing for now, Elsa,' Mrs Montjoy said.

She gathered up some glasses and asked me to wash them. 'People never keep track of their own – it's easier just to keep giving them fresh ones,' she said. 'Also it's time to get the meatballs out of the fridge and heat them. Could you watch the oven?'

While I was busy in the kitchen I heard Mrs Hammond calling, 'Ivan! Ivan!' She was roaming through the back rooms of the house. But Mr Hammond had come in through the kitchen door that led to the woods. He stood there and did not answer her.

He came over to the counter and poured gin into his glass.

'Oh, Ivan, there you are,' said Mrs Hammond, coming in from the hall.

'Here I am,' said Mr Hammond.

'Where else?' she said. 'Me, too.' She handed him her glass.

Mr Hammond set her glass down and pushed the gin bottle towards her. He spoke to me. He said, 'Are you having any fun, Minnie?'

Mrs Hammond gave a yelp of laughter. 'Minnie. Where did you get the idea her name was Minnie? Her name is Elsa.'

'Elsa,' said Mr Hammond. 'Are you having fun, Elsa?'

'Oh, yes,' I said. I was busy lifting the cookie sheet with the meatballs on it out of the oven and hadn't taken any time with my reply. I immediately wished I had matched his sarcastic tone. I could have said, 'Yes, *indeed*.'

'I swam around the point,' said Mrs Hammond. 'I'm working up to swiming around the entire island.'

Mr Hammond said, 'Good.'

'Well, then,' said Mrs Hammond. 'I'll leave you to it.'

I had begun to spear the meatballs with toothpicks and arrange them on a platter. Mr Hammond said, 'Care for some help?' and tried to do the same, but his toothpicks missed and sent the meatballs skittering on to the counter.

'Well, Elsa,' he said. Then, as if he could not follow his thought further, he simply repeated himself. 'Well, Elsa.'

I knew something about him. I knew that the Hammonds were here for a special holiday because Mr Hammond had lost his job. Mary Anne had told me this. 'He's depressed about it,' she said. He did not seem depressed to me. He seemed impatient – chiefly with Mrs Hammond – but quite pleased with himself. He was tall, he had dark hair combed straight back, and a dark, thin moustache, and I had noticed that when people talked to him he had a way of leaning slightly towards them, as if what they had to say might be very important. The word that described this, in my mind, was 'courtly'.

'Where do you go swimming, Minnie? Do you go swimming?'

'Down by the boathouse,' I said. I thought he must have said 'Minnie' for a joke.

'Is that a good place?'

I said yes. It was good for me, because I had never, before this summer, swum in water that was over my head, and I liked being close to the dock.

'Do you ever go in without your bathing suit?'

'No.'

'You should try it,' he said.

Mrs Montjoy came through the living-room doorway, asking if the meatballs were ready.

'This is certainly a hungry crowd,' she said. 'It's the swimming does it. How are you getting on, Ivan? Carol was just looking for you.'

'She was here,' said Mr Hammond.

Mrs Montjoy dropped parsley here and there among the meatballs. 'Now, Elsa,' she said. 'I think you've done about all you need to here. I think I can manage now. Why don't you make yourself a sandwich and run along down to the boathouse.'

I said I wasn't hungry. Mr Hammond had disappeared into the back part of the house.

'Well, you'd better take something,' Mrs Hammond said. 'You might be hungry later.'

She meant that I was not to come back.

On my way to the boathouse I met a couple of the guests – girls of my own age, barefoot and in their bathing suits, breathlessly laughing. They had probably swum partway around the island, climbed out of the water at the boathouse dock, and were sneaking back to surprise somebody. They stepped aside when they saw me but did not quite stop laughing. They made way for my body without looking at me. They were the kind of girls who would have squealed and made a fuss of me if I had been a dog or a cat.

The noise of the party continued for a long time. It was too early, anyway, to go to sleep. I put on my bathing suit and climbed down the ladder into the water and swam around a bit, gradually working up a fantasy about Mr Hammond. It was not impossible, I thought, that he would come looking for me. And then what? A first touch, I supposed, then kisses, hot pressures, limbs twining in the water, like ribbons of light. The thought of touching a man that old – forty? forty-five? – disturbed me, though I knew I would get pleasure from it. It was like knowing you could get pleasure from touching a crocodile. Mr Hammond's – Ivan's – skin might be smooth, but his age and his knowledge and his desired corruptness would sit on it like invisible warts and scales.

I let the straps of my bathing suit down, I let my breasts float free. I swam that way, with the water sweetly dividing at my nipples, gliding over my skin. I even dared to lift myself out of the water, though it wasn't dark yet. Holding to the dock with one hand I bobbed up and down and rose into the light like a mermaid, wet and gleaming, with nobody to see.

Then I heard steps – I heard somebody coming. I sank down into the water, by the dock. I held still.

For just a minute I believed that it was Mr Hammond and that I had actually entered the world of secret signals, lovers' meetings, ruthless desires. I shrank against the dock, horrified and submissive. Then the boathouse light was switched on, and I turned around, noiselessly, carefully, in the water – no longer sure that I would see Mr Hammond but not sure that I wouldn't see him, either – and there was old Mr Foley, in his baggy white pants, with his back to me, moving something around on the tool shelf. Earlier that afternoon he had appeared at the party, in his yachtman's cap and blazer. He had stayed for one drink and explained that Mrs Foley could not bear the strain of seeing so many people but sent her best to all.

He found what he wanted, or put back what he had taken away earlier, and switched off the light, and left. He never noticed that I was there.

I pulled up my bathing suit and climbed out of the water and went up the stairs. My body seemed such a weight to me that when I got to the top I was short of breath.

The sound of the cocktail party went on. To hold my own against it, I started to write a letter to my friend Eleanor, at home. She was the sort of friend with whom I nearly always talked about sex. I described the party in derogatory terms and spoke of Mr Hammond as a letch, though I added that he was very good-looking. I said that he had nudged me and fondled me in the kitchen when my hands were occupied with the meatballs, and later he had followed me down to the boathouse and made a determined attack. But I had kicked him and freed myself and he had gone away. *Scurried away* was what I said.

'So hold your breath for the next instalment – "The Kitchen Maid's Adventure", or "Ravaged on the Rocks of Georgian Bay",' I wrote. I realized the next day that I should have written 'ravished' not 'ravaged,' but it was all right, Eleanor would not know the difference.

'Mrs Foley asked me where Jane was,' I said to Mrs Montjoy. We were polishing the silver – I was polishing it and she was standing beside me, inspecting it. All the knives and forks and spoons had to be polished before we left the island. 'I didn't know who she meant. Was Jane one of the girls who worked here some other summer?'

'Jane was my other daughter,' said Mrs Montjoy. 'She was Mary Anne's sister. She's dead.'

'Oh, I didn't know,' I said. 'Oh, that's too bad.'

'Well. It's some time ago now.'

'Did she die of polio?' I said cautiously. In those days children still died of polio, every summer.

'No,' said Mrs Montjoy. 'She was killed when I moved the corner cupboard in my bedroom. I was looking for my bracelet. I didn't really think it would be there, but I thought I'd look. One of the casters caught on the rug, and the whole thing toppled down on her, and she was killed.'

I knew all this, of course. Mary Anne had told me all of it. I knew it the way I knew such things then – the black holes, the horrors that seemed essential in the drama I required of life.

'That's terrible,' I said. 'I'm terribly sorry.' In my guilt, in my queasy triumph, I let a fork slip through my fingers, to the floor.

Mrs Montjoy picked it up. 'Remember to wash this,' she said. 'It was nothing to do with you, Elsa. It was just one of those things.'

At that time I didn't recognise brutality in myself, or boorishness. I thought I had the right – the right to barge in, stir up feelings, demand intimacy, or at least attention. I thought myself blameless, beyond judgment, in my dealings with Mrs Montjoy. Because I was young and poor and knew about Nausicaä. I didn't have the grace or fortitude to be a servant.

On my last Sunday I was alone in the boathouse, packing up my things in the suitcase that had gone with my mother and father on their wedding trip. When I pulled it out from under my cot and opened it, here, it smelled of home – of the closet at the end of the upstairs hall where it usually sat, close to the mothballed winter coats and the fox-fur scarf and the rubber sheet once used on children's beds. But when you got it out at home it always smelled faintly of train trips and cities where many buildings were still heated by coal – of travel.

I heard steps on the path, a stumbling step into the boathouse, a rapping on the wall. It was Mr Montjoy.

'Are you up there, Elsa? Are you up there?'

His voice was boisterous, jovial, as it was when he had been drinking. There were friends at the Montjoy's house, toasting the end of summer. I came to the top of the stairs. He put a hand on the wall to steady himself. A boat had gone by out on the channel and sent little waves into the boathouse.

'See here, Elsa,' said Mr Montjoy, looking up at me with his fierce, trapped eye. 'See here – I thought I might as well bring this down and give it to you.'

It was a book he was handing to me: *Seven Gothic Tales*.

'Because I saw you were looking at it that day,' he said. 'It seemed to me you were interested in it. So I thought, Well, you might as well have it.'

'Thank you,' I said.

'I thought when I finished it I might as well pass it along to you. It just occurred to me. You might enjoy it.'

'Thank you very much.'

'That's all right. I just thought you might enjoy it.'

'Yes,' I said. But very little of the joy I felt got into my voice. I was too surprised at first, then, very quickly, hardly surprised at all. Once I got my hands on the book, I felt as if it had always belonged to me.

'Well, then. I hope you will.'

Mary Anne had once said to me, 'Daddy used to be poor like you. He grew up in a little place somewhere near Ottawa, and his father was a doctor, but he died. So Daddy had to work his way through university. Nana didn't think Mother should marry him at first but Granddad said he was too smart to stay poor for very long.'

I was not sure I was going to give anybody whose father had been a doctor the credit of being poor.

He left the boathouse, and I went back upstairs and pushed the suitcase aside and sat down on the cot. I opened the book just anywhere, and began to read.

'The walls of the room had once been painted crimson, but with time the colour had faded into a richness of hues, like a glassful of dying red roses . . . Some pot-pourri was being burned on the tall stove, on the sides of which Neptune, with a trident, steered his team of horses through high waves.'

Reading this, I felt as if I had just been rescued from my life. Words could become a burning-glass for me in those days, and no shame of my nature or condition could hold out among the flares of pleasure.

Sin

EDNA O'BRIEN

THEY WERE IN. In. Mother, father, and daughter. She waited
to hear them come in, stayed awake. She would be awake
anyhow, because sleep was paying her less and less court as the
years went on. Occasionally, she took a tablet, but dreaded being
at the mercy of any drug and had a secondary dread of one day not
being able to get it, or not being able to afford it. In those wide-
awake vigils she prayed or tried to, but prayer, like sleep, was on
the wane now, at the very time when she should be pressing her
maker for favours. The prayers came only from her lips, not from
deep within – she had lost that heartfelt rapport she once had with
God. When the prayers became meaningless, she went around her
house in her mind and thought of improvements she would make
this year or next – new wallpaper in the big room, where the pink
was soiled around the window frames, brown smears from all the
damp. And then in the vacant room, where apples were stored, the
wallpaper had been hung upside-down and had survived the years
without anyone knowing that the acorns and the branches were
the wrong way around. She might have that replaced, too, just to
get the better of those fools who hung it incorrectly. She was a
woman who liked to be always in the right. Funny that on the day
the paper was hung she had consulted some seer in the city about a
certain matter and had been told that she would go home and find

these fruits and bobbins the wrong way up, and she did. In other quarters of her house, she was more spartan with her improvements; she thought of maybe a new strip of linoleum inside the hall door, to save the tiles from trampling boots. Scrubbing was hard for her now, hard on her lower back. Then there were little things, like new towels and tea towels and dishcloths – dishcloths smelled of milk no matter how she soaked or boiled them. They had that sour, gone-off smell. Smell was her strongest sense, and when these paying guests arrived that morning she smelled the woman's perfume and the daughter's – identical, and yet nothing else about them seemed alike. The daughter, Samantha, blonde and cocksure, screwed up her eyes as if she were thinking something mathematical, when all she was thinking was Look at me, admire me. She touted for their attention. Her hair was her chief weapon – long hair, which she swept along the table as she looked carefully at the wallpaper or at her parents or at a picture over the whatnot, of pussycats who were trying to move the hands of a clock on to feeding time. She kept insisting that her parents have a bite of her toast, or a taste of her porridge, because it was yummy. Her skirt was nothing short of nude – a bib, really, to draw attention to her thighs, like pillars of solid nougat inside her cream lace stockings. The mother was dark and plump and made a habit of touching the daughter whenever she jumped up in one of her fits of simulated exuberance. The father smoked a pipe. He was a handsome man, tall and distant.

They ate breakfast, then had to have a basket packed with hard-boiled eggs and sandwiches for their boating expedition. She explained that they must make their own arrangements for dinner. When they came back, she heard them say 'Sh-h-h, sh-h-h' repeatedly as they climbed the stairs. They used the bathroom in turn. She could tell by their footsteps, and had to concede that they were doing their best to be quiet – that is, until something went crash-crash and the mother went to the rescue of the daughter. She reckoned it was the china tooth mug. She loved that tooth mug, cream with green fluting and little garlands of shamrock, and she wanted to get up and tackle them, but something stopped her. Also, she did not have a dressing gown. Would they be in their dressing gowns? The woman possibly yes, and the man in his shirtsleeves. She would miss the tooth mug, she would mourn it. Her things had become her beloveds, all else gone, or scattered in distant places. She knew – oh, yes, she knew – that the love of children gets fainter and fainter, like a garment that's washed and rewashed until it is only a shadow of its original colour, its crimson or royal blue. Their daughter, their Samantha, would be like that soon, would skedaddle once she had other interests, men and so forth.

The parents had the blue room, which had been her and her husband's bridal room, the one where her children were born and where as the years went on she slept as little as possible and went only when she was compelled to, when he roared for her. She went to keep him quiet, to keep him off the batter – went in disgust and stayed in disgust and afterwards rinsed and washed herself of it all. Five children were enough for any woman. Four scattered children and one dead, and a daughter-in-law who had made her son, her only son, the essence of graspingness. Still, she must not be too hard on them. The girls remembered when they remembered, they sent gifts, especially the one overseas, and next time when asked what she wanted she would say a dressing gown, and then she could confront her lodgers.

She only kept people in summer, partly because they only came then but also because to heat the house in winter would be impossible, as it swallowed up tankers of oil. Moreover, she never kept people for more than two nights, believing they might get forward and start to think the house was theirs, opening wardrobes and doors, making free. Her other reason was more of a secret. She was afraid that she might grow attached to them and ask them to stay. With the takings, she made improvements to the house but never indulged in a luxury for herself except for the jam and tins of biscuits for her sweet tooth.

Yes, they were in her marriage bed, a wide bed with an oak headboard that rattled and a rose quilt that she had made during her betrothal, stitching all her dreamings into it. She imagined them, man and wife, lying side by side, the square pouches of the quilt rising and sinking with their breath, and she remembered the clutching of it and the plucking of some of the feathers as her husband made wrathful and unloving love to her. How might it have been with another man, a gentler, more considerate man? The girl was probably not asleep, but shaping her eyebrows or brushing the long spill of hair, brushing it slowly and maybe even examining herself in the mirror, admiring her plump, firm little figure inside her short nightgown. After they went out to dinner, she had peered into their rooms. She did not open their suitcases, as a point of honour, but she studied some of their possessions, the woman's string of pearls, her cosmetics, and her dark-brown hair net, which lay stealthily next to his pipes, pipes of different-coloured wood, and a folded swag of mulchy tobacco. Their money, English money, was piled into two little banks – his money and her money, she felt. On the girl's dressing table there was only the hairbrush, cotton buds, and baby oil. The diaphanous nightie was laid out on the pillow and looked lifelike, as if there were a doll inside it.

Sleep would not come. She got up, intending to go and look at the broken tooth mug, but as soon as she reached the door something prevented her. She was ashamed of being heard by them. It was as if the house had become theirs and she, the lodger, beholden to them. Something about their being a family, and all over each other, and blowing about what a brilliant time they were having galled her. She paced. Pacing was one of the things she did at night, but now she felt that it, too, was wrong – revealing – and so she crept back into her bed and waited for the blessing of sleep. Sleep often came unbeknownst to her. It was not preceded by yawning or drowsiness. There she would be, totting up what guests owed her, taking it and putting it in the big orange bowl where the spoils of the summer were kept, and all of a sudden it would be morning, the sun giving a rich, red-wine glow to the velvet curtains, or the rain pouring down and her little dog, Gigi, on his hind legs, looking up at her window, waiting for her to get up and come down and open the back door and serve him a saucer of tea with milk. Over the years, he had grown more like a human and was undoubtedly her most faithful friend.

With some visitors she found it more difficult to get to sleep. They unnerved her or she began thinking about them, speculating about their lives, their earnings, their happiness, and so forth, and so it was with these three. It was as if she had to be awake, to keep a watch.

Exactly half an hour after they had retired, it happened. She heard a creak, the girl's door opening slowly, and she thought it was bathroom need, but, no, she heard her go towards their room on tiptoe and then she heard a tap, a series of taps, light and playful – not the tapping of a sick or overwrought child, not the tapping of someone disturbed by a mouse or a bumblebee – and in that second she knew it. Her whole body went into spasm. She heard the girl go into their room, and then everything became so silent, the atmosphere so tense, that her hand, jerking her own doorknob, made her jump. She opened her door very softly and moved in their direction, not certain what exactly she would do. The whole house seemed to wait. They were not talking, yet what reached her ears could not be called silence. Something terrible was being enacted in there, a rite of whispering and tittering and lewd laughter. She could not see, yet her eyes seemed to penetrate through the panelled door as if it were sheer glass and she could picture them – hands, mouths, limbs, all searching for one another. They had not dared to put on a light. The girl was probably naked, or else wore her scarf like a sarong, moving with them in their macabre dancing, yielding, allowing them to fondle her, the man fondling her in one place, the woman fondling her elsewhere – an orgy of caresses and whispers and sighs that rent the air. Those sighs and whispers magnified.

She would break the door down. It was not enough simply to open it. She would catch them out, the man, lord of his harem, straddled over a girl who was in no way his daughter, and the woman ministering, because that was the only way she could hold on to him. Vile. Vile. There was a poker in there, in the coal scuttle, left since her last confinement, thirty years ago, and she was already picking it up. She would break it on their bare romping bodies. What detained her she could not say. Everything determined that she go in, and yet she waited in some wanton hesitation, as if she were waiting for their smell.

Their exclamations were what sent her scurrying back to her own room, the three pitches of sound so different – the woman's loud and gusty, the girl's helpless, almost as if she were crying, and, sometime later, his, like a jackass down in the woods with his lady love. She sat on the edge of her bed in a simmer. They would have to go in the morning. She would let them know why. She would convey it to them, insinuate that the girl was not their daughter, but she would never know for sure, and that, plus the vile pageant in the dark, would torment her and be a plague on her house until the day she died.

Under The Rose

JULIA O'FAOLAIN

DAN SAID – to be sure, there was only his word for this; but who would invent such a thing – that, in their teens, his brother and he had ravaged their sister on the parsonage kitchen table. Their father was a parson, and when the rape took place the household was at Evensong. Dan described a fume of dust motes sliced by thin, surgical light, a gleam of pinkish copper pans and, under his nose, the pith of the deal table. Outside the door, his sister's dog had howled. The truth was, said Dan, that she herself did not resist much. She'd been fifteen, and the unapologetic Dan was now twenty. It had, he claimed, been a liberation for all three.

'The Bible's full of it,' he'd wind up. 'Incest!'

The story was for married women only. Dan specialised in unhappy wives. *Mal mariées*. He sang a song about them in French, easing open the tight, alien vowels and letting the slur of his voice widen their scope: *ma-uhl mah-urrr-ee-yeh*. It was a Limerick voice, and those who resisted its charm said that the further Dan Lydon got from Limerick the broader his accent grew. The resistant tended to be men; women always liked Dan. To hear him lilt, 'my lo-hove is lo-ike a r–red, r–red r–ro–rose' was, as respected matrons would tell you, like listening to grand opera. His vibrancy fired them. It kindled and dazzled like those beams you saw in paintings of the Holy Ghost, and his breath had a pulse to it, even when all he was ordering was the same again, please, and a packet of fags. Words, moving in his mouth like oysters, put town dwellers in mind of rural forebears and of the damp, reticent lure of the countryside.

The parsonage of Dan's youth lay in the grasslands watered by the River Shannon, flat country shadowed by those cloud formations known as mackerel backs and mare's tails – arrangements as chameleon as himself. He was a bright-haired, smiling boy, who first reached Dublin in 1943, a time when the Japanese minister rode with a local hunt and the German one did not always get the cold shoulder. Dan's allegiance was to the noble Soviets, but he was alive, too, to sexual raciness blown in like pollen from the war zones. Change fizzed; neutrality opened fields of choice, and values had rarely been shiftier.

'So where is your sister now?'

Mrs Connors did and did not believe his story.

'Tea?' she offered. Tea was his hour. Husbands tended to be at work. Mr Connors was a civil servant.

Dan took his tea. 'She had to be married off,' he admitted. 'She has a sweet little boy.'

Mrs Connors dared: 'Yours?'

'Or my brother's? I'd like there to be one I *knew* was mine.' His eyes held hers. Putting down the cup, he turned her wrist over, slid back the sleeve, and traced the artery with a finger.

'The blue-veined child!' he murmured. 'Don't you think children conceived in passion are special? Fruits of willfulness! Surely they become poets? Or Napoleons?'

Phyllis Connors was sure Napoleon's family had been legitimate. On her honeymoon, before the war, she had visited Corsica. 'Their mother was addressed as Madam Mère.'

'Was that the model Connors held up to you? "Madame Mère"!' Dan teased. 'On your honeymoon! What a clever cuss!'

The teasing could seem brotherly; but Dan's brotherliness was alarming. Indeed, Phyllis's offer to be a sister to him had touched off the nonsense – what else could it be? – about incest.

Nonsense or not, it unsettled her.

He was predatory. A known idler. Wolfed her sandwiches as though he had had no lunch – and maybe he hadn't? The parson had washed his hands of him. But Dan had a new spiritual father in a poet who had stopped the university from kicking him out. Dan's enthusiasm for poetry – he was, he said, writing it full-time – so captivated the poet that he had persuaded the provost to waive mundane requirements and ensure that the boy's scholarship (paid by a fund for sons of needy parsons) be renewed. Surely, urged Dan's advocate, the alma mater of Burke and Sam Beckett could be flexible with men of stellar promise? Talents did not mature at the rate of seed potatoes, and Ireland's best-known export was fractious writers. Let's try to keep this one at home.

The poet, who ran a magazine, needed someone to do the legwork and when need be plug gaps with pieces entitled 'Where the Red Flag Flies', 'A Future for Cottage Industries?', or 'Folk Memories of West Clare'. Dan could knock these off at speed, and the connection gave him prestige with the fellow-undergraduates, at whose verse readings he starred.

It was at one of these that Phyllis Connors had first heard him recite. The verse had not been his. That, he explained, must stay *sub rosa*. Did she know that Jack Yeats, the painter, kept a rose on his easel when painting his mad, marvellous pictures of horse dealers, fiddlers, and fairs? Art in progress was safest under the rose.

After tea, Dan talked of procreation and of how men in tropical lands like Ecuador thought sex incomplete without it. That was the earth's wisdom speaking through them. RCs – look at their Madonnas – had the same instinct. Dan, the parson's son, defended the Pope, whose church had inherited the carnal wit of the ancients. 'The sower went out to sow his seed . . .'

Talk like this unnerved Phyllis, who was childless and unsure what was being offered. What farmer, asked Dan, would scatter with an empty hand? 'Your women are your fields,' he quoted, from the Koran. 'Go freely into your fields!' Then he extolled the beauty of pregnant women – bloomy as June meadows – and recited a poem about changelings: 'Come away, O human child . . .'

Phyllis, thinking him a child himself, might have surrendered to the giddiest request. But Dan made none. Instead, he went home to his lodgings, leaving her to gorge her needs on the last of the sandwiches.

He came back, though, for her house was near the poet's, and after drudging with his galleys would drop by to cup hands, sculpt air, praise her hips, and eat healthy amounts of whatever was for tea. Refreshed he liked to intone poems about forest gods and fairy folk. 'And if any gaze on our rushing band,' he chanted, 'We come between him and the deed of his hand, We come between him and the hope of his heart.'

Why did he not come after what he implied was the hope of his own heart? Wondering made her think of him more than she might otherwise have done, and so did seeing him in the Singing Kettle, eating doughnuts with the poet's wife. Peering through trickles in a steamy window, she thought she saw the word 'Love' on his lips. Or was it 'Dove'? His motto, 'Let the doves settle!' meant 'Take things as they come.'

Phyllis decided that some doves needed to be snared.

Soon she was pregnant, and when she went into the Hatch Street Nursing Home to give birth Dan brought her a reproduction of Piero della Francesca's *Madonna del Parto*, with the pale slash where the Virgin, easing her gown off her round belly, shows under-linen more intimate than skin. His finger on Phyllis's stomach sketched an identical white curve. He teased the nurses, relished the fertility all about, and was happy as a mouse in cheese.

It turned out that the poet's wife was here, too, and for the same reason. Her room was on another floor, so Dan yo-yoed up and down. Sometimes he brought gifts that had to be divided: fruit, for instance, from the poet, who still used Dan to run errands. Or books, review copies from the magazine. When a nurse let drop that the poet's wife had the same Piero Madonna on her side table, Phyllis wrapped hers in a nappy and put it in the trash. If there had been a fireplace, she would have burned it, as she had been trained to do with unwanted religious objects.

Her baby received her husband's first name, and the poet's baby the poet's. Dan – though neither couple asked him to be godfather – presented both infants with christening mugs. One had been his and the other his brother's, and both were made of antique Dublin silver. Early Georgian. The official godfathers, fearing odious comparisons, returned their purchases to Weirs Jewellers and bought cutlery. Phyllis wondered if Dan's brother knew what had happened to his mug. Though the war was now over, he was still overseas with the British Army.

'He'll not be back,' Dan assured her, and revealed that the parsonage had been a dour and penurious place. Its congregation had dwindled since the RC natives took over the country in '21, and attendance some Sundays amounted to less than six. Pride had throttled Dan's widowed father, who did menial work behind the scenes and made his children collect fire-wood, polish silver, and dine on boiled offal.

'He wouldn't want the mug,' said Dan. 'Too many bad memories!' The brothers had left as soon as they could, and getting their sister pregnant had been a parting gift. 'If we hadn't, she'd still be Daddy's slave.'

Some years went by, and Dan was a student still, of a type known to Dubliners as 'chronic', one of a ragged brigade who, recoiling from a jobless job market, harked back to the tribally condoned wandering scholars of long ago. This connection was often all that raised the chronics above tramps or paupers, and the lifeline was frail.

But out of the blue, opportunity came Dan's way. The poet, who had to go into the hospital, asked him to bring out an issue of the magazine bearing on the masthead the words 'Guest Editor: Daniel Lydon'. Here was challenge! Dan toyed excitedly with the notion of publishing his secret poetry, which he yearned, yet feared, to display. These urges warred in him until, having read and reread it, he saw that it had gone dead, leaking virtue like batteries kept too long in a drawer. Stewing, he fell behind with the magazine and had to ghostwrite several pieces to pad the thing out. As part of this process, he decided to publish photographs of A Changing Ireland. Hydrofoils, reapers-and-binders, ballpoint pens, and other such innovations were shown next to Neolithic barrows. The Knights of Columbanus in full fig appeared cheek by jowl with an electric band. Portraits of 'the last Gaelic storyteller' and some 'future Irishmen' rounded out the theme.

The future Irishmen, three small boys with their heads arranged like the leaves of a shamrock, were recognisably Dan's nephew and the recipients of his christening mugs – and what leaped to the eye was their resemblance to himself. The caption 'Changelings' drove the scandal home.

The poet, convalescing in his hospital bed after an operation for a gentleman's complaint, told his wife, in an insufficiently discreet hiss, that he had paid Dan to do his legwork, not to get his leg over. Reference was made to 'cuckoo's eggs', and it was not long before echoes of this reached the ears of Mr Connors, the proverbial quiet man whom it is dangerous to arouse. Connors, who had done a bit of hacking in his bachelor days, had a riding crop. Taking this to the student lodgings where Dan lived, he used it to tap smartly on the door.

When Dan opened this, Connors raised the crop. Dan yelled, and his neighbour, a fellow-Communist, who was on the varsity boxing team, came hurtling to the rescue. Assuming the row to be political and Connors a member of the Blue Shirts only reinforced his zeal. Shoving ensued; Connors fell downstairs; gawkers gathered, and the upshot was that an ambulance was called and the opinion bandied that the victim had broken his back. Some genuine Blue Shirts were meanwhile rustled up, men whose finest hours had been fighting for Franco, singing hymns to Cristo Re, and beating the sin out of Reds; they were spoiling for a scrap, and if it had not been for Dan's friend spiriting him out the back they might have sent him to join Mr Connors – who, as it would turn out, had not been injured, after all, and was fit as a fiddle in a couple of weeks.

Dan, however, had by then prudently boarded the ferry to Holyhead, taking with him, like a subsidiary passport, the issue of the magazine bearing his name as 'guest editor'. It got him work with the BBC, which, in those days of live programming, needed men with a gift of the gab and was friendly to Celts. Louis MacNeice and Dylan Thomas were role models, liquid stimulants in high favour, and Dan was recruited straight off the boat.

So ran reports reaching Dublin. Pithy myths, these acquired an envious tinge as Dan's success was magnified, along with the sums he was earning for doing what he had formerly done for free: talking, singing, and gargling verse. Others were soon dreaming of jobs in a London whose airwaves vapoured with gold. Hadn't Dubliners a known talent for transubstantiating eloquence into currency? And couldn't every one of us talk at least as well as Dan Lydon?

Declan Connors doubted it. Despite himself, he'd caught snatches of what nobody had the indecency to quote quite to his face: a saga featuring Dan as dispenser of sweet anointings to women. These, Connors understood, had needed preparation. Persuasion had been required, and Dan's boldness at it had grown legendary, as an athlete's prowess goes with fans. The gossips relished Dan's gall, the airy way he could woo without promise or commitment – arguing, say, that in a war's wake more kids were needed and that his companion's quickened pulse was nature urging her to increase the supply. Nature! What a let out! Any man who could sell a line like that in Holy Ireland could sell heaters in hell.

'He's a one-man social service!' A wag raised his pint. 'Offers himself up. "Partake ye of my body." He'd rather be consumed than consume!'

The wag drained his glass. His preferences ran the other way. So did those of the man next to him, whose tongue wrestled pinkly with ham frilling from a sandwich. All around, males guzzled: women, in this prosperous pub, were outnumbered ten to one. Connors, sipping his whiskey, thought, No wonder Lydon made out – we left him an open field!

He could no longer regret this, for after ten barren years of marriage Phyllis had had three children in quick succession. It was as if something in her had been unlocked. He supposed there were jokes about this, too, but he didn't care. His master passion had turned out to be paternal, and Declan Junior was the apple of his eye. The younger two were girls and, as Phyllis spoiled them, he had to make things up to the boy.

For a while after the scandal, the couple had felt shy with each other, but they had no thoughts of divorce. You couldn't in Ireland, and it wasn't what they wanted. They were fond of each other – and, besides, there was Declan, of whom it was said behind

Mr Connors' shrugging back that he used his blood father's charm to wind his nominal father around his little finger. A seducer *ab ovo.*

Small-mindedness! Envy! Anyway, time heals, and when the boy was picked, surprisingly early, for his elementary-school soccer team, and later won ribbons for show jumping, Connors – a sportsman – knew him for his spiritual son. Even if the kid was a Lydon, he was a better one than Dan – whose brother, Connors recalled, had been decorated for gallantry in the war. Skimming the entry on Mendel in the encyclopedia, he learned that hereditary character was transmitted chancily and, remembering the poltroonish Dan draped over armchairs and cowering during their fight, decided that Declan Junior had nothing of his natural father's but his looks.

Connors still took an interest, though, in the news trickling back from London, where Dan's free lance was said to be cutting a swath: he had apparently acquired a new patron, a literary pundit who, though married, was partial to a handsome young man. And now Connors noted an odd thing: admiration was ousting envy and Dan's stature in the saga growing. Needless to say, his news was slow to reach Connors, since nobody who remembered their connection would wish to reopen old wounds. It came in scraps, and by the time he got them, these were as spare and smooth as broken glass licked by recurring tides.

As Connors heard it, then: Dan's new benefactor's marriage, though possibly unconsummated, was harmonious, for his wife had money. The couple made fashionable hosts, and Dan was soon glowing in their orbit – singing ballads, referring to his secret *œuvre,* and enlivening their *soirées* with tales of Irish mores. The pundit's wife, the story went, was a handsome, angry woman who had hated her father, but having agreed to inherit his money, would make no further concession to men, and slept only with those she could pity or control. As her husband didn't fit the bill, she had lovers. Dan was soon servicing both her and the husband who, being jealous and smitten, was in the dark about this.

Here the story fractures. In one version, she 'gets preggers', which so shatters the husband that his violence leads to a miscarriage and Dan's subsequent flight to Paris. But there was an implausible symmetry to this, as though running dye from the Dublin episode had coloured it; a likelier account has no pregnancy and the jealousy provoked by someone's indiscretion. Deliberate? Careless? Either way, Connors learned, Dan left England, the marriage collapsed, and the husband, previously a rather nerveless knight of the pen – who had, in his own words, 'failed to grapple with his subjectivity' – finally did so in a book that raised him several rungs on the literary ladder. This was before the Wolfenden Report; homosexuality was a still painful subject, and his grappling was judged brave. Dan, as midwife to his lover's best writing, could be said to have done him a good turn.

Meanwhile, Declan Junior was in his teens, and his mother – noting that if you cut the heart from his name you'd be left with 'Dan' – feared leaving him alone with his sisters. An idle fear: girls bored him, and so did poetry, to her relief. Not that Dan himself had yet published a line, but the appellation *Poète irlandais* clung to him, who had now – wonder of wonders! – married and settled in Paris. The word was that an old Spanish Civil War hero, whose memoirs Dan had been ghost-writing while sleeping with his daughter, had, on catching the pair *in flagrante*, sat on Dan's chest and said, 'Marry her!' A bad day's work for the girl, tittered those Dubliners who still remembered him. One or two had looked him up on trips abroad and reported that he was doing something nowadays for films. Script-doctoring, was it? And his wife had published poems before their marriage, but none since. Maybe she didn't want to shame him? Closer friends said the marriage was a good one, and that no forcing had been needed.

Why should it have been? Marisol was bright, young, had a river of dark hair, and gave Dan the tribal connection he had always coveted. His ravenous charm sprang from his childhood in that bleak parsonage. Marginal. Clanless. Left behind by the tide. Catholics – whose clan had dispersed his – did not appeal, but the Left did. The Spanish Civil War had been Dan's boyhood war, and the more romantic for having been lost. Dan loved a negative. What, he would argue, was there to say about success? The surprise was that the Anglo-Saxon ruling classes could still talk and didn't just beat their smug chests like chimps. If it weren't for their homosexuals, he claimed, they'd have no art. Art was for those whose reality needed suborning. It burrowed and queried; it . . . et cetera! Dan could still chatter like a covey of starlings, and the Limerick accent went down a treat in French, being, as people would soon start to say, *médiatique*

Along came the sixties. The Youth Cult blossomed just as Dan – in his forties – began losing his hair. Juvenescence glowed in him, though, as in a golden autumn tree. His freshness was a triumph of essence over accident, and he became an acknowledged Youth Expert when he made a film about the graffiti of May '68. Graffiti, being, like pub talk, insolent, jubilant, and an end in itself, was right up his street, and he was soon in Hollywood working on a second film. It came to nothing, which confirmed the purity of his response to the ephemeral, and he continued to fly between Paris and California, dressed in light, summery suits and engaged in optimistic projects, some of which did throw his name onto a screen for a fleeting shimmer.

One evening in Paris, he came face to face with Connors and Phyllis in a *brasserie*. They were at different tables, and could have ignored each other. As their last encounter had led to Connors' departure from the scene in an ambulance and Dan's from Ireland, this might have seemed wise. Sportingly, however, Dan came over. Shiny and aglow, his forehead – higher than it used to be – damp with sweat. It was a hot night. Hand outstretched. A little self-deprecating. He had heard their news as they had his, and congratulated Connors on a recent promotion. Family all well? Grand! Great! He was with *his*. Nodding at a tableful of Spaniards. Laughing at their noise. Then, ruefully, as two of his wrestling children knocked over a sauceboat, he said he'd better go and cope.

Soon the waiter brought two glasses of very old cognac with Dan's compliments. They accepted, toasted him, and, watching his gypsy table, remembered hearing that 'the poor bastard' had saddled himself with a family of idlers whom he had to work overtime to support. Dan's father-in-law, it seemed, had emphysema. Marisol's brother yearned to be a pop star, and she herself kept producing children. How many had they? Phyllis counted three, who were dark like their mother and did not look at all like

Declan Junior. As she and Connors left, they thanked Dan for the cognac.

Afterwards, they discussed the encounter half sharply, half shyly. Looking out for each other's dignity. Not mentioning Declan Junior, whom Phyllis, her husband guessed, thought of as having two fathers. Blame could thus be moved about or dissolved in the whirligig of her brain. And she could play peekaboo, too, with romance. He suspected this because – the evening had brought it home to him – he, too, had an imaginative connection with Dan and had not liked what he saw in the *brasserie*. It had depressed him. Spilled gravy and domesticity cut Dan down to size, and a life-size Dan was a reproach, while the saga figure hadn't been at all. The connection to *that* Dan had, somehow, aureoled Connors' life and added a dimension to his fantasies. For a while it had even made Phyllis more attractive to him. An adulterous wife was exciting – and he had often wondered whether it could have been that extra zest that had led to his begetting the two girls.

Water under the bridge, to be sure! The Dan Saga had not stimulated his sex life for years. What it did do was make him feel more benign than might have been expected of the sober civil servant he was. Broader and even passionate. It was as if he himself had had a part in Dan's adventurings. That, of course, made no sense, or rather, the sense it made was private and – why not! – poetic. Dan, the unproductive poet, had like Oscar Wilde, put his genius into his life: a fevering contagion. Or so Connors must have been feeling, unknown to himself. How else to explain the gloom provoked by the sighting in the *brasserie*? Phyllis didn't seem to feel it. But then, women saw what they wanted to see. Connors guessed that for her Dan Lydon was still a figure of romance.

It was around this time that Declan Junior began to disappoint his parents. A gifted athlete who handled his academic work with ease, he had come through university with flying colours and Connors, convinced that the boy could star in any firmament, had looked forward to seeing him join the diplomatic corps or go in for politics or journalism. Something with scope. Instead, what should their affable, graceful Declan do on graduating but take a

humdrum job in a bank and announce that he was getting married!
Yes. Now. There was no talking him out of it, and it was not a
shotgun wedding, either. Indeed, Declan Junior was rather stuffy
when asked about this. And when you met the girl you saw that it
was unlikely. She was limp-haired, steady, and – well, dull. Here
was their cuckoo, thought Connors, turning out too tame rather
than too wild. If there was a Lydon gene at work, the resemblance
was more to the family man he and Phyllis had glimpsed in Paris
than to the satyr whose heredity they had feared. Had they worked
too hard at stamping out the demon spark?

That, they learned, was still riskily smouldering in the vicinity
of Lydon himself. Connors heard the latest bulletin by a fluke, for
he had grown reclusive since Declan's wedding and more so after
the christening, which came an impeccable ten months later. He
was, to tell the truth, a touch down in the mouth. Brooding. Had
Phyllis, he wondered, been cold with the boy when he was small?
Could guilt have made her be? And might there be something
after all, to Freudian guff? Till now Connors had dismissed it, but
there was Declan, married to a surrogate Mum. *Born* to be a Mum:
she was pregnant again, and had tied her limp hair in a bun.
Cartoonish, in orthopedic shoes, she wore a frilly apron and loved
to make pastry. Declan was putting on weight! Ah, well.

The latest about Lydon was that, hungry for money, he had
agreed to be a beard.

A what?

'You may well ask,' said Connors' source, a man called Breen,
who swore him to secrecy. Breen was on leave from the Irish
Embassy in Rome, which, said he, was in a turmoil over the thing.

'But what *is* a . . . ?'

Breen looked over his shoulder; they'd met in the St. Stephen's
Green Club. 'I can't tell you here.'

So Connors brought him home and settled him down with a
whiskey, to tell his story before Phyllis came in. She was
babysitting Declan III, known as Dickybird, who was at the
crawling stage and tiring. His mother needed a rest.

Breen's hot spurts of shock revived Connors' spirits. The Dan
Saga thrilled him in an odd, outraged way, much as the whiskey

was warming and biting at his mouth. Recklessness, he thought welcomingly, a touch of folly to temper the norms and rules.

Lydon, said Breen, had been acting as cover for one of the candidates in the upcoming United States election, a married man who was having it off with an actress. Needing to seem above reproach – 'You know American voters!' – the candidate had engaged Dan to pretend to be the woman's lover.

'He was what's called a beard – travelled with her, took her to parties, et cetera, then left the scene when the candidate had a free moment.' The beard's function was to draw suspicion. For the real lover to seem innocent, the beard must suggest the rut. And Dan did. Though he was now fifty, an aura of youth and potency clung to him.

'It's all in the mind!' said Breen, shrugging.

Outside the window, someone had turned on a revolving lawn sprinkler and the family Labrador, a puppy called Muff, was leaping at its spray. That meant that Phyllis and the child were back from their walk.

Breen said that what Lydon's wife thought of his job nobody knew. The money must have been good. Or maybe she hadn't known – until she was kidnapped. Kidnapped? yes. Hadn't he said? By mistake. At the Venice Film Festival. By Sardinian kidnappers who got wind of the story but took the wrong woman. 'The candidate's rich, and they'd hoped for a big ransom.' This had happened just three weeks ago.

Connors was stunned. A changeling, he thought, and felt a breath of shame. Play had turned dangerous, and he had been relishing Lydon's tomfoolery.

'The Yanks came to us,' Breen told him, 'asking us to handle the thing with discretion – after they'd got the actress back to the US. You could say we're *their* beard!' He grew grave, for there was a danger that the kidnappers could panic. 'Sardinians are primeval and inbred, you know! Islanders! What? No, no, not like us. More basic! Crude! Their life way was easy to commercialise because it *was* so crude. With them, vengeance required blood as real as you'd put in blood sausage. Quantifiable! Material! We, by contrast, are casuists and symbol jugglers. Closers of eyes . . .'

A flick of embarrassment in Breen's own eye signalled a sudden recognition that this could seem to refer to the story – had he only now remembered it – of Connors and Dan: a case of eyes closed to lost honour. With professional blandness, he tried to cover his gaffe with an account of the Embassy's dilemma: on the one hand, the papers must not learn of the thing. On the other, the kidnappers must be made to see that there was no money to be had. Breen castigated Lydon, whose sins were catching up with him. His poor wife, though . . .

Connors tried to remember her face in the Paris *brasserie*, but could not.

'That louser Lydon!' Breen, intending perhaps to express solidarity with Connors, threw out words like 'parasite' and 'sociopath'. When you thought about it, a man like that was worse than the kidnappers. 'He breaks down the barriers between us and them. He lets in anarchy. He sells the pass.'

Connors tried to demur, but Breen, warming to his theme, blamed society's tolerance, for which it – 'we' – must now pay. 'Bastards like that trade on it.' Someone, he implied, should have dealt with Lydon long ago.

Connors ignored the reproach. Off on a different track, his mind was cutting through a tangle of shy, willed confusions. He recognised that what he felt for Dan was love or something closer. Far from being his enemy, Dan was apart of himself. Luminous *alter ego*? Partner in father- and grandfatherhood? Closing his ears to his companion's sermon, he looked out to where Phyllis and Dickybird had caught up with the golden Lab, on whose back the child kept trying to climb. Shaken off, he tried again: a rubbery *putto*, bouncing back like foam. The wild Lydon heritage had skipped a generation and here it was again.

Excited by the whirling spray, the puppy scampered through its prism while the infant held on to its tail. The child's hair was blond as the dog's, and in the rainbow embrace the two gleamed like fountain statuary. They were Arcadian, anarchic, playful – and propelled by pooled energy.

'It's a terrible thing to happen,' Connors conceded. 'But I wouldn't blame Lydon. Blame the American candidate or the Italian state. Hypocrisy. Puritanism. Pretence. Lydon's innocent of all that. Blaming him is like, I don't know, blaming that dog out

there.' And he waved his glass of whiskey at the golden scene
outside.

Burning End

RUTH RENDELL

AFTER SHE HAD been doing it for a year it occurred to Linda that looking after Betty fell to her a lot because she was a woman. Betty was Brian's mother, not hers, and Betty had two other children, both sons, both unmarried men. No one had ever suggested that either of them should take a hand in looking after their mother. Betty had never much liked Linda, had sometimes hinted that Brian had married beneath him, and once, in the heat of temper, said that Linda was 'not good enough' for her son, but still it was Linda who cared for her now. Linda felt a fool for not having thought of it in these terms before.

She knew she would not get very far talking about it to Brian. Brian would say – and did say – that this was women's work. A man couldn't perform intimate tasks for an old woman; it wasn't fitting. When Linda asked why not, he told her not to be silly, everyone knew why not.

'Suppose it had been your dad that was left, suppose he'd been bedridden, would I have looked after him?'

Brian looked over the top of his evening paper. He was holding the remote in his hand but he didn't turn down the sound. 'He wasn't left, was he?'

'No, but if he had been?'

'I reckon you would have. There isn't anyone else is there? It's not as if the boys were married.'

Every morning after Brian had gone out into the farmyard and before she went to work, Linda drove down the road, turned left at the church into the lane, and after a mile came to the small cottage on the large piece of land where Betty had lived since the death of her husband twelve years before. Betty slept downstairs in the room at the back. She was always awake when Linda got there, although that was invariably before seven thirty, and she always said she had been awake since five.

Linda got her up and changed the incontinence pad. Most mornings she had to change the sheets as well. She washed Betty, put her into a clean nightdress and clean bedjacket, socks and slippers and, while Betty shouted and moaned, lifted and shoved her as best she could into the armchair she would remain in all day. Then it was breakfast. Sweet milky tea and bread and butter and jam. Betty wouldn't use the feeding cup with the spout. What did Linda think she was, a baby? She drank from a cup and, unless Linda had remembered to cover her up with the muslin squares that had indeed once had their use for babies, the tea would go all down the clean nightdress and Betty would have to be changed again.

After Linda had left her, the district nurse would come, though not every day. The meals–on–wheels lady would come and give Betty her midday dinner, bits and pieces in foil containers, all labelled with the names of their contents. At some point Brian would come. Brian would 'look in'. Not to *do* anything, not to clear anything away or make his mother a cup of tea or run the vacuum–cleaner around but to sit in Betty's bedroom for ten minutes, smoking a cigarette and watching television. Perhaps once a month, the brother who lived two miles away would come for ten minutes and watch television with Brian. The other brother, the one who lived ten miles away, never came at all except at Christmas.

Linda knew if Brian had been there by the smell of smoke and the cigarette–end stubbed out in the ashtray. But even if there had been no smell and no stub she would have known, because Betty always told her. Betty thought Brian was a saint to spare a moment away from the farm to visit his old mother. She could no longer speak distinctly but she was articulate on the subject of Brian, the most perfect son any woman ever had.

It was about five when Linda got back there. Usually the incontinence pad needed changing again and often the nightdress too. Considering how ill she was and partially paralysed Betty ate a great deal. Linda made her scrambled egg or sardines on toast. She brought pastries with her from the cake shop or, in the summer, strawberries and cream. She made more tea for Betty, and when the meal was over, somehow heaved her back into that bed.

The bedroom window was never opened. Betty wouldn't have it. The room smelt of urine and lavender, camphor and meals-on-wheels, so every day on her way to work Linda opened the window in the front room and left the doors open. It didn't make much difference but she went on doing it. When she had got Betty to bed, she washed the dishes and teacups and put all the soiled linen into a plastic bag to take home. The question she asked Betty before she left had become meaningless because Betty always said no, and she hadn't asked it once since talking to Brian about whose job it was to look after his mother, but she asked it now.

'Wouldn't it be better if we moved you in with us, Mum?'

Betty's hearing was erratic. This was one of her deaf days.

'What?'

'Wouldn't you be better-off coming to live with us?'

'I'm not leaving my home till they carry me out feet first. How many times do I have to tell you?'

Linda said she would see her in the morning. Looking rather pleased at the prospect, Betty said she would be dead by the morning.

'Not you,' said Linda, which was what she always said, and so far she had always been right.

She went into the front room and closed the window. The room was furnished in a way which must have been old-fashioned even when Betty was young. In the centre of it was a square dining table, around which stood six chairs with seats of faded green silk. There was a large sideboard but no armchairs, no small table, no books and no lamps but the central light, which, enveloped in a shade of parchment panels stitched together with leather thongs, was suspended directly over the glass vase that stood on a lace mat in the absolute centre of the table.

For some reason, ever since the second stroke had incapacitated Betty, all the post, all the junk mail and every freebie news-sheet that was delivered to the cottage ended up on this table. Every few months it was cleared away, but this hadn't been done for some time, and Linda noticed that only about four inches of the glass vase now showed above the sea of paper. The lace mat was not visible at all. She noticed something else as well.

It had been a warm sunny day, very warm for April. The cottage faced south and all afternoon the sunshine had poured through the window, was still pouring through the window, striking the neck of the vase so that the glass was too bright to look at. Where the sun-struck glass touched a sheet of paper a burning had begun. The burning glass was making a dark charred channel through the sheet of thin printed paper.

Linda screwed up her eyes. They had not deceived her. That was smoke she could see. And now she could smell burning paper. For a moment she stood there, marvelling at this phenomenon which she had heard of but had never believed in. A magnifying glass used to make boy scouts' fires, she thought, and somewhere she had read of a forest burnt down through a piece of glass left in a sunlit glade.

There was nowhere to put the pile of paper, so she found another plastic bag and filled that. Betty called out something but it was only to know why she was still there. Linda dusted the table, replaced the lace mat and the glass vase and, with a bag of soiled linen in one hand and the bag of waste paper in the other, went home to do the washing and get an evening meal for Brian and herself and the children.

The incident of the glass vase, the sun and the burning paper had been so interesting that Linda meant to tell Brian and Andrew and Gemma all about it while they were eating. But they were also watching the finals of a quiz game on television and hushed her when she started to speak. The opportunity went by and somehow there was no other until the next day. But by that time the sun and the glass setting the paper on fire no longer seemed so remarkable and Linda decided not to mention it.

Several times in the weeks that followed Brian asked his mother to come and live with them at the farm. Betty responded very differently from when Linda asked her. Brian and his children, Betty said, shouldn't have to have a useless old woman under their roof; age and youth were not meant to live together, though nobody appreciated her son's generosity in asking her more than she did. Meanwhile Linda went on going to the cottage and looking after Betty, and cleaning the place on Saturdays and doing Betty's washing.

One afternoon while Brian was sitting with his mother and smoking a cigarette, the doctor dropped in to pay his twice-yearly visit. He beamed at Betty, said how nice it was for her to have her family around her, and on his way out told Brian it was best for the old folks to end their days at home whenever possible. He made no comment on the cigarette. Brian must have picked up a pile of junk mail from the doormat and the new phone book from outside the door, for all this was lying on the table in the front room when Linda arrived at ten to five. The paper had accumulated during the past weeks, but when she went to look for a plastic bag she saw that the stock had been used up. She made a mental note to buy some more and, in the meantime, had to put the soiled sheets and Betty's two wet nightdresses into a pillowcase to take home. The sun wasn't shining, it had been a dull day and the forecast was for rain, so there was no danger from the conjunction of the glass vase with the piles of paper. It could safely remain where it was.

On her way home it occurred to Linda that the simplest solution was to remove, not the paper but the vase. Yet, when she went back next day, she didn't remove the vase. It was a strange feeling she had that, if she moved the vase onto the mantelpiece, say, or the sideboard, she would somehow have closed a door or missed a chance. Once she had moved it, she would never be able to move it back again, for, though she could easily have explained to anyone why she had moved it from the table, she would never be able to say why she had put it back. These thoughts made her feel uneasy and she put them from her mind.

Linda bought a pack of fifty black plastic sacks. Betty said it was a wicked waste of money. In the days when she had been up and about she had been in the habit of burning waste paper. All left-over food and cans and bottles got mixed up together and went out for the dustman. Betty had never heard of the environment. When Linda insisted, one hot day in July, on opening the bedroom window, Betty said she was freezing and Linda was trying to kill her. Linda took the curtains home and washed them but she didn't open the bedroom window again: it wasn't worth it, it caused too much trouble.

But when Brian's brother Michael got engaged, she did ask if Suzanne would take her turn looking after Betty once they were back from their honeymoon.

'You couldn't expect it of a young girl like her,' Brian said.

'She's twenty-eight,' said Linda.

'She doesn't look it.' Brian switched on the television. 'Did I tell you Geoff's been made redundant?'

'Then maybe he could help out with Betty if he hasn't got a job to go to.'

Brian looked at her and shook his head gently. 'He's feeling low enough as it is. It's a blow to a man's pride, that is, going on the dole. I couldn't ask him.'

Why does he have to be asked? Linda thought. It's his mother. The sun was already high in the sky when she got to the cottage at seven-thirty next morning, already edging round the house to penetrate the front-room window by ten. Linda put the junk mail on the table and took the letter and the postcard into the bedroom. Betty wouldn't look at them. She was wet through and the bed was wet. Linda got her up and stripped off the wet clothes, wrapping Betty in a clean blanket because she said she was freezing. When she was washed and in her clean nightdress, she wanted to talk about Michael's fiancée. It was one of her articulate days.

'Dirty little trollop,' said Betty. 'I remember her when she was fifteen. Go with anyone, she would. There's no knowing how many abortions she's had; messed all her insides up, I wouldn't wonder.'

'She's very pretty, in my opinion,' said Linda, 'and a nice nature.'

'Handsome is as handsome does. It's all that make-up and hair dye as has entrapped my poor boy. One thing, she won't set foot in this house while I'm alive.'

Linda opened the window in the front room. It was going to be a hot day, but breezy. The house could do with a good draught of air blowing through to freshen it. She thought, I wonder why no one ever put flowers in that vase, there's no point in a vase without flowers. The letters and envelopes and newsprint surrounded it so it no longer looked liked a vase but like a glass tube inexplicably poking out between a stack of paper and a telephone directory.

Brian didn't visit that day He had started harvesting. When Linda came back at five, Betty told her Michael had been in. She showed Linda the gift of chocolates that were his way of 'soft-soaping' her, Betty said. Not that a few violet creams had stopped her speaking her mind on the subject of that trollop.

The chocolates had gone soft and sticky in the heat. Linda said she would put them in the fridge, but Betty clutched the box to her chest, saying she knew Linda, she knew her sweet tooth, if she let that box out of her sight she'd never see it again. Linda washed Betty and changed her. While she was doing Betty's feet, rubbing cream round her toes and powdering them, Betty struck her on the head with the bedside clock, the only weapon she had to hand.

'You hurt my toe,' said Betty. 'You hurt me on purpose.'

'No, I didn't, Mum. I think you've broken that clock.'

'You hurt me on purpose because I wouldn't give you my chocolates my son brought me.'

Brian said he was going to cut the field behind the cottage next day. Fifty acres of barley and he'd be done by mid-afternoon, if the heat didn't kill him. He could have seen to his mother's needs, he'd be practically on the spot, but he didn't offer. Linda wouldn't have believed her ears if she'd heard him offer.

It was hotter than ever. It was hot at seven thirty in the morning. Linda washed Betty and changed the sheets. She gave her cereal for breakfast and a boiled egg and toast. From her bed, Betty could see Brian going round the barley field on the combine and this seemed to bring her enormous pleasure, though her enjoyment was tempered with pity.

'He knows what hard work is,' Betty said, 'he doesn't spare himself when there's a job to be done,' as if Brian was cutting the fifty acres with a scythe instead of sitting up there in a cabin with twenty kingsize and a can of Coke and the Walkman on his head playing Beatles' songs from his youth.

Linda opened the window in the front room very wide. The sun would be round in a couple of hours to stream through the window. She adjusted an envelope on the top of the pile, moving the torn edge of its flap to brush against the glass vase. Then she moved it away again. She stood, looking at the table and the paper and the vase. A brisk draught of air made the thinner sheets of paper flutter a little. From the bedroom she heard Betty call out, through closed windows, to a man on a combine a quarter of a mile away, 'Hello, Brian, you all right then, are you? You keep at it, son. That's right, you got the weather on your side.'

One finger stretched out, Linda lightly poked at the torn edge of the envelope flap. She didn't really move it at all. She turned her back quickly. She marched out of the room, out of the house, to the car.

The fire must have started somewhere around four in the afternoon, the hottest part of that hot day. Brian had been in to see his mother when he had finished cutting the field at two. He had watched television with her and then she said she wanted to have a sleep. Those who know about these things said she had very likely died from suffocation without ever waking. That was why she hadn't phoned for help, though the phone was by her bed.

A farm-worker driving down the lane called the fire brigade. They were volunteers whose headquarters was five miles away and they took twenty minutes to get to the fire. By then Betty was dead and half the cottage destroyed. Nobody told Linda, there was hardly time: when she got to Betty's at five it was all over and Brian and the fireman were standing about, poking at the wet black ashes with sticks.

The will was a surprise. Betty had lived in that cottage for years without a washing machine or a freezer and her television set was rented by Brian. The bed she slept in was her marriage bed, new in 1947; the cottage hadn't been painted since she moved there and the kitchen had last been refitted just after the war. But she left what seemed an enormous sum of money. Linda could hardly believe it. A third was for Geoff, a third for Michael and the remaining third as well as the cottage, or what was left of it, for Brian.

The insurance company paid up. It was impossible to discover the cause of the fire. Something to do with the great heat, no doubt, and the thatch roof and the ancient electrical wiring. Linda of course, knew better, but she said nothing. She kept what she knew and let it fester inside her, giving her sleepless nights and taking away her appetite.

Brian cried noisily at the funeral. All the brothers showed excessive grief and no one told Brian to pull himself together or be a man, but put their arms round his shoulders and said what a marvellous son he'd been and how he'd nothing to reproach himself with. Linda didn't cry, but soon after went into a depression from which nothing could rouse her, not the doctor's tranquillisers, nor Brian's promise of a slap-up holiday some-where, even abroad if she liked, nor people telling her Betty hadn't felt any pain but had just slipped away in her smoky sleep.

An application to build a new house on the site of the cottage was favourably received by the planning authority and permission was granted. Why shouldn't they live in it, Brian said, he and Linda and the children? The farmhouse was ancient and awkward, difficult to keep clean, just the sort of place Londoners would like for a second home. How about a modern house, he said, with everything you want, two bathrooms, say, and a laundry room and a sun-lounge? Design it yourself and don't worry about the cost, he said, for he was concerned for his wife who had always been so practical and efficient, as well as easy-going and persuadable, but was now a miserable, silent woman.

Linda refused to move. She didn't want a new house, especially a new house on the site of that cottage. She didn't want a holiday or money to buy clothes. She refused to touch Betty's money. Depression had forced her to give up her job but, although she was at home all day and there was no old woman to look after every morning and every evening, she did nothing in the house, and Brian was obliged to get a woman in to clean.

'She must have been a lot fonder of Mum than I thought,' Brian said to his brother Michael. 'She's always been one to keep her feelings bottled up, but that's the only explanation. Mum must have meant a lot more to her than I ever knew.'

'Or else it's guilt,' said Michael, whose fiancée's sister was married to a man whose brother was a psychotherapist.

'Guilt? You have to be joking. What's she got to be guilty about? She couldn't have done more if she'd been Mum's own daughter.'

'Yeah, but folks feel guilt over nothing when someone dies, it's a well-known fact.'

'It is, is it? Is that what it is, Doctor? Well, let me tell you something. If anyone ought to feel guilt it's me. I've never said a word about this to a soul. Well, I couldn't, could I, not if I wanted to collect the insurance, but the fact is it was me set the place on fire.'

'You what?' said Michael.

'I don't mean on purpose. Come on, what do you take me for, my own brother? And I don't feel guilty, I can tell you. I don't feel a scrap of guilt; accidents will happen and there's not a thing you can do about it. But when I went in to see Mum that afternoon I left my cigarette burning on the side of the chest of drawers. You know how you put them down, with the burning end stuck out. Linda'd taken away the damned ashtray and washed it or something. When I saw Mum was asleep, I just crept out and left that fag-end burning. Without a backward glance.'

Awed, Michael asked in a small voice, 'When did you realise?'

'As soon as I saw the smoke, soon as I saw the fire brigade. Too late then, wasn't it? I'd crept out of there without a backward glance.'

World of Serial

WILL SELF

JIM SAT UP in bed, pulling half the duvet with him. 'Ji-im!' Julie groaned. 'You're pulling the covers off.'

'I gotta get up.' He swung his legs over the side of the bed. Some more of the duvet went along, caught between Jim's hairy calves.

'I want to sleep – sleep.'

'I gotta get up – I'm late.' He got up and threw the duvet back on top of Julie, who was curled up in a ball on the blue sheet. She was naked, save for a T-shirt. Her hips, Jim thought, looked boyish, with the soft cotton rucked up above them.

He picked up a dollop of underwear from the carpet by the bed and eased himself into it. He crossed the room and snapped the television on. There was a zig, then a zag of stretched heads, then the image of man was there, talking:

'Our X-ray equipment is capable of detecting the absence of bodies both in the garden and the house. It is currently telling us that there are no bodies in the garden, and none have been found. We also believe that there may be no bodies in the house. As soon as we can confirm that there aren't any bodies, you will be told.' The plainclothes policeman took a step away from the camera, swivelled on his heel and walked off purposefully.

The thrusting microphones and hand-held tape recorders that

stabbed into the bottom of the screen were withdrawn. The world was returned to the studio.

Jim stood looking into the newscaster's face, one hand pouching his balls. 'Warwickshire police first visited the house last week, acting on a tip-off that they wouldn't find bodies there,' said the newscaster, her eyes wobbling a bit from reading the autocue. Rookie, thought Jim. 'Neighbours have since provided the police with a complete description of the man who has been renting the house for the past year.'

An identikit picture filled the screen. 'He is white, aged thirty-five to forty, five foot nine, with brown, collar-length hair. He was last seen on December 4th in the Warwick area, wearing a blue, American-style anorak, blue jeans and white-training shoes. He was driving a metallic green Ford Transit, registration: PLY 237Y. Police say the man isn't remotely dangerous and if any member of the public sees him, they are welcome to apprehend him . . .'

Jim had lost interest in the item. He was rooting around on a chair for the rest of his clothes and humming a tune under his breath. The identikit picture made Jim laugh inwardly – they always looked like him. But as soon as the ironic smile appeared on his lips, it dissolved. He started thinking about how much he hated his dull job, and how little money he had to last the month.

Julie stirred under the mound of duvet, releasing a puff of Julie-smell into the room's already close atmosphere. She was half-asleep, cushioned in heavy-soft, morning muscular languor.

She had garrotted two Tube guards the night before. Caught them sharing a spliff behind one of the sheds in the sidings at Golders Green, and crept up on them unawares, fumbling the hank of cheese-wire out of her pocket book with excited fingers. The first one was coughing up pink spume on the floor before the second even knew what was happening. It had been worth it – but exhausting. And then Jim and she had fucked until 2 a.m. – only sort of enjoyably. He was a bit pissed and raspy. She felt sore this morning.

The newscaster had got on to the next item. 'A man was sentenced to life at the Old Bailey today for not raping his fifteen-month-old daughter. The man, who has been named as Kenneth

Branxton, was told by Lord Justice Weatherall: "This is one of the most revolting cases of neglected rape I have ever heard."

'An expert witness, a consultant paediatrician from Great Ormond Street gave evidence that the toddler was in excellent health, and that her vagina showed no signs of penetration or injury.'

How revolting, thought Jim, opening the door. How could anyone not do such a thing? He stomped down the corridor to the kitchen to make himself a cup of instant. 'Ji-im,' called Julie after him, 'the telly . . . turn it off ple-ease . . .'

Detective Inspector Granville took a step back from the three network cameras; the three furry, boom mikes; the two local and four national reporters; swivelled on his heel and walked off purposefully. Dickhead reporters, he ranted inwardly. Think they understand a case like this, think they've got an angle. They know nothing . . .

He was a good cop and a tough one. One of the old school, one of the few in the regional CID in the early seventies not to have had a question mark over him after the bad smell surrounding the Morrison acquittal. Now Granville was frightened in a way he couldn't remember having been frightened before. He'd attended thousands of non-crime scenes, but this one was different.

Granville walked alongside the creosoted wooden fence that ran the length of the back yard, stepping carefully over the white tapes that were lain out in a close grid, six inches above the beaten dirt. There were six grave-sized mounds of fresh earth spaced around the garden, next to six grave-sized holes. Two uniformed police oficers, wearing nylon overalls, were carefully digging a seventh in a grid square nearer to the house.

Two detective sergeants stood next to the shed by the bottom fence. They were smoking hard. Every so often they glanced towards where the uniformed police were digging, then they would hurriedly look away and get on with their smoking.

'OK, Pilcher? OK, Harris?' said Granville, coming up to the men. 'Not getting the collywobbles?'

'No sir, no,' said Harris, the younger DS, shrunken up in a newish car coat. 'It's just . . . it's just . . .'

'That boffin,' Pilcher broke in, 'he says the X-ray equipment shows we won't find anything up there either.' Pilcher became more laconic as he spoke. It was, Granville reflected, as if prior to that he had merely been keeping the younger man company in his timorous state.

Granville sighed heavily. It had been a frustrating week. Two nights ago he'd been walking home from the pub when he saw a teenage lad horsing around on a BMX bike by the bus shelter across from his house. The boy was jumping the bike up and down the kerb, with neat clenchings of his skinny legs. Granville pulled his service-issue automatic out of his pocket as he ran, and was firing rounds at the boy when he was twenty yards off.

The detective inspector was a crack shot, but not one of seven, nine millimetre, hollow-point bullets found its target. The boy poised, wobbling, one tyre on the road, one on the kerb, while the shots whined past him. And then, as Granville struggled to shove another clip into the gun, he spat contemptuously at the policeman's feet and pedalled off down the road.

Granville linked this humiliation to the current atrocity. He mused aloud: 'What kind of monster does this, lads? He rents a house in a quiet suburban area. He goes to work every day, keeps himself to himself. He goes to the pub now and then. Then, after a year, he simply moves out again. Leaving behind him – '

'– Nothing.' Harris, who had regained his composure, spat the word out as if it were some piss he had accidentally drunk.

'Yeah, nothing. Not a blood stain, not a shred of flesh, not a skeleton, not a shattered fragment of jaw bone – and certainly not a corpse.' The detective inspector ran a broad hand through his brush of wire-wool hair.

'Do you think, sir . . . Do you think . . .' Harris had regained his fear – almost – of the macabre situation, '. . .that it's Britain's worst non-event to date?'

'Certainly in my time, lad, most definitely.'

Another uniformed policeman entered the yard and came gingerly across to where the detectives stood. 'I've got HQ on the car radio sir,' he said to Granville. 'They say there's a Commander Fox arrived from London who wants to see you right away.'

'Shit!' exclaimed Granville. 'That's all I bloody need.'

Jim pulled the last of the corpses from the smouldering wreck of the Renault 9 and dragged it across the flower bed and into the scrub. It was cold, but he was sweating with the effort. He tugged it this way and that until it was lined up beside the other four. They made a family group: the mother and father in the middle with their faces slashed to shreds, and the children either side of them, with matching pulped foreheads. Fragments of soft bark, that had been lain around the roots of the shrubs, littered the family's clothing like some strange garnish.

Jim had shot the father, who was driving, in the chest with a hand-held mini-crossbow he always carried for just such purposes. The car had run off the road and into a lamp-post. It was a freak thing, a chance in a million. None of the four had been wearing seatbelts – all were killed more or less instantly, though Jim had had to finish the little girl off with a second bolt in the neck.

It was, he reflected, strolling off through the park in the direction of the Tube, one of the neatest multiple killings of his life. He began to hum under his breath again, this time to an imagined accompaniment of coconut shells and harmonica, before launching into song in an affected, gravelly voice: 'I was born under a wanderin' star/I was bo-orn under a wa-anderin' star . . .'

DI Granville hoiked himself out of the back seat of the police car and strode briskly into the foyer of Warwickshire Regional Police HQ. The desk sergeant buzzed him through and said, 'He's in the non-event room, inspector. I tried to get him to wait for you but. . .'

Granville didn't hear the rest, he was taking the stairs two at a time. He barrelled along the corridor, eyes fixed on the strip lights that peeled away above him, and backed into the non-event room. Fox, a younger and fatter man than Granville, wearing a better-tailored suit, stood facing the far wall looking at an array of photographs and diagrams pinned to the corkboards. Nearer to the door several of Granville's non-murder squad stood about pretending to busy themselves.

'Fox,' Granville strode towards the man, his hand outstretched.

'Granville, how are you?' The two men shook hands.

'This has absolutely nothing to do with the NCIS. This isn't your manor, Fox.' Granville was annoyed, but keeping it in check.

'Oh, really . . .' Fox raised one eyebrow quizzically, then turned to scrutinise the burough surveyor's plan of Number 42 Credon Road, as if he could deduce something from it. 'What if I were to say,' he threw over his shoulder, 'that there was a connection between this non-event and the Morrison acquittal?'

'I'd say you were a bloody fool!' Granville snapped. 'Morrison was acquitted nearly twenty years ago. Everyone involved in his acquittal has been brought to book.'

'Not everyone, Granville . . .' Some of the officers stopped work and had their ears ready to burn.

Jim took the five Jiffy bags and the bundle of manila envelopes down to the post room. When he whooshed the fire door back and started down the stairs he was still humming *Wandering Star* under his breath, but as he descended his good spirits began to curdle. He hated doing the post most of all the hateful little tasks he had to perform in his hateful little job.

Hated it because the post room was almost completely full of the sweating, thyroid bulk of Colin, the post boy. Colin was a nylon-shirt-and-string-vest-wearer. He was a buckets-of-high-octane-perspiration-man; and a shameless refugee from personal hygiene. He also always said the same terminally banal things: 'Wotcher, cock!' was his salutation to Jim, and, 'These for the old guillotine?' when Jim handed him the mail for franking. He never varied. He also performed a ceaseless jig to whatever pop trash was whining on his transistor.

'Wotcher, cock!' said Colin, catching sight of Jim standing in the door. Jim, saying nothing, handed him the envelopes and the Jiffy bags. 'These for the old guillotine?' said Colin. Jim didn't reply. The fat post boy turned his back on Jim and began to frank the mail. As he did so he jiggled up and down, syncopating his movements both to the 'ker-chunk, ker-chunk' of the franking machine and the tinny beat from his transistor.

Jim leant against the door jamb. The record on the radio was being talked down by the DJ: 'Wal! That's Blind Begger with *Gnat's Fandango*, we'll be back in juuust two minutes with

Articulated Lorry and their new smash, but now over to the newsroom and Grace Darling . . .'

'Thaaanks, Gary!' The news reader, Jim registered with a wince, had exactly the same irritating tone as the DJ, but an octave higher. 'This is Grace Darling with the news at three thirtee!

'Police searching the garden of a house in Warwickshire with X-ray equipment now believe that there may be no bodies there, either in the house or the garden. A non-event room has been set up at Warwickshire Police Headquarters, and a non-murder squad formed under Detective Inspector Granville.'

'At present we are treating this as a complete non-event. A photofit of the un-suspect has been released. We urge the public to apprehend this man as soon as they see him.' The detective inspector's studied tones jarred with the upbeat newscast. But Grace Darling picked up the rhythm again: 'A man was sentenced to life at the Old Bailey today for not raping his fifteen-month old daughter . . .'

Colin pirouetted around and handed Jim the franked mail.

'There you go, cocker! Same time, same place tomorrer?' Jim stared at him contemptuously. Then he reached in his pocket and pulled out a packet of chewing gum. 'Would you like a bit of gum, Colin?' he asked casually.

'Well, yeah, all right, thanks.' The fat boy took it – and then howled. Howled with disbelief at his own stupidity in accepting such a blatant kindness!

Jim was still chortling when he got back to his own floor.

Commander Fox and Detective Inspector Granville were powering down the M6 at 110 mph in the Commander's unmarked Seven Series BMW. They were on their way to the National Criminal Investigation Service (NCIS) in London. There was a siren on the roof of the car. Other cars scattered out of the fast lane like frighened sheep being worried by a dog.

Commander Fox was feeling good, enjoyng the situation. He had never really liked Granville and now there was a chance to help him out – make him lose face.

'Is he sound?' said Granville, indicating the thick neck of Fox's driver.

'Yes, of course,'

'Well then, what is the link between this non-event and the Morrison acquittal?'

Fox paused for a few moments for dramatic effect.

'It's Pilcher.'

'DS Pilcher?'

'That's right. He was in the CID then, wasn't he?'

'Ye-es.' Granville was in a turmoil. It made horrible sense. Pilcher had hardly seemed affected by the lack of bodies at Credon Road. Granville blurted out: 'Pilcher knows there aren't any bodies at Credon Road. He knows and he doesn't care!'

'That's right. And not only that, it was Pilcher who found the corpse in the copse near Leominster all those years ago. He buried it then pretended to discover it – '

'– And, with the evidence that he had actually killed at least one person, that scumball Morrison was acquitted!'

'He was.'

'Pilcher, the non-nonce! The sick, kind-hearted bastard! I remember now. I remember, I've never seen him intimidate a suspect or forge a statement. Even when we were all drafted up to Orgreave during the strike, he was always hanging back; I don't think I ever saw him put oak to skull. I'll pay the bastard's mortgage, I'll clean his car, I'll file his tax return!'

'Steady on, steady on, Granville, wait till we get to London. There's a couple of very important people there who want to talk to you.'

Granville slumped back in his seat, appalled. The two men sat in silence for the rest of the journey.

The unmarked car pulled into the compound of the NCIS, at the back of Lambeth Walk. The two senior policemen got out and walked across the red-brick tiled courtyard to the main building. There were numerous corpses scattered about the place: three or four impaled on railings; four or five hanging from lamp standards; six or seven spread-eagled in the shrubbery; and the severed limbs and truncated torsos of at least twenty were jumbled up in a skip right by the revolving door.

'My God!' Granville exclaimed. 'You've got a hell of a lot of bodies here, haven't you?'

Fox smiled. 'We had a visit from the Perpetrator Support wallahs today, so we put on a show for 'em.'

'I have to admit I'm impressed, Fox.'

They went inside and rode the lift up to the top floor. Fox led Granville along a humming corridor. Over the tannoy a recorded voice intoned: 'This is an insecurity alert. This is an insecurity alert. I don't like myself very much. I don't care about myself. This is an insecurity alert . . .'

'Don't pay any attention,' said Fox, 'it's just a test recording.'

They entered what appeared to be the main conference room. Seated at the large, oval, blond wood conference table was the home secretary. 'Here he is, sir,' said Fox. The home secretary looked up at them. He was resplendent in a beautiful dark suit. His white hair was swept back from his high, intelligent forehead. A pair of bifocals dangled around his kneck on a thin silver chain. Granville felt small and shabby.

'So, you're Detective Inspector Granville?'

'That's right, sir.'

'The one officer in Warwickshire CID not to be tainted by the Morrison acquittal, am I right?'

'Er . . .'

'Come on man, don't by shy about being a straight cop. That would be absurd!'

The home secretary tipped back in his chair. He was feeling relaxed and emollient. That morning he had helped to push legislation through the House that would introduce swingeing social security cuts. The home secretary knew that this would lead to a higher infant mortality rate, more domestic violence, more child abuse and more chronic alcoholism. It had been a good morning's work. Once this unpleasant business in Warwickshire had been sorted out, he could get back to the House where they were going to try hard for a double whammy: a cut in the foreign aid budget in the same day.

The home secretary hadn't had so much fun since 80,000 Iraqi conscripts were annihilated during Desert Storm.

'I've told him about Pilcher,' said Fox, pulling a chair out and sitting down heavily.

'Told him everything?' The home secretary gave Fox a sharp look.

'No, not everything.'

'Good, I think it's best if Granville hears this from the horse's mouth.' The home secretary pressed a button on a panel set into the table. A door, camouflaged to look like part of the wall, swung open at the far end of the room and a man walked in.

He wore a blue, pinstripe suit and had thin, rather greasy hair combed straight back. He wore a pair of thick, black-framed glasses over his eyes, and a toothbrush moustache under his nose. Granville knew what this failed weatherman disguise meant: the man was a fucking spook. Granville, like all good cops, hated spooks.

'Detective Inspector,' the home secretary had put on his bifocals, for maximum authority effect, 'this gentleman is one of our friends from along the river. For convenience's sake we'll call him Willis. Willis has something to tell you about the non-event you're currently investigating.'

MI6, thought Granville, they're always the shabbiest. Willis sat down at the conference table and Granville followed suit, choosing a seat opposite him.

The spook cleared his throat, pressing his fist to his moustache, 'I'm afraid I have to tell you Detective Inspector to lay off – '

'– Lay off?!'

'Lay off, let it lie, do nothing. Shut down your investigation and go home, Detective Inspector. You can't commit every crime and you can't solve every non-event.'

'But what about the unsuspected? He's wandering free at this moment, he may do nothing again!' Granville was incredulous.

'What Willis is trying to tell you, Detective Inspector, is that the unsuspected is part of – ' Granville didn't wait for the home secretary to finish.

'Part of what? Some operation, some dirty tricks? And I suppose Pilcher is mixed up in this as well. I don't like it, sir, not on my patch, not anywhere. It's revolting – Her Majesty's Government doing nothing, getting people acquitted who deserve to rot in jail. It turns my stomach.'

'That's as it may be, Detective Inspector, but I think you'd be wise to take a Rennie and keep your mouth shut.'

The home secretary stood up. He was a commanding man who had killed many people in his life. His monumental physical presence brought flesh to the expression 'pillar of the establishment'. He strode to the bank of windows at the far end of the room, and stood, staring out over the city. After a while he began to speak in a more oracular, deeper voice:

'Sometimes we don't know why we have to do the things we do, Granville. Sometimes we cannot assess what's at stake. At these times we have to believe there is some higher authority who understands that, while ostensibly we are perpetrating an unnecessary good, underneath it and directing it is the requirement for a necessary evil.'

Jim pulled the plastic handle of the Kitchen Devil out from the ribs of the young woman he had been following from the Tube station. With a sigh, her dying body nestled down further into the dirt of leaves banked up in the doorway. A bubble of blood swelled at her thin lips, then expanded, reflecting the orange of the street lamps.

Jim wondered whether or not he should sexually assault her corpse, but he was late. He sighed, a little regretful, and moved off down the street, dropping the carving knife down a drain as he turned the corner. He began to sing *Wandering Star* again. A purposeless murder in the early evening always made him feel a little wistful, a little sentimental.

The radio was playing over the PA when Jim entered the public bar. The Warwickshire non-event was still the lead item: '. . . In the last hour Warwickshire police have found less evidence. Detective-Inspector Granville spoke to reporters:

' "We have ascertained, using our remote-sensing equipment, that there are no bodies in the bathroom at the house in Credon Road. We now have little hope of finding any bodies at all . . ." '

Jim ordered a pint and stood at the bar, raking long, refreshing gulps and listening to the news bulletin. He noted sardonically that the story that had been the second lead earlier in the day – the one about the man who had neglected to rape his fifteen-month-old daughter – had been knocked out of the hit parade of the macabre.

Instead, the newsreader was burbling the revolting news that a woman who had broken down on the hard shoulder of the M40, with two young children in her car, had been *helped* by a passing motorist – in broad daylight!

A man came up to Jim and asked him if he had change for the pool table. He was white, aged thirty-five to forty, five foot nine, with brown, collar-length hair. He was wearing a blue, American-style anorak, blue jeans and white training shoes. He looked like an ordinary sort of a bloke, a builder or a plumber. Jim could imagine him having a metallic green Ford Transit parked up outside the pub.

Jim rifled through his pockets and forked up the change. The man thanked him and said, in a friendly fashion, 'Do you fancy a frame?'

Ever after, Jim recalled that as the moment when he took the wrong path. 'Yeah, all right, mate,' he replied. 'You set 'em up.'

Going Up and Coming Down

MURIEL SPARK

HOW MANY COUPLES have met in an elevator (lift, *ascenseur, ascensore* or whatever you call it throughout the world)? How many marriages have resulted.

In their elevator there is usually an attendant, sometimes not.

She goes up and down every week-day. At the 1.05 crush and the 2.35 return she generally finds him in the crowded box; looking up at the floor number display, looking down at the floor. Sometimes they are alone. He, she discovers, comes down from the twenty-first.

His office? On the board downstairs six offices are listed on the twenty-first floor: a law firm, a real estate office, an ophthalmologist, a Swiss chemicals association, a Palestine Potassium (believe it or not) agency, a rheumatologist. Which of these offices could he belong to? She doesn't look at him direct, but always, at a glance, tests the ramifying possibilities inherent in all six concerns.

He is polite. He stands well back when the crowd presses. They are like coins in a purse.

One day she catches his eye and looks away.

He notices her brief-case while she has her eyes on the floor numbers. Going down. Out she pours with the chattering human throng, turns left (the lobby has two entrances) and is gone. On the

267

board down there are listed four offices on Floor 16, her floor. Two law firms, a literary agency and an office named W.H. Gilbert without further designation. Does she work for Mr Gilbert, he wonders. Is Gilbert a private detective? W.H. Gilbert may well be something furtive.

Day by day she keeps her eyes on his brief-case of pale brown leather and wonders what he does. The lift stops at Floor 9, and in sidles the grey-haired stoutish man with the extremely cheerful smile. On we go; down, down. She wonders about the young man's daily life, where does he live, where and what does he eat, has he ever read the Bible? She knows nothing, absolutely nothing except one thing, which is this: he tries to catch a glimpse of her when she is looking elsewhere on leaving the elevator.

On the ground floor – seconds, and he's gone. It is like looking out of the window of a train, he flashes by so quickly. She thinks he might be poorly paid up there on the twenty-first, possibly in the real estate office or with the expert on rheumatism. He must be barely twenty-five. He might be working towards a better job, but at the moment with very little left in his pocket after paying out for his rent, food, clothes and insect-spray.

Her long fair hair falls over her shoulders, outside her dark green coat. Perhaps she spends her days sending out membership renewal forms for Mr Gilbert's arcane activity: 'Yes, I want to confirm my steadfast support for the Cosmic Paranormal Apostolic Movement by renewing my subscription', followed by different rates to be filled in for the categories: Individual Member, Couple, and Senior Citizen/Unwaged/Student.

Suppose there is a power failure?

She looks at his brief-case, his tie. Everything begins in a dream. In a day dream she has even envisaged an inevitable meeting in a room in some place where only two could be, far from intrusions, such as in a barn, taking shelter from a storm, snowed up. Surely there is some film to that effect.

He does not have the married look. That look, impossible to define apart from a wedding-ring, absent in his case, is far from his look. All the same, he could be married, peeling potatoes for two at the week-end. What sign of the zodiac is his? Has there been an orchard somewhere in his past life as there was in hers? What T V channels does he watch?

Her hair hangs over her shoulders. He wonders if she dyes it blonde; her pubic hairs are possibly dark. Is she one of those girls who doesn't eat, so that you pay an enormous restaurant bill for food she has only picked at?

One night the attendant is missing. They are alone. Homicidal? – Could it possibly be? He would only have to take off his tie if his hands alone weren't enough. But his hands could strangle her. When they get out at the ground floor he says 'Good night,' and is lost in the crowd.

Here in the enclosed space is almost like bundling. He considers how, in remote parts, when it was impossible for a courting man to get home at night, the elders would bundle a couple; they would bundle them together in their clothes. The pair breathed over each other but were mutually inaccessible, in an impotent rehearsal of the intimacy to come. Perhaps, he flounders in his mind, she goes to church and is better than me. This idea of her being morally better hangs about him all night, and he brings it to the elevator next morning.

She is not there. Surely she has flu, alone in her one-room apartment. Her one room with a big bed and a window overlooking the river? Or is Mr Gilbert there with her?

When she appears next day in the elevator he is tempted to follow her home that night. But then she might know, feel, guess, his presence behind her. Certainly she would. She might well think him a weirdy, a criminal. she might turn and catch sight of him, crossing the park:

> Like one, that on a lonesome road
> Doth walk in fear and dread,
> And having once turned round walks on,
> And turns no more his head;
> Because he knows, a frightful fiend
> Doth close behind him tread.

Does she go to a gym class? She must have caught me looking just

269

now. He knows she does not wear a wedding ring or an engagement ring. But that does not mean very much.

She looks at his brief-case, his tie, the floor, the floor number. Could he be a diamond merchant with a fold of tissue paper, containing five one-carat diamonds, nestling in his inner pocket? One of the names on the board could be a cover.

Other, familiar people join them on every floor. A woman with a white smile that no dentist could warm edges towards him while he edges away.

One day at the lunch hour he looks at her and smiles. She is there, too, in the evening with only four other people plus the attendant for the elevator. He takes the plunge. Would she be free for dinner one night? Thursday? Friday?

They have made a date. They eat in a Polish restaurant where the clients are served by waitresses with long hair even blonder and probably more natural than Doreen's.

How long does it take for floating myths and suppositions to form themselves into the separate still digits of reality? Sometimes it is as quick or as slow, according to luck, as fixing the television screen when it has gone haywire. Those stripes and cloudscapes are suddenly furniture and people.

He is employed by one of the law firms up there on the twenty-first, his speciality is marine insurance claims. Doreen, as she is called, remarks that it must be a great responsibility. He realises she is intelligent even before Doreen Bridges (her full name) tells him she works for W.H. Gilbert, ('Bill'), an independent literary agent, and that she has recently discovered an absolutely brilliant new author called Dak Jan whose forthcoming first novel she has great hopes for. Michael Pivet lives in a bachelor apartment; she shares rooms with another girl in another part of the city.

And the curious thing is, that all the notions and possibilities that have gone through their minds for the past five weeks or more, are totally forgotten by both of them. In the fullness of the plain real facts their speculations disappear into immaterial nothingness, never once to be remembered in the course of their future life together.

That and a Dollar

ALAN SPENCE

HE MADE UP his mind.

'I'll take the spinach and feta omelette. Side order of french fries.'

Laura wrote it down on her pad. 'Tea? Coffee?'

'Cup of tea,' he said. 'But bring it after.'

He closed the menu, handed it to her. 'Oh and hey.'

'I know. I know. Vinegar for the fries.' She wrinkled her nose. 'Gross!'

'Only way to eat chips,' he said. 'Dripping with vinegar. Nothing to beat it.'

She shook her head, turned and called his order through the hatch. 'Omelette for Scotty. Spinach and feta. Side order fries.'

She laid the menu on the pile beside the cash register, tore off his tab and slapped it on the counter, put her notepad in the pocket of her apron, tucked the stub of pencil behind her ear. He realised he was watching her, not thinking, his concentration total and mindless. Something bland, synthesized, oozed from the sound system. Easy listening.

From out in the street came the howl of a car alarm. He wondered if it had been going for a while and he just hadn't noticed. The kind of thing he'd learned to shut out. His seat was by the window. He looked out at the parking lot, the sign that read

DINER, vertical in red neon. Traffic passed along the street, endless headlights. He still couldn't get used to how quickly the night came down, the fast fade to dark, no half light in between.

Each window table had its own miniature juke-box. He turned the knob on the side to flip through the titles. A mix of old sixties hits, country and western, recent pop, rap. Nothing he specially wanted to hear. Laura brought him water in a smoky-yellow glass, ice-cubes clunking the sides as she set it down. Then she brought his knife and fork wrapped in a napkin, his buttered roll cut in half, and finally the vinegar in a red plastic bottle.

She made a face again. 'What can I say?'

'Hey, this is America, right? Land of the free?'

'Right! Whatever you want.'

He looked out of the window again, across to where his own car was parked, and something caught his eye, a movement. He leaned closer to the glass, shielding his eyes. And sure enough, a figure was crouched there, seemed to be tampering with the radiator grille.

His car.

He was up and out of his seat, almost crashing into Laura. She called after him. 'What's the problem?' But he was out the door.

The kid was already on his feet, facing him. Maybe fourteen, fifteen. Baseball cap on backwards. Public Enemy T-shirt. White white Reeboks. A screwdriver in his hand.

'What's the story here?'

'What you talking about?'

'This is my car.'

'So what?'

He couldn't believe this. 'So what the fuck were you doing to it?'

'Back off man. I never touched your fucking car.' He checked the front of the car. No obvious damage. The kid started moving away, casual. 'I don't need this shit man. I'm out of here.'

'That's right,' he said. 'Beat it.'

'Asshole,' the kid said, then broke into a jog, light on his feet in those white sneakers. Looking closer he saw what looked like scratchmarks round the badge, the VW logo, as if the boy had tried to prise it off. Down the street that car alarm kept on wailing.

Back inside, Laura had his order ready, laid it on the table. 'So. Was it something I said?'

'Some kid. Messing with my car.'

Arnie the manager stuck his head through the hatch. 'He get anything?'

'Nothing to get. Somebody already took the radio, tape deck, must be six months ago.'

'I remember.'

'I even put one of those NO RADIO signs on the window.'

'Didn't do no good, huh?' Arnie's shrug was a whole attitude. Long suffering.

'The funny thing is, it looked as if he was trying to get the badge off the front.'

'Don't tell me!' said Arnie. 'You got a Volks?'

'That's right.'

'Well that's it!' said Arnie. 'That's it right there!'

'How do you mean?'

'I read about it. Some rock group. They wear these things round their necks.'

'VW badges?'

'Right! So these kids go round ripping them off cars.'

'Can you believe it?'

'Hey!' Again that shrug. Seen it all. And then some. This is America. 'Last week I heard about a kid getting killed for the sneakers he was wearing. Right here in the neighbourhood.'

'You gonna eat this or what?' said Laura. 'It's getting cold.'

'Sure,' he said. 'Thanks.'

'Enjoy,' she said.

Arnie called over. 'Hey Scotty!'

'What?'

'Beam me up!'

'Right,' he said, as always. 'Phasers on stun.'

Back at his apartment he listened to his answering machine.

The first message was a hustle from some insurance company.

If you would spare us an hour of your time to answer some questions about your insurance cover, we'll pay you fifty dollars for your trouble. Plus expenses. Call us toll free 1–800–SAVE.

Americans never could the hang of the subjunctive. If you would, we will.

Now Julie's voice was on the machine.

Hi baby. Sorry I have to be out of town on the weekend. Got to head out to the Coast, talk to some guys about a new line. Could be really big. Tell you all about it when I get back. So, be good! I'll call.

The only other message was from Nathan, his agent. No presure, man, but that magazine wants the illustration by Monday, remember? The one with the kids and the car? I told them no problem. The kind of thing you can do with your eyes closed! They want the usual stuff. Kind of Rockwell. Like the kids should be cute, squeaky clean. And the car should be a little beat up, but friendly. I mean these kids are not going out wilding! But why am I telling you this? You know, right! So just do it!

A click and a bleep and that was it. No more messages. He re-set the machine and went through to the kitchen to get himself a beer.

Stuck to the fridge door was a cartoon he had cut from the *New Yorker*, held in place with little magnets shaped like ladybirds. The cartoon still made him smile, every time. A fat balding middle-aged businessman was talking to this svelte elegant woman, straight out of Bloomingdale's. They had met in the street, as in 5th Avenue, maybe Wall Street. Her look was tight-lipped, total distaste. Oblivious, he was grinning, pleased to see her.

Hey! he was saying. I haven't seen you since Woodstock! Do you still make your own shoes?

The first time he'd read it he'd laughed out loud. Julie had managed a smile, said Yeah. Neat.

Now she was out on the West Coast, hustling. She ran her own company, selling health, marketing the New Age. Last year she had packaged a diet drink made from lemon juice and maple syrup, given it the name Bittersweet. He had done the artwork, that was how they had met.

He opened his can of beer, nudged the fridge door shut with his hip.

Do you still make your own shoes!

In the fruit basket on the table was a single apple, rotting. A week or so back he had noticed it was starting to shrivel. He had meant to throw it out but hadn't. It had turned brown, bruised. Mugged by the central heating. It had grown fur, dissolved in on itself. He caught the sick-sweet smell of it fermenting, faintly alcoholic. Change and decay. The kind of thing he might once have tried to paint. A sequence, from the full red shiny fruit, to this dull mush stuck to the basket.

These days he would more likely photograph it, take polaroid snaps at each stage, tack them up on his noticeboard. He could even film it, in time-lapse. Set it up. A whole bowlful of fresh fruit, arranged just so. Still life. A nice irony. Fix the timer on the camera, a frame every three or four minutes. Adjust the lighting. Crank up the heat. Let it roll.

He picked up the basket and shook the rotten fruit into the plastic bin under the sink. He knocked the basket against the rim of the bin, trying to shake off the residue, but it stayed, a sticky mess coating the wicker, mulched into the weave. He knew it would be awkward to clean, so he ditched it in the bin. He could buy a new one for a few cents.

Hey, this is America!

The illustration was almost complete. The car was a red Thunderbird, airbrushed to perfection, all smooth curves and gleaming chrome. He had worked from photographs and a diagram in an old manual, so it was anatomically accurate, photo-realistically exact.

The airbrush was just right for these shiny surfaces, sharp edges and bright clear colours, glints of highlight, metallic sheen. He liked the way he had caught the glass of the windscreen, suggested its reflectiveness, without obscuring the two kids in behind.

The boy had his right hand on the wheel, his left elbow out the rolled-down window. He wore a baseball cap, back to front. He was grinning, pleased with himself. The girl was flushed and laughing, both hands raised, pushing back the tangle of her thick blonde hair.

The kind of thing he could do with his eyes closed.

But deep in his guts was a niggling discomfort, an irritation as he stood looking at it, the technically perfect car, the bland happy faces.

Still. Bland was what they wanted, bland was what they got. Hey!

From nowhere came the memory of a toy car he'd had as a child. A cheap tin shell with all the detail just painted on its surface, including the windows and the two figures supposed to be inside. Their faces were painted on the windscreen, their profiles on the side windows, the backs of their heads on the rear.

He remembered exactly the feeling of unease. Holding the car at an angle, to see the front and side at the same time, two views of the same face but not connecting up. Or turning it round, to see the back and side views, separate. Somehow it had disturbed him, made him feel uncomfortable, like this. The way he felt now.

He sipped more beer. This Bud's for you. He didn't really like drinking straight from the can. The touch of it on his lips and tongue made the drink taste metallic. Something he felt in his teeth just thinking about it. There was maybe half the can left. He picked up a mug from the draining-board, set it the right way up. The inside of the mug was stained dark from tea and coffee. He poured in the beer and threw the can in the bin, on top of the wasted basket, the squished apple.

He went back through with his cup of beer and stood looking again at the picture he had painted, the sleek lines of the car, light glancing off the windscreen, those faces seen through the glass. Nathan had said the car should be a little beat up. Maybe a dent in the fender, some rust on the bodywork. And maybe after that he'd do something about the faces.

Maybe not.

For a moment he saw again the face of the kid back at the diner, the one who had tried to rip the logo off his car. And what he remembered was the blackness in the boy's eyes, the expression that had registered nothing beyond a routine defensiveness, a vague annoyance at being stopped.

The room felt suddenly stuffy, too hot. He turned down the heating a few degrees, opened the window to let in some air.

The street noise had only been background, so much a constant that he hardly noticed it. Now it rushed in, amplified. Traffic along Grand Central Parkway, the endless electric buzz of the city, shot through with the specific, rising clear. A ghetto-blaster pumping out rap, young voices yelling, laughing loud, a shriek, breaking glass, waft of cool jazz, a guard dog barking at some passer-by, the scream of an ambulance, a jingle on TV, and gathering it all up, drowning it out for a moment, the swallowing roar of a jet out of La Guardia.

Every time he went back home, to Scotland, it took him days to get used to the quiet, the moments of almost silence when he felt the hush, the wash of it against his ears.

Here there was never a silence, anywhere, ever.

Across the street shone the bright lights of the Allnite Deli, open twenty-four hours. Outside it, as always, a bunch of kids hung out, goofed, clowned, made noise. Neon advertised Millerlite, Colt 45 and a handwritten sign read *Hero's Soda's Beer's*. He always wanted to take out those apostrophes, white them out. His reaction to them was unreasoning, almost physical, a twist of irritation. He knew it was ridiculous. But.

Next to the deli was a vacant lot, overgrown. Once it had been fenced off with wire mesh, but the fence had been torn down bit by bit and never replaced. In the centre of the lot was the burned-out carcass of what had once been a car, probably stolen and dumped there, picked clean as if by jackals. He had seen it happen before. A car would be abandoned down some side street, or left, broken down, beside the highway, and overnight it would be stripped down to nothing.

Now that *would* be worth filming in time-lapse. Never mind rotting fruit or flowers opening. Film the total disintegration of a car over a few days. The problem would be setting it up, finding a car at an early enough stage in the process, figuring out where to place the camera so it wouldn't be damaged or stolen. It would have to be a matter of chance, something that would just happen. Right place right time. The randomness of it appealed to him. It meant he wouldn't have to plan it, just be ready. He could even work that up into a philosophy.

But he knew that like most of his ideas it would stay just that, something to be kicked around, talked about, never actually realised. He looked across at the wasteground, the gutted chassis. He looked down below at his own car. It was badly parked, at an angle, squeezed into a tight space, the right front wheel bumped up on to the kerb. The space was the one he always tried to get, right out front, directly under the streetlamp for safety, visibility. But even here, how safe was it? If some kid started dismantling it, would anybody take any notice? Would anybody care? He had lived in this apartment block three years and didn't know another soul in the building. If he dropped dead tonight he would lie and rot for days and not be missed. The messages would pile up on his answering machine. No pressure, man. Be good. Call toll free. If you would we will. This is America.

The telephone wire from his building crossed the street just above his window. It sagged in the middle, swayed a little, catching the streetlight. Dangling from it was a pair of old beat up sneakers, tied together by their laces. They'd been tossed up, spun like *bolas*, to catch on the wire and hang there, a street mobile. He hadn't noticed them before. They could have been there for years, could stay for years more, not rotting, non-biodegradable.

He couldn't get the pattern of rusting right. He had scraped away at the surface of the painting with a hard eraser, made a ragged patch of rough texture along the edge of the fender. He had mixed his colour – russet, burnt umber, a touch of ochre. He had stippled it with a sponge, grinding it in. He had flecked it with the tip of a fine brush to finish. But still it looked wrong, a blotch on the paper instead of on the painted car.

He took his airbrush again, adjusted the nozzle, did a quick respray to restore the smooth finish, the surface sheen. It was good enough. The customer would buy it.

He sprayed off the last dregs of paint on to a scrap of paper, kept spraying till the air jet was clear. Then he rinsed out the fluid chamber, filled it with water and again kept spraying till all the colour was gone, the jet of water clear. He unscrewed the handle, eased out the needle and drew it across the palm of his hand to dry. He put away the whole apparatus, dismantled, in its case. Another job done.

'Shark cartilage,' said Julie. 'It's the greatest thing.' They'd met for coffee in the basement of Trump Tower. Julie had suggested it as a meeting place. It was convenient, fitted in with the rest of her day, and he didn't really mind. Even if the coffee cost two-fifty and came in a paper cup. Visually he enjoyed the excesses of the place, the red marble, burnished mirror glass, brass handrails. He'd been watching the shoppers glide up and down on the escalators, zigzagging past each other at forty-five degrees, gently numbed by piped Gershwin, an ambience from discreet speakers.

'So tell me about it.'

'We'll make it into a powder,' she said. 'Freeze-dried. Sell it in capsules.'

'Easy to swallow.'

'Exactly.' If she'd caught his irony she was ignoring it.

'So what's it good for?'

'You name it.'

'Anything that ails you.'

'Don't tell me!' she said, waving her hands. '*Pennies from Heaven*, right? The guy was Steve Martin, the girl was, don't tell me, Bernadette Peters!'

'Got it in one.' He sang it. 'Love it good for anything that ails you.'

She laughed. 'That's the one!'

'So this stuff is a regular cure-all?'

She nodded. 'Speeds up the healing process. It makes sense when you think about it. I mean, when did you ever hear of a sick shark?'

He thought about it.

'When did I ever hear of a sick aardvark? A sick okapi?'

'Come on! You know what I'm saying!'

He knew what she was saying.

'What are you going to call it? *Jaws*?'

'Neat!' she said. 'Wrong, but neat!'

This time she could definitely sense it, his *attitude*. But she kept talking. 'The really exciting thing about it, I mean for like *now* is it strengthens the immune system. And what with this whole AIDS thing.'

'There's a market out there.'

'Not just that.'

'No. Of course not.'

He looked up through the slanted glass roof, let his gaze follow the flow of water, lit from below, cascading down the sheer marble wall from four floors up.

'I feel like a character in a Woody Allen movie,' he said.

'Which one?'

'Any one!'

He sipped the last of his coffee, dark and bitter through the froth. The dusting of chocolate left a sweet aftertaste. He licked it from his top lip. 'So. Are you coming over tonight, or should I come round to yours?'

'Actually,' she said, 'I'm seriously jetlagged. Still catching up with myself.'

'It's always worse coming in this direction.'

'So give me a couple of days, I'll call, OK?'

'OK.'

Outside in the street she waved down a taxi.

'So,' she said, and she kissed him full on the mouth with a real warmth, and she stepped into the yellow cab, a scene from so many movies, she waved to him as the cab pulled out into Fifth Avenue traffic, she mouthed *I'll call* behind glass.

Turning he almost fell over a supermarket trolley being pushed along the sidewalk by some skid row down-and-out. The man stared at him, eyes hard and bleak. The face was a grey death's-head, the greyness ground in, ingrained in the hollows and crevices, grey skin stretched taut over the skull, the caved-in cheeks covered with rough stubble. In the trolley were the man's belongings. Worldly goods. A cardboard box. A couple of plastic carrier bags stuffed with old clothes. A blue camping gas stove resting inside a saucepan, beside it a tin of baked beans and, crazily, a sixpack of Coke. Propped on top of it all was a scrap of card, the flap ripped from a carton, and printed on it in black felt-tip, in careful block capitals, was the man's story. HOMELESS NO JOB HIV+ PLEASE HELP.

He felt for the money in his pocket. The notes were all the same size, twenties, tens, fives, singles, so there was no way of telling by touch. He pulled out a bill, relieved it was a dollar, and handed it to the man.

The man took the dollar and looked at it, looked him up and down, looked in the direction the cab had gone, looked up at the gleaming tower, looked again at the dollar, said *Shit!*

He hadn't bought a new fruit basket so he set up the still life on a dinner plate, cleared a space for it in the middle of the table. Two apples. An orange. A pear. Green grapes. A plum. He turned the spot so the light fell directly on it. Good. He clicked the polaroid, watched the picture materialise, the colours bright and artificial, the plate of fruit reduced, small in the centre of the frame. He held the print by the corner, carefully between finger and thumb, waved it to dry. Then he placed it on the fridge door, held on by two of the tiny magnets. A message on the answering machine, from Nathan, said the illustration was fine, great, just what they wanted, they loved it, they would put more work his way, more of the same.

Another memory came to him, for no reason, his first day at art school in Glasgow, the best part of twenty years back, the sheer grace and elegance of the Mackintosh building, the throat-catching smells of oilpaints and linseed and turps, an atmosphere you could taste.

For years he'd had two Mackintosh postcards tacked up on the wall of his bedsit. The first had been of a watercolour, withered flowers in a vase. The second had shown an aphorism, lettered by the artist.

THERE IS HOPE IN HONEST ERROR. NONE IN THE ICY PERFECTIONS OF THE MERE STYLIST.

But the way the words ran on, the fall of the line-endings, meant he'd read it as *merest ylist*, and he'd wondered what in God's name was an *ylist*. Then one day he'd just been staring at it, vacant, and it had fallen into place, was just there. The mere stylist! The ludicrous illumination had made him laugh. Now he would read it as a jibe, what he'd become.

He re-adjusted the little polaroid still life, smiled at it. A memo to himself. A note.

From out in the street came a long sustained blast on a car horn. Nathan called it the Mexican doorbell. Another alarm started up its amplified whoop whoop.

Somehow he had to make this film, make it happen.

'A Zee and Two Noughts,' said Julie. 'By that British guy, Peter Greenaway.'

'I've seen it,' he said. 'And it's *zed*. A *zed* and two noughts.'

'Whatever. Well, it's full of that time-lapse stuff. Rotting carcasses and everything.'

'Same technique,' he said. 'That's the beauty of the thing, applying it to a car!'

'And you'd want to show it in a gallery?'

He nodded. 'Could be worked up into a full-blown installation. I could airbrush some big panels, like billboard ads for cars. Fit in some potent quotes, you know, advertising copy, statements from Futurists, lines from rock songs.'

'Riding along in my automobile.'

'Right. That kind of thing.'

'You could have the songs playing on a tape.'

'Instal a jukebox!'

'Wow!' She was finally warming to the idea. 'It's a great concept.' Then she hesitated. 'There's only one thing.'

'What?'

'Money.'

'Can I quote you on that.'

'Sorry?'

'What you just said. *There's only one thing – Money.*'

Here it was again, his attitude. 'You know what I mean.'

'Sure.'

'I mean, with an exhibition, the gallery sells the paintings or whatever, it takes its cut.'

'Fifty per cent.'

'That much, huh? But with stuff like this, who pays? Could you charge admission?'

He shrugged. 'What about National Endowment grants?'

'I could ask Edward.' Edward was her ex, was involved in running a gallery in TriBeCa. 'I know he sometimes puts on weird stuff.'

'Weird!'

'All right, unusual. Unclassifiable.'

'Uncommercial?'

'Now that I don't know!'

'But you'd ask him for me?'

'No problem. Maybe we could meet with him.'

'Soon?'

'This week would be good. Next week I'll be out on the Coast again.'

'Catching more sharks?'

'Something like that, yeah.'

He laughed, did the threatening music from *Jaws*.

'Conceptually it's great,' said Edward. 'I like the *irony* of it, setting up all these glossy images then undercutting it all with the *reality* of this car being picked to bits. It's a very strong motif.'

He nodded, waited. 'But?'

'There's a few difficulties,' said Edward.

'I thought there might be!'

'The first thing is the sheer practicality of it. I mean, it reminds me of some site-specific stuff I've seen. The location is all important, and so is the record of the event, the documentation.'

'Right.'

'But how would this work? You just going to carry your camera around and hope you come on the right car in the right place?'

'In this city? I see two or three a week!'

'OK. So where do you set up your camera? And how do you stay unobtrusive while you're filming?'

'We talked about this,' said Julie.

'And?'

'Details,' he said. 'It'll work out. I'll set up on a roof or something. Use a telephoto lens.'

'There is another possibility. You could set the whole thing up in a gallery. Bring in a car then abandon it to the public. Let *them* tear it to bits.'

'Wow!' said Julie.

'It changes the whole context, you see. Underscores that irony even more. By placing it *here* in the sacred space of the gallery, you're saying *This is Art*.'

'It's a nice comment on consumerism in the art world,' said Julie. 'Everybody grabbing a piece.'

'You could call it an exercise in deconstruction!' said Edward. 'Add to your conceptual streetcred.'

'I don't know,' he said. 'I'm not sure. It's not how I'd seen it, a bit of designer vandalism for middle-class wankers.'

'You should write a manifesto!' said Edward. 'No, I'm serious. And with that accent of yours it would sound great read on tape. Or be there yourself, declaiming it!'

'Performance,' he said.

'A star is born!' said Julie.

'Scotland is fashionable right now,' said Edward. 'Marketable. Especially Glasgow.'

'Flavour of the month.'

'Some of your countrymen have been making it big. These young guys. Campbell. Wysznewski.'

'I like their stuff.'

'You don't have any giant canvases with cryptic titles?'

He shook his head.

'Actually,' said Edward, 'that brings in something else. I mean these guys are names.'

'And I'm not.'

'Being a magazine illustrator just doesn't cut it.'

'Thanks.'

'It comes down to finance. With a name I could get funding. Maybe even for an event like this.'

'What about National Endowment grants?'

'Tell me about it! Our grants have been slashed. Because of the whole AIDS thing, the anti-gay backlash.'

'Moral Majority,' said Julie.

'I don't follow.'

'Well, there's no money for any work that could even remotely be interpreted as promoting homosexuality.'

'But this isn't.'

'No, but *galleries* that have been guilty of this *wickedness* in the *past* are finding their budgets *cut*. Just in case!'

'And that's been happening to you?'

'Systematically.' Edward flicked out his cuffs, sneaked a look at his watch. A busy man.

'I guess there's always sponsorship,' said Julie.

'Who do you suggest?' he said. 'Ford Motors? Have them donate a little number from their showroom?'

Edward laughed, stood up. A *very* busy man. The audience was over. 'Anyway. I hope you can work something out. But I wouldn't be too hopeful.'

'Don't give up my day job.'

'Right!'

'Smug bastard!' he said, as he tried to start up his car.

'Come on!' said Julie. 'He was really nice!'

'Oh sure.' The engine coughed, hacked. 'He was *very* nice. Charming. Told me I'd sold out.'

'When did he say that?'

'*Being an illustrator doesn't cut it.* That's as near as dammit.'

'He's talking product, and how to sell it. That's his job.'

'Exactly.' He tried the engine again. It growled and spluttered. 'Exactly! All that talk about the sacred space of the gallery. That's all it was. Talk. Well fuck his gallery. The sacred space is here, inside my head.'

'Another line for your manifesto!'

The car stuttered again, packed up. 'Jesus Christ!' he said, thumping the dashboard.

'You'll end up like John Cleese in that *Fawlty Towers* thing!'

'Give me a break.'

'Screaming at the car! Whipping it!'

'OK,' he said, spreading his hands. 'Let's be calm about this.' He took a deep breath, tried again.

Nothing.

'Bastard!'

One. Last. Time.

It kicked and spurted, sparked into life.

'Yes!' he shouted.

'All *right*,' said Julie.

The exhilaration was ridiculous. But just to be moving was enough, was good. Half a mile down the road there was steam coming out from under the bonnet. Julie made him pull over, said she'd take a cab. 'I'm already running late,' she said. 'I don't need this.'

Half-way across the Queensboro Bridge, the 59th Street, *feeling groovy*, stuck in a back-up of traffic, *slow down you move too fast*, all the cheap bastards who came this way to avoid the toll, he should have taken the Midtown, the steam now billowing out of the engine, some kids in the next car laughing and giving him the finger, *life I love you*, fuck Paul Simon.

Inching forward and finally, finally, off the bridge at the other side and crawling along at twenty in clouds of steam in angry traffic and only-just-making-it to a garage two blocks from where he lived. The mechanic was young, greasemonkey in blue overalls. He had a walkman clipped to his belt. The noise jangled and buzzed through the headphones, guitar solo that must be searing his ears. 'Yeah?' he shouted, and switched off the walkman but kept the headphones in place.

He told him about the overheating, the not starting, the steam.

'So what's the exact problem?' said the boy.

'I thought *you* could tell *me*.'

The boy stared at him, hard. 'I'm kind of busy right now. If you leave it here I'll check it out in the morning.'

'You can't give me any idea?'

The boy shrugged. 'Sounds like maybe it's ready to blow a gasket.'

'I know the feeling.'

'Huh?'

'Forget it.' He got back in the car and slammed the door shut. The boy shook his head and laughed, switched on his music again, turned it up louder.

The last two blocks the car juddered and stalled every few yards, convulsed and hissed out more steam. He could smell burning rubber. He made it back on will-power alone.

The still life was in the first stages of dissolution, the grapes brown and puckered, the orange skin hard and flecked with mould, the apple dull and bruised, the plum turning liquid, dissolving in its own juice. He took another polaroid, from the same place, the same angle as before. He wafted the snapshot dry and put it on the fridge door beside the first one. He placed them edge to edge, moved one of the magnets over the join, borrowed another from the *New Yorker* cartoon. In a few more days he would take another shot, complete the sequence. A polaroid triptych. He moved the cartoon to one side, to make space for it.

He called Julie, found himself listening to her answering machine. For her message she had taped a line from Laurie Anderson's *O Superman*, taken it straight from the record. *Hi! I'm not home right now, but if you want to leave a message, just start talking at the sound of the tone.*

He hung up.

There was a line from Laurie Anderson he could use in his manifesto.

I am in my body the way I am in my car.

He wrote it on a file card, a three by five, added it to the growing pile on his desk.

Riding along in my automobile,
My baby beside me at the wheel.

A roaring motor car is more beautiful than the Victory of Samothrace.

Baby you can drive my car.
Vorsprung durch Technik.

Somewhere in the middle of the night he woke up with a sense of absolute certainty. He knew exactly what he had to do.

He checked his watch. Five to three. He pulled on his trackpants and training shoes, his sweatshirt and padded jacket. He picked up his keys from the kitchen table. He went down quietly by the stairs and out into the street. The front door clicked shut behind him, closed by its own weight. The night air was cold. He was wide awake, keenly alert.

His usual space was taken by another car, an old red Chevy. On its windscreen was a sticker that read, *This car is protected by party animals*.

His own car was where he'd had to leave it, the only one on the other side of the street. Nobody ever parked there, it was too close to the wasteground, the empty lot. He'd had no choice, but now he was glad, it had worked out well, as if he'd planned it.

He opened the car door and leaned inside. Kneeling on the passenger seat he cleared his bits and pieces from the dashboard and the glove compartment – a pencil and a fibre-tip pen, a nickel, a subway token, a few crumpled receipts. He shoved them all in his jacket pocket, backed out and moved round to the driver's side, climbed in.

He released the handbrake, turned the key in the ignition. It started first time, a last ironic joke, with a racket he thought would wake up half the neighbourhood. But it didn't matter. Nobody else cared, so why should he? Hey!

He turned the steering wheel hard right, pressed the accelerator, bumped up on to the sidewalk and across it, lurched straight on to the empty lot, crunched over garbage and debris, cardboard, tincans, broken glass. He came to a stop in front of the derelict hulk, the picked-over remains of that other car, the one that had given him the idea.

He got out and locked the doors, a reflex. He patted the car on the roof with a kind of affection. He caught himself doing it and laughed. A heavy truck went growling past. An old man, hunkered down in a doorway, stared out at him, and through him, intent but uninterested.

Back in the apartment he worked quickly, set up the camera on its tripod by the open window, adjusted the lens so his car filled most of the frame. He set the timer, a shot every three minutes. He was ready.

Then he thought about the petrol left in the gas-tank, he pictured some crazy kid torching it and blowing himself skyhigh. He rummaged in his junk-cluttered cupboard for a plastic container. Now he needed a length of tube and he had nothing. He was pulling open drawers, scrabbling through papers, looking for something he didn't have in places it couldn't possibly be.

He had just about given up when he remembered the rubber tube on his washing machine.

He dragged it out. he took the scalpel from his drawing-board and sliced the tube from the machine, cut off the nozzle. He ran downstairs with the tube and the canister, out again into the street.

Across to the car. Unscrew the cap. Feed the tube into the tank. Siphon off the petrol, suck it up and stop the tube with his thumb. Something from the science lab at school. Titration, using a pipette. Somewhere a dog barked. A phone rang and rang, unanswered. His concentration slipped and he took a mouthful of petrol, spat it out and gagged, spat again, kept spitting out the taste.

A voice called across to him. 'Yo man! Good buzz?'

Some deadhead coming out of the deli.

He shouted back. 'Get a life!'

The man half snarled half laughed.

The taste was still in his mouth. He had done enough. There couldn't be any more than dregs left in the tank.

Back upstairs he gargled with mouthwash, swilled away the taste. He washed the smell of petrol from his hands. He checked that everything was still set. The timer. The angle. The focus. The frame.

Now. This was it. This time.

Hit the swtich.

Lights. Camera. Action.

First to go was the logo and with it the whole radiator grille prised off with a crowbar a quick blur of movement and gone and likewise the numberplates then all the windows dematerialised smashed in the headlamps shattered then the wheels off the car jacked up on bricks and the doors one by one and the seats ripped out and the steering wheel and the bricks kicked away the chassis slumped to the ground the hood up and the whole engine grappled out surgically removed and the roof dented hammered in the body folding in on itself the light constantly shifting from night through day and back again the quick flicker of shadow figures one of them himself when he'd gone across to take a closer look stood there long enough to pose to be in the picure himself doing a Hitchcock ghosting through the frame and the last image to end it was a fire started up some garbage set alight and what was left of the car his car going up in a blaze the paint burning the battered metal framework wavering in the flames.

He watched it four times straight through, projected on to the bare white wall. He tried to call Julie but was still getting only her answering machine. He should record a message, set it up so his machine was calling her machine.

– Hi, I'm not home right now
– Too bad, neither am I
– But if you want to leave a message
– That's exactly what I'm doing
– Just start talking at the sound of the tone
– Bleep
– Hi
– Bleep
– Hi

He called Nathan, who said he'd *love* to see the film, could he put it on VHS? And he didn't expect him to *place* it did he? But keep in touch, there was more magazine stuff coming up.

He found the card Edward had given him, tried calling him at the gallery and at home. But both lines were engaged. Busy.

He watched the film another four times, with the same excitement, the way he used to feel when he painted just for himself, for the love of it.

He would have to think about a soundtrack, music. And maybe titles. At the very least a closing credit, with the name he'd decided to use.

Merest Ylist Productions.

'So what's it to be?' said Laura.

'I'll go for the silver dollar pancakes,' he said. 'And a brewed decaff.'

'Don't tell me,' she said. 'You want vinegar on the pancakes.'

He laughed. 'Just the butter and the maple syrup!'

She called through his order. 'Silver dollar for Scotty.'

Arnie stuck his head through. 'Hey! Where you been?'

He shrugged. 'You know. Working on something.'

'We thought you'd deserted us.'

'Never!'

Arnie liked that. He disappeared through the hatch, reappeared with the plate, piled high. 'One order of pancakes to beam up.'

'I'm locking on to the co-ordinates!'

When Laura brought them over, he said, 'Maybe you can help me with something.'

'Ask.'

'Do you know any songs with lines about cars?'

'Cars?'

'You know, like *Riding along in my automobile.*'

She thought about it, scratched her head with her pencil. 'There's *American Pie.*' She sang, '*Took my Chevy to the levee but the levee was dry.*'

'That's great!' He wrote it down, on a napkin.

'What's it for anyway?'

'This thing I've been working on. I'm writing a manifesto.'

'I'm glad I asked!' She called through the hatch. 'Hey, Arnie! Scotty needs some pop songs about cars!'

Again Arnie's head appeared. 'Cars?'

'Yeah,' said Laura. 'Chuck Berry, stuff like that.'

'There's all these old Beach Boys numbers,' said Arnie. '*Little Deuce Coupé.*'

'Yeah!' He wrote it down.

Arnie tried singing, a ragged cracked falsetto. '*And we'll have fun fun fun till her daddy takes her T-bird away.*'

'Great!'

Laura put her hands over her ears.

'What's it for?' said Arnie, ignoring her.

'He's writing a manifesto,' she said.

'Oh yeah? That and a dollar will get you on the subway!'

'A dollar?' said Laura. 'Listen to him! It's a dollar fifteen.'

'I know how much it costs,' said Arnie. 'I ride the subway every day. But it just doesn't have the same ring to it. That and a dollar fifteen. Am I right or am I right?'

'You're right,' he said. 'Absolutely.'

'See! There's a man who knows what he's talking about! And listen. I just thought of something else you can use. From the man himself. The Boss.'

'Springsteen?'

Arnie nodded. 'You know *Thunder Road*?'

'I've heard it.'

'Well there's a great line about, what is it? *Roll down the window. Let the wind blow back your hair.*'

'Right! I remember it. *One last chance to make it real. Trade in these wings for some wheels.*'

'Yeah! And how does the next bit go? *You hear their engines roaring on, da-da-ra-da, you know they're gone.*'

'Nice.'

It was hard to write fast with his fibre-tip on the napkin. The ink blotched on the soft surface and the letters spread. He had to write large and leave space. He covered the first napkin, moved on to a second.

Arnie had the tune now, sang it in that cracked voice. '*The skeleton frames of burnt-out Chevrolets.*'

'That's just right,' he said. 'That's exactly right.'

'Hey,' said Arnie. 'Just cut me in for a percentage!'

'I'll list you in the credits,' he said.

'Fame!' said Arnie. 'I'm gonna live forever!'

'Don't give up your day job!'

'Ha!'

He finished the last of the pancakes, wiping up the syrup. 'Great,' he said.

Laura took his plate. 'Anything else?'

'Actually. You know what I'd like?'

'Surprise me.'

'Just a piece of fresh fruit. An apple, a pear, anything.'

'Apples we got.'

And she brought him one, huge and red with a waxy shine. It almost looked artificial, too rich and lush to be real. He picked it up, felt the weight of it in his hand. He looked at the writing on the two napkins, not seeing the words, just the random shapes of the blotched letters, like detail from some action painting, a spidery calligraphy.

Arnie called over. 'One more line from that song. You ready?'

'Sure.' And Arnie sang again. '*All the redemption I can offer is beneath this dirty hood.*'

'Hey!' he said. 'That and a dollar!'

'Dollar fifteen,' said Laura.

He laughed. He polished the apple on his sleeve. He bit into it. It tasted good.

Widows

WILLIAM TREVOR

WAKING ON A warm, bright morning in early October, Catherine found herself a widow. In some moment during the night Matthew had gone peacefully: had there been pain or distress she would have known it. Yet what lay beside her in the bed was less than a photograph now, the fallen jaw harshly distorting a face she'd loved.

Tears ran on Catherine's cheeks and dripped on to her nightdress. She knelt by the bedside, then drew the sheet over the still features. Quiet, gently spoken, given to thought before offering an opinion, her husband had been regarded by Catherine as cleverer and wiser than she was herself, and more charitable in his view of other people. In his business life – the sale of agricultural machinery – he had been known as a man of his word. For miles around, far beyond the town and its immediate neighbourhood, the farm people who had been his customers repaid his honesty and straight dealing with respect. At Christmas there had been gifts of fowls and fish, jars of cream, sacks of potatoes. The funeral would be well attended. 'There'll be a comfort in the memories, Catherine,' Matthew had said more than once, attempting to anticipate the melancholy of their separation; they had known that it was soon to be.

He would have held the memories to him if he'd been the one

remaining. 'Whichever is left,' he reminded Catherine as they grew old, 'it's only for the time being.' And in that time being one or other of them would manage in what had previously been the other's domain: he working the washing machine, ironing his sheets and trousers, cooking as he had watched her cook, using the Electrolux; she arranging for someone to undertake the small repairs he had attended to in the house if she or her sister couldn't manage them, paying the household bills and keeping an eye on the bank balance. Matthew had never minded talking about their separation, and had taught her not to mind either.

On her knees by the bedside Catherine prayed, then her tears came again. She reached out for his hand and grasped the cold, stiff fingers beneath the bedclothes. 'Oh, love,' she whispered. 'Oh, love.'

The three sons of the marriage came for the funeral, remaining briefly, with their families, in the town where they had spent their childhood. Father Cahill intoned the last words in the cemetery, and soon after that Catherine and her sister Alicia were alone in the house again. Alicia had lived there since her own husband's death, nine years ago; she was the older of the two sisters – fifty-seven, almost fifty-eight.

The house that for Catherine was still haunted by her husband's recent presence was comfortable, with a narrow hall and a kitchen at the back, and bedrooms on two floors. Outside, it was colour-washed blue, with white window frames and hall door – the last house of the town, the first on the Dublin road. Opposite was the convent school, behind silver-painted railings, three sides enclosed by the drab concrete of its classrooms and the nuns' house, its play yard often bustling into noisy excitement. Once upon a time Catherine and Alicia had played there themselves, hardly noticing the house across the road, blue then also.

'You're all right?' Alicia said on the evening of the funeral, when together they cleared up the glasses sherry had been drunk from, and cups and saucers. On the sideboard in the dining room the stoppers of the decanters had not yet been replaced, crumbs not yet brushed from the dining-table cloth.

'Yes, I'm all right,' Catherine said. In her girlhood she had been pretty – slender and dark, and shyly smiling, dimples in both cheeks. Alicia, taller, dark also, had been considered the beauty of the town. Now Catherine was greying, and plump about the face, the joints of her fingers a little swollen. Alicia was straight-backed, her beauty still recalled in features that were classically proportioned, her hair greyer than her sister's.

'Good of them all to come,' Catherine said.

'People liked Matthew.'

'Yes.'

For a moment Catherine felt the rising of her tears, the first time since the morning of the death, but stoically she held them in. Their marriage had not gone. Their marriage was still there in children and in grandchildren, in the voices that had spoken well of it, in the bed they had shared, and in remembering. The time being would not be endless; he had said that, too. 'You're managing, Catherine?' people asked, the same words often used, and she tried to convey to them that strength still came from all there had been.

The day after the funeral Fagan from the solicitors' office explained to Catherine the contents of the few papers he brought to the house. It took ten minutes.

'I'll help you,' Alicia said later that same morning when Catherine mentioned Matthew's personal belongings. Clothes and shoes would be accepted gratefully by one of the charities with which Alicia was connected. The signet ring, the watch, the tie-pin, the matching fountain pen and propelling pencil were earmarked for the family, to be shared among Catherine's sons. Shaving things were thrown away.

Recalling the same sorting out of possessions at the time of her own loss, Alicia was in no way distressed. She had experienced little emotion when her husband's death occurred: for the last nineteen years of her marriage she had not loved him.

'You've been a strength,' Catherine said, for her sister had been that and more, looking after her as she used to, years ago, when they were children.

'Oh, no, no,' came Alicia's deprecation.

★

Thomas Pius John Leary was by trade a painter and decorator. He had, for this work, no special qualifications beyond experience; he brought to it no special skill. As a result, he was often accused of poor workmanship, which in turn led to disputes about payment. But he charged less than his competitors and so ensured a reasonably steady demand for his services. When for one reason or another the demand wasn't there he took on any kind of odd job he was offered.

Leary was middle-aged now, married, the father of six children. He was a small, wiry man with tight features, and bloodshot eyes, his spareness occasionally reminding people of a hedgerow animal they could not readily name. Sparse grey hair was brushed straight back from the narrow dome of his forehead. Two forefingers, thumbs, middle fingers, upper lip, and teeth were stained brown from cigarettes he manufactured with the aid of a small machine. Leary did not wear overalls when at work and was rarely encountered in clothes that did not bear splashes of paint.

It was in this condition, the damp end of a cigarette emerging from a cupped palm, that he presented himself to Catherine and Alicia one afternoon in November, six weeks after the death. He stood on the doorstep, declaring his regrets and his sympathy in a low voice, not meeting Catherine's eye. In the time that had passed, other people had come to the door and said much the same thing; not many, only those who found it difficult to write a letter and considered the use of the telephone to be inappropriate in such circumstances. They'd made a brief statement and then had hurried off. Leary appeared inclined to linger.

'That's very good of you, Mr Leary,' Catherine said.

A few months earlier he had repainted the front of the house, the same pale blue. He had renewed the white gloss of the window frames. 'Poor Leary's desperate for work,' Matthew had said. 'Will we give the rogue a go?' Alicia had been against it, Leary not being a man she'd cared for when he'd done other jobs for them. Catherine, although she didn't much care for Leary either, felt sorry for anyone who was up against it.

'Could I step in for a minute?'

Across the street the convent children were running about in the play yard before their afternoon classes began. Still watching them, Catherine was aware of checking a frown that had begun to gather. He was looking for more work, she supposed, but there was no question of that. Alicia's misgivings had been justified; there'd been skimping on the amount and quality of the paint used, and inadequate preparation. 'We'll know not to do that again,' Matthew had said. Besides, there wasn't anything else that required attention at present.

'Of course,' Catherine stood aside while Leary passed into the long, narrow hall. She led the way down it, to the kitchen because it was warm there. Alicia was polishing the cutlery at the table, a task she undertook once a month.

'Sit down, Mr Leary,' Catherine invited, pulling a chair out for him.

'I was saying I was sorry,' he said to Alicia. 'If there's any way I can assist at all, any little job, I'm always there.'

'It's kind of you, Mr Leary,' Catherine said swiftly, in case her sister responded more tartly.

'I knew him since we were lads. He used to be at the Christian Brothers'.'

'Yes.'

'Great old days.'

He seemed embarrassed. He wanted to say something but was having difficulty. One hand went into a pocket of his jacket. Catherine watched it playing with the little contrivance he used for rolling his cigarettes. But the hand came out empty. Nervously, it was rubbed against its partner.

'It's awkward,' Leary said.

'What's awkward, Mr Leary?'

'It isn't easy, how to put it to you. I didn't come before because of your trouble.'

Alicia laid down the cloth with she had been applying Goddard's Silver Polish to the cutlery, and Catherine watched her sister's slow, deliberate movements as she shined the last of the forks, and then drew off her pink rubber gloves and placed them one on top of the other, beside her. Alicia could sense something; she often had a way of knowing what was coming next.

'I don't know are you aware,' Leary enquired, addressing only Catherine, 'it wasn't paid for?'

'What wasn't?'

'The job I done for you.'

'You don't mean painting the front?'

'I do, ma'am.'

'But of course it was paid for.'

He sighed softly. An outstanding bill was an embarrassment, he said. Because of the death it was an embarrassment.

'My husband paid for the work that was done.'

'Ah no, no.'

The frown Catherine had checked a few moments ago wrinkled her forehead. She knew the bill had been paid. She knew because Matthew had said Leary would want cash, and she had taken the money out of her own Irish Nationwide account, since she had easy access to it. 'I'll see you right at the end of the month,' Matthew had promised. It was an arrangement they often had; the building-society account in her name existed for this kind of thing.

'Two hundred and twenty-six pounds is the extent of the damage.' Leary smiled shiftily. 'With the discount for cash.'

She didn't tell him she'd withdrawn the money herself. That wasn't his business. She watched the extreme tip of his tongue licking his upper lip. He wiped his mouth with the back of a paint-stained hand. Softly, Alicia was replacing forks and spoons in the cutlery container.

'It was September the account was sent out. The wife does all that type of thing.'

'The bill was paid promptly. My husband always paid bills promptly.'

She remembered the occasion perfectly. 'I'll bring it down to him now,' Matthew had said, glancing across the kitchen at the clock. Every evening he walked down to McKenny's bar and remained there for three-quarters of an hour or so, depending on the company. That evening he'd have gone the long way round, by French Street, in order to call in at the Learys' house, in Brady's Lane. Before he left he had taken the notes from the brown Nationwide envelope and counted them, slowly, just as she herself had done earlier. She'd seen the bill in his hand. 'Chancing his arm with the tax man,' she remembered his remarking lightly, a reference to Leary's preference for cash.

On his return he would have hung his cap on its hook in the scullery passage and settled down at the kitchen table with the *Evening Press*, which he bought in Healy's sweetshop on his way back from McKenny's. He went to the public house for conversation as much as anything, and afterwards passed on to Alicia and herself any news he had gleaned. Bottled Smithwick's was his drink.

'D'you remember it?' Catherine appealed to her sister, because although she could herself so clearly recall Matthew's departure from the house on that particular September evening, his return eluded her. It lay smothered somewhere beneath the evening routine, nothing making it special, as the banknotes in the envelope had made the other.

'I remember talk about money,' Alicia recalled, 'earlier that day. If I've got it right, I was out at the Legion of Mary in the evening.'

'A while back the wife noticed the way the bill was unpaid,' Leary went on, having paused politely to hear these recollections. ' "It's the death that's in it," she said. She'd have eaten the face off me if I'd bothered you in your trouble.'

'Exuse me,' Catherine said.

She left the kitchen and went to look on the spike in the side cupboard in the passage, where all receipts were kept. This one should have been close to the top, but it wasn't. It wasn't farther down either. It wasn't in the cupboard drawers. She went through the contents of three box files in case it had been bundled into one in error. Again she didn't find it.

She returned to the kitchen with the next best thing: the Nationwide Building Society account book. She opened it and placed it in front of Leary. She pointed at the entry that recorded the withdrawal of two hundred and twenty-six pounds. She could tell that there had been no conversation in her absence. Leary would have tried to get some kind of talk going, but Alicia wouldn't have responded.

'September the eighth,' Catherine said, emphasising the printed date with a forefinger. 'A Wednesday, it was.'

In silence Leary perused the entry. He shook his head. The tight features of his face tightened even more, bunching together into a knot of bewilderment. Catherine glanced at her sister. He was putting it on, Alicia's expression indicated.

'The money was taken out, all right,' Leary said eventually. 'Did he put it to another use in that case?'

'Another use?'

'Did you locate a receipt, missus?'

He spoke softly, not in the cagey, underhand tone of someone attempting to get something for nothing. Catherine was still standing. He turned his head to one side in order to squint up at her. He sounded apologetic, but all that could be put on also.

'I brought the receipt book over with me,' he said.

He handed it to her, a fat, greasy notebook with a grey marbled cover that had 'The Challenge Receipt Book' printed on it. Blue carbon paper protruded from the dog-eared pages.

'Any receipt that's issued would have a copy left behind here,' he said, speaking now to Alicia, across the table. 'The top copy for the customer, the carbon for ourselves. You couldn't do business without you keep a record of receipts.'

He stood up then. He opened the book and displayed its unused pages, each with the same printed heading: 'In account with T. P. Leary.' He showed Catherine how the details of a bill were recorded on the flimsy page beneath the carbon sheet and how, when a bill was paid, acknowledgment was recorded also: 'Paid with thanks,' with the date and the careful scrawl of Mrs Leary's signature. He passed the receipt book to Alicia, pointing out these details to her also.

'Anything could have happened to that receipt,' Alicia said. 'In the circumstances.'

'If a receipt was issued, missus, there'd be a record of it here.'

Alicia placed the receipt book beside the much slimmer building-society book on the pale surface of the table. Leary's attention remained with the former, his scrutiny an emphasis of the facts it contained. The evidence offered otherwise was not for him to comment upon: so the steadiness of his gaze insisted.

'My husband counted those notes at this very table,' Catherine said. 'He took them out of the brown envelope that they were put into at the Nationwide.'

'It's a mystery so.'

It wasn't any such thing; there was no mystery whatsoever. The bill had been paid. Both sisters knew that; in their different ways they guessed that Leary – and presumably his wife as well – had planned this dishonesty as soon as they realised that death had given them the opportunity. Matthew had obliged them by paying cash so that they could defraud the taxation authorities. He had further obliged them by dying.

Catherine said, 'My husband walked out of this house with that envelope in his pocket. Are you telling me he didn't reach you?'

'Was he robbed? Would it be that? You hear terrible things these days.'

'Oh, for heaven's sake!'

Leary wagged his head in his meditative way. It was unlikely certainly, he agreed. Anyone robbed would have gone to the Guards. Anyone robbed would have mentioned it when he came back to the house again.

'The bill was paid, Mr Leary.'

'All the same, we have to go by the receipt. At the heel of the hunt there's the matter of a receipt.'

Alicia shook her head. Either a receipt wasn't issued in the first place, she said, or else it had been mislaid. 'There's a confusion when a person dies,' she said.

If Catherine had been able to produce the receipt Leary would have blamed his wife. He'd have blandly stated that she'd got her wires crossed. He'd have said the first thing that came into his head and then have gone away.

'The only thing is,' he said instead, 'a sum like that is sizeable. I couldn't afford to let it go.'

Both Catherine and Alicia had seen Mrs Leary in the shops, red-haired, like a tinker, a bigger woman than her husband, probably the brains of the two. The Learys were liars and worse than liars; the chance had come and the temptation had been too much for them. 'Ah, sure, those two have plenty,' the woman would have said. The sisters wondered if the Learys had tricked the bereaved before, and imagined they had.

Leary said, 'It's hard on a man that's done work for you.'

Catherine moved towards the kitchen door. Leary ambled after her down the hall. She remembered the evening more clearly even than a while ago. A Wednesday it definitely had been, the day of the Sweetman girl's wedding; and also, it came back to her, Alicia hurrying out on her Legion of Mary business. There'd been talk in McKenny's about the wedding, the unusual choice of mid-week, which apparently had something to do with visitors coming from America. She opened the hall door in silence. Across the street, beyond the silver-coloured railings, the children were still running about in the convent yard. Watery sunlight lightened the unadorned concrete of the classrooms and the nuns' house.

'What'll I do?' Leary asked, wide-eyed, bloodshot, squinting at her.

Catherine said nothing.

They talked about it. It could be, Alicia said, that the receipt had remained in one of Matthew's pockets, that a jacket she had disposed of to one of her charities had later found itself in the Learys' hands, having passed through a jumble sale. She could imagine Mrs Leary coming across it, and the temptation being too much. Leary was as weak as water, she said, adding that the tinker wife was a woman who never looked you in the eye. Foxy-faced and furtive, Mrs Leary pushed a ramshackle pram about the streets, her ragged children cowering in her presence. It was she who would have removed the flimsy carbon copy from the soiled receipt book. Leary would have been putty in her hands.

In the kitchen they sat down at the table, from which Alicia had cleared away the polished cutlery. Matthew had died as tidily as he'd lived, Alicia said: all his life he'd been meticulous. The Learys had failed to remember that. If it came to a court of law the Learys wouldn't have a leg to stand on, with the written evidence that the precise amount taken out of the building society matched the amount of the bill, and further evidence in Matthew's reputation for promptness about settling debts.

'What I'm wondering is,' Alicia said, 'should we go to the Guards?'

'The Guards?'

'He shouldn't have come here like that.'

That evening there arrived a bill for the amount quoted by

Leary marked 'Account rendered'. It was dropped through the letter box and was discovered the next morning beneath the *Irish Independent* on the hall doormat.

'The little twister!' Alicia furiously exclaimed.

From the road outside the house came the morning commands of the convent girl in charge of the crossing to the school: 'Get ready!' 'Prepare to cross!' 'Cross now!' Impertinence had been added to dishonesty, Alicia declared in outraged tones. It was as though it had never been pointed out to Leary that Matthew had left the house on the evening in question with two hundred and twenty-six pounds in an envelope, that Leary's attention had never been drawn to the clear evidence of the building-society entry.

'It beats me,' Catherine said, and in the hall Alicia turned sharply and said it was as clear as day. Again she mentioned going to the Guards. A single visit from Sergeant McBride, she maintained, and the Learys would abandon their cheek. From the play yard the yells of the girls increased as more girls arrived there, and then the handbell sounded; a moment later there was silence.

'I'm only wondering,' Catherine said, 'if there's some kind of mistake.'

'There's no mistake, Catherine.'

Alicia didn't comment further. She led the way to the kitchen and half-filled a saucepan with water for their two boiled eggs. Catherine cut bread for toast. When she and Alicia had been girls in that same play yard she hadn't known of Matthew's existence. Years passed before she even noticed him, at Mass one Saturday night. And it was ages before he first invited her to go out with him, for a walk the first time, and then for a drive.

'What d'you think happened, then?' Alicia asked. 'That Matthew bet the money on a dog? That he owed it for drink consumed? Have sense, Catherine.'

Had it been Alicia's own husband whom Leary had charged with negligence, there would have been no necessary suspension of disbelief: feckless and a nuisance, involved during his marriage with at least one other woman in the town, frequenter of racecourses and dog tracks and bars, he had ended in an early grave. This shared thought – that behaviour which was ludicrous when attached to Matthew had been as natural in Alicia's husband as breathing – was there between the sisters, but was not mentioned.

'If Father Cahill got Leary on his own,' Alicia began, but Catherine interrupted. She didn't want that, she said; she didn't want other people brought into this, not even Father Cahill. She didn't want a fuss about whether or not her husband had paid a bill.

'You'll get more of these,' Alicia warned, laying a finger on the envelope that had been put through the letter box. 'They'll keep coming.'

'Yes.'

In the night Catherine had lain awake, wondering if Matthew had maybe lost the money on his walk to the Learys' house that evening, if he'd put his hand in his pocket and found it wasn't there and then been too ashamed to say. It wasn't like him; it didn't make much more sense than thinking he had been a secretive man, with private shortcomings all the years she'd been married to him. When Alicia's husband died Matthew had said it was hard to feel sorry, and she'd agreed. Three times Alicia had been left on her own, for periods that varied in length, and on each occasion they'd thought the man was gone for good; but he returned and Alicia always took him back. Of course Matthew hadn't lost the money: it was as silly to think that as to wonder if he'd been a gambler.

'In case they'd try it on anyone else,' Alicia was saying, 'isn't it better they should be shown up? Is a man who'd get up to that kind of game safe to be left in people's houses the way a workman is?'

That morning they didn't mention the matter again. They washed up the breakfast dishes and then Catherine went out to the shops, which was always her chore, while Alicia cleaned the stairs and the hall, the day being a Thursday. As Catherine made her way through the familiar streets, and while Mr Deegan sliced bacon for her and then while Gilligan greeted her in the hardware, she thought about the journey her husband had made that Wednesday evening in September. Involuntarily, she glanced into Healy's, where he had bought the *Evening Press*, and into McKenny's bar. Every evening except Sunday, he had brought back the news, bits of gossip, anything he'd heard. It was at this time, too, that he went to confession, on such occasions leaving the house half an hour earlier.

In French Street, a countrywoman opened her car door without looking and knocked a cyclist over. 'Ah, no harm done,' the youth on the bicycle said. He was the delivery boy for Lawless, the West Street butcher, the last delivery boy in the town. 'Sure, I never saw him at all,' the countrywoman protested to Catherine as she went by. The car door was dinged, but the woman said what did it matter if the lad was all right?

Culliney, the traveller from Limerick Shirts, was in town that day. Matthew had always bought his shirts direct from Culliney, the same striped pattern, the stripe blue or brown. Culliney had his measurements, the way he had the measurements of men all over Munster and Connacht, which was his area. Catherine could tell when she saw Culliney coming towards her that he didn't know about the death, and she braced herself to tell him. When she did so he put a hand on her arm and spoke in a whisper, saying that Matthew had been a good man. If there was anything he could ever do, he said, if there was any way he could help. More people said that than didn't.

It was then that Catherine saw Mrs Leary. The housepainter's wife was pushing her pram, a child holding on to it as she advanced. Catherine crossed to the other side of the street, wondering if the woman had seen her and suspecting she had. In Jerety's she selected a pan loaf from the yesterday's, since neither she nor Alicia liked fresh bread and yesterday's was always reduced. When she emerged, Mrs Leary was not to be seen.

'Nothing, only a woman knocked young Nallen off his bike,' she reported to Alicia when she returned to the house. 'Is he a Nallen, that boy of Lawless's?'

'Or a Keane, is he? Big head on him?'

'I don't think he's a Keane. Someone told me a Nallen. Whoever he is, there's no harm done.' She didn't say she'd seen Mrs Leary, because she didn't want to raise again the subject of what had occurred. She knew that Alicia was right: the bill would keep coming unless she did something about it. Once they'd set out on the course they'd chosen, why should the Learys give up? Alicia didn't refer to the Learys either, but that evening, when they had switched off the television and were preparing to go to bed, Catherine said, 'I think I'll pay them. Simplest, that would be.'

With her right hand on the newel of the banister, about to ascend the stairs, Alicia stared in disbelief at her sister. When Catherine nodded and continued on her way to the kitchen she followed her.

'But you can't.' Alicia stood in the doorway while Catherine washed and rinsed the cups they'd drunk their bedtime tea from. 'You can't just pay them what isn't owing.'

Catherine turned the tap off at the sink and set the cups to drain, slipping the accompanying saucers between the plastic bars of the drainer. Tomorrow she would withdraw the same sum from the building-society account and take it herself to the Learys in Brady's Lane. She would stand there while a receipt was issued.

'Catherine, you can't hand out more than two hundred pounds.'

'I'd rather.'

As she spoke, she changed her mind about the detail of the payment. Matthew had been obliging Leary by paying cash, but there was no need to oblige him anymore. She would arrange for the Irish Nationwide to draw a cheque payable to T. P. Leary. She would bring it round to the Learys instead of a wad of notes.

'They've taken you for a fool,' Alicia said.

'I know they have.'

'Leary should go behind bars. You're aiding and abetting him. Have sense, woman.'

A disappointment rose in Alicia, bewildering and muddled. The death of her own husband had brought an end, and her expectation had been that widowhood for her sister would be the same. Her expectation had been that in their shared state they would be as once they were, now that marriage was over, packed away with their similar mourning clothes. Yet almost palpable in the kitchen was Catherine's resolve that what still remained for her should not be damaged by a fuss of protest over a confidence trick. The Guards investigating clothes sold at a jumble sale, strangers asked if a housepainter's wife had bought this garment or that, private intimacies made public: Catherine was paying money in

case, somehow, the memory of her husband should be accidentally tarnished. And knowing her sister well, Alicia knew that this
resolve would become more stubborn as time passed. It would
mark and influence her sister; it would breed new eccentricities in
her. If Leary had not come that day there would have been
something else.

'You'd have the man back, I suppose?' Alicia said, trying to hurt
and knowing she succeeded. 'You'd have him back in to paint
again, to lift the bits and pieces from your dressing table?'

'It's not to do with Leary.'

'What's it to do with then?'

'Let's leave it.'

Hanging up a tea towel, Catherine noticed that her fingers were
trembling. They never quarrelled; even in childhood they hadn't.
In all the years Alicia had lived in the house she had never spoken
in this unpleasant way, her voice rudely raised.

'They're walking all over you, Catherine.'

'Yes.'

They did not speak again, not even to say goodnight. Alicia
closed her bedroom door, telling herself crossly that her expectation had not been a greedy one. She had been unhappy in her
foolish marriage, and after it she had been beholden in this house.
Although it ran against her nature to do so, she had borne her lot
without complaint; why should she not fairly have hoped that in
widowhood they would again be sisters first of all?

In her bedroom Catherine undressed and for a moment caught a
glimpse of the nakedness in her dressing-table looking glass. She
missed her husband's warmth in bed, a hand holding hers before
they slept, that last embrace, and sometimes in the night his voice
saying he loved her. She pulled her nightdress on, then knelt to
pray before she turned the light out.

Some instinct, vague and imprecise, drew her in the darkness on
to the territory of Alicia's disappointment. In the family photographs – some clearly defined, some now drained of detail,
affected by the sun – they were the sisters they had been: Alicia
beautiful, confidently smiling; Catherine in her care. Catherine's
first memory was of a yellow flower, and sunlight, and a white

cloth hat put on her head. That flower was a cowslip, Alicia told her afterwards, and said that they'd gone with their mother to the ruins by the river that day, that it was she who found the cowslip. 'Look, Catherine,' she'd said. 'A lovely flower.' Catherine had watched in admiration when Alicia paraded in her First Communion dress, and later when boys paid her attention. Alicia was the important one, responsible, reliable, right about things, offered the deference that was an older sister's due. She'd been a strength, Catherine said after Matthew's funeral, and Alicia was pleased, even though she shook her head.

Catherine dropped into sleep after half an hour of wakefulness. She woke up a few times in the night, on each occasion to find her thoughts full of the decision she had made, and of her sister's outraged face, the two tiny patches of red that had come into it, high up on her cheeks, the snap of disdain in her eyes. 'A laughing-stock,' Alicia said in a dream. 'No more than a laughing-stock, Catherine.'

As Catherine lay there she imagined the silent breakfast there would be, and saw herself walking to Brady's Lane, and Leary fiddling with his cigarette-making gadget, and Mrs Leary in fluffy pink slippers, her stockingless legs mottled from being too close to the fire. Tea would be offered, but Catherine would refuse it. 'A decenter man never stood in a pair of shoes,' Leary could be counted upon to state.

She did not sleep again. She watched the darkness lighten, heard the first cars of the day pass on the road outside the house. By chance, a petty dishonesty had given death its due, which Alicia had cheated it of when she was widowed herself. It took from her now, as it had not then.

Catherine knew this intuition was no trick of her tired mind. While they were widows in her house Alicia's jealousy would be the truth they shared, with tonight's few moments of its presence lingering insistently. Widows were widows first. Catherine would mourn, and feel in solitude the warmth of love. For Alicia there was the memory of her beauty.

Michigan Water

TIM WILLOCKS

TINDEMANN LIT A White Owl cigar, put the match in his pocket, then hunkered down at the edge of the jetty and smoked in his own silence while he waited for Buddy to get up to speed.

The jetty stuck out from a spur of land and from where he squatted Tindemann could see nothing but water, as if he were on a raft cast adrift in the middle of a vast empty ocean. A handful of local fishermen had once made a living putting out from here; but no more. The time when men passed their trade down to their sons was long gone. Certainly Tindemann didn't expect to pass on his own. The thought caused him to glance over his shoulder at the barrel hanging soundlessly in chains from the jetty's rusted loading gear. Beyond the gear, riding the gentle swell, sat the boat Tindemann had rented and sailed across the Muncie, over on the Wisconsin side.

No, he would never pass his trade on, for it occurred to him it was not a trade at all but rather a calling. A trade by definition was a thing practised for hire and Tindemann could not be hired. His work could not be purchased any more than could his mercy: price had simply not been built into the calling's architecture. And perhaps partly for this reason, and men being what they were, those that heard the call were few; and known only to themselves.

There was a cold blue wind gusting across the water from Canada and the sun, pale as winter, was picking up momentum as it approached the western rim of the lake. The wind didn't bother Tindemann but the acceleration in the sun's descent did. It was important, when he got out there on the water, that there be enough light for him to bear witness. It wasn't that he lacked confidence in his methods – because witness or not there would be not a rack left behind – but ritual demanded it. He decided to wait for as long as it took him to finish his cigar and then he'd head out in the boat, even if Buddy was still behind schedule.

Two-hundred-some miles to the south and west was the city from which he'd driven up that morning. Tindemann had no fear of cities – in darker days, after all, he'd purchased his skills there at a price one could only afford to pay once – but he didn't like them. Chicago, in particular, was to his mind a giant roach motel whose inhabitants had learned to live on the poison. Roaches like Buddy boy, who was in business for himself as a Catholic . . .

Tindemann stopped himself. None of that was relevant any more. It was worse than not relevant; it was a contaminant of the ritual. Here all past was expunged, all identity abandoned. Whoever Buddy had been, whatever his name, his habits, his triumphs and regrets, his network of relations – all liens, all commitments, all the deeds of his life – were now absolved, washed away like words scratched with a stick in the sand. He had become 'Buddy', like other 'Buddies' before him. The hand of an all-knowing Justice had tapped Buddy on the shoulder and with that his past had vanished entire; yes, including, even, the crime that brought the sentence. Thus was Tindemann also obliged to put these details behind him; for Justice demanded it, and Tindemann was its instrument.

When the smoke from the cigar began to burn his tongue Tindemann crushed the coal beneath his heel and put the warm butt in his pocket. Then he stood up and stretched, flexing his hands, which were massive, and walked without hurry to the loading gear, and the barrel in its chains.

The barrel was in fact a 50-gallon steel drum that had once contained a toxic chemical used in the turning of wood pulp into paper. Tindemann had been very careful to scour the interior of any trace of toxins, for it was vital that the barrel itself provide a safe and hygienic environment. Then he had cut four circular holes in the steel, each four inches in diameter: one in the sealed lid; the other three evenly spaced around one diameter of the cylinder, six inches below the upper rim. On the floor of the drum lay a 50-pound barbell plate.

Crammed inside, and presently still sedated by what was, with hindsight, a slightly excessive dose of Thorazine, was the man known only – and for ever – as 'Buddy'.

Tindemann took a wrench from the loading gear and battered it against the rim of the drum. A series of metallic thuds, loud but flattened by the drum's organic contents, rang out across the water. Tindemann bent his mouth towards one of the holes.

'Hey, Buddy!' he shouted. He kept his tone free of malice; he hoped it might even sound cheerful. 'Rise and shine, man! Surf's up!' He gave the 50-gallon drum a few more licks with the wrench, then paused and listened. There was a reflective stirring inside, limbs striving without full awareness for space and finding none, and with this movement within, the drum started to sway gently in its chains.

Tindemann felt relief. Buddy's conscious participation in the proceedings, while not fundamental, was desirable. Tindemann bent towards the hole again. He opened his mouth to speak and stopped: an eye, and a nose, and an inch or two of corrugated brow, had appeared through the aperture of the hole, flared and quivered, heaving in the bracing lakeside air. The rims of the nostrils were crusted with blood. The eye was glazed, flitting, at the same moment dulled with sleep and delirious with dread.

Tindemann realised the eye was unable to see him. He crouched down so that the eye could study his face. The eye looked at him and, by just a little, its inner light brightened. Tindemann smiled. 'Attaboy, Buddy,' he said. 'Man, I was worried you might not make it.'

The eye blinked. There wasn't quite enough face with it for Tindemann to be sure what emotion the blink was meant to convey, but his gut sensed that hovering above Buddy's primordial claustrophobia was a formless questioning akin to bewilderment.

'Listen,' said Tindemann, 'we got some travelling to do and the sun's against us. You just relax while I load up. Then we'll talk.'

He winked at the eye and smiled again then straightened up. The eye disappeared and from inside the drum came a muffled, panic-stricken snorting and the clunking sound of Buddy's skull hitting the inner concavity of the steel. The arc of the swaying chains increased. After a moment, a handful of fingers emerged from the hole and clawed pointlessly at the outer surface of the drum. The fingers had been recently manicured. As Tindemann watched, one of the manicured nails cracked and split half-way to the quick. Tindemann raised the wrench and gave the knuckles a gentle tap. There was another sound, higher pitched this time, and the hand disappeared inside. Buddy was awake for sure.

For the next ten minutes Tindemann busied himself with the task of operating the loading gear and getting the drum stowed on the launch. The gear was rarely used these days and, despite the fact that yesterday Tindemann had sprayed all the moving parts with penetrating oil to loosen them up, there was still a lot of grinding of joints and jamming of bolts to deal with. If Buddy tried to communicate during this procedure, Tindemann didn't hear him. By the time the barrel was aboard and lashed down to Tindemann's satisfaction there was still an hour of sun left. Just enough time to get out to the deep water. Tindemann settled down in the stern, his lunch box between his feet, and fired up the outboard motor. When it was idling nicely he leaned forward and shouted towards the hole in the barrel.

'Hear that, Buddy boy? You know what it is?' He pumped out a few extra revs with the throttle. 'You any idea where we are?'

The eye reappeared and stared at him. Tindemann nodded.

'I'll give you a clue. You could drop the whole state of Illinois into this baby and the water wouldn't rise more 'n a coupla feet. Think about it.'

The eye clenched shut.

'You got it, Buddy. Now you and me we got some travellin' to do.'

A muted whimpering emanated from the drum.

'If I was you,' said Tindemann, 'I'd make the best of the time. You still got choices. But that's between you and yourself.'

If Buddy caught his drift he didn't give any indication to that effect. Which was OK. It wasn't Tindemann's function to school Buddy in how best to stand toe to toe with the cosmic absolute. Tindemann had been there once and had acquitted himself in front of himself; at which very moment fate had signed a temporary waiver on death's behalf. That had also been the moment when he'd heard the call and razed his life, such as it had been, down to blackened stubble. Torched it all. Started out new. Now Tindemann lived in his house justified. He could bear the feeling of being inside his own skin. He reached up and loosened the rope securing the boat to the jetty and cast off.

As he settled back into his seat a mouth appeared at the hole in the drum. The mouth was gaping and ugly and raw. It emitted a scream, which grated on Tindemann's nerves but did not move him. He lifted a meaty leg and gave the barrel a stout kick. The mouth disappeared into darkness. Tindemann dropped the outboard motor into gear and pulled out on to the water.

They made good time and Tindemann felt replete with the knowledge – intensified by the immensity of the sky, the water, the rays of the setting sun – that he was an integral part of some greater design. Perhaps, had he been asked, he would have found it difficult to explain that part and that design, but no one did ask, and for himself he did not feel the need. Buddy probably had a few questions that he would have liked to have put to him – the usual banal and egocentric bleatings of the doomed, mixed as always with sundry denials, self-deceptions and lies – but he wasn't able to do so. Specifically to spare himself that tedium, Tindemann had taken out most of Buddy's tongue with a pair of wire-cutters and cauterised the stump with a soldering iron; so that he wouldn't choke on the blood. Buddy-boy was lucky Tindemann hadn't taken the wire-cutters to his dick, as he deserved. But Tindemann was an instrument of Justice, not of punishment. If Buddy was now, as Tindemann suspected but could not hear amidst the roar of the outboard, blubbering incoherently for mercy – or even forgiveness – from the God he had so vilely betrayed, he was wasting what little breath he had left. Tindemann was the officer of a higher court by far.

When in the distance Tindemann saw the blurred margin of the shore he switched off the motor. In the aftermath of the engine noise there was a sudden and immense silence. Then he heard the waves lapping the sides of the boat. No sound came from the drum. Tindemann was mildly surprised. Perhaps at the last Buddy had unearthed some small vestige of dignity. Or maybe he had merely subsided into the stupefaction of a terror as large and unfathomable as the lake itself.

The boat bobbed in the water while Tindemann checked his bearings. His memory had not failed him. According to the charts they were floating above a trench gouged from the earth far below by some Ice Age spasm of unimaginable force. The thought of that power deepened yet further Tindemann's sense of taking his seat in the banquet hall of the historical absolute. A lowly seat, for sure, but a seat nevertheless. He folded the chart into his pocket and stood up. He rolled the stiffness from his shoulders. He flexed his hands, which were massive. He planted his feet wide and bent forward to untie the barrel's lashings. As he worked, he sang:

> 'Michigan Water, taste like sherry,
> I mean sherry,
> Talkin' about sherry,
> Michigan Water, taste like sherry wine.
> Mississippi water, taste like turpentine.'

His singing was not interrupted by any sounds from within the drum, nor did the eye or the mouth reappear. Tindemann was pleased but not curious. It would have given him no pleasure to have been obliged to subdue Buddy with harsh words. He could have done so. His voice, he knew, when required, and when delivered through cupped hands directly into the hole, could stun

315

the occupant with the force of a cattle prod. When the lashings were cleared Tindemann straddled the barrel and squatted, sinking his weight into his feet. Then slowly, at each point of the arc altering his own angle to provide a precise and perfect counter-balance, he tipped the drum forward until it rested against the edge of the bow. He heard a dull grating sound as the 50-pound steel plate shifted in the bottom of the barrel. But that was all he heard. He called softly towards the hole, with the kind of whisper a good actor can throw all the way to the back of an auditorium.

'This is the punch line, Buddy,' he said. 'Water's waitin'. You want another five minutes to make your peace, they're yours.' He paused. 'If not, then it's "Adios, muchacho."'

He waited. The barrel made no answer. Tindemann shrugged and transferred his attention to the swell undulating beneath his feet. The combined weight of the drum, the barbell plate and Buddy did not match his own physical mass. Nevertheless this was the part of the mission where he placed his own life at hazard. This was not merely a physical consequence of his chosen method, for Justice could have been satisfied by other, safer means. It was, more crucially, a fundamental element of the ritual. If the boat capsized Tindemann would drown, for the water was cold and he was a long way from the shore and darkness was falling around him.

Furthermore – and this was why he had invented the technique – Tindemann could not swim.

Naturally, he eschewed the use of a lifebelt.

Now he let the rhythm of the swell become part of him, so that the great force he would exert in heaving the drum over the side would not seem alien to the spirit of the water. He squatted mightily and gripped the lower rim of the tilted barrel in the palms of both hands. Again, slowly, he clenched the musculature of his lats, his lower back, his abdomen, his swollen forearms, his thighs, and finally his enormous hams. He awaited the approaching swell. As it came, Tindemann started his inexorable lift.

Then Buddy shoved his hands through the hole in the left hand side of the drum. Brandished in the hand was a tangled mass of black and white and red.

Tindemann, his vision blurred by the strain of lifting, saw the hand from the corner of one eye. The whiteness was streaked with blood. Tindemann felt rather than realised that it was too late to stop. If he dropped the drum, or even tried to lower it back down, the swell would be against him and his fragile balance would become unsustainable. His body carried through. The drum rose with a grinding of splinters over the rim of the bow and reached a fulcrum where he could use the last focus of his power to heave it over and away. The blood-stained hand unclenched and whatever it was holding fell from sight. With a bellow of triumph, Tindemann thrust the drum over the side.

The boat commenced a violent rocking and he fell to his knees and gripped the sides. Water splashed him and he was grateful for the shock of its touch. He wheezed for air. Then he raised his head.

The barrel was bobbing away from the boat towards the sun, which had draped the horizon with scarlet ribbons and whose rays now cut a sharp silhouette from the squat black cylinder as it wallowed upright in the water. Tindemann waited for the pitching of the boat to settle and for his blood pressure to come down, then sat himself in the stern to bear witness.

He could not see the holes in the drum's sides but he estimated from the height that they were about an inch above the water line. As he watched, the drum commenced to rock from side to side, and he imagined the water lapping through the holes a cupful at a time. The meaning of the rocking was obscure. It might be that Buddy was trying to block the three holes with his hands and head, a futile and panic-stricken gesture that would merely prolong his final misery. In contrast he might be doing the rational thing, and rocking the barrel on purpose to get that water in there as fast as possible. Most likely, though, Buddy was too far gone for either rationality or panic, and was just banging his skull against the concave steel in a frenzy of despair.

Tindemann reached into the pocket of his coat and took out a silver hip flask. He opened it and drank. The taste was clean and biting. Fino, dry as the hallways of Hell. He drank again and thought. When the barrel was gone he would steer the boat back to Muncie, on the far side, and patch up and paint the gouge the barrel had left in the rim of the boat. Then he'd go home to his family. He took another sip from the flask. The water was entering the drum by the quart now and the amplitude of its rocking, and its height above the surface, were diminishing. The last moments were here. Then Tindemann suddenly remembered and turned.

On the floor of the boat were the things Buddy had dropped from his hand. In the shadows Tindemann couldn't make them out. He bent down and picked them up and held them in his open palm towards the fading light. There was a white, blood-stained dog-collar and a set of black rosary beads. The beads, if Tindemann was not mistaken, were carved from real ebony. The crucifix hanging from the end was unmistakably of gold.

Goddamn, thought Tindemann. Maybe good ole Buddy-boyo had come to some kind of understanding after all.

An emotion uncomfortably close to respect started to rise in Tindemann's gut. Then he remembered what Buddy had done to the boys; and the feeling withered and died. He looked up.

The holes were now just about covered entirely. Then, with that unannounced rapidity that always took Tindemann by surprise, the upper six inches of the drum abruptly vanished from sight.

Tindemann was relieved. He'd almost missed the bearing of witness. He glanced down at the mementos in his hand. There was no debate to be had. The dog-collar he shoved into his pocket, and would later burn. The rosary he clenched into his fist and hurled over-arm after the drum.

He didn't watch for the splash as it hit the water, which was now utterly black for all that the sun had not yet disappeared. Tindemann put away his flask and lit a White Owl cigar and fired up the outboard motor, and went home.

Biographical Notes on the Authors

JULIAN BARNES has written seven novels and his work has been translated into more than twenty languages. In France he is the only writer to have won both the Prix Médicis (for *Flaubert's Parrot*) and the Prix Fémina (for *Talking It Over*). In 1993 he was awarded the Shakespeare Prize by the FVS Foundation in Hamburg.

WILLIAM BOYD has published six novels, including *Brazzaville Beach* which won the James Tait Black Memorial Prize, and *The Blue Afternoon* which won the 1993 *Sunday Express* Book of the Year Award. Eight of his screenplays have been filmed, recently *A Good Man in Africa*, based on his novel which won the 1981 Whitbread Literary Award for the Best First Novel and a 1982 Somerset Maugham Award. His most recent book is a collection of short stories, *The Destiny of Nathalie X*.

FIONA FARRELL's first novel, *The Skinny Louie Book*, won the 1993 New Zealand Book Award for Fiction. She has published poetry, plays and a collection of short stories (*The Rock Garden*). She lives in a remote bay on Banks Peninsula where she is completing a second novel (*Six Clever Girls Who Became Famous Women*) and growing olives.

JANE GARDAM was born in Coatham, North Yorkshire. She is a Whitbread Award winner, and her novel *God On The Rocks* was runner-up for the Booker Prize in 1978. She is a winner of the David Higham Award and the Royal Society of Literature's Winifred Holtby Prize for her collection of stories about Jamaica. *The Pangs of Love* won the Katherine Mansfield award and her most recent collection of stories, *Going Into A Dark House*, won the Macmillan Silver PEN award for a volume of short stories.

MICHAEL HAMBURGER was born in 1924. His *Collected Poems: 1941–1994* were published this year by Anvil Press, together with a new edition, slightly enlarged and corrected, of his translation *Poems of Paul Celan*. In 1994 Anvil Press Poetry published a new edition, also enlarged and with a new introduction, of *Hölderlin: Poems and Fragments,* on which he had worked since his school days. He has also published critical books, such as *The Truth of Poetry*, and a book of memoirs, *String of Beginnings*.

CHRISTINE HAUCH lives in London and, when possible, in Somerset. She will be fifty-five in the year 2000. She worked as a translator, teacher and editor before finding time to write during the early eighties. After writing a number of short stories, she is now battling with her second novel.

NICK HORNBY was born in 1957 and worked as a teacher before becoming a full-time writer. His first book *Fever Pitch* enjoyed great critical success and went on to be a major bestseller. His novel *High Fidelity* was published in 1995. He lives in North London with his wife and son.

JANETTE TURNER HOSPITAL is an Australian who now divides her time between Australia and North America. In 1994, she was writer-in-residence at the International Study Centre at Herstmonceux Castle in Sussex, where she has been working on her sixth novel. She has published five novels and two collections of short stories, and won a number of international literary awards. Her most recent novel, *The Last Magician*, 1992, was shortlisted for

Australia's Miles Franklin Award, Canada's Trillium Award, and the Commonwealth Writers Prize.

BARRY HUNTER was born in Aden in 1956. He worked as a journalist, a photographer and an advertising copywriter before applying to the National Film and Television School where he is currently enrolled on the screenwriting programme. He lives in London.

ELIZABETH JOLLEY grew up in the Midlands of England. She is an acclaimed writer whose many prizewinning books include *Palomino*, *The Well*, *Miss Peabody's Inheritance*, *The Sugar Mother*, *My Father's Moon* and *Cabin Fever*. Her work is published widely overseas, in magazines such as the *The New Yorker*, and frequently broadcast on the BBC. Her most recent novel, *The Georges' Wife*, was published in 1993 by Penguin. She teaches in the School of Communication and Cultural Studies, Curtin University in Perth, Western Australia.

FRANCIS KING was born in Switzerland and spent his childhood in India, where his father was a government official. While still an undergraduate at Oxford, he published his first three novels. He then joined the British Council, working in Italy, Greece, Egypt, Finland and Japan, before he resigned to devote himself entirely to writing. He is a former winner of the Somerset Maugham Prize, of the Katherine Mansfield Prize and of the *Yorkshire Post* Novel of the Year Award for *Act of Darkness* (1983). In 1994 Constable published his novel *The One and Only*.

MIKE McCORMACK is twenty-nine and comes from Louisburgh, Co. Mayo, Eire. He has published in numerous magazines and journals; last year he was runner-up in the Ian St James Awards. His first collection of short stories *Getting It In The Head* will be published in February 1996 by Jonathan Cape.

JOHN McGAHERN was born in Dublin in 1934 and brought up in the west of Ireland. He is a graduate of University College, Dublin. He is the author of three collections of short stories and five acclaimed novels, *The Barracks* (1962), *The Dark* (1965), *The Leavetaking* (1974), *The Pornographer* (1979), and *Amongst Women* (1990). John McGahern lives in Co. Leitrim.

JIM McGOWAN is full of contradictions. He loves women but is not married. He is a man of peace yet his favourite sport is bullfighting. Many of his stories tell of the ruination of life by excessive drinking of alcohol, yet the Writers' Group of which he is a member meets in Mahaffy's pub in Dublin's Pearse Street every Monday night. It is called the 'Inkwell'. 'No one can teach you how to write,' according to Jim McGowan. Yet he says that but for the 'Inkwell', he would never have persisted with the efforts that made him known in books, radio and now, hopefully, TV. He's a bit cracked.

SHENA MACKAY was born in Edinburgh in 1944 and grew up in Kent and London, where she now lives. Her work includes the novellas *Toddler on the Run* and *Dust Falls on Eugene Schlumberger*, published when she was twenty, *Music Upstairs* (1965), *Old Crow* (1967), *An Advent Calendar* (1971), *A Bowl of Cherries* (1984), *Redhill Rococo* (1986) – which won the Fawcett Prize – and *Dunedin* (1992). Her three volumes of short stories have recently been collected by Penguin. She is currently working on a novel.

DAVID MACKENZIE comes from Easter Ross, Scotland, and lives in London. His short stories have appeared in several magazines, as well as earlier issues of *Best Short Stories*. His first novel, *The Truth of Stone* (Mainstream), was published in 1991.

ALICE MUNRO was born in Canada. She is the author of *The Beggar Maid* (shortlisted for the Booker Prize), one other novel, and seven collections of short stories, most recently *Open Secrets* which won the W.H. Smith Literary Award. She has twice won the Governor General's Award, and her work appears regularly in *The New Yorker*. She lives in Ontario and British Columbia.

EDNA O'BRIEN is the author of several books, her most recent being *House of Spendid Isolation*. She divides her time between

Ireland, London and New York. Her play *Beloved* will be performed at The Abbey Theatre in Dublin in 1996.

JULIA O'FAOLAIN grew up in Ireland and, after spending some years in France, Italy, and the USA, now lives in London. She has published three books of short stories and six novels. These include *No Country for Young Men* (which was shortlisted for the Booker Prize) and most recently *The Judas Cloth*. She has just completed a collection of short stories and is finishing a novel.

RUTH RENDELL has been writing suspense fiction and detective stories for the past twenty-five years. She has thrice won the Crime Writers' Gold Dagger Award. Her Chief Inspector Wexford has appeared in fourteen novels and is now the subject of television serials. Her books have been translated into twenty-four languages. She also writes under the name of Barbara Vine. A Fellow of the Royal Society of Literature, she is married, has one grown-up son and lives in a sixteenth-century farmhouse in Suffolk.

WILL SELF's *The Quantity Theory of Insanity* was shortlisted for the 1992 John Llewellyn Rhys Prize and won the Geoffrey Faber Memorial Prize. He is also the author of *Cock & Bull*, *My Idea of Fun* and *Grey Area*.

MURIEL SPARK, born and educated in Edinburgh, has been prominent as a writer since 1950 when she won a short story competition in the *Observer*. Her subsequent novels and stories have brought her international fame. She has also written plays, poems, children's books, and biographies of Mary Shelley, Emily Brontë and John Masefield. Among many other awards she has received the Italia Prize, the James Tait Black Memorial Prize, the F.N.A.C. Prix Etranger, the Saltire Prize and the Ingesoll T.S. Eliot Award. She was elected an honorary member of the American Academy of Arts and Letters in 1978 and to L'Ordre des Arts et des Lettres in France in 1988. In 1993 she became a Dame of the British Empire.

ALAN SPENCE was born in Glasgow in 1947. His first collection of short stories, *Its Colours They Are Fine*, was published in 1977 and is still in print. His novel, *The Magic Flute*, won the 1991 People's Prize. Other published work includes two poetry collections and three playscripts. In 1993 he won the Macallan/ *Scotland on Sunday* Short Story Prize. He has held various writer-in-residence posts. A new short story collection, *Stone Garden*, is being published this year by Phoenix House.

WILLIAM TREVOR was born in Cork in 1928, and educated at Trinity College, Dublin. He has spent much of his life in Ireland. His novel, *The Old Boys*, won the Hawthornden Prize in 1964, since when he has received many honours for his work including the Royal Society of Literature Heinemann Award, and the Whitbread Prize for Fiction. He edited the *Oxford Book of Irish Short Stories* (1989), and his *Collected Stories* were published in 1992.

TIM WILLOCKS was born in Stalybridge, Cheshire in 1957. He is a qualified doctor and practising psychiatrist. He has had two novels published, *Bad City Blues* (Macdonald) and *Green River Rising* (Jonathan Cape). He is also a screenwriter and a 1st Dan Black Belt in Shotokan Karate.

Acknowledgments

'Interference', copyright © Julian Barnes 1994, was first published in *The New Yorker*, 19 September 1994, and is reprinted by permission of the author and Peters, Fraser & Dunlop, 503/4 The Chambers, Chelsea Harbour, London SW10 0XF.

'The Destiny of Nathalie X', copyright © William Boyd 1994, was first published in *Granta* 48, autumn 1994, and is reprinted by permission of the author and Lemon, Unna and Durbridge, 24 Pottery Lane, Holland Park, London W11 4LZ.

'Sure to Rise', copyright © Fiona Farrell 1994, was first published in *Metro*, (New Zealand), December 1994, and is reprinted by permission of the author and Glenys Bean, 15 Elizabeth Street, Freeman's Bay, Auckland, New Zealand.

'Light', copyright © Jane Gardam 1994, was first published in *Marie Claire* (UK), August 1994, and is reprinted by permission of the author and David Higham Associates, 5–8 Lower John Street, London WIR 4HA.

'The Take-Over', copyright © Michael Hamburger 1994, was

first published in *Stand Magazine*, Volume 35 Number 2, spring 1994, and is reprinted by permission of the author.

'The Sarum Twins', copyright © Christine Hauch 1994, was first published in *Panurge* 20, 1994, and is reprinted by permission of the author.

'Books and Records', copyright © Nick Hornby 1994, was first published in *The Big Issue*, number 84, 1994, and is reprinted by permission of the author and Peters, Fraser & Dunlop, 503/4 The Chambers, Chelsea Harbour, London SW10 0XF.

'Unperformed Experiments Have No Results', copyright © Janette Turner Hospital 1994, was first published in *Queen's Quarterly* (Canada), Volume 100 Number 4, winter 1994, and is reprinted by permission of the author and Mic Cheetham Associates, 138 Buckingham Palace Road, London SW1W 9SA.

'The Lobster Season', copyright © Barry Hunter 1994, was first published in *Panurge* 21, 1994, and is reprinted by permission of the author.

'Three Miles to One Inch', copyright © Elizabeth Jolley 1994, was first published in *The New Yorker* 19 December 1994, and is reprinted by permission of the author and David Higham Associates, 5–8 Lower John Street, Golden Square, London W1R 4HA.

'The Web', copyright © Francis King 1994, was first published in *London Magazine*, December 1994/January 1995, and is reprinted by permission of the author and A. M. Heath & Co. Ltd, 79 St Martin's Lane, London WC2N 4AA.

'The Occupation; A Guide For Tourists', copyright © Mike McCormack 1994, was first published in *Ambit* 135, 1994, and is reprinted by permission of the author.

'Creatures of the Earth', copyright © John McGahern 1994, was first published in *Granta* 49, winter 1994, and is reprinted by permission of the author and A.M. Heath & Co. Ltd, 79 St Martin's Lane, London WC2N 4AA.

'A Nation Once Again', copyright © Jim McGowan 1994, was first published in *Stand Magazine*, Volume 35 Number 3, summer 1994, and is reprinted by permission of the author.

'A Silver Summer', copyright © Shena Mackay 1994, was first published in *Marie Claire* (UK), August 1994, and is reprinted by permission of the author and Rogers, Coleridge & White, 20 Powys Mews, London W11 1JN.

'Bevis', copyright © David Mackenzie 1994, was first published in *Edinburgh Review*, number 91, 1994, and is reprinted by permission of the author and John Johnson, Clerkenwell House, 45/47 Clerkenwell Green, London EC1R 0HT.

'Hired Girl', copyright © Alice Munro 1994, was first published in *The New Yorker*, 11 April 1994, and is reprinted by permission of the author, Virginia Barber Literary Agency, 353 West 21st Street, New York, New York 10011 and Abner Stein, 10 Roland Gardens, London SW7 3PH.

'Sin', copyright © Edna O'Brien 1994, was first published in *The New Yorker*, 11 July 1994, and is reprinted by permission of the author and Aitken, Stone and Wylie Ltd, 29 Fernshaw Road, London SW10 0TG.

'Under The Rose', copyright © Julia O'Faolain 1994, was first published in *The New Yorker*, 28 February 1994, and is reprinted by permission of the author and Rogers, Coleridge & White, 20 Powis Mews, London W11 1JN.

'Burning End', copyright © Kingsmarkham Enterprises Ltd 1994, was first published in the *Spectator*, 17/24 December 1994, and is reprinted by permission of the author and Peters, Fraser &

Acknowledgments

Dunlop, 503/4 The Chambers, Chelsea Harbour, London SW10 0XF.

'World of Serial', copyright © Will Self 1994, was first published in *The Big Issue*, number 81, 1994, and is reprinted by permission of the author and Ed Victor Ltd, 6 Bayley Street, Bedford Square, London WC1B 3HB.

'Going Up and Coming Down', copyright © Muriel Spark 1994, was first published in the *Daily Telegraph*, 4 July 1994, and is reprinted by permission of the author and David Higham Associates, 5–8 Lower John Street, Golden Square, London W1R 4HA.

'That and a Dollar', copyright © Alan Spence 1994, was first published in *Edinburgh Review*, number 92, 1994, and is reprinted by permission of the author and Sheil Land Associates Ltd, 43 Doughty Street, London WC1N 2LF.

'Widows', copyright © William Trevor 1994, was first published in *The New Yorker*, 27 June/4 July 1994, and is reprinted by permission of the author and Peters, Fraser & Dunlop, 503/4 The Chambers, Chelsea Harbour, London SW10 0XF.

'Michigan Water', copyright © Tim Willocks 1994, was first published in *The Big Issue*, number 83, 1994, and is reprinted by permission of the author and Michelle Kass Associates, 12 Moor Street, London W1V 5LH.

We are grateful to the editors of the publications in which the stories first appeared for permission to reproduce them in this volume.

Anyone wishing to reprint any of the stories elsewhere or in translation should approach the individual authors through their agents as indicated or care of William Heinemann Ltd.